2009 B2

WITHDRAWN

HOLLYWOOD
MOON

ALSO BY JOSEPH WAMBAUGH

FICTION
Hollywood Crows
Hollywood Station
Floaters
Finnegan's Week
Fugitive Nights
The Golden Orange
The Secrets of Harry Bright
The Delta Star
The Glitter Dome
The Black Marble
The Choirboys
The Blue Knight
The New Centurions

NONFICTION
Fire Lover
The Blooding
Echoes in the Darkness
Lines and Shadows
The Onion Field

HOLLYWOOD MOON

A NOVEL

JOSEPH WAMBAUGH

Little, Brown and Company

New York   Boston   London

Little, Brown and Company
Hachette Book Group
237 Park Avenue, New York, NY 10017
Visit our Web site at www.HachetteBookGroup.com

First Edition: November 2009

Little, Brown and Company is a division of Hachette Book Group, Inc.
The Little, Brown name and logo are trademarks of Hachette Book Group, Inc.

The characters and events in this book are fictitious. Any similarity to real persons, living or dead, is coincidental and not intended by the author.

Library of Congress Cataloging-in-Publication Data
Wambaugh, Joseph.
    Hollywood moon : a novel / Joseph Wambaugh. — 1st ed.
       p. cm.
    ISBN 978-0-316-04518-6
    1. Police—California—Los Angeles—Fiction.   2. Hollywood (Los Angeles, Calif.) —Fiction.   I. Title.
    PS3573.A475H649 2009
    813'.54—dc22   2008043793

10 9 8 7 6 5 4 3 2 1

RRD-IN

Printed in the United States of America

ACKNOWLEDGMENTS

As ever, special thanks for the terrific anecdotes and great cop talk goes to officers of the Los Angeles Police Department:

Randy Barr, Gabriel Blanco, Sue Brandstetter, Alma Burke, Vicki Bynum, Holly Daniel, Bob Deamer, Mike Diaz, Bill Duke, Bob Duretto (ret.), Klaus Edgell, Irma Foster, Dan Gomez, Brett Goodkin, Craig Herron, Diana Herron, Lin Hom, John Incontro, LaMont Jerrett, Corina Lee, J. J. Leonard (ret.), Sig Lo, Al Lopez, Kathy McAnany, Steve McClain, Paul McKechnie, Joan McNamara, Greg Nichols, Maligi Nua Jr., Bill Pack, Kim Porter, Armando Romero, Ken Smith (ret.), Nick Titiriga, Terri Utley, Ray Valois, Jody Wakefield, Ed Whyte, Tracy Wolfe, Eddie Yoon

And to officers of the San Diego Police Department:

J. B. Boyd, Silvia Brown, Laurie Cairncross, Paul Conley, Carlton Hershman, Mike Holden, Lou Johns, Howard Labroe, Duane Malinowski, Vic Morel, Paul Phillips, Tony Puente (ret.), Cori Queen, Dani Resch, Dave Speck, John Teft

And to Officer Arvar Elkins of the Huntington Beach Police Department

ACKNOWLEDGMENTS

And to investigators of the San Diego District Attorney's Office: Joe Cargel, Paul Libassi

And to San Diego deputy district attorney Joan K. Stein

And to special agent of the Bureau of Alcohol, Tobacco, Firearms and Explosives Mike Matassa (ret.)

And to special agent of the Secret Service Elizabeth McCaffree

HOLLYWOOD
MOON

★ ONE ★

"**H**OLLYWOOD NATE RENTS midgets," the long-legged, sunbaked surfer cop whom the others called Flotsam said to his partner while 6-X-32 was passing Grauman's Chinese Theatre, cruising east on Hollywood Boulevard at twilight.

The dying spangled sunlight ricocheted off the windows of the taller buildings, and his shorter surfer partner, also weathered and singed, whom of course they called Jetsam, glanced at the driver through the smoked lenses of his wraparound shades and said, "What?"

Flotsam wore his two-inch hair gelled up in front like a baby cockatoo, and Jetsam's was semispiked, both coifs streaked with highlights not provided by sun, sea, or nature. And with just enough gel to get it done and still not annoy the watch commander, a lieutenant in his early fifties, twenty years their senior, and very old-school.

"In fact," Flotsam continued, "last Wednesday, Nate hired one to bowl with him for twenty bucks an hour. That's when five coppers from the midwatch and Watch 2 got together at the bowling alley in the Kodak Centre with a bunch from north Hollywood and Wilshire. I heard that Nate, like, stole the spotlight with his midget."

"Where did you hear about Hollywood Nate and midget love?" Jetsam wanted to know.

"I got it from Sheila," Flotsam said, referring to Officer Sheila Montez, a midwatch P2 whom both surfer cops lusted for. "And I ain't saying he loves little people, but, dude, he's so cinematically dialed-in, he devised this way to capture the attention of all the bowling alley Sallys. His little fella gets all flirty and cute with the Sallys, and it sets things up for Nate to move in and close the deal."

Officer Nathan Weiss, a hawkishly handsome thirty-seven-year-old, physically fit gym rat, was called Hollywood Nate because he possessed a SAG card and had actually appeared briefly in a few TV movies. And he always volunteered to work every red carpet event at the Kodak Theatre in his thus-far futile quest for cinematic discovery and eventual stardom.

Jetsam envisioned those feverishly hot Sallys as he shot a casual glance toward the Walk of Fame, where lots of curb creatures were already out. He saw a tweaker sidling closer toward the purse of an obese tourist who was busy yelling at her much smaller husband. The tweaker backed off and slithered into the crowd when Jetsam gave him the stink eye as the black-and-white passed. The Street Characters—Batman, Superman (two Supermans, actually), Darth Vader, Spider-Man, Bart Simpson, SpongeBob, and Catwoman—were all mingling with tourists in the forecourt of Grauman's Chinese Theatre, posing for camera shots in an endless quest for tourist bucks.

"Maybe we oughtta hire a midget too," Jetsam said. "I used to bowl a lot when I was married to my second ex-wife, who I miss like a prostate infection. It was a low-rent bowling alley in Long Beach, and I was, like, the only bowler in the whole place who wasn't sleazed-out. Even my second ex—who loved bowling, Leonardo DiCaprio, and pharmaceuticals—was inked-up, a butterfly on her belly and my name on her ass. Her girlfriend told me how that prescription zombie screamed like a cat when they lasered my name off. I'da coughed up two weeks' pay for a video of it. Her exotic girlfriend, by the way, might be worth your attention, bro. She's an Indian."

"Feather or dot?"

"Dot."

"No way, dude," Flotsam said. "Every time my laptop goes sideways, I get one of them on the line and always end up tossing my cell phone against the wall in frustration. I buy more cells than every cartel in

Colombia. But I agree, we should definitely not overlook the target-rich environment at the Kodak Centre."

Jetsam said, "Being where it's located makes it, like, the most lavish bowling alley this side of the palace of Dubai. Maybe we can't afford it?"

" 'Can't' is a frame of mind that don't hold our photo," Flotsam said. "Hollywood Nate claims that on certain nights, it's full of bowling alley Sallys hoping Matt Damon will come in to roll a line or two, or maybe Brad Pitt when Angelina's in Africa looking for sainthood with people even skinnier than she is."

Jetsam said, "I hear what you're saying, bro. I mean, there's gotta be opportunities on those lanes for coppers as coolaphonic and hormonally imaginative as the almost four hundred pounds of male heat riding in this car."

Flotsam thought about it some more and then said, "There's a midget that works at the newsstand on Cahuenga. And there's that roller-skating midget at Hollywood and Highland. The one that throws water balloons at tourists? He'd crawl in a clothes dryer for twenty bucks an hour."

"A *plethora* of midgets ain't gonna get us our way," Jetsam said, showing off the new vocabulary he was acquiring from his community college class. "We gotta think original. Maybe we could, like, hire a clown to bowl with us. That would amaze those ten-pin tootsies."

"I'm scared of clowns," Flotsam blurted, and it was out of his mouth before he could take it back.

"You're what?" Jetsam said, and this time he turned fully toward his partner as the late-summer sun dropped into the Pacific and lights came on in Hollywood, the fluorescent glow making the boulevard scene look even weirder to the swarming tourists.

Flotsam and Jetsam had been midwatch partners and fellow surfers for more than two years, but this was the first time Jetsam had learned this incredible secret: His tall, rugged partner was afraid of clowns!

"Maybe I said it wrong, dude," Flotsam quickly added. "It's just that they, like, shiver me. The way a snake creeps you out, know what I mean?"

"Snakes don't creep me out, bro," Jetsam said.

"Rats, then. I seen you that time we got the dead-body call where rats were all eating the guy's eyeballs. You were ready to blow chunks, dude."

"It wasn't the rats themselves, bro," Jetsam said. "I just wasn't ready for an all-out rodent luau."

"Anyways, I'm just saying, clowns, like, make me, like, all . . . goose-bumpy. I mean, maybe I saw too many movies about slasher clowns or something, I don't know."

"This goes on my desktop," Jetsam said with a grin. "I'm holding on to this."

"What happens in our shop stays in our shop, dude," Flotsam said grimly, referring to their car with its "shop number" on the roof and doors. "So hit your delete key."

"I feel ya, bro," Jetsam said. "No need to go all aggro. Next time a boulevard clown squirts a tourist with a water gun, just stay in the car and roll your window up and lock the doors. I'll man-up for both of us. And I'll taze the first asshole that calls my partner a sissified, whimpering bitch."

While 6-X-32 was cruising the boulevard, two homeless middle-aged panhandlers in east Hollywood named Axel Minton and Bootsie Brown were pushing a man in a wheelchair along the sidewalk to a graffiti-tagged neighborhood market frequented by local pensioners. It was a store where Axel and Bootsie often begged for change from the residents of the neighborhood, mostly Latino and Asian, who bought groceries there.

Axel was a spindly white man with sprigs of gray hair who would drink anything from a bottle if the label indicated any alcohol content. Bootsie was a black man blind in one eye who slept in a storage shed behind the apartment building where eighty-eight-year-old pensioner Coleman O'Toole lived. They both wore layers, sooty and drab, molded to their forms like fungus until it wasn't clear where the fabrics left off and they began. And neither was many gallons away from wandering Hollywood Boulevard—like all those other self-lobotomized colorless specters in pull-tab necklaces and football helmets, or maybe wearing bikini bottoms on their heads—pushing a trash-laden shopping cart, chanting gibberish, or yodeling at terrified tourists. The Hollywood cops called it "gone to Dizzyland."

Each transient had wheeled Coleman O'Toole to the store many times for a modest fee. This time they were both pushing the wheelchair, and they were bickering when they stopped in front and entered, leaving Coleman O'Toole parked in the shadows.

While Axel and Bootsie were inside loading up on shelf items, which included three quarts of 100-proof vodka and three quarts of gin, another octogenarian transient, known as Trombone Teddy, shuffled by. He'd been a good bebop sideman back in the day, or, as he put it, "when I was a real person." Teddy, who was well known to officers at Hollywood Station, looked curiously at the figure in the wheelchair. Then he used his last few coins to phone the police, and the call was given to 6-X-32 of the midwatch.

Axel and Bootsie's bottles of liquor and several bags of snacks were piled on the counter. The part-time clerk, who called herself Lucy, was a white transsexual in a blinged-out T-shirt, low-rise jeans, nosebleed stilettos, and magenta hair extensions piled so high she wouldn't have felt being conked by a bottle of Corona, which could easily happen in that store. She adjusted her silk scarf to better conceal the healing from recent surgery to remove her manly apple and looked at the transients curiously.

Being acquainted with both of them as well as with Coleman O'Toole, she said, "Is Coley throwing a party or what?"

"It's his birthday," Bootsie said.

"No, it isn't," the tranny said. "His birthday was last month, same as mine. He brought me a card."

"It ain't his birthday, dummy," Axel said to Bootsie. "It's the anniversary of his retirement from the railroad. He has a party every year to celebrate his current life of comfort and ease."

Lucy looked at Coleman O'Toole's pension check and at the endorsement. The signature looked like the old man's scrawl. "Why don't you wheel Coley inside?" the tranny said, squinting out the window at the wheelchair figure alone in the darkness.

"You wanna check his ID, see if he's old enough to buy booze?" Bootsie said with a wet, nearly toothless grin.

"Yeah, you wanna card old Coleman?" Axel said, snuffling and grinning wider than Bootsie. "Actually, the old bugger's sick. Puked halfway down the street. You don't want him in here unless you got a bucket and mop."

"And all this booze is gonna cure him?" Lucy said, then shrugged and started ringing up the items just as 6-X-32 parked in front of the store and was met by Trombone Teddy.

The cops hardly noticed the old guy in the wheelchair, and Flotsam said, "Did you make the call, Teddy?"

"Yes, sir," Teddy said. "Is there a reward for capturing a couple of crooks for check fraud?"

"Whadda you mean?" Jetsam said.

"If you would put in a word to the store owner, would he give me a few bucks for blowing the whistle on a pair of thugs?"

"High-level business negotiations are above my pay grade, Teddy," said Flotsam. "But I gotta think somebody'd buy you a forty or two."

"Okay," Teddy said. "I'll take a chance that generosity still exists in this ungrateful, goddamn world. Go inside and you'll find two thieves cashing a stolen check."

"This better be righteous, Teddy," Flotsam said, walking inside with Jetsam at his back.

The tranny, who was as tall as Flotsam in those heels, was surprised when the cop appeared and said, "Can I see that check?"

Pushing the check across the counter, Lucy said, "Something wrong, Officer?"

"That's what we wanna know," Jetsam said.

Flotsam examined the check and said, "Are either of you Coleman O'Toole?"

It was Lucy who said, "No, they're not, Officer. Coley's the one out there in the wheelchair. These two sometimes wheel him down here to buy groceries."

"Coley's the salt of the earth," Axel said, looking uneasy. "I'd fight a whole pack of pit bulls for old Coley. He's a fellow wine connoisseur."

"Connoisseurs don't drink wine in a paper bag," Jetsam noted.

"Coley's my man," Bootsie said. "When some no-account neighbor put lye in his gin bottle one time and he ended up wif a tube in his stomach, it was me that poured some good whiskey into the tube so he could get drunk."

"That's a touching testament to friendship," Flotsam said, putting the check on the counter.

He walked to the door, nodding to Jetsam, who stayed inside while the grocery transaction was being completed. Lucy was counting out the change when Flotsam came back inside.

Axel Minton looked at the cop's expression and said, "Uh-oh."

The tranny's eyes were theatrically made-up so as to be seen from balcony seats, and those amazing orbs moved from Flotsam to the transients and back again before she said, "Don't tell me that's not Coleman O'Toole out there in the wheelchair!"

"Oh, yeah," said Flotsam. "I'm sure it's him. He's strapped in and rigged up nice as you please."

"What's the problem, then?" Lucy asked.

"It's that he won't be needing all this booze," Flotsam said. "Him being deceased and all."

"Uh-oh," said Bootsie, who pointed at Axel. "It was his idea after we found Coley layin' on the floor, colder than Aunt Ruby's poon." Then he looked at the tranny and said, "Sorry for my rude mouf, Miss Lucy."

"You lying rat!" Axel said to Bootsie. Then to the cops, "He was the one noticed Coley had already signed his check!"

"Tha's right, Officer," Bootsie said, "but it was this here pissant that pointed to Coley layin' there quiet as a bedbug on your pilla and said ol' Coley woulda wanted us to cash it and have a Irish wake!"

"Okay, you two turn around and put your hands behind your backs," Flotsam said. And sotto to Jetsam, "Better notify the night-watch detective about the corpse in the wheelchair and our two grave robbers. While we're waiting for the body snatchers, I'll take care of Teddy."

As Jetsam led the handcuffed miscreants out to their car to await the arrival of the coroner's van, Flotsam bought a pint of Jack for Trombone Teddy to show that generosity still exists in this ungrateful, goddamn world.

The woman officer with the smartest mouth at Hollywood Station was Dana Vaughn, and Hollywood Nate was stuck with her for at least one deployment period, an unhappy way to spend his first month back on the midwatch. He'd spent a year at the Community Relations Office (acronym CRO, pronounced "crow"), tending to touchy-feely quality-of-life issues and getting a little bump in pay for the easy work. But when fellow crow Bix Ramstead shot himself after being involved in a scandal, a lot of the fun was gone from the job and Nate felt like returning to real police work. Besides, he needed to work nights in order to keep his days free to pursue and torment casting agents. At age thirty-seven, it was now or never.

With sixteen years on the LAPD, Nate Weiss figured he'd have to stick around for at least four more years to ensure a vested pension, but one he couldn't draw until the age of fifty, which kept most cops on the job long past twenty years. He wondered what he'd do if his acting career finally caught fire in the next four years? Would it be worth it to resign from the LAPD and lose that pension for an uncertain career as an actor? He might damn well need the pension after he turned fifty and his pecs were falling and he couldn't suck in his gut any longer. Hollywood Nate felt that he was way too handsome to make it as an older character actor, and the mere thought of it made Nate unconsciously pass his hand over his abdominals, well covered by a T-shirt, a Kevlar vest, and his uniform shirt.

Dana Vaughn, also a P2, who was driving 6-X-76's Ford Crown Vic late that afternoon, hadn't missed it. She never missed a thing, which was one of the reasons Hollywood Nate didn't quite feel relaxed around her.

After noticing that subtle move to his belly, Dana said, "Yeah, you're ripped, Nate. Abs to die for. Must be tough being as smokin' hot as you. Who cleans all the mirrors in your house?"

"I just have a slight stomachache is all," said Hollywood Nate lamely.

"Sure, honey," Dana said with that throaty, tinkling chuckle of hers, which irritated him all the more because he actually liked the sound of it.

When he muttered, "I'd sure hate to work for you when you make sergeant," she laughed, and that pissed him off more than when she snarked him about his vanity.

Another thing he disliked about Dana Vaughn was that she called him honey in the way that his aunt Ruthie called him honey. Like the old woman at the donut stand in Farmers Market, his usual destination for a croissant and coffee in the morning.

Dana was six years older than Nate, with twenty-one years on the job, but she acted like she was from the WW II generation or something. Almost every damn thing she said to him somehow sounded patronizing and made Nate feel like a kid. And to make matters worse, she still looked good. She was fit, with great shoulders and only faint lines starting around her alert golden-brown eyes and at the sides of her mouth when she smirked at him.

Dana used the workout room nearly as much as Nate, always in a tight tank and spandex shorts. She didn't even bother to dye her salt-and-pepper ear-length bob, and it looked just right on her, emphasizing the woman she was, not the girl she had once been. If she'd been what the surfer cops called a yuckbabe or one of those always griping about "JFH," meaning just-fucked hairdo, instead of an older woman who still looked hot and knew it, Nate figured she'd have been easier to take.

The first time Nate had ever seen Dana was in the station parking lot when he happened to be loading his war bag and shotgun into his shop after he'd just come back to patrol from his stint at the Community Relations Office. Dana was also new to Watch 5, the midwatch, and had been working for the first time that night with young Harris Triplett, a phase-three probationer whose field training officer was on a day off. Since the P1 was in the last phase of his eighteen months of probation, he could be put with a P2 like Dana instead of with a P3 FTO. In fact, Harris was scheduled to complete his probation in a matter of days, and Nate had intended to buy him a burger to celebrate.

Nate remembered seeing her dead-stare the kid just before she got behind the wheel that first night, and he heard her say to Harris, "Boy, I need to know right out front. Do you intend to fanny burp in my presence or in our shop?"

"Of course not, ma'am!" Harris Triplett said, stunned.

Then Dana said, deadpan, "Do you intend to crank up loogies? You got loogie problems, I suggest you swallow them. To spit them out the window and have them blow back on our shop would be highly unprofessional and might jeopardize your probation."

"I don't do things like that!" Harris said.

"I want you to remember a few basics about curb creatures," she said. "Rock cocaine is either in their mouths or in their butts. Watch the breathing of the chest for a tip-off. It's a built-in lie detector. And throw their keys on the roof of their car if you're gonna return to our shop to run their records."

"Yes, ma'am. Okay," Harris said.

"And if they got booty rock, it's your job to deal with it. There are dark and scary places where I won't go."

"Right," Harris said earnestly.

Dana wasn't through. "One more thing: Most males have no shame, but you need to remember there're EEO laws on the books regarding age and gender. Do you resent working with me because my badge and handcuffs're older than you? And do you think you can get away with making sexual innuendos and maybe touching me in an inappropriate way because I'm an old woman?"

His face flushed, Harris Triplett looked around for help at that moment, and the passing surfer cops stepped in to save him.

"She's just honking on you, dude," Flotsam said to the boot.

Still deadpan, Dana continued, "On second thought, I'm pretty much EEO-proof. You can fanny burp if you want to, but no loogies. And about the sexual harassment, if I happen to touch *you* in a lewd or offensive way, you have every right to complain to the watch commander." A long pause. "But tell me you won't, honey. *Please* tell me you won't!"

"Get in the car, bro. She won't hurt you . . . very much," Jetsam said to the utterly bewildered rookie, and for the first time, Hollywood Nate got to see Dana Vaughn flash that annoying half-smile of hers when she slid in behind the wheel.

Remembering that episode, Hollywood Nate had to admit that Dana was sometimes entertaining, even though she could be a major pain in the ass. A good thing about her was that, like Nate, she preferred Starbucks latte with biscotti to the usual Winchell's cuppa joe with two sugars, two creams, and a raspberry jelly donut. Moreover, Nate knew that she'd been in a fatal shooting the month prior, when she'd worked Watch 3.

That late-night watch was a graveyard shift for three days a week, lasting twelve hours. It overlapped the hours of the four-day-a-week, ten-hour midwatch. Two weeks after the shooting, Dana had asked to be assigned to the midwatch, and her request was granted. As an authentic gunfighter and a senior officer on the sergeants list, she was entitled to great respect.

For twelve years prior to her assignment to night-watch patrol at Hollywood Station, Dana Vaughn had been away from patrolling the streets. She'd worked at the police academy for eight years as an instructor, teaching computer classes and report writing and reviewing the academic curriculum. Then, after leaving the academy, she'd spent four more years across the street from Hollywood Station in the Hollywood narcotics unit, housed in a small building at the corner of De Longpre and Wilcox. There she did mostly administrative chores and helped the UC coordinators who handled the undercover officers.

Being a single mom, Dana Vaughn had tried for most of her career to keep from working the streets, seeking jobs that would allow her to have evenings at home and weekends off in order to properly raise her daughter. Late in her career, Dana had decided to take the sergeants exams, passed them easily, and was on the sergeants list. Now that her eighteen-year-old daughter, Pamela, was going off to Cal in September, Dana had decided that it was time to get more street experience in a black-and-white. After her promotion, she'd be sent to a patrol division as a supervisor, and she wanted to be ready for the new job.

Dana's ex-husband, a lawyer at a firm in the city's tallest downtown office building, at Fifth and Grand, had bought their daughter a new Acura for high school graduation and assured them both that all through her university studies, he'd send $1,500 a month for Pamela, and he'd promised to continue the payments through graduate school if she sought an advanced degree. All of this made Dana despise the philandering bastard a little less than she had during their brief marriage.

An incident that Hollywood Nate found very strange happened the very first night that he worked with Dana Vaughn. They'd received a "prowler there now" call in the Hollywood Hills on a street below the famous Hollywood sign. They were the first and, Nate assumed, the only car to arrive. After checking the property on foot with flashlights, and after interviewing a nervous neighbor who thought she'd heard somebody knock over a trash can, they decided that it was probably a coyote or a raccoon or even a deer, since the hills were full of critters.

When Nate and Dana were returning to their shop, Nate noticed another Crown Vic, parked half a block farther down the unlit street. Silhouetted across the roof was a light bar.

"That doesn't look like a midwatch unit," he'd said to Dana Vaughn, trying to peer through the darkness. "Must be somebody from Watch Three."

"It is," she said.

"You got infrared eyeballs or what?" Nate said. "How do you know?"

"I know," she said.

"Why're they sitting there in the dark like that?"

"That's how a guardian angel does it," Dana said, starting the engine and driving back down to the flats, passing the parked black-and-white without a word and without looking its way.

"It's great working with you," Nate said. "I just love a mystery."

Dana Vaughn heaved a sigh and said, "I'm sure you remember the OIS I got involved in when I was working Watch Three."

"Yeah, everyone knows you smoked a guy that was doing a death grapple with...what's his name."

"Leon Calloway is his name," Dana said. "That's him in the parked unit, with his partner."

"You gonna enlighten me or what?" Nate asked.

And then Dana Vaughn said, "Yeah, I guess I've gotta." And she slowly began to tell Hollywood Nate the story of her officer-involved shooting, which had endeared her to even the most hard-core anti-female coppers on Watch 3, one of whom had been Leon Calloway.

Calloway was a hulking, flat-nosed, twenty-five-year P2 with a jutting jaw that pushed into a room ahead of him, and a meticulously shaved head the size of a beach ball. He'd spent his last ten years working the night watch at Hollywood Station. When Dana Vaughn transferred to Hollywood patrol, some of the women officers told her which guys were good to work with and which were not. Calloway was in the latter group. When he occasionally worked with women officers who were in phase three of their probation, he was a mouth-breathing nightmare who scared the hell out of them.

Calloway would usually start the evening by saying to a female rookie, "I hope you can hold your pee or do it in an alley like a man. I don't like looking for a *ladies' room* when I'm doing police work."

That might be followed by "Velcro crotches would solve the problem. I think I'll invent police pants with a Velcro crotch for all you... *ladies*."

It wouldn't take long either before he'd look at the young boot, and no matter how feminine she appeared, he'd say, "Are you a lesbian?"

The first time they encountered Latino gang members in Southeast Hollywood, he'd always tell the probationer, "I don't chase. If they run, *you* chase. I'll drive after them. Try to keep up."

Or he'd say, "Do you carry D batteries in your war bag?"

And when the perplexed female rookie said, "No, sir, why?" Calloway would say, "To throw at any little asshole that disses us by running. I hope you got a good arm, sis."

And all young boots were warned by the older female officers that if they got an upset stomach from eating greasy tacos fried in lard from a stand on Normandie Avenue—which Calloway liked because it was a "full pop," meaning it was free to cops—or if they were under the weather for any other reason, he was sure to say, "Oh, you're not feeling well? Is it *that time?*"

The young women learned very quickly that they'd chosen a career in what was still a man's world, and Leon Calloway never let them forget it.

He didn't try any of this with women cops as senior as Dana Vaughn, but he was a hellish partner for rookie Sarah Messinger, who happened to be riding shotgun with Calloway on the night that Dana Vaughn got into the only officer-involved shooting of her career.

A business dispute had taken place between a streetwalking prostitute on the east Sunset Boulevard track and a customer who happened to be a parolee-at-large. The parolee was a large black man, even bigger than Leon Calloway and, as it turned out, considerably stronger. Although Hollywood had a very small African-American population, it was a nighttime destination for many black men from south L.A. because it was, well, Hollywood. The parolee, whose name was Rupert Moore, was one of those, and he was specifically looking for transsexuals or drag queens, having gotten a taste for them during his twelve-year jolt in Folsom Prison.

The detectives later learned that earlier in the evening, Rupert Moore had been turned away by at least one tranny and two dragons on the Santa Monica Boulevard track. After drinking in a bar on Western Avenue for three hours, Rupert Moore had decided to try east Sunset Boulevard, where he'd met a Latino tranny named Javier Molina, aka Josefina Lamour. A drag queen who was working a short distance farther east saw and heard the encounter and later gave details to homicide detectives.

Apparently Josefina didn't like the look of Rupert Moore any more than the other trannies and dragons had. Josefina waved him off when he pulled his green Mazda to the curb, slurring his words and saying, "Say, baby, how 'bout you and me go for some sweet time in any motel you want."

Josefina had never been known to take black tricks and wasn't about to start with this supersize drunk. "Uh-uh, sorry," Josefina said.

Rupert Moore had heard too many "uh-uhs" that evening, and he turned off the engine and got out.

Josefina tried walking away fast in sky-high wedges, but Rupert Moore, with his much longer stride, caught up and said, "Sweet stuff, I got forty-five dollars and it's all for you."

Josefina kept walking until Rupert Moore grabbed the tranny by the arm and said, "You think you're too good for this nigger? Is that it, bitch?"

"I'm sorry," Josefina said, very frightened, looking around for a black-and-white, a vice car, anything! But the headlights kept passing swiftly by on Sunset Boulevard, and nobody seemed to notice or care that a large man was holding a small woman by the arm as she struggled to break free.

The Pakistani owner of a nearby liquor store later said that he heard a scream, and when he ran outside, he saw Josefina Lamour trying to hold her spilling intestines inside her belly as Rupert Moore ran to his car, brandishing a bloody knife. Josefina Lamour was dead when the ambulance arrived eight minutes later.

Six-Adam-Seventy-nine, driven by Leon Calloway with his female rookie as passenger, was the first to spot the Mazda, moments after the call came out. It was his P1 partner's first pursuit, and it was memorable for the way things ended for all concerned.

With light bar flashing and siren howling, Calloway drove a nine-minute pursuit that made the rookie regret not having taken her partner's advice about going to the bathroom before leaving the station. The pursuit ended in Rampart Division west of Alvarado, where, after a turn onto a one-way street, Rupert Moore crashed the Mazda into a row of trash cans sitting curbside in front of an apartment house. Two tires blew, and the parolee leaped from the damaged car and ran in panic into the darkness.

Within minutes, sixteen cops from Hollywood and Rampart Divisions were swarming the neighborhood with flashlights, searching yards and stairwells of apartment buildings, scanning fire escapes, and climbing walls and fences to check neighboring yards. But their murder suspect was nowhere to be found.

A voice on the tactical frequency said, "Airship up!" And soon they heard the police helicopter overhead and knew the spotter was trying to use night vision lenses to find their suspect.

Bored with it all, Leon Calloway decided to amuse himself at the expense of young Sarah Messinger. The rookie was just about to go into a dark alley, remove her Sam Browne in the darkness, and probably drop her radio and half her other gear in order to have an urgently needed pee.

The two of them had been searching as a team and were now half a block from the nearest assistance. They had entered a seedy apartment complex from the street side, climbing over a security gate. After searching alcoves and stairwells, they'd emerged in a poorly tended public area that fed onto the alley and was protected by a ten-foot-high wrought-iron fence with razor wire across the top. The gate could be opened from the yard side but was keyed on the alley side, a good thing given the number of Latino gang members who lived in houses and apartments bordering that alley.

When the partners got to the imposing security fence and Sarah was ready to scurry into the alley for the nature call, the big veteran cop backed against the wall of an adjoining garage, paused, and held a vertical finger to his lips, as though he'd heard something. Of course, his young partner froze and listened also, but all she could hear were the hum of traffic, meringue music coming from one of the second-floor apartments, and the faint sound of other cops calling to one another somewhere east in the alley.

Suddenly Leon Calloway began to bark. The sound came from his chest and passed up to his throat, where it took on a gravelly resonance that made Sarah Messinger actually spin around, expecting to face a gangbanger's pit bull. Leon Calloway's face looked flushed in the moonlight as he continued to strain and bark.

Then he yelled, "Come out, asshole, or we'll turn the dog loose. This is your last chance."

His astonished young partner gaped at this amazing performance until Leon Calloway whispered to her, "For chrissake, boot, tap on the side of the garage!" Then he began barking again.

Sarah Messinger obeyed in confusion by knocking twice on the clapboard with her knuckles.

Leon Calloway stopped barking and whispered urgently, "What the hell's the matter with you? I said 'tap.' Use your baton, and don't stop till I tell you." Then he watched her draw her baton and knock on the wood siding: *tap-tap-tap-tap.*

It seemed to satisfy him and he shouted, "Last chance, dipshit! I'm taking the leash off Rambo right this second, hear me?" After that, he resumed barking.

Sarah Messinger was miserable. She had to pee desperately, and there was a killer on the loose, and she was tapping on the side of a ramshackle garage, and her goofy-ass partner was barking like a crazed Doberman, and finally, she'd had enough.

"Sir," said Sarah Messinger, "why am I tapping on the side of this garage?"

"Why do you think, dummy?" said Leon Calloway. "It's our dog wagging its tail!"

The rookie cop never got a chance to respond to this new information, or to Leon Calloway's canine performance in general, because the instant she stopped tapping and he stopped barking, she heard a scraping above her. And when she looked up, Rupert Moore, who had been lying flat on the garage roof, legs and arms spread as he tried to hang on to the broken composite shingles, lost his grip completely and slid down, tumbling off the roof and landing with all 280 pounds on Sarah Messinger, slamming her skull onto the concrete and partially paralyzing her.

Officer Messinger finally got to release the few hundred cubic centimeters of urine from her bladder while she flopped on the walkway like a fish, and Officer Leon Calloway found himself fighting for his life with a man even bigger and stronger than he was. Rupert Moore had dropped the murder weapon on the walkway next to the flailing young woman who was trying in vain to get her limbs to obey and whose body happened to cover the knife, preventing the killer from grabbing it before he scrambled to his feet.

Then Leon Calloway began shouting for help and trying to draw his Beretta, but Rupert Moore, surging with adrenaline, had the cop's hand in both of his, and there began what looked to the semiconscious young partner like a macabre death dance. Two big men, one of them shouting for help, the other screaming curses, both clawing at the pistol, lunging forward and jerking backward in a lunatic fox-trot, banging into the wrought-iron gate, falling to their knees, and then crashing down onto the walkway. The killer was on his back and the cop on top of him, the pistol at chest level of both men, whose grunts and raspy breathing sounded to the still-helpless rookie like noises in the hog pen on her grandparents' farm in Stockton.

Instantly, there were flashlight beams and more shouts. Men were yelling, as was a woman, who had all run down the alley in the direction of Leon Calloway's cries for help. But they couldn't help him. They were locked out of the yard by the tall iron barrier and the razor wire.

One male voice hollered, "Run around to the front, Sam! Hurry up!"

Another yelled, "I'll climb the fence next door! Get some light up there!"

Another screamed to the still-floundering rookie, "Shoot him! Shoot the bastard!"

Then there were more voices screaming at both Leon Calloway and Sarah Messinger: "Shoot! Shoot! Kill the fucker! Kill him! Kill him! Kill him!"

But Sarah Messinger couldn't shoot anybody. Her entire focus was on getting her knees under her, and she couldn't even manage that.

By this time, the three cops still standing outside the fence had guns pointed and were lighting Rupert Moore and Leon Calloway with crisscrossing flashlight beams, but nobody dared take a shot, not with heads bobbing and the big cop on top. Leon Calloway hadn't enough strength left to do anything but hang on to the gun, with the tip of his index finger jammed between the trigger and the grip to keep it from firing. From one second to the next, Leon Calloway didn't know if the muzzle was pointed toward Rupert Moore's face or at his own, but he sensed it was at himself.

Now the helicopter was hovering right above them, lighting the life-or-death struggle with an aerial spotlight, and Sarah Messinger resumed her battle with cerebral contusion and the law of gravity, managing to get to her knees. And when she looked up, there in a literal spotlight, she was uncertain if this was reality or just another Hollywood production. Then she began vomiting all over her uniform shirt while voices were still screaming at her, "Kill him! Kill him! Kill him!"

But Officer Sarah Messinger just had to ignore them all, and she lay back down, her cheek pressed to the concrete, and in a moment went into the deepest slumber of her young life, one from which she would not awaken for ten days.

In agony, Leon Calloway tried to muscle the gun down, but Rupert Moore kept bending his wrist inexorably, and the muzzle kept moving back, back toward the face of the cop, who felt Rupert Moore's powerful fingers gouging, prying his own away from the trigger guard. And then there was nothing he could do to stop this powerful force.

During those last seconds, Leon Calloway was certain he would die, and he tried to remember the words he'd learned at catechism: "O my God, I am sorry for having offended..."

One blast, one fireball, one echoing .40 caliber round ringing in their ears, and it stopped the praying, the shouting, the Hollywood fantasy, everything.

It came from the yard next door, also fenced off with wrought iron, which Dana Vaughn and her male partner had entered from three properties away during all the screaming. By climbing the fences, they'd managed to get to the adjoining yard of a stucco triplex, where they had a better view. They were right in the kill zone, with Rupert Moore lying at an angle where one of them could risk a head shot. Maybe.

And that's what Dana Vaughn had done. While her partner was unholstering his nine, she was already at the fence, aiming her Glock with both hands as the airship's spotlight bounced and the crisscrossing beams from flashlights danced over the two men, making her dizzy. She took a long breath, held it, and squeezed off the only shot she'd ever fired outside the police pistol range.

The .40 caliber round did not strike the intended target, which was the skull of Rupert Moore, but was close enough, entering the side of his throat, ripping apart the carotid arteries and bathing Leon Calloway first in spatter, then in spurt, when he fell face forward onto the gurgling killer, who began quickly to drown in his own blood.

The first rescue ambulance that roared into the alley whisked Sarah Messinger from the scene, followed by a second. One of the cops waiting outside the now-open security gate worried that Rupert Moore hadn't bled out yet and said to the paramedics, "Did you happen to hear the Dodgers game? Did they win tonight? Who was pitching?"

The paramedics declined the invitation to discuss Dodgers box scores and instead ran to the side of Rupert Moore, who might not have finished bleeding out but who was very dead nonetheless.

At that point in the story, Dana said to Hollywood Nate, "The watch commander sent me downtown to the BSS shrink, and I had to show up without a weapon and sit around with a bunch of other cops who were supposed to talk about emotional trauma they were supposed to've experienced. Nobody had much to say, and when it was my turn, I had *nothing* to say. So I had to go for a private session, where the shrink said, 'Tell me about your childhood.' And 'Tell me about your relationship with your parents.' I said to him, 'A cop was about to get killed. What do my parents have to do with it?' He said, 'Well, then, tell me what you felt when you pulled that trigger.' I said, 'First of all, I didn't pull, I squeezed. And I felt the Glock buck in my hand. And I also felt an acrylic nail snap off when my finger got snagged on the wire fence. And I felt pissed off because I paid forty bucks for those acrylics. Those are the things I felt.' Finally, he seemed to think I was hopeless and gave up."

"What happened to the young boot?" Nate asked.

"She's okay," Dana said. "She was in a coma for ten days, but she's in physical therapy and doing fine now. She was brand-new to Watch Three when it happened, so I didn't know her at all and had never spoken to her, not even in the locker room."

"And that was Calloway in the black-and-white?"

"He's the main reason I requested to come to Watch Five. I thought that if he didn't see me at roll call every day, he might stop dogging me."

"So he's your guardian angel," Nate said.

"On Watch Three, whenever he was clear, he'd roll on every call of mine that he figured had the slightest element of danger involved. I'm sure it drove his partners crazy. I know it drove me crazy."

"And now you have someone to watch over you, just like in the song."

"Much to my discomfort," Dana said. "I tried talking to him about it, but he claims he backs up everyone like this. I finally talked confidentially to the watch commander and got to come to Watch Five."

It was close to midnight when Dana Vaughn and Nate Weiss got a "man with a gun" call to the parking lot near the border with West Hollywood. It involved an elderly resident shooting at feral cats with a pellet gun. The pensioner explained that the cats were keeping him awake with their cries at night.

After giving the appropriate warnings and hearing promises from the old guy's daughter that it would never happen again, Dana and Nate were walking to their car, and there it was again: 6-A-79 parked a few houses away, lights out, watching.

"Okay, that's it!" Dana Vaughn said.

While Nate waited beside their shop, she crossed the street and approached the driver's side, saying, "Leon, can I talk to you for a minute?"

The hulking cop said something to his partner, got out of the black-and-white, and trudged off with Dana Vaughn until they were alone.

She said to him, "Leon, don't get me wrong, I appreciate that you think you're taking care of me, and I know why, but you gotta stop."

"I back up everyone on code two and code three calls if I can," he said, avoiding her eyes.

"Not like this, you don't," Dana said. "And it's embarrassing."

Leon Calloway, looking in the direction of his shoes, said, "You saved my life, Dana. I was two seconds from having my face blown apart. When I go home at night and peek in at my son sleeping, I think, I get to do this because of Dana Vaughn. When I wake up in the morning after a bad dream—and I have lots of bad dreams now—I think, I get to wake up this morning because of what Dana Vaughn did for me. That's what I think."

"Have you talked to our BSS guy?" Dana asked, referring to the Behavioral Science Services shrink who was assigned to the officers of Hollywood Station, a man with a lonely job, because cops, being members of a macho tribe, feared a stigma of being soft and needy.

"That's for sick people," the big cop said. "I'm not sick."

"Leon, this is over, hear me?" Dana said. "You've gotta move on with your life. Leave it behind. Let it go. If you do this again, I'm gonna have to complain to the captain."

Leon Calloway kept his head bowed for several seconds and finally turned and shuffled toward his waiting black-and-white.

"Roger that," he said without looking back. "But I'll never forget. And if you need anything, you just call Six-Adam-Seventy-nine. I'll be all over it."

When Dana got back to their shop and they resumed patrol, she said to Hollywood Nate, "There was one thing about the BSS shrink that I didn't tell you about. He said that women aren't so afraid to admit it when we can use a little help. I told him for the third time that I had no regrets about capping that guy, and that he did lots of bad things in his life, and I had no choice and no remorse. The shrink said, nevertheless, I killed a human being, and that means something to me in a certain part of my brain. He predicted that I might have night sweats and recurring dreams about trying to fire my gun and having the round dribble out and fall on the ground. He said that kind of dream is common to cops, especially after a fatal OIS." She paused, looked over at Nate, and said, "Do you ever have dreams like that?"

Nate studied Dana Vaughn as she drove, observing that the wise-cracking veteran had morphed. Now her mouth was pulled down at the corners, and her voice had lost some of its timbre, and in a peculiar way she looked younger. He liked being with this Dana more but thought it was time to bring his partner back from that other place.

Hollywood Nate cocked an eyebrow and said to Dana, "My gun *never* dribbles, partner. It's always locked and loaded and ready for action."

That did it. The tension faded, and she grinned mischievously, saying, "Ah, so all the Hollywood Nate gossip I hear from the girls in the locker room is true? Well, when you're ready for show 'n' tell, be sure to drop a dime, honey!"

TWO

"A RED FLAG UP on a mailbox is like a party invitation," Tristan Hawkins said to the man he called his apprentice, Jerzy Szarpowicz. "Outgoing mail. Come and get it."

His passenger flipped down the car's visor when the afternoon sun hit him in the eyes, surprisingly harsh rays given the layer of summertime smog they had to penetrate, smog lying low over the Hollywood Hills.

Jerzy Szarpowicz was the second Jerzy who'd worked for the boss, Jakob Kessler. The boss told Tristan that he liked to hire people of Eastern European ethnicity and also said that he was born and raised in the former East Germany and believed that Poles, Serbs, Hungarians, Czechs, Romanians, and those from other former Soviet-bloc countries were more reliable than Americans. He said, however, that he never hired Russians or Armenians, who were too ambitious and dangerous, too given to extortion and violence.

But the only thing Polish about Jerzy Szarpowicz was his name, thanks to a Polish great-grandfather who'd immigrated to America from just outside of Radom, Poland. On one of his meetings with Tristan, Jakob Kessler admitted that he was sorry to learn that he hadn't hired a real Pole, but he'd decided to give Jerzy a chance anyway.

Until the older Jerzy, whose surname was Krakowski, failed to show up on a scheduled job and was not seen again, having two Jerzys in the group confused some of the other runners. So Krakowski was called Old

Jerzy, and Szarpowicz New Jerzy. When Tristan inquired after the fate of Old Jerzy, Jakob Kessler simply said that his employment had been terminated.

New Jerzy seldom spoke to Tristan, communicating with grunts and mumbles in response to the running commentary from the loquacious driver of the battered sixteen-year-old Chevy Caprice. Jerzy knew his partner only as Creole. When the car slowed and stopped at the next street mailbox with the flag up, Jerzy opened the box and scooped all of the outgoing mail through the open car window into his own lap.

Tristan said, "Man, I knew a crew of tweakers that used to steal the blue mailboxes right off the street corners. Took some tools, a pickup truck, and lots of sweat, but they'd do it. Or they'd break into a mail truck and steal keys and mail. I knew one street whore that was blowin' a mail carrier, and she made her own key from his and sold that to the tweakers."

"So what happened to the tweakers?" Jerzy muttered.

"What always happens to tweakers? Their teeth fall out and they end up in the joint. They're doin' federal time. How about you? Smokin' much crystal these days?"

The fucking nerve of this dude, interrogating him, Jerzy thought, but he said, "I do pot and booze. And maybe I do a little crack or crystal once in a while."

"Mr. Kessler will let you go if he thinks you're a tweaker," Tristan said. "He don't like tweakers."

Jerzy gave a noncommittal grunt while eyeing the multimillion-dollar homes on both sides as the car snaked its way along the residential streets overlooking Hollywood. As he saw it, the problem with stealing mail was that down in the flats, there weren't street mailboxes. Most down there were attached to the walls of homes or businesses, and mail thieves would have to get out of the car and run to the box, taking a chance of being gang-tackled by some fucking neighborhood heroes or of giving some nosy neighbor enough time to take down their license number. That's why they were cruising these fancy streets in the Hollywood Hills, but it was risky because the only people who drove crap cars like this one were Mexican gardeners or housekeepers. And since neither of them was a greaser, Jerzy didn't like it a bit. Any cop who took a close look would jack them up for sure.

Jerzy Szarpowicz had been in Los Angeles for twenty years, having drifted in at the age of nineteen after receiving a bad-conduct discharge from the US Navy for grand theft. He'd thought about returning home to Arkansas but decided that with his dicey discharge and the several run-ins he'd had with LAPD narcs that got him three trips to L.A. County Jail for selling meth and crack, he wouldn't even be able to get a shitty construction job like his father and both his brothers. Besides, he liked the climate in L.A.

What he didn't like were all the goddamn nonwhite foreigners who lived in the city, and what he especially didn't like was this dude next to him, who said Creole was his "nom de guerre" instead of just his street name. Creole seemed to think he was some kind of master criminal and Jerzy was his lackey. What Jerzy said behind Creole's back to the few other runners he'd met was that Creole seemed to forget which one of them was the nigger.

Creole, who was nine years younger than Jerzy, wore his hair in dreads to his shoulders, and Jerzy thought his skin was the color of a buckskin mare his uncle used to own. Creole had delicate, almost feminine features and could nearly pass if he shaved his head. Jerzy decided that Creole's momma was fucking white men and that's how she ended up with a buckskin boy.

Creole claimed he'd lived for a time in New Orleans, long before Hurricane Katrina, and seemed to think he was some kind of artiste, always going on about some dance or other he'd choreographed back when he worked in a dance studio part-time. That's when he wasn't yapping about something he'd learned "back in college." Jerzy figured him for a closet faggot that never got out of high school. His dance studio was probably a three-room rat hole he shared with streetwalking dragons, and the only dancing he did was when he got a ten-inch cucumber up his ass.

Tristan Hawkins didn't like Jerzy Szarpowicz any more than Jerzy liked him, but he was under orders to train the surly redneck, and that's what he was doing. Tristan looked at the pile of mail accumulating at his partner's feet and said, "Okay, let's call it a day up here. We gotta get our other job done and head back to the office."

That's another thing that made Jerzy sneer. The "office" was what he called the duplex apartment in east Hollywood where meetings were held with the boss in order to trade loot for pay.

"About time," Jerzy said. "This is way stupid to be cruisin' up here." And he waved his hand to indicate the hills of Hollywood with all the multimillion-dollar homes. "Maybe you figure to outrun any cops that might come after this piece-of-shit car of yours?"

Tristan couldn't contain his own sneer. This biker-ugly cracker calling *him* stupid? Tristan looked at Jerzy's belly, hanging in two blubber rolls under his sweaty black T-shirt. Jerzy was tatted-out on both arms, Navy shit and women's tits. And of course the dumb Polack wore a baseball cap backward on his football-shaped skull, with tufts of rhubarb-red hair sticking out over his wing-nut ears, and with eyebrows like balls of rust clinging to his lumpy forehead under the cap band. And those faded blue eyes of his, Tristan thought they looked too shallow to drown an ant, but the grungy little teeth were the worst, like you'd see on the pancaked carcass of roadkill that spent its life eating grubs, insects, and worms. When they went on certain jobs, Jerzy wore a long-sleeve shirt to cover the ink and turned the bill to the front, but it didn't help at all, and Tristan hated to be seen with him and always walked several paces ahead.

"Never fear, my Polish apprentice," Tristan said with a smirk. "I won't try to get away in this piece-of-shit car. I'll bail and get away on my two feet. You can try it too. You can waddle up one of them steep streets fast as you can and see how far you get. You'll drop dead of a heart attack and the cops won't end up with nothin' but a pile of mail and a car that's registered to a dude that died two years ago. And three bills of dead goober coolin' out on the curb. So I don't see no problem with this here car, wood."

"You're gonna woof on me once too often," Jerzy said. "I ain't no goober. And I don't weigh no three bills."

"Hey, if it don't apply, let it fly," Tristan said.

"And I warned you before, I don't like bein' called a peckerwood."

Tristan's mouth smiled and he said, "I dropped the pecker. You okay with that, wood?"

Jerzy glared with watery blue eyes at the brazen little nigger, the scar across Jerzy's eyebrow flushing through the frown, and said, "Someday, Mr. Bojangles, you're gonna dance too far."

"Somehow I get the idea that us two ain't never gonna get all 'Kum Bay Ya,'" said Tristan Hawkins.

The next and final job of their long working day was at a popular Gym-and-Swim in the San Fernando Valley. It boasted an enormous workout room with state-of-the-art equipment and an indoor pool, and Jakob Kessler had arranged a membership card for Tristan under a fictitious name. This kind of job was not for Jerzy, who looked too much like street trash to get through the door without someone grabbing weapons of self-defense. Tristan, on the other hand, was clean-shaven and untatted, wore wire-rim glasses even though he didn't really need them, and always dressed in a clean Polo shirt and Banana Republic jeans and the kind of Nike sneaks that white men wore. He figured that his dreads even enhanced his aura of respectability, making him look more like the sensitive artistic type he felt he was.

Tristan parked the car in the Gym-and-Swim lot, where Jerzy pulled his baseball hat over his eyes to snooze. Tristan opened the trunk, took out his gym bag, and entered, showing his card to the kid at the desk, who barely glanced at it before giving him a locker key and a towel.

There were no members in the locker room, so Tristan walked along the double rows of laminated wood lockers and tried them all before putting down his bag. You never knew when somebody might forget to lock his, but not today. He put the bag on one of the benches and took out his tiny eyeglass screwdriver and a pick. He could open a locker in less than a minute, and he opened two that turned out to be empty before he found one that was in use. The clothes hanging there looked promising, and the Rolex inside one of the Ferragamo loafers looked very promising, possibly indicating a large line of credit for this dude. It took all of Tristan's self-control not to steal the Rolex and the wallet, but Jakob Kessler had drilled it into his head that discipline would make money for them and keep them out of jail. And that greed would get them jailed, "or worse."

Jakob Kessler, which Tristan figured was a bogus name, looked to Tristan like an accountant. He was an unimposing guy, maybe in his late fifties, with a full head of slicked-back silver hair, and maybe six feet tall but with posture somewhat stooped. There was something about those eyes, so pale that the irises looked more white than blue. Tristan thought from the beginning that he shouldn't fuck with the guy, at least not until he saw how much money he was going to make through their association. He took the "or worse" to mean something very bad might happen to him if he disobeyed orders.

Kessler had explained the game to Tristan in that accent of his, saying, "If you steal money, the man can figure out how it happened. If you replace the card and steal nothing, he will be confused and try to think, when was it he had his last restaurant meal and mistakenly got given back the wrong card?"

"What if he goes to a gas station right after his workout and finds out he's got a wrong card?" Tristan had asked Kessler.

His employer had said, "Even if he discovers the replacement card today, he is going to take time to ponder and to maybe call the last restaurant he visited. He will not think that the card could have been stolen from his wallet, because nothing else is missing—not his money, nothing. His belief will be that the restaurant made a mistake. And we may have the use of the card for perhaps one day. Perhaps two. Perhaps longer, you never know. So you see, Creole, why we do not steal money, rings, or wristwatches? It would end that specific game for us."

When he spoke to Kessler, Tristan was conscious of his own grammar and diction, never talking street to the man. He said, "You mean at that specific location?"

"Exactly," Kessler said. "We can visit the Gym-and-Swim at least once a week for a very long time if we are patient and not greedy. You must never surrender to greed." Then his employer said, "There must be discipline."

Tristan did not like the way Kessler's eyes bore into his when he uttered that last word, and he didn't think it wise to push it. Instead he said, "What's the longest you ever had a card before it got canceled?"

"For almost a month," Kessler said.

"And how much did your people charge on it?" Tristan asked.

Kessler chuckled and said, "You have a curious mind, Creole. I don't mind that. I like curiosity in a man as long as he is loyal and obedient. To answer your question, many thousands were charged in small amounts for three weeks before the switched card was discovered and reported."

"That ain't—that's not bad," Tristan said. "Not bad at all."

"Think of what one location like Gym-and-Swim could do for us in a few months, Creole," Kessler said to him, "if we never surrender to greed."

There it was again: *greed*. When Kessler said it that time, his eyes seemed to grow deader than Old Jerzy Krakowski. That's where Tristan figured Old Jerzy was—dead. He figured that's what Kessler really meant when he'd said that Old Jerzy's employment had been terminated. He wondered if Old Jerzy had surrendered to greed.

Tempted though he was, memories of all of those conversations with Jakob Kessler made Tristan leave the Rolex inside the loafer. Tristan opened the wallet and found three credit cards. He removed the American Express card and, choosing from among the several cards that Kessler had given to him, replaced it with a stolen and expired American Express card.

Tristan picked six more lockers and was disappointed that only one had clothes inside. He removed a Visa card from the wallet in that locker, and was in the process of replacing it with a stolen and expired Visa card, when a customer in a Speedo walked into the locker room, drying off with a towel. Tristan was ready to bolt if this was the guy's locker and he started yelling.

But the man, a flabby fifty-something with a bad transplant and a worse dye job, just smiled and said, "The pool's too cold today in case you plan to try it." He went to a locker on the other side of the benches and unlocked a lower one.

Tristan said to the guy, "I just had a workout on the treadmill. I'm ready to go home."

Then a naked bodybuilder suddenly entered from the pool area, a white guy with shoulders like a buffalo who was all sleeved-out with tatts, from his wrists to his bulging biceps. On his belly he had an attention-getting tattoo of a semiautomatic pistol, muzzle down. With his shirt hanging open, it would look like he was packing, a handgun tucked inside his waistband. His head was shaved, and even his skull was inked-up. Just over his left ear, where a gold loop dangled, a tatt on his skull said, "What're you looking at, bitch?"

Tristan froze. The guy was between him and the exit. If he was into this 'roid monster's locker, he was one dead identity thief. But the guy walked past him and opened a locker near the end of the row.

Tristan hurriedly completed the switch, closed the locker, and left the locker room, making sure to slip past the desk when the kid was on the phone and not looking, because he hadn't been in there long enough for a workout or a swim. His only regret was that the Rolex would've looked very fine on his wrist. He was definitely a Rolex type of dude.

Officer Sheila Montez, the heavy-lashed, sloe-eyed P2 who was currently the heartthrob of both surfer cops as well as half the midwatch, had just finished doing her nails with clear polish, all the while shooting peevish glances at her slightly older partner. Aaron Sloane, at age twenty-nine and with eight years on the LAPD, certainly did not look older than Sheila Montez, nor anyone else at Hollywood Station, and that included twenty-two-year-old rookies. The boyish-looking cop was too heavy-footed on brake and throttle for Sheila's taste, and he caused her to smear polish on her fingertip.

Both partners had the windows rolled down on this warm summer twilight as Aaron drove through the streets in the Hollywood Hills, where a number of car burglaries had taken place during early evening hours. After Sheila finished with her nails, she held all ten fingers in front of her, blowing lightly on them. Like all women patrol officers at LAPD, she had her hair pinned up so that it did not hang below her collar. And like all women officers who favored lip gloss and nail polish, she wore a pale unobtrusive shade while on duty. Aaron Sloane liked watching her do her lips and nails and thought her dusky good looks could be enhanced by a more crimson shade, especially if those lustrous umber tresses were unpinned and draped across her shoulders.

Sheila had almost seven years on the Job, and though she'd recently transferred to Hollywood from Pacific Division, she was comfortable enough with Aaron to be tending to nails and makeup while riding shotgun in unit 6-X-66. When she'd been a rookie at Northeast Division, her field training officer, an old P3 named Tim Brannigan, would've had apoplexy if she'd tried this in his shop. Tim Brannigan had been the kind of FTO who resented women working patrol in the first place, never talked to her when he could yell, and made her call him sir right to the end of her probationary period.

Since he'd hated writing reports, Tim Brannigan had let her drive only about once every four or five days. The rest of the time she was the passenger, doing the report writing. His favorite response to her requests to drive had been, "Rookie, you're taking the paper."

Sheila figured the old bastard probably wasn't breast-fed as a baby, so he never learned to appreciate or respect women. But at least he wasn't one of the handsy partners who'd "accidentally" touch her when reaching for the MDC dashboard computer. There had been more than a few of those in her career.

Sheila recalled a night two weeks earlier when Aaron Sloane was driving and a code 3 call had interrupted her nail polishing. She'd had to hang her wet nails out the window to dry while he drove with lights and siren to a check-cashing store where a clerk had accidentally tripped the silent robbery alarm. Aaron never complained about her dangling fingers and never told the others about what he called her girl stuff and she called her ablutions. And he never complained about the car mirror being turned so she could touch up her lips.

Part of the reason Aaron never protested about anything was that he was one of the smitten ones, as Sheila had suspected from their first night together. But she'd never encouraged him, even though now, glancing over at him, she had to admit that he had boy-next-door good looks and was buff from a lot of iron pumping. It was just that the sandy-haired, baby-faced reticent types like Aaron had never appealed to her.

And as though he had read her mind at that moment, Aaron said, "I got carded Saturday night when I had a date with a girl I met in my poly sci class."

Like many of the young cops at Hollywood Station, Aaron was taking college classes, and he was only six units away from a bachelor's degree.

"Does that surprise you?" Sheila asked. "Getting carded? I wish I could get carded once in a while."

"Don't tell me you're worried about getting old," Aaron said, gazing at her with that moony expression of his.

"Less than two years from now I'll be thirty," she said. "It's hard to believe."

"I'll be thirty in four months," Aaron said. "And I get carded just about every damn time I go to a bar. It's embarrassing when I have a date."

"You'll be glad someday to be looking like a perennial frat rat." To tweak him she added, "Do you have to shave every day, Aaron, or just a couple times a week?"

Aaron reddened and said, "You know, my youthful DNA almost got me killed before I got off probation. Did you know I worked UC for a while? I mean deep undercover."

"No," she said, quite surprised. "Where was that?"

"I was one they took right from the academy and put into the buy program," he said, "back when they still liked to do that. I was twenty-one but looked sixteen. They put me in high school in the Valley, where teenage gangsters were selling pot and meth on campus. It was when a couple kids got killed in a four-car TC after they'd smoked crystal in the gym. It was mostly an intelligence-gathering job rather than making buys of dime bags. I was in school for two months as a senior transfer. My UC name was Scott Taylor, and I actually tried out for the baseball team. One time a very aggressive LAPD officer stopped a few of us in the school parking lot after a game, and he yelled to me, 'Get your hands up!' I put them up really high, thinking, if he shoots me, the trajectory test would get my mom and dad some big bucks in the lawsuit."

With a sly smile Sheila said, "Did you score with any of the cheerleaders?"

"I was warned about fraternizing with the other kids, especially of the female persuasion," Aaron replied. "And just as I was getting close to the adult gangster that was supplying the high school kids, I screwed up and ended my UC career."

"How'd you do that?"

"By getting in a fight in shop class. Some little dude in one of the Hispanic gangs kept picking on me, always calling me *puto* and *maricón,* shit like that. I got sick of it, and one afternoon he dumped a soda on me and I kicked his ass. Beat him bad right there in class. Our instructor called Security and had us both taken to the vice principal's office. He happened to be the only one that knew I was cop."

"Damn, Aaron!" Sheila said. "There's another side to you. Where do you park your Batmobile?"

"We were both given a suspension," Aaron continued with a self-conscious smile. "Which was fine with me, except when I drove home from school that afternoon, I got tailed by two tricked-out lowriders packed with crew. I figured they were tooled-up, so I tried to call for help, but my cell was dead. And that happened to be the day I was so late for school I ran out the door, leaving my Beretta on the kitchen table instead of taping it under the seat of my UC car like I was supposed to. With that posse driving up my ass, and me all helpless, I can tell you I was *scared.*"

"So what happened?"

"Of course, there's never a cop around when you need one, so I drove that shitty UC car straight to the nearest mall with the lead lowrider locking bumpers with me, and me thinking the crowds of people might scare them off. When I got there, I looked in the mirror and saw one dude leaning out the window, aiming what looked like a TEC-nine at me. And I kinda panicked and burned a fast left but lost it and went skidding through the window of a Big Five store, where luckily nobody got hurt but me. Two cracked ribs and a busted collarbone."

"What happened to the gangsters?"

"They split and got away. I wasn't really able to ID any of them later when gang cops showed me six-packs. I got removed from school real fast and from the buy program too. And after I recovered, I got sent to Wilshire patrol, where I finished my probation. All that drama because I looked way young. I've never found any advantage to it."

"That's quite a story, Aaron," Sheila said.

Aaron was pleased to see that for the first time, Sheila Montez seemed to be watching him with a bit of interest. Known for being supercool and unflappable, she'd told him she'd worked down south at both the busy Seventy-seventh Street Division as well as at Newton Street for three years. And she'd also done a couple of dangerous UC assignments where they'd needed Hispanic women. Aaron had felt that his police career had been tame next to Sheila's.

Aaron had also heard that she'd been married to a sergeant at Mission Division for about a year but had divorced him shortly after her baby was stillborn. It was not something she'd ever talked about to him, but nowhere on the planet was gossip as rife as in the police world, and secrets were nearly impossible to keep. Well, now he'd shown her that he too was someone with a history. It wasn't everyone that was chased through the window of a Big 5 store.

"My picture and UC name are in the high school yearbook," Aaron said. "I have one at home. I'll bring it in if you'd like to see it. I look really dorky."

"Sure, let's have a peek," Sheila said.

Their second call just after dark gave Aaron Sloane a chance to see another side of supercool Sheila Montez. After reading the southeast Hollywood address on the computer screen, she rogered the message and hit the en route key. When they arrived at the call, they saw a rescue ambulance already parked on the street, and a Latina in a lavender dress was waiting under a streetlight in front of a stucco duplex that had been tagged from roof to concrete slab with gang graffiti.

When she saw Sheila Montez, the woman started to speak Spanish, then saw that the male cop was a gringo and said in English, "My neighbor. Her baby..." Then the woman shook her head and walked back to her apartment.

The two cops entered just as the paramedics were leaving. Before exiting, the older paramedic said, "The baby's probably been dead for a few hours. Letting a sick infant with a respiratory infection sleep next to a broken-out window night after night wasn't helpful, that's for sure. And today Little Momma gave the baby a child's dose of medication, not an infant's dose. Then she put the baby facedown on a bulky quilt and decided to take a long nap after downing a glass or two of cheap chardonnay. It looks like the baby's illness, the overdose of meds, and the quilt around the baby's face resulted in accidental asphyxiation. But it's yours now. Catch you later."

The young mother was not Latina. She was rosy-cheeked and freckled, the teenage wife of a Marine deployed in Iraq. She was sitting on a kitchen chair, crying, a wineglass beside her on the table. The crib was in the only bedroom. Sheila Montez hesitated for a moment but walked to the crib to look at the infant.

The baby might have had her mother's rosy cheeks in life, but in death she was already turning gray, now lying faceup, nesting in the heavy quilt. Sheila Montez stared down at the baby for a long time, and Aaron Sloane was more than happy to let her take charge, figuring this was a job for a woman.

"She was like that when I woke up," the young mother said between sobs, looking at Aaron. "She was ice-cold, and I knew right away she was gone!"

Sheila Montez picked up the medicine bottle from a table beside the crib, looked at it, and put it back. For no apparent reason, she reached down and lifted the baby from the quilt that had smothered her and put her back down on the sheet. She adjusted the pink pajama across the infant's chest and, using a towel that was draped over the crib, wiped some dried mucus from the baby's face and smoothed back her corn-silk hair.

Aaron Sloane didn't learn until later that night that this was the first dead baby Sheila Montez had seen since the night that her own lay lifeless in her arms, when a nurse had let Sheila hold her dead baby for a few minutes before taking it away forever. He was just getting ready to put in an obligatory call to the night-watch detective so he could verify onscene that it was an accidental death before the body snatchers took her away.

All of a sudden his partner advanced toward the young mother. Sheila's wide-set dark brown eyes looked black now, and her face had gone very pale around the mouth. Trembling with rage, Sheila Montez said, "You...ignorant...pathetic...little—"

She didn't get a chance to say more because Aaron Sloane leaped forward, grabbed his partner by the arm, and dragged her outside, from where he could hear the young mother sobbing loudly. And there on the sidewalk in the darkness, Sheila tried to say something to him. She tried, but her fury utterly overwhelmed her and she started to weep. Aaron put his arms around her for a moment and she didn't resist, her body shuddering against him.

He saw the headlights as another patrol unit drove up, and he said, "Come on, partner, let's get you back to our shop."

While she was sitting in their car, trying to control the tears, Aaron waved off the second patrol car, indicating that no assistance was needed, returned to the duplex, made the calls, and did the paperwork until the coroner's van arrived.

Later, Sheila apologized to Aaron Sloane for what she wryly called "the Montez meltdown." She also told him about her own dead baby, and a little bit about her bad marriage to the sergeant from Mission Division, something she'd never spoken about with any other officer, male or female, at Hollywood Station. She did it because she had to, and she could only hope that Aaron Sloane was that most rare of creatures, a partner who could actually keep a secret in the gossip-riddled world of street cops.

"What happens in our shop stays in our shop," Aaron Sloane at last said to Sheila Montez, trying to reassure her when he saw the anguish in her eyes.

As for Aaron Sloane, he realized that he had been her confessor that night only because he was there, such being the strange and unique intimacy that can develop quite by chance within a police partnership. But in this case, it was an intimacy that set his heart racing. And being true to his word, nobody but Aaron Sloane ever learned what had happened to imperturbable Sheila Montez the night she stood in silence beside a dead baby's crib.

★ THREE ★

THERE WAS MORE THAN THE USUAL amount of complaining going on at the midwatch roll call the next afternoon, especially concerning Officer Hall from Watch 3, who had been bitten on the thumb by a gay hooker on Friday night. His taller brother, who worked Watch 5, had started the gripe session on behalf of his little brother. The cops called them Short Hall and Long Hall. The prisoner wouldn't consent to a blood test, so a search warrant would have to be obtained in order to take the prisoner's blood. The cop's vacation had to be postponed, and Long Hall was so livid that Sergeant Murillo assigned him to the desk, feeling that he might go all junkyard dog if turned loose on the streets.

Long Hall said to Sergeant Murillo, "Twenty years of fighting 'roided-up street savages and my brother gets taken down by Tiny Tim with a germ in his ass. They shoulda just cut his thumb off so the AIDS bug couldn't crawl up his arm."

Everyone in general was grouchy too because they were only able to field six cars, what with the perennial personnel shortages at LAPD. The midwatch should've had a dozen. It was to be expected, given that the bulk of the probationary rookies were on Watch 2 and Watch 3, leaving the Watch 5 midwatch to the saltier cops. And then someone mentioned the name of the despised US district judge who for more than six years had been ramrodding the federal consent decree, under which the LAPD was compelled to function as a result of the Rodney King riots and the so-called Rampart scandal a decade earlier.

The federal jurist had publicly commented that a recent criminal case involving a series of home invasions where drug dealers were ripped off by a trio of cops, two from LAPD, indicated that the draconian consent decree policies should not be lifted. The judge felt that this case proved that the consent decree was an essential tool in policing the police, bringing with it an endless paper blizzard devoted to audits and oversight and micromanaging minutiae. The private "monitoring" firm, which received a cool $2.4 million a year from a teetering city budget to oversee compliance, could not have been unhappy with the judge's comments, which implicitly encouraged more milking of the municipal cash cow with no end in sight.

"Does anybody ever point out that there were only two crooked cops in that whole freaking Rampart deal?" Flotsam rhetorically asked the acting watch commander, not expecting an answer and not getting one.

"And how about this latest case?" Hollywood Nate said. "Two cops again. We're a police department of ninety-three hundred, for chrissake! A total of four thieving cops in ten years, and the judge thinks LAPD corruption is pervasive? I wonder how many corrupt lawyers are out there in our fair city?"

Jetsam said, "And who caught the bad Rampart cops? It was us. LAPD caught them!"

"It's a catch-twenty-two," Dana Vaughn said. "There's no financial incentive for the auditing firm to ever say that LAPD's taken all the steps required under the consent decree. We might be still using hundreds of coppers doing useless and redundant paperwork for another ten years. No wonder the midwatch can only field six cars on a weekend night!"

Sheila Montez said, "When LAPD was forced to break up the Rampart Crash unit, *Mara Salvatrucha* gangsters from L.A. to El Salvador were dancing in the streets."

Hollywood Nate said, "Why can't all those cop haters be satisfied? They broke our sword, why do they have to bury it up our ass?"

The acting watch commander was Sergeant Lee Murillo, a wiry, sharp-eyed, third-generation Mexican-American with prematurely gray wavy hair who had almost made an L.A. Dodgers farm team fifteen years prior, before his arm lost its elasticity and his fastball went from ninety-plus to a hanging balloon that his grandmother could've hit.

He'd been a cop for thirteen years and a sergeant for three, all of his supervisory years having been spent at Hollywood Division, now officially called Hollywood Area to sound less military. Of course, the troops said that anyone, including the brass, who would replace *division* with *area* was a pussy, and Sergeant Murillo always referred to their piece of Los Angeles geography as Hollywood Division.

The fact was, he agreed with everything they said, but being a supervisor, he wasn't supposed to validate the bitching. He just sat in front of the room and gazed over the heads of the dozen seated troops at the one-sheet movie posters decorating the walls, posters that could be found in other parts of the building as well in case anyone didn't know that this police station was in Hollywood, USA. In the roll call room were the posters for *L.A. Confidential* and *Sunset Boulevard*. Downstairs there was *Hollywood Homicide*.

Lee Murillo wondered when they'd start in on their latest complaint. That would be the brouhaha over the judge's wanting "confidential financial disclosure" by all LAPD officers who worked gang enforcement details and narcotics field enforcement. The rant came from Johnny Lanier, the only black cop on Watch 5. Johnny was a compact, outspoken P3 with fourteen years on the Job. He was a veteran of the first Gulf War who liked to say, "This job has all the good things about the Army: a uniform, weapons, camaraderie, ball-busting fun, and I don't have to go back to Iraq." He was next up to work the Gang Impact Team, but he didn't know if he wanted to work GIT now that there was the financial disclosure issue.

"Who's the problem out there, gangbangers or us?" he said. "You think I want some gangster or his lawyer getting his hands on my bank account number? How does that keep me honest in the first place?"

"No other law enforcement agency has to reveal their assets or bank accounts," Hollywood Nate said. "Do you think those few crooked LAPD cops put their loot in their bank accounts? The only ones that get their privacy violated here are the honest cops!"

Sergeant Lee Murillo looked at his watch then, and they took it as a cue. They ceased grumbling and settled down so he could call roll and read the crimes. But before he started, Sergeant Murillo earned a bit of applause when he said quietly, "I'd like to tell the federal judge that if I was a crooked cop, I would certainly never put the hot money in my bank account. I'd stuff it in my freezer, just like your average US congressman."

Six-X-Seventy-six decided to write their first ticket of the watch at 6:30 P.M., shortly after clearing from roll call, when they saw a ten-year-old GMC pickup blow a stoplight on Melrose Avenue near Paramount Studios. There was still plenty of daylight on this hot summer evening, and the setting sun was certainly not in the eyes of the driver who was heading east.

Hollywood Nate was driving and said to Dana Vaughn, "You're up."

Dana grabbed her citation book, and after Nate tooted at the guy to pull over, he parked behind the pickup. She got out and approached the car while Nate crossed behind her and stepped up on the sidewalk to look in through the passenger window.

The driver was a wide-bodied working stiff in his late twenties dressed in a gray work uniform. His fingernails were grease-caked, and smudges showed on his ruddy cheeks, as though he'd been crawling under a car.

"Your license and registration, please," Dana Vaughn said, and the guy fumbled with his wallet.

The smell of stale beer hit her, and when he handed over his driver's license, she said, "How much have you had to drink today?"

The guy looked up with bloodshot, unfocused eyes, brushed his light brown hair off his forehead, and said, "The boss let me off early because my wife had twins yesterday. A boy and a girl. Two of the mechanics I work with bought me some beers to celebrate."

"How many beers did you drink?"

"Seven," he said. "Or eight. I'm not used to drinking."

Dana looked over the bed of the truck at Hollywood Nate and said, "Whadda you know? A forthright man." Then she opened the door of the pickup and said, "Step out, sir. Up onto the sidewalk."

When the new father stepped onto the sidewalk, he stumbled, and Nate reached out, grabbing his elbow. "Whoa, cowboy," Nate said.

"What've you been arrested for?" Dana asked.

"Nothing," the young man said. "Never. You can check. And I only had one ticket for speeding in my whole life."

"Your whole life is gonna be cut short if you keep drinking seven or eight beers and driving," Dana said.

She looked at Nate, knowing that he hated booking drunk drivers, believing it was too much paperwork for a misdemeanor and that it probably meant court time. He was always looking for something that could get his name in the news. Something that could make a casting agent see it and remember him.

The mechanic stood on the sidewalk, facing the two cops and reeling slightly, taking out his cell phone. "I can call and have my brother come get me," he said boozily. "I'm a father now. I can't afford to go to jail. Besides, Officer, I'm not really drunk."

"You're not, huh," Dana said. "Let's see you count backward from seventy-five to fifty-five. If you can do it, we'll let you lock up your truck and call your brother."

The mechanic said, "Yes, Officer." And turning around unsteadily until his back was to the astonished cops, he said slowly over his shoulder, "Can you please tell me again what number I should start with?"

Hollywood Nate stared dumbfounded, and when he'd recovered, he said to Dana, "Partner, there's no way we can book this guy. I can dine out on this story."

Dana Vaughn said to the new father, "Okay, honey, turn back around and call your brother to come get you."

The trio standing on the sidewalk never noticed the nondescript gray Honda Civic motoring slowly past them on Melrose, where the mechanic had earned his freedom by unintentionally providing the officers of 6-X-76 with a locker-room tale. The man that Tristan and Jerzy knew as Jakob Kessler glanced their way but was not curious, checking his watch because he had to be at the restaurant before Suzie got off shift.

Suzie was waiting for Kessler when he got there. She was a recent college graduate who'd majored in art history and, like thousands before her, had gotten employment where she could, usually in Hollywood eateries. The young woman looked nervous and was fiddling with her auburn ponytail when Kessler walked into the chain eatery on Sunset Boulevard. The stools were all taken, as were most of the tables, and Jakob Kessler, wearing his usual dark suit and plain necktie, waited until a customer vacated one of the stools.

He sat, ordered a cup of coffee, and used a paper napkin when he lifted the cup to his lips, so as not to leave fingerprints when he was working a job. As for DNA on the cup, there was nothing he could do about it short of carrying a spray bottle and washing it. He dismissed his action as a silly example of his growing anxiety with the work overload being forced upon him, and he dropped the paper napkin.

Suzie brushed past him, touching his back when she took an order to the kitchen, and when she returned, she paused behind his stool, removed the skimmer from under her apron, and handed it to him. Jakob Kessler took the skimmer, which was the size of a cigarette pack, and put it under his suit coat in a small bag hanging from his shoulder. As Suzie was walking away, she had her hands behind her and held up four fingers on one hand and five on the other, meaning that she'd skimmed nine credit cards.

Jakob Kessler put money on the counter for his coffee and counted out two $50 bills for Suzie. He felt he was being overly generous, but she was new and he wanted to keep her in the game. They passed close to each other when he headed for the door and she freed her right hand from a tray of dessert and grabbed the money, slipping it into her apron pocket. He didn't have a replacement skimmer with him and made a mental note to have his wife go on the Internet and buy several new ones. After all, they were only $50 each and worth their weight in diamonds.

For his next stop he had to drive over the hill to a mall in Sherman Oaks. Once again he considered the way he was doing business, wearing out tires and shoe leather when there were competitors doing it the easy way. He knew several Hollywood Armenians who were putting their skimmers inside service station gasoline pumps. He'd been told that it was ridiculously easy to do, since one key opened all pumps. The Armenians would simply wait until the service station was closed, then install the skimmer. After a few days they'd return to the pump and remove it as easily as they'd installed it.

The Romanians were more ingenious, and experts in Bluetooth technology. They'd simply aim their device, which would seek, find, and connect, relaying the information from the skimmer. They didn't even have to take the risk of dealing with a device that might get discovered by a service station owner who'd then alert police. The city was full of cyber thieves trolling the airwaves.

He drove to a Hollywood shopping center and entered a hardware store, one of the chains that employed at least a hundred employees in each store. He picked out a roll of duct tape that he did not need and headed for the checkout line manned by a longtime store employee named Harold Swanson, a man who spent far too much on the horses at Hollywood Park and Santa Anita.

This was another case that caused Jakob Kessler vexation after his suggestion to install a skimmer in the POS machine was summarily dismissed by his wife as "stupid and risky." He knew that none of the Eastern European teams would have hesitated to bribe Harold Swanson to install a skimmer there at the point of sale, to be removed at a propitious moment, thereby eliminating all these daily trips over the hill into the San Fernando Valley.

When Harold Swanson saw Jakob Kessler in line at his counter, he worked a little faster to finish with another customer and said to Kessler, "Evening, sir, is that all you're purchasing this evening?"

"Just the duct tape," Jakob Kessler said in his German accent.

"Yes, sir," the clerk said. "Sometimes we have sales on duct tape where you can buy six rolls at half price. Six."

Jakob Kessler said, "Six. I shall remember that." Then he put down a $10 bill for the tape along with six $50 bills from his wallet.

Harold Swanson put the duct tape and the skimmer in a plastic bag, pocketed the six President Grants, and handed the bag to Jakob Kessler, saying, "Have a nice evening, sir."

Tristan Hawkins and Jerzy Szarpowicz were waiting at the duplex/office with two of the three Latino runners that Kessler had hired for their skill in passing bogus checks at the many stores catering to illegal immigrants from Mexico and Latin America. Tristan and Jerzy were speaking to each other by then, as much as they ever did, Jerzy sitting in one of the secondhand overstuffed chairs, when all at once he slapped at a flea and leaped to his feet.

"Goddamn it!" he yelled and did a dance, his wattles bouncing as he slapped at his belly and reached around to his back, brushing away more imaginary fleas.

"Why do you think I never sit on nothin' here unless it's made of wood or plastic?" Tristan said. "How 'bout you, Diego?"

One of the two young Mexicans sitting at the table in the kitchenette looked up and grinned, a gold tooth gleaming, and said, "Las *pulgas*. They don' be hurting you, man. If they ain't scorpions, I don' say nothing."

He was doing freelance work, "washing" a stolen check with acetone. The larger Mexican next to him, a placid mestizo teenager, was doing the same to another check, but he was washing it with nail polish remover. Both men worked with great patience and care.

Tristan said to them, "Don't let Mr. Kessler see you doin' that. Nobody with any class bleaches checks these days. It's too easy to make your own."

The smaller Mexican shrugged and said, "This how we do it back in Cuernavaca. I still make some money like this."

Jerzy walked to the kitchen, opened the little refrigerator, found nothing but two strawberry sodas inside, and took one without asking and popped it open. He eased his bulk onto the floor, leaned against the plasterboard wall, and drank.

Tristan said to the Mexican, "Can I have one too, Diego?"

"Okay," said the Mexican, not looking up from his work.

Tristan put two dollars on the kitchen table and took the last soda. When he sat down beside his partner, he said, "So how do you like the job, wood?"

"It's okay," Jerzy said. "Till somethin' better comes along." He gulped down the drink, crushed the can in his big beefy mitts, and said, "How long you been workin' here, anyways?"

"Almost two months," Tristan said. "Old Jerzy was somebody I used to see at Pablo's Tacos when I'd go there to score a couple rocks. He told me about Jakob Kessler. Now Old Jerzy's gone."

"This job don't look like a place where you form long-term relationships," Jerzy said.

"How'd you meet the man?" Tristan asked.

"This basehead named Stella told me about him. She used to live in the room next to me at Cochran's Hotel. Said I could make some serious coin, but I ain't seen nothin' serious yet."

"I don't know a Stella workin' for him," Tristan said.

"She's brain-fried, man. Here one day, spun out and gone the next."

"Jakob Kessler is one weird dude," Tristan said, realizing that this was the first time in four days working together that he and Jerzy had spoken more than a dozen words at a time.

Jerzy just grunted and scratched his balls, looking as though he'd like to throw one of the Mexicans out of a kitchen chair so he could get off the floor.

"Way he got me," Tristan said, "he saw me lookin' at some shiny spinners on a pimpmobile at Pablo's. He says to me in that Hitler accent of his, 'You don't have to steal spinners. If you want them, you can walk in a store and buy them with a credit card.' Then he bought me a taco plate and we talked."

"He never bought me nothin'," Jerzy said.

"The man can talk," Tristan said. "Do those weird eyes of his ever get on your nerves?"

"I don't pay no attention to nobody's eyes," Jerzy said. "Unless I think the guy's an undercover cop and he's lookin' at me too close."

Tristan then said to the smaller Mexican, "How long you been at work here for the boss?"

The Mexican shrugged and said, "Three, four week. I think."

"And your amigo?" Tristan said.

"The same."

"See?" Tristan said to Jerzy. "Nobody works long for Kessler. Then they're gone, like Old Jerzy. I'll bet this fuckin' apartment is rented week to week."

"What, you were hopin' for a pension and health plan?" Jerzy said.

"I just don't wanna suddenly not be here someday," Tristan said. "Like Old Jerzy."

The Mexicans completed their check washing and hid their work in a laundry bag just before Jakob Kessler arrived. He still looked neat and eminently presentable in his suit and white shirt and tie, a businessman finishing up a long day but still ready in case a sale had to be made.

Tristan got to his feet, but Jerzy didn't bother. Tristan pointed to a paper bag on a little table by the flea-infested chair in the living room. "We didn't go through the real mail, Mr. Kessler. It's all there 'cept for the junk stuff. And the two credit cards I got from—"

"Never mind where you got them from," Jakob Kessler interrupted, glancing quickly at the two Mexicans.

"Oh, yeah," Tristan said, remembering that Kessler kept his teams of runners segregated for security. "Anyways, it's all there, Mr. Kessler."

"I was hoping you'd get more than two cards," Jakob Kessler said.

"The locker room—I mean the *place* was pretty busy. I'll do better next time," Tristan said.

Jakob Kessler picked up the bag, looked inside, and said, "How many mailboxes did you visit?"

"About fifteen or twenty," Jerzy said, finally standing up.

"Twenty-two," Tristan said. "There's bound to be some good stuff in there."

"We'll see," Kessler said. Then he reached into his inside jacket pocket, withdrew a leather wallet, and removed eight $100 bills, giving two to each man in the room. Then he removed one more $100 bill and gave it to Tristan, saying, "Your extra work was more risky."

"I could cash checks for you, Mr. Kessler," Tristan said. "If you'd get me a driver's license and a credit card. I always make a good impression, and people don't question me. Or I could be a great shopper if you'd give me a chance."

"I shall keep that in mind, Creole," Kessler said. "Perhaps in a few days."

"That's it?" Jerzy said. "I was with him. I only get two Ben Franklins for all our labor?"

Kessler said, "If your bags of material and the credit cards work out, you are going to get ten percent of what we net from them, as promised."

"How will I know how much you net?" Jerzy demanded.

"I shall tell you how much," Kessler said, annoyance in his voice, turning those pale lasers on his fat mail thief.

"That don't seem right, Mr. Kessler," Jerzy murmured, but when he glanced at the man's strange eyes, he looked away and was silent.

"You know where to take the merchandise after you shop tomorrow, don't you, Diego?" Jakob Kessler said to the smaller Mexican, who looked at Tristan and Jerzy and said, "I know, boss. The new place."

"Good lad," said Kessler.

"When we suppose to meet tomorrow, boss?" the Mexican asked.

"I can't do it tomorrow. Just wait for my call."

"Okay, boss," said the Mexican.

And then Kessler was out the door and gone.

"That man talks to people like we're all niggers," Jerzy said to the Mexicans.

"Fuck you, peckerwood," said Tristan.

For the first time all day, Jerzy smiled and replied, "As a famous member of your tribe once said, 'Can't we all jist get along?'"

There was a remarkable part of the story of the Rupert Moore shooting that Dana Vaughn did not share with Hollywood Nate. He'd learned it from Sergeant Lee Murillo at end-of-watch after Dana had gone home. The story made it that much more difficult for Nate to get annoyed with her for all her witty remarks at his expense. Only a few officers at Hollywood Station knew about it, yet it was considered a small miracle by the parents of Officer Sarah Messinger.

For each of the ten days that the rookie was at Cedars-Sinai Medical Center in a coma, Dana Vaughn had visited her, a woman she'd never met. Sarah Messinger was only a few years older than Dana Vaughn's daughter, and there was something about what the rookie had undergone that made Dana bond with that helpless young woman who was sustained by feeding tubes and monitors.

Dana introduced herself to the ward nurses on the first night, nurses who knew about the incident that put Officer Sarah Messinger in their care. And each day or evening, when she was sure that there would be no one else but nurses present, Officer Dana Vaughn, usually in uniform, would go to the bedside of the young woman and speak to her for ten minutes or more. Sometimes she told Sarah Messinger about the happenings on Watch 3. Sometimes she talked about teaming up with Sarah when she came back to work and was off probation. Sometimes she just did girl talk. But she never missed a day.

On one of those visits, when Dana was in uniform, an elderly Irish priest entered while Dana was talking to the young woman. The shoulders of the priest's black coat were flaked with dandruff, and Dana thought she could smell liquor on his breath. She stopped talking when he entered.

"Don't stop, Officer," he said with a thick brogue. "Please don't let me bother you. I only make the rounds to see if I'm needed by anyone."

Dana was embarrassed and said, "I know it's silly of me. The nurses say she can't hear me, but . . . well, I know it's silly."

"It's not silly," the priest said, and when he walked closer to the bed, Dana could see right through his wispy white hair to his scaly pink scalp, and she smelled liquor on his breath for sure. "Doctors don't know everything. I believe that people in comas are like dolphins that dive deep into the waters, fathoms deeper than we can imagine, but they are still capable of receiving signals from the surface. You keep talking to your young friend, and she will hear you in ways that we cannot understand."

"I'm not a Catholic, Father," Dana said, "but I'd like to think you're right."

"I'm not a *good* Catholic," the old priest said, "but I know I'm right."

The remarkable event happened at 8 P.M. on the evening of the tenth day, when Sarah Messinger awakened from her coma. Dana Vaughn was on a night off and dressed in civilian clothes when she rushed from home after getting a call and hearing the wonderful news. As she entered the hospital room, the parents of Sarah Messinger and a young neurosurgeon were standing by the young woman's bed, all overjoyed.

The Messingers had been apprised of the many visits by the police officer who'd shot the man that injured their child, and when they saw Dana Vaughn, Sarah's mother embraced her. Sarah was lying propped up on pillows, and she looked at Dana curiously.

Dana said, "Hello, Sarah. I'm so *very* happy tonight! You're looking just fine!"

"Thank you," Sarah said faintly.

"Do you know who this is, Sarah?" her mother asked.

"No," Sarah said, studying Dana for a moment. "But somehow I know her voice."

# FOUR

ONE OF THE NEWER COPPERS on the midwatch was forty-two-year-old R.T. Dibney. He'd worked patrol at Southeast, Hollenbeck, Newton Street, Mission, and North Hollywood Divisions during his nineteen-year career prior to his transfer to Hollywood Station. Three of those moves were "administrative transfers," which could mean almost anything but generally signaled that the officer hadn't done (or hadn't been caught doing) anything so serious that it could bring about heavyweight disciplinary action. But it was nevertheless an indication that the officer was persona non grata at the former station. It was the police version of "no convictions," and nobody liked finding administrative transfers in a personnel package.

R.T. Dibney was broad-shouldered and wore his chestnut hair in a kind of retro seventies cut, blow-dried, heavily sprayed, and just touching the ears, with sideburns long but not so long that he caught crap from the supervisors about shaving them shorter. He had a thin mustache that also was retro, unlike the macho growths that most cops sported, and, like his sideburns, it required a bit of L'Oréal to hide the gray. The thing about his mustache was that whenever he was in a tense situation, his upper lip twitched and the slender stash started jumping, a dead giveaway that something was amiss. As to his looks, according to Dana Vaughn he was "okay-looking in an infomercial-guy-selling-steak-knives sort of way."

His most recent transfer, the one from North Hollywood Division, resulted from his possibly having had a relationship with the wife of a Pacific Division watch commander, an allegation that could not be proved. The aggrieved watch commander, Lieutenant Edgar Lamb, had tried to set elaborate traps to catch his wife and her lover, certain that she was cheating on him with a police officer. One of the neighbors on his North Hollywood residential street told him confidentially that a black-and-white police car had been parked in front of his house several times during the deployment period when the lieutenant was on Watch 3 at Pacific Division, working all night and not getting home until late morning.

Then, a month later, when Lieutenant Lamb was at home on a day off and had occasion to report a raucous juvenile drinking party on his street, the call happened to be assigned to R.T. Dibney and his partner. When the two cops entered Lieutenant Lamb's house, the lieutenant identified himself as a watch commander at Pacific Division and introduced the two cops to his wife. The family cat, a wary and suspicious Persian, hissed at the partner who was first in the house, arched her back as she always did with strangers, and ran behind the sofa to hide.

But upon hearing R.T. Dibney's voice saying to Lieutenant Lamb's voluptuous wife, "Pleased to meet you, Mrs. Lamb," the cat ran from her safe haven directly to R.T. Dibney and purred, rubbed, and curled her body against and around his blue uniform trousers until it looked like he was wearing angora leg warmers.

As the lieutenant gawked, R.T. Dibney said, "What a friendly cat!"

Lieutenant Lamb said, "No, she's a very unfriendly cat. She hates strangers."

"I had a tuna sandwich before coming to work and musta spilled a little fish juice on my pants," R.T. Dibney said as his slender mustache jumped and twitched.

Thus began the suspicion that, though never conclusively proved, put R.T. Dibney on the short list for an administrative transfer, and he was assigned to the desk during part of his last deployment period at North Hollywood Division. At the urging of Lieutenant Edgar Lamb, Internal Affairs agreed to monitor a video camera in the station lobby to determine whether or not R.T. Dibney was making on-duty phone calls to Lieutenant Lamb's wife.

To set the trap, R.T. Dibney was specifically told by a North Hollywood sergeant that the camera in the lobby was strictly for officer safety because of an incident wherein a deranged person had walked into Rampart Station with a can of gasoline and tried to set the place on fire. And would have, except that he couldn't strike a match while wearing gloves.

After the sergeant's rather suspiciously timed and unnecessary remarks about the camera, R.T. Dibney whispered to the other desk officer, "Know what? We're on reality TV."

And during that tour of duty at the desk, when nobody was in the North Hollywood lobby but R.T. Dibney and that desk partner—a black veteran P2 named Otis Maxwell—R.T. Dibney suddenly began humming and rocking slowly, his mustache twitching, and then did a weird and spooky dance while staring at the camera lens as Officer Maxwell watched, stupefied.

When R.T. Dibney puckered his lips sensually and pinched his own nipples, Officer Maxwell cried, "What're you doin', Dibney? Your fuckin' stash is jumpin' like a tap dancer's nuts."

"Who am I?" R.T. Dibney said.

"Who are you?" Maxwell sputtered. "You're a fifty-one-fifty wack job is who you are."

"This is a charade. You gotta guess the famous movie. Come on, it's been on TV a hundred times."

"This is about a movie?" said Maxwell.

"I'll give you a hint," R.T. Dibney said. "I kill women and strip off their skin."

"Boy, we better get you down to the BSS shrink," said Maxwell. "You're weirded out. Gone bug shit."

"Okay, another hint," Dibney said. "My moniker in the movie is Buffalo Bill. The movie stars Jodie Foster and Anthony Hopkins, who won an Oscar."

Officer Maxwell could only gawk wordlessly when R.T. Dibney once again began the lascivious writhing and lubricious posing, all the time panting at the camera, and he only stopped when Maxwell cried, "*Silence of the Fuckin' Lambs*! Now step off! You're freakin' me!"

Internal Affairs later viewed the eerie video, and an IA investigator informed Lieutenant Edgar Lamb that this officer was not going to be caught so easily and that maybe the lieutenant should seek marriage counseling.

The end of R.T. Dibney's tour at North Hollywood Division and his administrative transfer finally came when he was ordered to transport to jail a Beverly Hills attorney whom a motor officer had arrested for DUI. The attorney, who'd been berating the motor cop, then directed the tirade against R.T. Dibney the moment the lawyer was put into the back-seat of his black-and-white. According to the lawyer's formal complaint, halfway to the station after the attorney demanded an answer to a legiti-mate question, "The officer farted at me. Twice." And since this hap-pened while the LAPD was laboring under the draconian federal consent decree, by which every accusation had to be taken seriously, a personnel complaint was initiated and had to be fully investigated.

According to the attorney's statement alleging the officer's unbecom-ing conduct, as well as during later verbal testimony before a trial board heard by a tribunal consisting of two command officers and a civilian, the lawyer said of the incident, "It was rude. It was insulting. It was dis-gusting. It was unprofessional. It was outrageous."

When it was his turn, Officer R.T. Dibney simply said, "It was frijoles."

Thus, R.T. Dibney's explanation for the infamous caboose chirps made him a minor LAPD legend after the tribunal cleared him of mis-conduct through what eventually became known throughout the Depart-ment as "the frijoles defense."

On his midwatch deployment at Hollywood Station, R.T. Dibney was assigned to 6-X-46 with P2 Mindy Ling, a twenty-eight-year-old Chinese-American cop with six years on the LAPD, the last three being at Hollywood Station. Mindy Ling was as tall as R.T. Dibney and studi-ous, ambitious, and serious, everything that R.T. Dibney was not. She wore her black hair pulled back severely and rolled into a bun, and she was one of the few cops of either gender at Hollywood Station to wear an easy-access shoulder mike, while others simply carried the radio on their Sam Browne belt. Mindy Ling used that kind of caution in everything she did in life. She hated to make mistakes.

One of the reasons that Sergeant Lee Murillo assigned them together for the current deployment period was that he didn't want someone riding with R.T. Dibney who could be influenced by his lothario ways. Sergeant Murillo didn't want to end up creating another pair like the surfer cops, whom the sergeant called his Tylenol Team. That particular pair of supervisory headaches made quality arrests but were always just a big toe away from stepping over the line while getting it done. As long as no-nonsense P2 Mindy Ling was riding with R.T. Dibney, Sergeant Murillo figured he'd be under control, and the slightest romantic overture toward her or anyone else would be dealt with instantly. Sergeant Murillo felt certain of that.

This was brought home on their first night working together in 6-X-46. Mindy Ling, who usually stayed home on her nights off to study for a master's degree in public administration, occasionally watched Turner Classic Movies with her parents. While R.T. Dibney was loading up their black-and-white with their gear, Mindy began conversing with the cinematic scholar, Hollywood Nate Weiss, about her partner's style choices. R.T. Dibney saw them looking his way from across the parking lot but didn't know they were discussing his lounge-lizard mustache and tinted puffy coif reminiscent of yesteryear's movie stars.

Because the gossipy world of street cops brooks no secrets, Hollywood Nate was also informing her that R.T. Dibney lost his most recent wife by going to Las Vegas with his buddies after telling her he was on a fishing trip. He blew $2,000 on a weekend of fun and frolic at the tables and in hotel bedrooms, and it just about cleaned out their bank balance. Nearly broke and remorseful, he'd returned to L.A. and gone straight downtown to the diamond district, where two Iranian jewelers called Eddie and Freddie sold him a beautiful cubic zirconium ring for his last $200. R.T. Dibney told his wife that the ring had cost $2,500, and though it broke their piggy bank temporarily, he'd felt compelled to purchase it in order to renew their wedding vows, so deep was his love for her.

That particular wife had a cousin in the jewelry business, and when she showed the cousin her ring, he pointed out to her that her diamond was bogus and her husband was a conniving turd that she should flush away before spawning something that carried his genetic profile. R.T. Dibney's divorce lawyer told the cop that he alone was putting the lawyer's kid through college and in essence thanked him for being such a conniving turd.

Mindy Ling thanked Hollywood Nate for the information on R.T. Dibney, and by way of introduction that ultimately left her new partner gob-smacked, she got behind the wheel of their car, turned to R.T. Dibney, and said, "I've heard a lot about you and your devil-may-care swashbuckling exploits. Tell me, how many times have you been married?"

"I've been married three-point-five times," R.T. Dibney said with a semi-leer. "It must be that I give off a certain musk that makes me a marriage target, but I'm technically still on the market...in case anyone's interested."

R.T. Dibney was enjoying this unexpected attention from Mindy Ling until she added, "Partner, I'm as much into nostalgia as the next girl, so I gotta respect someone in this day and age with the chutzpah to sport a toothbrush stash and a Lady Clairol blow-dried do. But while you're with me, I'd like you to keep in mind that no matter how hard you try channeling Errol Flynn, he's dead and gone, and nobody gives a damn how many women he balled. Now, let's try to concentrate on good police work the whole time we're together, shall we?"

Late that afternoon, while 6-X-46 was still in the parking lot with the rest of the midwatch, fourteen-year-old Naomi Teller was near Fairfax High School, walking home to Ogden Drive, when a slender, smiling boy in a light blue T-shirt and jeans, who she thought was at least eighteen years old, walked up behind her on the sidewalk and said, "Yo, Goldilocks, you can't be just getting out of summer school this late."

Naomi hesitated but was reassured by his brilliant smile, which produced deep dimples in his cheeks. She liked the way his black hair curled over his ears and on his neck, and she liked his flaming dark eyes and tawny cheeks, which sported a young man's light growth of soft dark whiskers. She felt that he might be Hispanic, but he had no accent, so she wasn't sure. It was flattering to have such a very cute older boy paying attention to her.

Naomi had small bones, narrow shoulders, and still-developing breasts. Eyes too large and mouth too small, she hadn't received much attention from the boys in middle school, but this older boy was looking at her and talking to her in a way that no one had before, and it was superexciting.

"I won't be going to Fairfax until September," Naomi Teller said truthfully, even though she was tempted to lie about her age.

"You and me should maybe go someplace and hang out," he said. "I'd like to get to know you and make some friends around here. Most girls with hair like yours have to dye it to get it so gold, but I can see that yours was a gift from God. My name's Clark, what's yours?"

"Naomi," she said, and she couldn't help smiling back at him, his dimpled smile was so infectious. "That's the name of the guy in Superman, Clark Kent."

"That's why my adopted parents named me that when they found me near a crashed spaceship."

Naomi giggled, and he smiled more broadly and said, "Your hair is exactly the color of the honey I spread on my peanut butter sandwiches."

That made her laugh. "I guess that's a compliment."

"Yours is a natural color," he said. "Anybody can see that. I hate all those old women who try to make their hair look like yours. They can't do it and shouldn't try."

"My mom tries," Naomi said.

"Maybe we should go to the movies sometime, Naomi," he said. "Can I have your number?"

"Well...," she said.

"What time do you go to bed?"

"In the summer? About eleven. My mom's strict."

"I'll call you at ten forty-five to say good night," he said.

Naomi thought those dimples and that smile were to die for. And his teeth? So straight and white, natural white, not that phony bleached white that so many older people like her father were doing these days.

She said, "Okay, you can call me." And she gave him her cell number, which he wrote on the back of his hand with a ballpoint pen.

He looked at her quite seriously then, as though he wanted to say something more, but an older couple walked out of a nearby apartment building and looked their way. Then he smiled again and said, "Got to bounce. Call you later. I'll think of you when I make my peanut butter and honey sandwich tonight."

She giggled again and gave a little wave and continued home, except she hadn't gone half a block when her cell rang. She took it out of her purse and didn't recognize the number.

"Hello?" she said, thinking it was a wrong number.

"It's Clark," he said.

She turned around, but there was nobody walking on the street, only lots of traffic roaring by. "I thought you were going to call me tonight," Naomi said. "Where are you?"

"I'm watching you, Naomi," he said. "You're so beautiful, I can't help it. And I called just to make sure you gave me the right number. If you hadn't, my heart would be broken."

She looked around uneasily then, peering through exhaust smoke from a large truck passing on the street, and said, "Where are you? I can't see you."

"Nowhere," he said. "I'll call later. Don't forget me. Don't ever forget me."

The man that Tristan and Jerzy knew as Jakob Kessler was exhausted by the time he got back to his apartment on Franklin Avenue that night. His wife, Eunice Gleason, was waiting for him, poisoning the air with her chain-smoking. He entered, unlocking both dead-bolt locks, and removed his suit coat and the booster bag that contained the skimmer, the bag of mail, and the credit cards. His feet were killing him, so he took off the custom-made shoes with the three-inch lifts, and arching his back, he stretched. And he was no longer stooped.

"I'm home, Eunice," he yelled with no trace of a German accent.

"No shit," Eunice said, a cigarette protruding from her teeth as her hands flew over the computer keys. An ashtray beside her on the table was full of butts, and with shades drawn, under the harsh glare from the gooseneck lamp, she looked to him like she should have been onstage, maybe stirring a kettle in *Macbeth*.

Eunice was fifty-five years old, a coppery blonde with gray roots that she seldom bothered dyeing anymore until there was at least an inch showing. She was fifteen pounds heavier than when they'd married nine years earlier, and her tits and ass were starting to nose-dive, but when she fixed herself up, she could be passably attractive. The four packs a day she smoked sent her to a spa for regular Botox injections to smooth out the lines and wrinkles, but there was no reasoning with a nicotine addict, especially a hardhead like Eunice, so he'd given up long ago. Anyway, he figured that the world's best plastic surgeon could never erase her natural scowl lines.

Their "workroom" was what for most people would have been the living room. There was a long table with three computers and mail trays taking up every inch of the tabletop. On the other side of the room was a cheap metal desk with another computer as well as a stack of mail trays, all of them full of neatly catalogued envelopes with current work inside them. Eunice had reserved the table nearest to the window for the machine that she bought online to reencode information on magnetic strips.

She had a genius for recovering information from online public information sources. By no means did runners stealing mail or credit cards accomplish most of her information collecting. And Eunice had acting talent when it came to telephonically posing as a store employee where a purchase had been made, or as a bank employee requiring account information from a gullible bank customer.

He'd watch her with admiration when she'd do her "social engineering" calls, such as phoning the gas company in order to pay "her husband's" gas bill. She'd ask which credit card he used last time, and the gas company employee would almost always tell her the last four digits on the card. It was childishly simple for her to obtain needed data.

She'd frequently go on MySpace, where she could often learn a woman's full name along with her year and place of birth. Then she'd contact that city, claim to have lost her birth certificate, and obtain a new one. She'd go to the DMV with the birth certificate and get a driver's license. After that, she'd claim to have lost her Social Security card, and with all of the identity documents she'd already gotten, a new one would be issued. She could start all of this by just going to websites, doing nothing more than that.

The information that legal entities such as convention centers or cruise lines acquired from customers for access cards that their machines could read often ended up in the hands of Eunice Gleason and others like her. There was much valuable information to be gained from these and countless sources, and yet she was relentless in still requiring old-fashioned hands-on collecting from skimmers that she'd bought and provided. If her husband wasn't of use to her in this collecting phase of their enterprise, he wondered if he'd still be her husband.

He walked into the second bedroom, where he slept alone, loosened his tie, and entered the bathroom. After urinating, he washed his hands and face and, carefully pulling away the tape holding it in place, removed the silvery wig. Then he opened the medicine cabinet, found the contact lens case, and groaned with relief when he got the pale lenses out of his eyes. He looked at his normal light brown eyes for signs of irritation and squeezed some lubricating drops into both eyes. He took the jowl-enhancing gauze pads out of his mouth and, after brushing back his own gray-brown hair, examined himself. Without the dark shadows and tiny lines he'd drawn so carefully around his eyes, and after losing the wig, he figured he looked thirty-nine years old, although he was actually forty-eight.

When he reentered the workroom, he went straight to a window and opened it to let out some of the smoke that the electronic smoke eater hadn't removed. Eunice was too paranoid to ever let the shades be raised.

"Hey, don't let in the hot air," Eunice said. "The electric bill's killing us as it is, with all these computers going."

"I can't breathe in here," he said. "Edward R. Murrow didn't smoke this much. Nor did the Malibu Canyon fires, for that matter."

"Instead of standing here whining about it, just go in your bedroom and start phoning the college kids. And you got some shoppers to work before you go to bed tonight, so you better get into costume ASAP." Then she said, "By the way, did you buy another couple of prepaid cells?"

"Yes, I bought more GoPhones," he said with disgust. "I don't have dementia yet."

"How many kids you got for tonight?"

"Two. They both park cars at restaurants and love to act. They're perfect."

"Do they look like the faces on the driver's licenses?"

"Of course they do! You made the damn IDs, didn't you? Gimme a little credit."

"Yeah, I made them, but the last time you gave me photos to work with, the little bastard was five years younger in the pictures. Remember?"

"Okay, I shoulda paid attention to the photos he gave me. Gimme a break, Eunice!"

"That kid got busted behind it, Dewey," she said. "He went to jail."

"It didn't come back on us, did it?"

"It's stupid to get your people arrested," she said. "It's bad business and it's risky, Hugo always said."

"Hugo!" Dewey Gleason said. "I'm a writer and an actor, not a life-long grifter like Hugo. And look how that big-shot ex of yours ended up. In San Quentin and nearly dead from emphysema, with a criminal record from here to Baltimore. Anyway, that kid didn't know who I am or where I live, nothing. So stop worrying."

"So who were you on that one, Jakob Kessler?"

"No, I think I was the Jew, Felix Cohen, then. I hadn't created Jakob Kessler yet."

"You should uncreate him," she said. "That German accent sounds phony."

"It sounds just like Arnold!" Dewey said. "It's an Austrian's German accent."

"It sounds phony on Arnold too," she said. "And that cotton you stuff in your cheeks doesn't make you look like the Godfather. It makes you look like a man with a mouthful of disgusting food he can't swallow.

Kill the Kraut like you killed the Hebe. Stick with American characters. You're not actor enough to pull off the accents."

His jaws clenched and he said, "I can't do it till I use up the new guys, Creole and Jerzy. They only know me as Kessler."

"By the way, what happened to the old Polish guy that got pinched in Santa Monica?"

"That's Old Jerzy," Dewey said. "He was a parolee. Probably sent back to Pelican Bay or wherever. I use his memory to keep the new team in line." With a bit of pride in his voice, he said, "They think scary Jakob Kessler had Old Jerzy eliminated because he got greedy. I used some imagination on that one."

With her iguana smile: "Imagination? That's so goddamn lame, Dewey. It's the reason you failed as a screenwriter and as an actor. Kessler's a walking cliché. Why don't you face your limitations and concentrate on something you can do?"

Eyes moistening, Dewey said, "You can pull the guts right out of a man sometimes! I put in a ten-hour day already!"

"I put in *twelve* hours already," she said. "And you got problems with relationships, take it up with Dear Abby."

Malcolm Rojas wondered why he'd told young Naomi Teller that his name was Clark. He didn't have a conscious reason to lie to her, and yet he had. Something deep inside him made him do that, and he didn't quite understand it. There were lots of things about himself that he did not understand lately, lots of things that he had to do and did not know why. For instance, he did not consciously understand why he'd taken the box cutter home today from his job opening cardboard boxes at the massive home improvement center on Victory Boulevard in the San Fernando Valley. It wasn't for protection. Since he and his mother had moved to the apartment building a few blocks west of Highland Avenue, he'd felt very safe. He'd never felt safe when they lived in Boyle Heights, not in the middle of Latino gang turf, where he'd been raised until a year earlier, when he'd finished high school and got the job at the shopping center, far from Boyle Heights.

Malcolm Rojas didn't know why he'd pulled over and parked his red fifteen-year-old Mustang when he'd seen Naomi Teller on the street. Couldn't fathom why he'd gotten out and followed her and stopped her to talk. She didn't really appeal to him. She was too young, too skinny. She wasn't his type at all. Why did he say he'd call her? There were many conflicting emotions roiling inside him as he drove north on Highland Avenue toward Hollywood High School.

He parked and looked at the place. Why couldn't he have gone to high school there? Why did his father keep him and his mother all those years in a shitty house in Boyle Heights so his father could be close to his shitty job at the scrap yard? That wasn't reason enough. Malcolm had always been frightened there, of tattooed gang members, of barrio life in general, especially with a mother who was a very white American and who didn't understand more than a few words of Spanish. He'd felt like an outsider and had stayed home a lot with her, paying the price for it when he had to endure the names the other kids called him at school, especially after they found out that Malcolm's father was Honduran, not Mexican like theirs. One of the names they'd called him was Li'l Hondoo, and he hated it. He hated all those *cholo* bastards.

Malcolm well remembered the conflicting emotions he'd felt when his father had been fatally injured at work after a drunken crane operator dropped a mangled Ford station wagon on top of him and another worker. A local attorney had contacted his mother, and because of the gross negligence of the company, she ended up with a $400,000 settlement, which allowed them to move away from the barrio and into a modest apartment in Hollywood. The move made him feel that at last he was home.

As a baby he'd been christened Ruben after his father. His middle name was Malcolm, the name of his maternal grandfather, who'd died before the boy was born. Early in life, young Ruben had decided that he wasn't Honduran like his father, even though he knew how very much he looked like the man. After his father's death, young Ruben Rojas came to hate his Hispanic name and insisted that his mother call him Malcolm in honor of her late father. She always indulged her only child's whims, but it was hard for her even now to remember that he was Malcolm and not Ruben.

When she'd get drunk, his mother would endlessly repeat the story of how she'd first arrived in L.A. from Tulsa and moved into a hotel apartment near downtown. The man who would become Malcolm's father was her neighbor. She'd laugh when telling Malcolm how she didn't even know where Honduras was but believed it to be somewhere near Spain. Her handsome Honduran neighbor had an old car, and he would drive her to various cafeterias that were hiring waitresses and was always kind to her, and eventually they fell in love.

Malcolm hated those stories and tried to ignore them, and he hated being anything like his father. Malcolm was from his mother's womb, so he was his mother's son, and she was white and blue-eyed and blonde and...

Suddenly he was angry, very angry, for no reason at all. The bouts of anger had begun when he was about thirteen years old and had grown gradually over the past six years. He'd never talked to anyone about it, especially not to his mother. Once he thought about talking to a counselor at school but changed his mind. It was far better to work things out on your own, he decided. Why not? He'd been a loner all his life. Sometimes he could quell the anger by masturbating, but he didn't feel like doing that now.

He started the Mustang again and began driving. The sun had set and the mauve and persimmon sky over Hollywood was turning dark. He took one hand from the steering wheel and held it in front of him. The hand was shaking for no reason at all. He didn't even know what street he was on now, but there were apartment buildings on both sides. Three of them had parking garages down below and electric security gates that could be opened by the residents as they drove inside. He remembered a TV movie where a contract killer waited outside such a building, hiding behind some bushes, and then followed a car inside to shoot the driver before escaping in the victim's car.

He felt the anger growing, and his hands trembled more. His armpits were damp and he felt a bit light-headed, like when he'd sniffed glue back in middle school. He saw an apartment building that looked just like the one in the movie. There were even big clumps of bougainvillea growing beside the security gate that led to the underground parking. A contract killer could hide there, Malcolm thought. Just like in the movie.

★ ★ FIVE ★

NIGHT HAD FALLEN, and it was going to be a dark one, with low, hanging smog concealing the moon and stars. The residential street was adequately lighted, but the apartment building was situated in the middle of the line of streetlights and settled in deep shadow. The security lights on the front of the building were timed not to go on for another thirty minutes in order to save electricity. It was a quiet street, the only noise coming from the incessant traffic hum on Sunset Boulevard.

A white Pathfinder SUV drove south from Sunset toward the apartment building. There were plenty of cars parked on both sides of the residential street, but the Pathfinder was the only moving vehicle at the moment. The SUV slowed at the apartment building, and the driver touched the remote button and the heavy security gate began to rise and roll back. Beside the entrance to the parking garage was the large growth of bougainvillea as well as some azaleas. Crouching behind the flowering plants was Malcolm Rojas.

He had been hiding there for half an hour. It wasn't a particularly hot summer evening, yet he was burning up. He felt feverish, and as angry as he'd ever been in his life. He'd watched four other cars drive in during the past thirty minutes. One of them was driven by a man, one by a young woman, one by a middle-aged woman who looked Hispanic. None of those had propelled Malcolm Rojas into action. A stab of pain, sizzling and fizzing, began somewhere behind his eyes. He was in a rage.

A forty-seven-year-old Realtor named Sharon Gillespie drove the Pathfinder. She lived with a man who was also in real-estate sales, and she was just coming home from her office. She parked in her usual space, number 33, at the south wall of the parking garage. When she got out and was preparing to lock the SUV, a hand was clamped across her mouth, and another hand, this one holding a box cutter, flashed before her eyes. She dropped her briefcase onto the garage floor but had no chance to scream.

The call to the apartment garage was given twenty-three minutes later to 6-X-76, the shop driven by Dana Vaughn, with Hollywood Nate writing the reports, or, as the cops referred to it, "keeping books." And 6-X-66, with Sheila Montez driving and Aaron Sloane riding shotgun, arrived right behind them, all of them wanting to get more of a description. The radio call had only given the sketchy description of a male in his twenties, possibly of Middle Eastern descent, and wearing a light blue T-shirt, who'd fled on foot through a fire exit door that accessed the street, a door that was locked on the street side.

The apartment manager, a frightened woman in her sixties, was pacing in front of the building when the two patrol units parked in front. It went without saying that the female officer would question the victim and take the crime report in this kind of case, even though ordinarily that would be the passenger officer's job. Dana grabbed the reports binder, and Hollywood Nate tagged behind when his partner approached the security gate.

As Dana Vaughn put it, "If there's a vagina involved, we women get the case."

"How long ago did the suspect leave here?" Dana asked the apartment manager.

"About fifteen minutes, I think," the woman said. "She's up in apartment thirty-three, waiting for you. Sharon Gillespie is her name. The poor woman!"

"Nobody saw a car?" Sheila said, entering through the walk-in security gate and following Dana.

The apartment manager shook her head, saying, "It's the element that's taking over. Arabs, Iranians, they're everywhere around here."

A fifteen-minute head start in this most traffic-clogged city in North America might as well have been fifteen hours. As far as the cops were concerned, the suspect was probably in a car and long gone.

Dana Vaughn said to Sheila, "How about you and your partner help Nate secure the crime scene. I'll get a description out as soon as I can."

Sheila nodded and said to the manager, "Has anybody else touched anything in her vehicle or exited through the fire exit door since it happened?"

The apartment manager shook her head, and Hollywood Nate said, "Good. Take us there and open the car gate. Some crime lab people will be arriving soon. I hope."

"Like *CSI*?" the woman said.

Aaron fought the urge to heave a sigh but only said, "Don't expect their kind of results, but we'll do our best."

Matthew Harwood, a fifty-year-old real-estate broker who was the roommate and lover of Sharon Gillespie, admitted Dana to apartment 33. He'd been crying with her and was wiping his eyes with his fingertips when Dana arrived. Sharon Gillespie was sitting in a kitchen chair, holding a cup of coffee in her trembling hands, her highlighted blonde hair damp, her face washed clean of makeup. A contusion on her left cheekbone was swollen and discolored.

Too late, Dana thought. She'd already bathed. Dana turned to Matthew Harwood and said, "I'll talk to you later, sir, but do you mind if I talk to Ms. Gillespie alone? You might wait right outside with my partner. He'll need some information."

After Matthew Harwood was gone, Dana had a fleeting thought that this woman was not much older than she, and that made it more troubling. Dana said, "I know how...I have an *idea* how you're feeling right now, but we'll need to take you to the hospital to tend to your injuries and to get some evidence swabs. Is your underwear here or down where it happened?"

"He never made me remove my underwear," Sharon Gillespie said. "It didn't get that far. And this bruise on my face is my only injury. I'm not going to a hospital. I'm going to bed."

"Okay, what do you mean, 'It didn't get that far'?"

"He held the weapon in front of my eyes. A box knife, like the nine-eleven hijackers used. He pushed me into the backseat of my SUV. He pushed my head down. He said he'd cut my eyes out if I didn't..."

"Tell me the exact words that he said to you."

"He said, 'Suck my cock or I'll cut your eyes out, you filthy slut.'"

"And then what happened?"

"What do you think happened? I did it."

"I know this is very difficult," Dana said. "But I have to know details. If we can collect any semen at all, we can get his DNA profile. His genetic fingerprint."

"I know all that," Sharon Gillespie said. "I'm not stupid. But he didn't ejaculate. He didn't even get hard. He got angry. Furious. He called me all kinds of things. 'Whore, slut, pig, drunk, bitch.' I don't know what else."

"Drunk?" Dana said, writing in her notebook. "Had you been drinking?"

"No, I'd just come from work."

"Okay," Dana said, "so there was no ejaculation?"

"No," she said. "After a few minutes, he jerked me up by the hair and with that box knife in his fist punched me in the face and jumped out and ran toward the fire exit door."

"Would you be able to recognize the man if you saw him again?"

"No. He was a Middle Eastern guy in his twenties. Close to six feet tall, wearing a light blue T-shirt and jeans. He had black, curly hair and he looked like the nine-eleven hijackers. With that same kind of box knife."

"A box cutter," Dana said. "You're sure?"

"Yes," Sharon Gillespie said, "I've seen the guys at Home Depot cutting open boxes with those things."

"Did he have a Middle Eastern accent?" Dana asked.

"No, he had no accent that I could make out. He didn't say much. Only those filthy obscenities."

"About calling you a drunk," Dana said, "could he be someone who'd seen you at a bar or restaurant when you were having a few drinks? Maybe a busboy or waiter?"

"I go to a lot of restaurants in my business, but I never get drunk," Sharon Gillespie said. "Now, please go out there and catch that god-damn Arab!" Then she started to weep.

After Dana put out a further description of the suspect to the RTO at Communications Division, she walked down to the parking garage. There she found the lazy night-watch detective "Compassionate Charlie" Gilford, a lanky, middle-aged veteran D2 notorious for his horrible taste in neckties and acerbic comments at crime scenes.

The detective said, "SID's gonna have to crawl that SUV with a black light."

"No, they aren't," Dana said. "There's no semen in there."

Charlie Gilford, who had a thing for well-preserved fortyish woman like Dana, said to her, "What, no dribble in the withdraw mode? You got the panties?"

"Nope," Dana said, and before she could explain, Charlie Gilford said, "Those drawers and what was in them is a crime scene. Where are they?"

"He didn't ejaculate," Dana said, unsure which was more distasteful, his manner or his necktie.

"How can she be sure?" the detective said.

"Because his penis was in her mouth and it was flaccid," Dana said. "That means it wasn't hard."

"I know what it means," Charlie Gilford said, but Dana doubted it. Then he added, "How come the only sex maniac that leaves all the evidence where you can't miss it is Bill Clinton?"

Dana Vaughn and Hollywood Nate didn't immediately hear the further description of the apartment garage rapist when the Communications RTO broadcast her follow-up info. Since violent assailants often seem older or larger to their victims, Dana said to Nate, "He might not be that old, and he might not be that tall. And in fact, he might not be Middle Eastern. Just because the guy had a box cutter doesn't mean he works for Osama bin Laden."

"Might even be a Jew," Nate said. "His description sounds like my cousin Morris."

None of the Hollywood cops expected to find the guy on foot in the area, and of course they were right. Dana and Hollywood Nate cleared from their call, but before heading for the station, they immediately received another one.

At Nate's insistence, Dana had to speed to this one. It was the kind of call that brought out black-and-whites from all over the division, not to mention gang cops, motor cops, and any other male officers who happened to be on the radio frequency. It was a "311 woman," the penal code designation defining indecent exposure. The call sent 6-X-76 to a Laundromat on Santa Monica Boulevard.

Dana said en route to Hollywood Nate, "I know this is the most important call that you pathetically desperate males will roll on this month, but would you be terribly upset if I slowed down? My motto is 'Drive to Arrive.'"

Three female customers waited outside on the sidewalk for the police before venturing back inside to retrieve their clothes from the coin-operated dryers. Dana parked the Ford Crown Vic in front of the Laundromat and took her time emerging, not wanting to get in the way of horny male coppers like Hollywood Nate, who might trample her.

The Asian woman who'd made the call said, "She's still inside. She scared us to death when she took off all her clothes."

When Nate ran into the Laundromat, he found the 311 woman sitting on a folding chair. Rather, she was sitting on two folding chairs that had been pushed together. She was naked and milky white with long, stringy brown hair, and she weighed approximately 350 pounds. She was crying, her mascara running down her swollen cheeks and dripping off her pug nose onto her pendulous bosom.

Nate gaped, then turned to Dana and held up four fingers, meaning "code 4," no further help needed at the scene. Dana jogged out to their car and put out the code 4 broadcast, knowing that it wouldn't stop the other horny bastards from arriving. Not unless she said that the 311 woman was "GOA," or "gone-on-arrival," in which case they'd fan out and start looking for her.

The woman on the sidewalk who'd put in the call said to Dana, "Why is that woman naked, Officer?"

"We're gonna find out," Dana said. "Be patient."

When she reentered the Laundromat, Nate said to her, "I got a feeling you should handle this one."

Hollywood Nate walked out to the sidewalk, when, predictably, a car from Watch 3 squealed to the curb, despite the code 4 broadcast.

"You don't wanna go in there," he said to the cops inside. "She's naked all right, but she weighs at least three bills. Her jelly rolls hang like a loincloth. You don't wanna go in there."

Without comment, the night-watch car drove off, and a second one arrived and received the same eyewitness commentary, resulting in the same rapid departure. But the third black-and-white to arrive belonged to the midwatch surfer cops, and they stayed briefly.

After Hollywood Nate explained what he'd encountered inside the Laundromat, Flotsam tried to give Hollywood Nate his cell phone camera, saying, "Dude, you gotta get me a couple shots of her! Frontal and reverse!"

"I'm over this," Nate said.

"It might be worth a buck on YouTube!" Jetsam urged.

"Paddle off, you surfboard pervs!" Hollywood Nate said, and the surfer cops reluctantly drove away.

When Nate got back inside the Laundromat, Dana Vaughn was sitting in a folding chair next to the 311 woman, who made no effort to hide her nakedness from Hollywood Nate. Not that it would have been possible, since she only had a small hand towel, which she was using to dab at her lacerated and swollen lip and to wipe away her tears. She appeared to Nate to be in her late thirties.

She said to Dana between sobs, "He said he was leaving me and would never come back. And I'd always believed him when he said we were going to get married and have a family."

"How long have you been together, Reba?" Dana asked.

"Over a year. I spent most of my trust fund on him." Then she started crying openly again.

Dana looked up at Hollywood Nate and said, "This is Reba Costello. Her boyfriend Lester's a piece of work. He drops her here to do their laundry, and then he goes out and hits a couple bars on Western Avenue.

Then he comes back, and when the second load of laundry's not started, he starts ragging on her, and when they're alone, he ends up punching her in the mouth."

"Where's Lester now?" Nate asked.

"Probably back on Western Avenue," Dana said, answering for the sobbing woman.

"She gonna sign a report?"

Reba looked up at Nate and said, "I don't wanna have him arrested. I just want him to get a job and not get drunk all the time!"

"You don't have to be his punching bag," Dana said. "He should be in jail, Reba."

"No, please!" the woman said. "As soon as the clothes're dry, I'll just go home. I can walk from here."

"So why is she naked?" Hollywood Nate asked Dana, just as the dryer alarm sounded and the drum stopped turning.

Dana walked him a few steps away from the woman and whispered, "When he knocked her down on the floor here, the drunken bastard whipped it out and pissed on her. All she had on was her cotton dress and underwear. They're in the dryer with the second load."

Nate raised his voice, saying, "After that, she's not gonna sign a crime report?"

"No, no!" Reba said, overhearing him. "I think maybe I can persuade Lester to go to AA. Then everything will be fine. Honest."

Dana said to Reba Costello, "The load's done. Take your dress out and put it on. We'll give you a lift to your apartment."

"You've been real nice," Reba said, getting painfully to her feet and opening the dryer. "You don't have to do that."

"I'll help you fold your things," Dana said. "And then we'll get you home."

Fifteen minutes later, 6-X-76 dropped Reba Costello and her laundry at her apartment, a few blocks from the Hollywood Cemetery. Dana helped the obese woman out of the car, along with her bags of laundry.

"He wouldn't by chance be home by now, would he?" Dana said. "I'd like to have a little chat with him."

"No, no, he'll be out till the bars close when he's like this," Reba said. "I'll be okay. Thank you, Officers, for being so kind."

"Take care of yourself, honey," Dana said. "Call us if he ever lays a hand on you again."

When they had driven away, Hollywood Nate said, "Let's request seven," referring to code 7, the LAPD radio designation for a meal break.

"Okay," Dana said, "and you can be sure I won't be eating anything with a lot of fat grams or calories. Not tonight."

Nate said, "How come our Hollywood romances never end happy like the ones in the movies?"

"Does anything?" Dana Vaughn said.

By the time Malcolm Rojas arrived home that night, his mother was sound asleep and snoring on the sofa while the TV blared. Malcolm was exhausted, and his fury had waned. He was ravenously hungry and hoped that his mother had prepared something and put it in the fridge for him, but she had not. He went to the cupboard and began eating cereal out of the box. Then he ate an apple, and after that, some cottage cheese that had already started to turn.

Malcolm was not yet ready to relive the events of the evening. Tomorrow would be the best time for that. He knew instinctively that the thing in the parking garage was something momentous. He was changed and he'd never be the same again. He felt like a failure for not having consummated his experience with that fat whore, but on the other hand, he felt that he'd been brave. If that feeling ever came over him again, he believed he'd be up to the task. It wasn't his fault that he couldn't do it. He should've picked someone more attractive, someone more his type, for his first sexual experience with a woman.

After he'd eaten a peanut butter and honey sandwich, he thought about going to bed and masturbating. He looked at his mother lying on the sofa with her mouth hanging open, drool running down her cheek, and he was repulsed. They were all alike, women like her, sickeningly soft with flesh like jelly. Smelly drunkards who always tried to put their hands on him. He was sure that the woman in the SUV would've begged him to fuck her if they'd been in the right place at the right time. But she was disgusting, and thinking of her made the anger start to rise again. Instead of letting it overwhelm him, he opened his cell phone and impulsively dialed young Naomi Teller.

He smiled when a voice that sounded like a small child's said, "Hello?"

"It's me, Clark Kent," he said. "Strange visitor from the planet Krypton."

"Clark!" she said. "I was getting ready to go to bed. I didn't think you'd call."

"I told you I would, didn't I?"

"It's nice to talk to you," Naomi said. "Where are you?"

"I'm at home," Malcolm said, "thinking of you."

"No way," Naomi said. "You're not thinking of me."

"Yes way," Malcolm said. "I'm thinking that you and me're gonna hop in my Mustang and go to the mall in North Hollywood or wherever there's a good movie playing. And we're gonna eat popcorn, and then I'm gonna buy you a burger or pizza afterwards. Which do you want?"

"Pizza," she said.

"Deal," Malcolm said.

"But my parents can't know about this date, so I gotta plan how we're gonna do it," Naomi said.

"Why can't your parents know?"

"I'm not old enough to go out with a guy your age," Naomi said. "You're an adult."

That made him chuckle. He wasn't used to thinking of himself as an adult. "If we were both ten years older, our age difference wouldn't mean a thing," he said.

She was quiet for several seconds and then she said, "It doesn't mean a thing now. Not to me. You're a very easy person to talk to, Clark."

"I'll be calling you in a day or two, Naomi," he said. "Payday's coming up and I wanna have some money to spend on you."

"You don't have to spend money on me," Naomi said. "I'm not that kind of girl."

"You're a special kind of girl to me," Malcolm said. "I'll be calling you."

"I'll be here," Naomi said.

Before ending his call, Malcolm said, "Don't forget me. Don't ever forget me."

"Of course I won't forget you!" Naomi said. "How could I?"

Hollywood Nate said passionately to Kenny, the thirtyish, flamboyant waiter at Hamburger Hamlet, "Why can't I just quit you? Why?"

"Pick a newer movie line," Kenny said. "So what're you having?"

"I'll have a salad, honey," Dana Vaughn said. "Low-fat dressing. And a Coke."

"High-octane or diet?" Kenny asked.

"Diet, of course," Dana said.

"With voltage or without?" Kenny asked.

"What?" Dana said.

"Caffeine," Kenny said.

"With," Dana said. "I'm feeling dangerous tonight."

"How about you, Nate?" Kenny said.

The waiter wore a trendy "emo chic" cut, with his highlighted hair falling over one eye, a style that was said to express deep emotions.

With his best Bogie accent, Hollywood Nate said to Kenny. "If she can take it, so can I. You're doing it for her, do it for me. Serve it again, Ken."

"Two skinny salads," Kenny said. Then to Dana, "I wish he'd find an agent that could get him a job. Nate's a lot easier to take when he's got a gig to worry about. Has he done Cary Grant for you yet? And his Jack Nicholson is just awful."

"I might be reading for a cable movie next month," Nate said to Kenny. "Remember the producer you introduced me to when we were extras on that biker show?"

"He's a porn producer, Nate," Kenny said. "Is it straight porn or gay for pay?" Then he looked at Dana and said, "I figured Nate would cross over someday."

"How many times I gotta tell you, Kenny, I *am* gay except for the sex part," Nate said, adding, "Not the porn producer. I'm talking about the fat guy who told us he had a TV pilot he was prepping. The one who's into aromatherapy? That guy."

Unimpressed, Kenny said, "He comes in here once or twice a month. A notoriously bad tipper. Lots of luck with him, bucko."

"Are you an aspiring actor too?" Dana asked.

"Isn't everybody?" Kenny said. "Be right back with your drinks."

When the waiter was gone, Dana said to Nate, "How long have you been knocking at the door of stardom?"

"I've had my SAG card more than a year. I've done TV movies."

"Speaking parts?"

"Yeah, sort of. In a couple of them I had a line or two. But I've done lots of extra work."

"You enjoy it?"

Clearly uncomfortable discussing his show-business struggles with a woman he was not trying to seduce, Nate said, "Sure. It's, you know, better than most...hobbies."

"Is that what it is?" she asked in that penetrating way of hers that made him feel like a kid.

"Yeah, and maybe if it turns into something...well, you never know."

Dana nodded and said, "Hollywood is more than several square miles in the middle of L.A. Hollywood is a state of mind, isn't it?"

When Kenny returned with the drinks, he said, "I didn't mean to sound pessimistic about that fat producer, Nate. I just don't trust guys that stiff restaurant people."

By now, Hollywood Nate was getting depressed talking about it and said, "Maybe I'm kidding myself. Hell, I'm thirty-seven years old, with sixteen years on the Job. I might end up like the Oracle and die on the Walk with my boots on."

"Who's the Oracle?" Kenny asked.

"The late legendary sergeant of the midwatch," Dana Vaughn said. "I never worked for him, but his picture's hanging in the roll call room. Forty-six years on the LAPD and died of a massive heart attack on the police Walk of Fame, right in front of Hollywood Station."

"Yeah, you guys have your own stars in the marble, don't you?'

Kenny said. "Just like on Hollywood Boulevard. Once I went to Hollywood Station when somebody stole my bike, and I saw those stars. For the officers from the station that were killed on duty, right?"

"A heart attack after forty-six years of this?" Nate said. "That's being killed on duty in my book."

Kenny studied Hollywood Nate for a moment, and seeing how dejected he seemed now, the waiter said, "Don't give up your hopes and dreams, Nate. Gloria Stuart was an eighty-seven-year-old actress when *Titanic* was released, and she got a lotta good gigs out of it. You gotta be patient."

"What a silly goose I've been," said Hollywood Nate. "Here I am, studying the trades and paying parking tickets for casting agents who think I can fix them, when all I gotta do for success is wait fifty years. Cue the *Rocky* theme!" Then he pushed his plate away and added ruefully, "My appetite's gone."

"I'll eat your salad, honey," Dana said cheerily. "I need plenty of roughage if I'm gonna keep my ballerina body for your first red carpet appearance."

★ SIX ★

A WARNING POSTED on the board said, "Don't go to Taco Bell!" That was because a cook who worked there had gotten booked by vice cops the previous night for snogging a hooker in his car. The cook had been an extremely resentful arrestee, since many of the cops ate at Taco Bell regularly and he'd figured that gave him a get-out-of-jail-free card. The midwatch feared he'd take his revenge in their tacos.

Sergeant Lee Murillo was conducting the midwatch roll call without any other supervisors present, so the troops were really airing it out. The bitching started this time because an officer on Watch 2 was being disciplined for choking out a combative suspect. The carotid restraint, or "choke hold," had been the salvation of cops since the forming of the LAPD, but in the era of the federal consent decree, it was considered a use of lethal force. It would trigger the same sort of exhaustive investigation as an officer-involved shooting. This resulted in cops believing that if things came down to one or the other, they'd be better off using guns. Or, as the troops put it, "If you can choke 'em, you can smoke 'em."

After the kvetching had drained off most of the bile, Sergeant Lee Murillo read the crimes and talked about the sexual assault on Sharon Gillespie in the parking garage the prior evening. He read the description of the assailant and said, "The victim believes the suspect was of Middle Eastern descent, so you might keep that in mind."

"That only takes in half the employees of every liquor store, gas station, and taxi company in Hollywood, Sarge," Flotsam said.

Jetsam said, "Not to mention the wealthier nightclub patrons from countries where donkeys and camels are beasts of burden and occasional lovers. They park their Beemers and Benzes in every freaking no-parking zone within two blocks of the boulevards."

"No ethnic wisecracks," Sergeant Murillo said. "All I need is another complaint to investigate."

Rather than sounding off like the surfer cops, Dana Vaughn raised her hand, and when Sergeant Murillo nodded at her, she said, "I'm not sure about the Middle Eastern part of it. The young guy had dark, curly hair, a dark complexion, and dark eyes, but he had no accent of any kind."

R.T. Dibney chimed in and said, "That description fits Sanchez, Sarge." Then he pointed to the former rookie partner of P3 Johnny Lanier and said to the black cop, "Sorry to racially profile your boy, but where was he last night at—"

"Okay, Dibney," Sergeant Murillo said, while several of the troops sniggered, "save your humorous asides for the next retirement party."

While Dana Vaughn dead-stared R.T. Dibney for interrupting her, Sergeant Murillo said, "What was the point you wanted to make, Vaughn?"

"Actually, Dibney just made it," she said. "The description does fit lots of Hispanics as well. My opinion is that the box cutter influenced her. She mentioned the nine-eleven hijackers more than once. So the suspect could be a young guy of Middle Eastern descent or maybe of Hispanic descent, or maybe something else."

Sergeant Murillo said, "Okay, one thing is certain. Guys like that don't stop on their own, so give a little extra patrol in the early evening to streets with likely apartment buildings, especially around that area. The citizens in those reporting districts get a little jumpy about people roaming around with cutting instruments."

When he saw some quizzical looks, he added, "For you people who weren't around here a few years ago, the location is close to where we had a pair of real bogeyman murders. A former dancer and personal trainer entered the house of a ninety-one-year-old retired screenwriter, someone he'd never seen before, and cut the guy's head off with a meat cleaver he found in the kitchen."

Hollywood Nate, ever the cinematic authority, added, "That old man was one of the first screenwriters to be blacklisted during the McCarthy era—not that you dummies know anything about movie history." He stirred some interest when he added, "He also cowrote *Abbott and Costello Meet Frankenstein*."

"Yeah?" R.T. Dibney said. "I saw that on TV a hundred times when I was kid. What a great movie. The Wolf Man, Dracula, Frankenstein, they were all in it."

Sergeant Murillo continued, "Then he carried the old screenwriter's head and some of his organs over a back fence onto the next street, entered another house, and slashed a sixty-nine-year-old doctor to death. The doctor was making airline reservations at the time, and after he was killed, the nut job picked up the phone and said to the airline employee, 'Everything's fine now.' Then he went to Paramount Studios and tried to get in."

"He musta been, like, writing a way weird movie in his head and figured Paramount would give him a job," Flotsam observed.

"Back when the poor old guy wrote about movie monsters, I bet he never thought he'd meet a real one," Sergeant Murillo said. "It's something to always keep in mind. There're *real* monsters out there." Then he noticed R.T. Dibney turned sideways in his chair, whispering on his cell phone, no doubt to this week's bimbo of choice, and he said, "Dibney, the city is paying for *both* of your ears. Now, let's go to work."

The dozen cops that made up the shorthanded midwatch gathered their war bags and headed for the door. And every one of them, even those who'd never known the man, stopped to touch for luck the framed photograph of the late sergeant they called the Oracle, whose frame bore a brass plate that said

THE ORACLE
APPOINTED: FEB 1960
END-OF-WATCH: AUG 2006
SEMPER COP

* * *

Many things had changed at LAPD since back in the day when the Oracle was doing street police work. The shooting of a black teenager in a stolen car that nearly ran over an officer introduced a policy of not shooting at moving vehicles. The striking of a combative black suspect with a five-cell flashlight by a Latino officer resulted in the firing of the cop and a massive purchase of little ten-ounce flashlights for the entire Department.

All of this was designed to alter what the *L.A. Times* had long called the "warrior cop ethos" of the LAPD. Much hand-wringing at City Hall resulted in wholesale policy changes by the police commission, whose African-American president had spent a good deal of his prior life as head of the Urban League, denouncing the LAPD's proactive policies. This was one reason that the LAPD cops referred to him, and the rest of the Mexican-American mayor's police commission appointees, as the "anti-police commission."

Despite all this, some of the cops, especially those of a "frisky disposition," which is how R.T. Dibney described himself, kept their old five-cell flashlights in their nylon war bags and still used them when there wasn't a supervisor around. The zipper compartment of the war bag also contained a ticket book, notebook, and a street guide. In the other compartment was a helmet and chemical face mask. The surfer cops had observed R.T. Dibney on several occasions searching alleys and yards, walking behind the beam of the old five-cell flashlight.

The midwatch units, including Mindy Ling and R.T. Dibney, were busy loading up their cars with rover radios as well as PODDs, the handheld devices in which they could enter all sorts of useless data, some of it fictitious, for the auditors and overseers. The kit room also provided them with Tasers, Remington 870 shotguns, and beanbag shotguns. Mindy's war bag was actually a huge carrier on wheels, like a flight attendant's.

While all of this was going on, Jetsam was outside the parking lot, scurrying around a growth of curbside planting where he'd observed something interesting.

When he came back inside the lot to his waiting partner, he said, "Got it! Sweeeeet!"

"You are easily amused, dude," Flotsam said.

"Wanna see it? Or are you scared of these too?"

"Fucking donk," Flotsam said.

"You are seriously aggro, bro. Chill and enjoy. It's showtime."

Jetsam ran over to the black-and-white belonging to 6-X-46 and said, "My partner thinks he might have an idea who the rapist with the box cutter is. He'd like to talk to you."

Mindy Ling said, "Yeah?" and immediately walked toward Flotsam, who was standing outside his car.

"He said he'd like to share it with both of you," Jetsam said, so R.T. Dibney shrugged, and followed his partner to the surfers' black-and-white.

When they were gone, Jetsam quickly opened the door on the passenger side and, reaching under the seat, found R.T. Dibney's five-cell flashlight tucked away there. He removed the D-cell batteries from the big flashlight, replaced them with what he'd recovered from the planted area, dropped the batteries into the still-open trunk, and then strolled back over to Flotsam, who was just finishing up with his "clue."

"So anyways," Flotsam was saying, "I saw this dude hanging beside the parking gate of that other building half a block north of where the deal went down last night. He could be the same guy."

Mindy Ling said, "You say that was last Tuesday when you saw him?"

"Yeah," Flotsam said. "Right, partner?"

Jetsam, who had just arrived on cue, said, "Tuesday, yeah."

"Did you talk to the sex crime detectives at West Bureau?"

"Not yet," Flotsam said. "Coulda just been a guy trimming the bushes. I'm not sure. Maybe it's nothing, but he was right on. Light blue T-shirt and all."

"Okay," Mindy Ling said, "we'll be cruising that RD for the next few nights."

When they were walking back to their shop, R.T. Dibney said, "Some clue. The description fits half the gardeners from here to Malibu. Which is where those two belong, hanging ten and chasing surf bunnies instead of trying to do real police work."

R.T. Dibney acted highly critical of slackers and pranksters now that he was working with super serious Mindy Ling. But she wasn't impressed by much of anything that R.T. Dibney did or said. She was determined that she'd work another car for the next deployment period.

The first part of their watch was routine. They got a few calls on their MDC and dealt with them. One was a family dispute in southeast Hollywood involving a Latina with eight children, all of them boys. The woman was being driven to near violence by her two oldest, high school dropouts who were not working and didn't care to try. The yelling in that house had alarmed the neighbors. Their second call involved perennial parking problems everywhere near Sunset and Hollywood Boulevards.

After writing a speeder on Highland Avenue just before sunset, they got their first hotshot call. The RTO's voice said, "All units in the vicinity and Six-X-Forty-six, see the woman. Prowler there now..."

The address given was close to the area of the previous night's violent sexual assault, and as with most hotshot calls these days, the designation was code 3. The current chief had initiated this code 3 policy in order to keep other speeding responders, who were not using sirens, from crashing into one other. The cops enjoyed code 3 rides.

"Let's hit it," R.T. Dibney said, and Mindy Ling turned on the light bar and, with her usual caution, drove only as fast as she ever did, cutting off the siren when they got close to the address in order to arrive quietly.

When they parked, it was dark enough that lights were on in most of the apartments on the street, and the passing traffic was using headlights.

As Mindy Ling was removing the key, R.T. Dibney said, "I want some *real* light for this one."

He reached under the seat for his five-cell flashlight and said, "Hey, this feels lightweight. Where's the batteries?"

He clicked the switch, then unscrewed the battery cover, and out jumped a very pissed-off lizard. It landed in the lap of Mindy Ling, who screamed and leaped from the car with the lizard right behind her, the reptile hightailing it into the nearest vegetation.

This happened just as the surfer cops were pulling up in front of the apartment building, and Jetsam said, "Maybe this wasn't a good time for it."

"I warned you, dude," Flotsam said. "What if it happened when she was driving?"

"Jolly up, bro," Jetsam said. "The Oracle always said that doing police work was the most fun we'd ever have in our whole lives."

"Correction, dude," said Flotsam. "The Oracle said *good* police work. This don't exactly qualify."

It turned out that whoever had been roaming through the darkened parking area behind the building was long gone, but three cops from the midwatch and four more from Watch 3 had the opportunity of seeing Mindy Ling shaking and sputtering, trying to pull herself together.

R.T. Dibney looked with suspicion at the surfer cops and said, "Somebody put a lizard in my flashlight."

"Heavens!" said Flotsam.

"Gracious!" said Jetsam.

"Goddamn son of a bitch! I want the name of the asshole that did this!" Mindy Ling said to R.T. Dibney, who'd never heard her swear like this.

"Don't look at me!" he said. "I didn't do it to my own flashlight!"

She shivered and looked a bit nauseous as she turned abruptly and headed to the apartment of the person reporting.

R.T. Dibney hung back for a moment and said to the surfer cops, "Whoever did it better not brag about it. Mindy'll hunt them down and they will die a slow death by chopstick torture. After working with that babe, I am sure that China will eventually rule the world."

"I think it was a way juvenile prank," Flotsam said.

"Childish to the max," Jetsam said.

"I ain't mad at whoever did it," R.T. Dibney said. "This incident taught me something important. Mindy Ling is a girl. She's a real girl, after all. Now I might even start to like her a little bit."

After a few minutes, Mindy Ling returned, and when all officers were heading for their cars, she said to R.T. Dibney, "You ready to go, or do you wanna stay here and look for your lizard?"

"Hey, it wasn't *my* lizard!" R.T. Dibney said, his mustache twitching. "I was the intended victim of this here outrage."

Jetsam said, "Mindy, don't, like, go all bleak about your lizard phobia. I know a copper that's scared of clowns."

"Dude!" Flotsam said, reddening.

"Get outta my face, you surf rats," Mindy Ling blurted, storming to her car.

After 6-X-46 had driven away, Jetsam walked to the lushly planted area in front of the apartment building, shined his flashlight beam under a camellia bush, and said, "Bro, you are one lucky reptile. Your travel accommodations sucked, but this is a way cooler 'hood than the one you left behind."

Business was good at Pablo's Tacos early that evening. Parking was scarce in the little strip mall on Santa Monica Boulevard, and Malcolm Rojas, who had recently gotten off work at the home improvement center, had to park two blocks away on a residential side street. He knew from his prior visits to the taco stand that cops cruised by regularly and hassled any tweakers who looked like they might be holding or scoring crystal meth or other drugs. Malcolm had never eaten the lard-fried tacos from Pablo's and seldom ate Mexican fare at all, intent on leaving the Latino part of him back in Boyle Heights.

Still, Malcolm decided maybe he should try smoking a blunt when the anger grew too fierce. Before he got out of his Mustang, he took the box cutter from his pocket and put it under the front seat in case the cops stopped by and started jacking up people. He'd buy a little bit of weed and get out of there fast.

He'd gotten paid today, so he had plenty of money, no thanks to his mother. She was always yammering about him paying room and board now that he was almost twenty years old, as if their apartment was a damn boardinghouse or something. She still had settlement money left from his father's accidental death, and she was making good tips working part-time at Du-par's coffee shop in Farmers Market, so he couldn't understand why he should have to pay her.

It was just like his mother. Everything was all about her. He told her if she'd quit drinking a quart of Jim Beam every other day, she'd have more money, and she told him he was being cruel. Malcolm longed for the day when he could leave her, cut all ties, be his own man. That day would come.

There was nobody hanging around Pablo's that he'd seen or dealt with in the past. Pablo's mostly did a takeout business, but there were a few small tables inside, so he decided to sit and wait for a pot dealer to arrive. He needed something to make him feel more in charge of his emotions. He was still troubled about what had happened in the parking garage — troubled, but also more excited than he'd ever been in his entire life.

He'd wanted to come in that bitch's mouth, that's what he'd wanted to do, but he'd been too scared. There had been too many cars passing by, and he'd feared that at any minute one of the other residents would drive in. Then he might've had to fight for his life. How would that have been? With only a box cutter against a grown man? That's how Malcolm Rojas saw himself in such an encounter. Fighting for survival against *a grown man*.

But he didn't think he'd ever need to do that again. He'd never again let the anger rule him. He'd masturbate or smoke a blunt and everything would be okay.

Yet he'd brought his box cutter from the home improvement store again today. Why did he do that? He didn't want to think about it now. He just wanted a taste, only something to take the edge off. And if his mother bitched about him smoking it, maybe he'd tell her to go dive in her bottle of Jim Beam and shut the fuck up. Malcolm ordered a cup of coffee and sat down at one of the little tables inside to watch and wait for a dealer to show.

Dewey Gleason had been Bernie Graham all day. Bernie Graham was no challenge at all and in fact was a bit boring to his creator. Bernie was an L.A. guy, born and raised, and as Dewey saw him, Bernie had come from money, the son of a successful plastic surgeon who catered to a glamorous Westside trade. Bernie had an MBA from USC and had been a highly successful investment adviser, but he had suffered through two bad marriages with a gambling problem that necessitated his foray into illegal activity.

Dewey felt he had to establish this plausible backstory when dealing with college kids. They asked questions that the likes of Creole and Jerzy would never ask. The college boys were paranoid about getting caught and mentioned their parents a lot, and Dewey had to share fictional background information to reassure them. Or rather, paternalistic Bernie Graham had to.

At least Bernie Graham didn't need to be imposing, so Dewey didn't have to wear the shoes with lifts and suffer from ankle pain for two days, as he did when he was Jakob Kessler. Nor did he need the contact lenses, because Bernie Graham seldom needed to intimidate anybody. And Bernie Graham didn't have to be an older man, so Dewey could lose the gray wig. About all he'd done for Bernie Graham was use a rinse in his hair to make it a few shades darker and apply a stick-on mustache along with trendy eyeglasses.

His Bernie Graham character always dressed well—thanks to Nordstrom's no-questions-asked return policy—usually in a blazer and chinos. Dewey had considered creating a small but noticeable scar across Bernie's forehead that a college kid would undoubtedly describe for the cops if the kid was ever arrested. Ultimately, he'd decided that the scar would be overkill, but he affected a right-legged limp that he claimed was the result of a skiing accident on Mammoth Mountain, where he'd gone with fraternity brothers.

Meeting college kids wasn't hard to do. The previous year, Dewey had cultivated one who'd been working part-time at a Starbucks in West L.A., and he'd parlayed that meeting into several others with students who were cash-strapped. Soon he knew a dozen kids he could nurture and train. To begin with, he'd simply buy their debit cards and their PINs. The card-selling student would have to be in good standing with his bank. Dewey could almost always buy the card for $300 or less, but sometimes the more assertive kids chiseled another $100 out of him.

Then Dewey as Bernie Graham would use a "deposit runner" unknown to the first kid to deposit several of Eunice's counterfeit checks into the account of the kid who'd sold him the card. The deposit runner would have good bogus ID created by Eunice, so that any photo taken by a bank security camera would not match the student who'd sold Dewey the card. Then a third student, one who Dewey called his "bucks-up runner," not known by either of the first two, would be hired to travel to San Diego County, or out to the Palm Springs area, where there were some very big Indian casinos. That student, with another of Eunice's bogus IDs, would gamble a little, and through a clever phone call to override the card's daily limit, he would loot the debit account until it was dry. Any security video taken at the casinos would likewise not match the legitimate owner of the debit card, nor the one who'd deposited the bogus checks.

When the bank finally contacted the original student, the kid would say, "Oh, my gosh, my debit card isn't in my wallet! And I had my PIN number taped to it! Oh, my gosh!"

When the bank tried telling the kid that he owed the bank payback for the thousands they'd lost, the kid would recite lines fed by Bernie Graham: "But I didn't even know it was missing until you called me!"

The security at Indian casinos was generally lax, and none of Bernie's runners had gotten arrested so far. The security people at the casinos were concerned with customers cheating the house, not with cheating the banks. They'd look diligently for elaborate devices designed to beat the slot machines, but ATM scams were of little concern to them, and, most important, there were no close-up cameras at the ATM machines in the casinos, which made them desirable targets.

Dewey Gleason's favorite line as a closer to a new college kid was, "Look, the banks take the hits, so the Injuns don't give a shit. You think the banks can't afford to lose a few thousand here and there? Who needs it more, you or Bank of America?"

Dewey had no doubt that every one of the students skimmed some of the cash they were supposed to be returning to their mentor. Most of them would say something like, "Mr. Graham, there was a guy eyeballing me, so I had to gamble more than I wanted to. But I didn't lose too much."

But what they ended up giving him made the whole gag surprisingly profitable. The college kids didn't want to lose this new and fascinating source of income, so they were careful not to kill the golden goose. It made Eunice happy, but Dewey complained that he'd ended up being nothing more than a coach and collector. There was no challenge for a man who'd spent most of his adult life chasing casting agents and reading for uninterested TV producers and auditioning for parts he never got. At least with Jakob Kessler he got to give a real performance, and it was exhilarating, especially when he turned those pale contact lenses on someone like Creole and talked about greed. That's when he felt he was doing what he was born to do. He was giving a great performance every time, no matter what that jealous bitch had to say about it.

His last stop late that afternoon was in West Hollywood, but after a long day spent collecting, Dewey got a phone call on one of the eight GoPhones he kept on his person and in his briefcase.

Eunice, who could never resist belittling him, said, "Hello. Am I speaking with the tall and fearsome Jakob Kessler or gimpy little Bernie Graham?"

"How do I hate thee?" Dewey replied. "Let me count the ways."

"What?" she said. "You're breaking up."

"Get to the fucking point, Ethel," he said, using her GoPhone name. "Whadda you want?"

"Stop by the Mexican joint after you're all done," she said, which they both knew to mean Pablo's Tacos, the notorious Santa Monica Boulevard meeting place for tweakers, crackheads, and others with illicit goods to sell. "Look for a black guy who calls himself John. He's supposed to show up at around eight fifteen with the goods I talked to you about on Monday."

Eunice had never shut her fucking mouth on Monday or any other day, and most of what she'd said had passed him by. She had one idea after another, one job after another for him to do, while she just sat there in the apartment and "created," and smoked herself into an early grave. The last part would be just fine with him if it could happen sooner. Monday? Which gag was that? Finally, he had to admit the truth and take what she'd surely dump on him.

He said, "Okay, Ethel, I don't remember what you told me on fucking Monday, okay?"

"You don't remember. Why doesn't that surprise me?" she said. "Why do I knock myself out for you?"

"Please let *me* knock you out sometime," he said, slamming on the brakes after almost blowing the light at Cahuenga and Sunset because she had him so upset.

"The guy with the goods from his office? Sweet Jesus! Do I have to spell it out for you on the goddamn phone?"

Then he remembered. A Nigerian night janitor who was acquainted with one of Dewey's Mexican runners claimed to have access to his company's checks, and he'd suggested that some checks could temporarily disappear from the office, no problem. His company employed several hundred Latino workers, and Eunice intended to make duplicates of the paychecks and then have the janitor return the originals to the check file. She was curious to see how many could be cashed by Dewey's Mexicans with bogus IDs she supplied before the company and the company's bank discovered that some paychecks were being cashed twice.

"Okay, Ethel, I'm all dialed-in now," Dewey said after he remembered her instructions regarding the Nigerian. "I'll go by the joint and look for some black dude, which might include half the people I see in the parking lot, what with so many silverbacks coming up to Hollywood from South L.A. every goddamn night. Do you have a better description?"

"Your runner said he's forty, fat, and nervous, remember?" Then she said, "No, of course you don't remember. Offer one Franklin to him and see how it goes from there."

"This is just great," Dewey said. "Somebody walks into that parking lot looking suspicious and the first cop cruising by will be on him like maggots on the horse meat they sell in that joint. And of course, being a black foreigner from his fucked-up country, he'll be an hour late."

Ignoring his complaints, Eunice said, "And after you finish with that job, stop and get me a Whopper with fries. No, make it two Whoppers. I'm hungry."

Then she clicked off, and Dewey threw the phone on the seat beside him, muttering all the way to West Hollywood, for what he'd previously thought would be the last stop of the day.

Dewey was leery about dealing with a Nigerian. They had their own scams and didn't work well with outsiders. Dewey thought that by now everyone with the brain of a chicken would be onto the big Nigerian eBay scams, such as the one where an item, like a golf cart, would be listed for sale by a legitimate US seller. The Nigerians would send a check to the seller made out for five times the asking price of the item. Many honest but gullible sellers would send the item and the balance of the huge check to the Nigerian, who the seller figured was just not attuned to our American way. Of course, the seller's check would be legitimate but the Nigerian's original check would be bogus.

Dewey had seen a notice on the online classifieds site craigslist from a seller who'd been stung. He'd posted a message saying that his item was "not for sale to any Nigerian." Dewey figured he should be cautious when dealing with the Nigerian tonight and would look and listen very carefully to determine if the sheet of checks was legitimate.

He was lucky to find a parking space for his Honda Civic just off the Sunset Strip, and he spotted his depositor runner sitting outside at a sidewalk table, where he could sip a $5 cup of coffee and pretend that he was going to amount to something in the world as soon as he got his degree in anthropology or whatever useless fucking thing he was studying. Dewey hadn't met one yet who he thought would end up as anything but a valet parking attendant or a busboy at some Wolfgang Puck restaurant, if he got lucky.

This one was a smallish kid, and of course he was wearing wraparound shades, cargo pants, and a baseball cap pulled low, as if he were someone who didn't want to be recognized by the adoring public. Dewey wondered where he got the T-shirt with the Warner Bros. logo on the back. That, the cargoes and retro sneakers, and the inability to get out of his car without a bottle of designer water said, "I am employed in some capacity at the studio!" Dewey Gleason was sick to death of doing business with these pathetic little fucks.

When Dewey took the chair across the table, the kid smiled nervously and said, "Hi, Mr. Graham. I'm ready to go to work."

Dewey, ever cautious, removed the envelope he was carrying inside the pocket of his summer blazer, holding it by the corner between the tip of his thumb and forefinger, and slid it across the table.

"Everything is there, Michael," he said quietly after glancing to his right at a young woman with a leopard headband who might have overheard them if she hadn't been jabbering on her cell phone.

"Mitchell," the student corrected.

"Yes, Mitchell," Dewey agreed. "You'll find two checks each for three banks. The debit cards and the driver's licenses are in the name of Seymour Belmont, Josh Davidson, and Ralph Tanazzi. Instructions are very clear. Make sure you carry the correct ID and debit card for each bank and then deposit the checks as though you do it every day. The PIN number is taped on the card for you."

"I'm sorta blonde," Mitchell said, concerned. "I don't look like a Ralph Tanazzi."

"You look like the photo ID," Dewey said. "That's all you have to worry about."

"I hope the pictures on the driver's licenses turned out okay," Mitchell said. "That guy in the camera shop you sent me to was drunk."

"He did a good job," Dewey said. "Don't sweat it."

"And my . . . pay?"

"Is in the envelope," Dewey said. "Three hundred dollars for walking into three banks. A couple hours of your time, driving included."

"You said four hundred dollars, Mr. Graham," Mitchell said.

"Did I?" said Dewey disingenuously. He withdrew his wallet from the pocket of his blazer, removed a $100 bill, and put it on the table, saying, "My mistake."

An Asian waiter approached and said to Dewey, "Sir, what can I get you?"

"You'll buy me a coffee, won't you, Mitchell?" Dewey said.

Happily the kid replied, "Of course, Mr. Graham. And how about a croissant?"

Later, while driving to Pablo's Tacos, Dewey had to admit that Eunice had some impressive talents she'd learned from her first husband, Hugo.

She could legally shop on the Internet and buy whatever she needed. Legitimate companies sold her magnetic ink and high-end printers with different color inks, as well as other card-altering devices. Dewey was amazed the first time he watched her redo a mag number and slide a new mag strip in place of the old one.

She had very valuable information that she sometimes kept in the virtual storage she got when buying new computers. She claimed that the cops were able to get links to Internet sites, but that was all, and that Dewey, who was nearly computer-illiterate, should stop worrying and leave the thinking to her. Of course, a deprecating crack or two would top off any admonishment she directed his way.

Eunice kept much of her information in a Yahoo account, including names, credit-card numbers, and Social Security numbers, so that she could just log in and bring up the information as needed. Sometimes she went to Office Depot to buy Mips VersaChecks with computer programs, along with plenty of check stock. With that she could produce her own checks, account numbers, and routing numbers. She believed it was risky and didn't like to do it too often, but Eunice had never spent a day in jail, except for a DUI, and Dewey had been jailed only twice, for traffic warrants back when he was a struggling actor, before meeting Eunice.

When Dewey parked in the little strip mall and walked inside Pablo's Tacos, he saw no black man who was forty, fat, and nervous. The people at the tables were a Latino couple with two small children, all of them eating tacos and refried beans, and a young Latino guy sitting by himself, drinking coffee.

Dewey ordered a taco he didn't really want and a Coke. Then he sat at the table next to the young man, who was no older than Dewey's college kids. In fact, this boy could very well be in college. He was a good-looking, slender young guy with great curly hair, wearing a red T-shirt, clean jeans, and Adidas running shoes. He had no tatts, earrings, or face jewelry, but being at Pablo's Tacos in an apparently expectant mode might mean that he had a drug issue and could use some fast and easy bucks.

While waiting for the Nigerian, Dewey figured he might as well work the kid and see what was what. Dewey nibbled at the taco and felt the heat instantly. He grabbed his Coke, took a couple of gulps, and said, "Damn, they didn't warn me about the jalapeños!"

Malcolm Rojas said, "You have to tell them no heat."

"I can't eat this," Dewey said, dropping the taco onto the paper plate.

"Take it back to the counter," Malcolm said. "They'll give you another."

"I'm not hungry anyway," Dewey said with an affable smile, "but thanks for the tip."

Malcolm looked at him curiously. In Hollywood, when a middle-aged white stranger started being friendly, Malcolm figured he was probably gay. This guy looked straight enough, but you never knew, especially on Santa Monica Boulevard.

Dewey said to Malcolm, "I'm looking for ambitious young college students who're interested in some very profitable part-time work. Would you be a student by any chance?"

Malcolm, who hadn't taken a single course even at a community college since graduating from high school, now figured the guy for some kind of pervert and said guardedly, "What kind of work?"

"Just some easy jobs to help with tuition and books, with a lot of money left over."

Even more curious now, Malcolm lied and said, "I'm only a part-time student at City College. Does that work for you?"

"Certainly," Dewey said. "If I told you that you could make between five hundred and a thousand dollars working just a couple of days a week, would you be interested?"

Now Malcolm was sure the guy was a perv. He said, "I don't do fuck films, man."

Dewey chuckled and said, "You wouldn't make such easy money in such a short time doing fuck films." He broke off a piece of the fried taco shell and said, "Are you willing to work with cards?"

"How do you mean?" Malcolm asked.

"Do you have a debit card?"

"No," Malcolm said.

"How old're you?"

"Nineteen," Malcolm said truthfully.

"That's fine," Dewey said. "You can pass for twenty-one, no problem."

"Whadda you mean, 'pass'?"

"If I gave you a debit card, a PIN number, and good ID with your picture on it, but with a bogus name, would you be willing to use it to draw out money at certain places that're very safe? Or would you be willing to go on a fun shopping trip and buy all kinds of great things with a credit card that has someone else's name on it?"

"I don't know," Malcolm said. "I got a job. I never done anything with debit cards or credit cards."

"I'll bet your job pays minimum wage," Dewey said.

A bit offended, Malcolm said, "It's a living."

There was something about this young man. He had a straightforward sincerity about him that Dewey seldom found in young people these days. Something told him that he could use this forthright young Latino to great advantage. He drew a business card from his wallet with the name Bernie Graham on it along with the number of one of his GoPhones, and slid it across the table to Malcolm.

"Think about a shopping trip as a starter," Dewey said. "Buying great merchandise is what it amounts to. You'd buy things at places I send you to, and you'd deliver the items to a place that I select. Call me tomorrow at five P.M. if you're interested. If I don't hear from you, I'll figure it's a no-go."

"I work till five," Malcolm said. "Can I call you at five thirty?"

"Certainly," Dewey said, confident that he'd hooked his fish. "I'm Bernie Graham. What's your name?"

"You can call me Clark," said Malcolm, standing up to leave. "Clark Jones."

"I hope to hear from you, Clark Jones," said Dewey as the young man exited the taco shop.

Six-X-Thirty-two was driven by Flotsam, whose partner had gotten permission from Sergeant Murillo to go home early after telling the supervisor that his dog had disappeared from the yard and his landlady was in a panic. It was a lie hastily dreamed up by the surfer cop after his waitress du jour at IHOP agreed to go surfing with him the next morning at Malibu but only if the surfer cop could get to the beach by 8 A.M. Because Watch 5 didn't end until 0400 hours, Jetsam had been in a tizzy, worrying about sleep deprivation that might make him less than magnificent the next day. So he concocted the dog story for Sergeant Murillo, even though the only pet he had was a turtle.

Flotsam, who of course was privy to his partner's scheme, asked the sergeant what he should do for the remainder of the watch, and it turned out that P1 rookie Harris Triplett's usual field training officer was on a special day off. The probationer had been assigned to assist the desk officer that night, just to give him something to do, so Sergeant Murillo decided to let him work with Flotsam for the remainder of the watch. The sergeant would ordinarily have been reluctant to put even a last-phase probationer like Harris Triplett with either of the surfer cops, but being down to five cars on the midwatch, he thought he'd take a chance.

Young Harris Triplett found himself riding the rest of the watch with Flotsam, and they happened to be cruising past Pablo's Tacos when Malcolm Rojas was walking away from the strip mall. Malcolm didn't interest Flotsam at all. What interested Flotsam was a portly black man driving an old Toyota who'd managed to find a parking place in the mall and who emerged from his car with a small paper-wrapped parcel in his hand, which he tucked under his jacket before approaching the entry door.

"First thing, dude," Flotsam said. "That year Toyota you can start with a screwdriver or a pair of scissors. Anything will turn the ignition on. So we're suspicious right away that the car could be hot, right?"

"Yes, sir," said the unsuspicious boot.

"And we know from long experience that Pablo's is a place where tweakers, baseheads, and every other kind of doper hangs out and does deals, right?"

"Yes, sir," said the rookie, who had no long experience about anything but who agreed with everything a P2 or P3 said.

"Don't call me 'sir.' It makes me feel like a shoobie."

"A what?"

"A lame-oh that wears socks and sandals on the beach."

"Oh," Harris said.

"Sometimes they bring their baloney sandwiches in a shoe box. Shoobie, get it? Way wack."

"I see," Harris said.

"So okay, for a dude in a place like this to be sticking a small package under his coat, that, like, sets off all kinds of alarms on our blue radar, don't it?"

"Yes, sir," Harris said, with conviction this time.

"Goddamnit!"

"Sorry, sorry!"

Flotsam said, "Something about the way that dude dresses says to me he's an immigrant. It's like all these Armenian gangsters? Unibrows in Armani Exchange and Members Only jackets, right? You know they ain't from around here."

"Got it."

"Look at that dude's shoes. Are they plastic or what? And those pants pulled up to his chest bone? And a white dress shirt and horse-blanket coat? He's from somewheres else too."

"Got it," Harris said.

"What if this black guy turns out to be Puerto Rican or Dominican?" Flotsam said. "I heard you can speak Spanish, right?"

"Yes," the rookie said. Then he hesitated and added, "Well, I get a two-point-seventy-five-percent pay bump for speaking Spanish. I minored in Spanish at Cal State L.A., but I'm not so good at the reading and writing."

"We won't have to write to the guy," Flotsam said.

"To be honest, I sort of speak Spanglish."

"Close enough," Flotsam said. "Let's go hear his story, whatever language it's in."

Flotsam parked the car in the red zone in front of the strip mall, and both cops collected their batons and entered the parking lot.

The Nigerian and Dewey Gleason made eye contact the moment the man entered the taco shop. Dewey was about to speak, when he spotted two uniformed cops—one a tall blond with gelled hair, and a younger athletic-looking partner—walking fast across the parking lot. His instincts told him to avert his gaze from the Nigerian's and to get the hell out of there ASAP.

Sure enough, the cops entered and the tall cop said to the Nigerian, "Sir, we'd like you to step outside for a minute."

"What for?" the Nigerian said in accented English, eyes widening.

Flotsam said, "We need to have a few words, sir." Then more firmly, "Step outside, please."

Reluctantly, the Nigerian walked outside with the cops, and after the glass door swung shut, Dewey Gleason rose and dumped his uneaten taco plate into a trash receptacle. He exited in time to see the cops walking the man toward an old Toyota at the far side of the parking lot. Dewey saw a parcel drop from under the man's checked sport coat and fall onto the asphalt. The younger cop picked it up and the Nigerian acted as though he'd never seen it before.

Dewey slowed when passing the trio, and he could see that the package had torn open and several sheets of checks had spilled onto the ground. The dumb shit had only needed to bring one sheet of checks for Eunice to duplicate! Dewey quickened his pace, not bothering with the Bernie Graham limp and not looking back. He wasn't sure, but when he reached the street, he thought he could hear the sound of handcuff ratchets chattering closed. It was a sound that chilled his blood.

★ SEVEN ★

MALCOLM ROJAS COULD HEAR his mother in the living room watching TV when he finally got home. That's all she did when she wasn't at work. He could hear the ice cubes tinkling in her glass of Jim Beam. She was laughing at some dumb show she was watching and might be half drunk by now. He thought he'd call in sick tomorrow. He hated working on weekends. The card belonging to that guy Bernie Graham was on his mind. He decided to make an appointment with the man and hear more about the debit cards and the real money he could make. It scared him to think about it, but it also excited him.

Excitement. That made him think once again of the woman in the apartment garage. Of how she'd been down on his lap. Of how he'd *owned* her. She'd promised she'd do whatever he wanted if he didn't hurt her with the box cutter. For a second he remembered that he hadn't done what he'd wanted to do with her, something he'd never done in his life. He'd wanted to come in her mouth, that fat old bitch. And he didn't, couldn't. He pushed it from his mind. He listened to his mother laughing again, but he didn't want to let her make him angry. He began to listen to heavy metal on his iPod.

Music made him start thinking about that girl Naomi. He almost called her but changed his mind. He wanted to see her again and promised himself that he would. He even liked the retainer on her teeth. It made her look . . . what was the word? *Vulnerable,* that was it. She looked so vulnerable. Naomi didn't seem to go with heavy metal, so he turned off the iPod. He wondered what she'd do if he kissed her and tried to touch her small breasts. He began getting an erection.

Then he heard his mother laughing again. He started to become angry, despite himself. He tried to think of Naomi again, but he could not. He pictured that fat bitch in the parking garage and thought of what he'd wanted to do to her, and that made him remember his failure. His fury grew powerful and he put his pillow over his head and tried to will himself to sleep.

It took him an hour, and when he awoke he was sweat-drenched. He could recall bits and pieces of a recurring dream. He was younger in the dream, and he was in bed with...he couldn't say who. He smelled the booze on her, and she kept stroking his body, starting with his hair, until her hands slid down his hips. She was murmuring "Ruben...my sweet Ruben." The dream was always like that. He awoke with an erection, and even after he masturbated, he could not go back to sleep for hours. The rage wouldn't let him.

Because the Pacific Dining Car on Sixth Street near downtown was open 24/7, Dewey Gleason chose it instead of Musso & Frank on Hollywood Boulevard, which was much closer to home. He preferred the city's oldest eateries, where little had changed since the likes of Gable and Tracy and Raymond Chandler had dined there. It was 1 A.M., and he was fatigued, waiting in the clubby little bar for the college kid, after having delivered two Whoppers to Eunice and changed his disguise. He loved old drinking spots like this, all mahogany, brass, and faux leather, offering timeless reassurance. He sat sipping a Manhattan, his first drink at the end of a very long day. There were three other men having cocktails, along with a bickering couple at the other end of the bar, no doubt having just come from somewhere that had gotten them juiced enough to fight it out in public.

What was the kid's name? Christ, he'd dealt with four of them since he'd hit the streets this morning and they'd begun to look and sound alike. When contact was just getting started with these kids, they were all positively thrumming with nervous energy, and not a little fear. Eventually they became laconic and lazy and even insolent when the greed set in. That's when Dewey had to dump them and look for a new set of faces, new college boys eager to sell their debit cards.

He asked himself again, What was the kid's fucking name? One time last month when Dewey was this exhausted and it was this late, he'd almost forgotten his *own* name, or rather the name of the character he was playing. Now, at 1 A.M. in the Pacific Dining Car, he had to think for a moment and touch the eyeglasses he was wearing. They belonged to Ambrose Willis, who in his past fictional life had been a lecturer in business management at an Ivy League university. Dewey was always vague about which university until he was sure it was not one with which the kid had familiarity. Ambrose Willis wore an auburn toupee and had a large mole on his left cheek near his mouth.

It reminded Dewey that when he was applying it earlier that evening, Eunice had slouched into the bathroom in her tatty pink robe, the one with cigarette burns on the front. Her frizz of coppery blonde hair was so grown out at the roots that she looked like a clown in a fright wig, and he'd noticed that she was starting to get two chins.

With the perennial cigarette dangling, Eunice looked at him working on his makeup and said, "That's quite a mole. It reminds me of that movie on TV the other night, *Dangerous Liaisons*."

"John Malkovich didn't have a mole in that movie," said Dewey, who was a lifelong movie buff.

Eunice said, "I was thinking of the whores in the French court. That's what you remind me of with that spot of shit on your face."

Get in the fucking moment! he told himself. Christ, what's that kid's name? He was just so damn tired.

"Evening, Mr. Willis," the young man said and took a stool next to him at the bar.

He was a lanky kid, an inch or so over six feet, as most of them were. Dewey wondered how it happened that this generation was a couple of inches taller than his. About half of his college runners were emos, with heavy hair flopping onto their foreheads so it bounced in time to the tunes of Morrissey, which they seemed to favor. This kid looked more metrosexual in a white linen dress shirt with the sleeves rolled above his elbows, a lavender T-shirt showing, and designer jeans he couldn't have afforded without working for Dewey.

"What'll you have?" Dewey said, and then it came to him and he added, "Stuart."

Stuart, who had plenty of bogus ID attesting to his being of age, said, "The same thing you're having."

Without being asked, Stuart put a bogus driver's license on the bar, which the bartender examined before making another Manhattan.

When the drink was in front of them, Dewey said, "Let's go to a table and chat."

After they got settled, Dewey said, "Would you like something to eat? How about a nice steak? They serve good food here at any hour of the night or day."

"I had a big supper," Stuart said, sipping his Manhattan. From his frowning response, Dewey was sure the Manhattan was a first for him.

"This place looks like a train car from the outside," Stuart said. "Like you're getting on a train."

"It's been too long since you've reported," Dewey said. "I think you have something for me, do you not?"

"That's the problem, Mr. Willis," Stuart said.

"What...problem?" Dewey said, the bonhomie gone. Screw the steak. He began eye-fucking the kid behind those steel frames.

"Don't get excited, Mr. Willis," Stuart said. "I have money for you."

"Then we don't have a problem, do we?" Dewey said.

"I just don't have it all. I had to gamble more than I intended to. Have you spent much time in those casinos, Mr. Willis?"

Unblinking, "Yes, I've been in all of them."

"Well, there was this big Indian guy in the second casino, the one just outside Palm Springs? I think he was a security officer. He started following me after I withdrew the first bunch of money with my debit card. I was pretty sure he was watching, so I put way more in the slots than I wanted to. See what I mean?"

"Oh, yes, I see what you mean," Dewey said. "It's perfectly clear to me."

"Okay, to start with, I followed your instructions, Mr. Willis. When

I arrived, I got the five-hundred-dollar limit from the account, and then at one minute after midnight, I got another five hundred. And then I went back to the motel and went to bed. The next day, I went to the second casino and used the second card. You were right about the casinos. I don't think there was a camera at the ATM machines like in the machines around here."

"Only the general cameras surveying the wide areas," Dewey said. "Nothing for you to worry about."

"Then I went to the third casino and used the third card," the kid said. "I just felt a lot better doing it like that instead of using all three debit cards in one casino. You were right about that too."

"Smart boy," Dewey said. "Get to the point."

Stuart took another sip from his cocktail and said, "I only played the slot machines to make it look good. I was actually thinking about playing something else in order to make it look even better."

"I told you, only slots," Dewey said. "And very few of those."

"Right, so I maybe spent an extra two, two-fifty, in the slots that I didn't wanna spend."

Dewey was silent for a moment, knowing this was a lie, and said, "You spent over two hundred dollars of my money in slot machines? I don't suppose you won anything in any of the three casinos, did you, Stuart?"

"No," Stuart said. "Are you sure those machines aren't rigged?"

"No, they're not," Dewey said, controlling his anger. "Where's my money?"

"In the trunk of my car in an envelope."

"Let's go get it," Dewey said.

When they got to the parking lot, Stuart opened the trunk of his Mazda and removed a large envelope, saying, "Everything is accounted for, just like you said, Mr. Willis. In the three casinos for the three days, I took out forty-five hundred dollars altogether. I spent two hundred for gas. I know it sounds like a lot, but my car needs a tune-up. I spent three hundred dollars for the three nights in a motel and only two hundred dollars for meals I was too tense to eat. I gambled two-fifty in the slots in the casinos. That left me with three thousand five hundred fifty. I deducted my thirty percent from the balance and had a few incidentals, including a new tire, and that came to four hundred fifty-five dollars. There's twenty-five hundred for you, Mr. Willis. It came out a nice round number, and the cards are in the envelope with the money."

"Nice round number," Dewey said. "It always comes out a nice round number. And I wonder why so many of you young men claim that you had to gamble so much more than you were told to gamble? Is that because you are afflicted by compulsive gambling disorder or by inherent greed?"

"I swear to God, Mr. Willis—," the kid said, but Dewey put up a hand to silence him.

"My...organization went to a lot of expense to set this whole thing up," Dewey said. "It hardly seems worthwhile now, Stuart."

"I worked three days for that money, Mr. Willis," Stuart said, "when you consider the driving time."

"How long do you think my organization spent setting it up?"

"Maybe I could do another part of the work next time," Stuart said. "Maybe I could make the deposits for you. Somebody has to put checks into the debit accounts. Why not me?"

"Ambitious," Dewey said. "You're an ambitious lad, Stuart. Well, it's getting late and I have to report to the boss of our organization. I hope he's not unhappy with your work. If he is, you'll be hearing from...somebody."

"Mr. Willis," the kid said, "I worked hard and did the best I could. I wouldn't cheat you!"

"Of course not," Dewey said. "Go home and get some sleep. We'll be in touch."

After Stuart was clear of the parking lot, Dewey went to his car, started it up, and began the drive home to Hollywood. The $2,500 wasn't bad, considering he had two more kids like Stuart to collect from before the month ended. The "organization boss"—that smoke-reeking, foul-tempered bitch—was someone he could almost live with, as long as the calendar month netted them at least $10,000 after expenses. Any less than that and she was so horrible, it was all he could do to keep from packing up and running away for good. Maybe then he'd have a chance of living a normal life span instead of dying of emphysema or lung cancer. And he would do it too, except that Eunice had sole access to the so-called retirement account.

For the first five years of their marriage, he'd secretly searched for an account number, a routing number, or an online password—anything that might open the door to her treasure vault. But he was never even able to discover in which bank she hoarded their money. He reckoned that by now she'd accumulated about $500,000, give or take. Currently he was running six bank accounts under several names, where money from their various gags could be deposited, transferred to another bank, and withdrawn before their victims' own banks ever discovered a problem. And Eunice did in-person as well as online banking. On one of his snooping forays, he'd found four checkbooks from local Hollywood banks.

Something had always bothered him about the "retirement account" story she'd fed him. It was that she was the momma bird protecting the nest egg that was going to see them through to a comfortable retirement in San Francisco. It was there that she owned an inherited family home on Russian Hill, currently leased out, but which would be theirs during their golden years. The thought of all that made him shiver with revulsion.

And then one day in March, after they'd gone out for a dress-up dinner at the Polo Lounge in the Beverly Hills Hotel, where she didn't see a single celebrity and got drunk instead, he'd found a brass key. He'd spotted it while snooping in her wallet after she'd passed out in her bedroom, and it looked to him like a padlock key. He'd hardly slept that night, thinking about the lock that the key would fit. There had been too many occasions over the years when she'd nagged and harangued Dewey about making banking errors that could lead back to him, or rather to one of the characters he played when he did in-person banking.

The fact was, she was distrustful of banks and always overestimated the employees, always fearing "red flags," as she put it. As far as Dewey could see, a few zeros added to a number meant nothing at all to the young tellers, most of whom looked like they'd rather be bartenders or cocktail waitresses or anything else where they could make a few bucks and meet some interesting people. He had persistent thoughts that someone like Eunice would keep her retirement fund in a safe deposit box rather than in an account where she'd surrender control to people she obsessively feared.

But the key he'd found in her wallet was not to a safe deposit box. It looked like an ordinary brass padlock key, the kind he used at storage facilities where he kept the merchandise that his runners bought with bogus checks and credit cards. He began thinking a lot about that key. There could be a huge amount of cash in storage somewhere in Los Angeles. That key provoked endless fantasies for Dewey Gleason.

In recent months he'd often awakened in the middle of the night and imagined ways in which he could kill Eunice, even though he'd never had the stomach for violence. In his most recent fantasy, one that gave him enormous pleasure, he envisioned holding her captive in an escape-proof basement, maybe in a cabin up near Angeles National Forest. Each morning he'd supply her all the water she needed, along with the choice of four Burger King Whoppers or four packs of cigarettes, which is what she ate and smoked on an average day. Whoppers or cancer tubes — either or, her choice. Dewey was confident that the miserable cunt would die of starvation within a month.

While Dewey Gleason was at the Pacific Dining Car, Dana Vaughn and Hollywood Nate got a call to meet 6-L-20 in the alley behind the Pantages Theater. Traffic on Hollywood Boulevard was heavy, and it took an extra few minutes to get there. The sergeant was Miriam Hermann, an LAPD old-timer with thirty-six years on the Job. They saw her car parked on Vine Street, and she was outside, leaning against it. Sergeant Hermann was a chunky woman of sixty-one years with black caterpillar eyebrows and iron-gray hair trimmed shorter than Dana's. Sergeant Murillo, the best-read supervisor at Hollywood Station, thought she looked like Gertrude Stein. But Miriam Hermann had no Alice B. Toklas, only rescued animals: two dogs and three cats. It was said that she'd had an unhappy childless marriage to a veterinarian before she was a cop, but she wasn't chatty about her past and no one knew for sure.

When Dana and Nate got out of their car, Sergeant Hermann said to them, "There's something going on back by the trash Dumpster. I saw some guys walk outta the nightclub and into the alley."

"A drug deal?" Nate said.

"Maybe," the sergeant said. "Let's have a look."

While they were walking, Dana said, "They're like lions waiting for prey in these nightclubs. A girl turns her back and they hit her drink with an eyedropper full of GHB. She awakes in a hotel room, raped and sodomized."

"Never take your hands off your drinks in Hollywood," Nate agreed. "If necessary, use a sippy cup."

They entered the alley, staying in the shadows of the buildings with their flashlights off. There was plenty of street noise to muffle their footsteps, but they needn't have worried. Somebody in a car on Vine Street was screaming at somebody else who was stalled in traffic. Soon horns were blowing and engines were racing. When the cops got close to the Dumpster, they saw that a man had a woman pinned up against it and was humping her from behind while two other men watched, probably waiting their turns.

The men were all well dressed and so drunk that none of them even noticed three cops approaching. Sergeant Hermann signaled to Dana and Nate, who circled the Dumpster to cut off retreat, and the sergeant turned her flashlight on the woman, who might as well have worn a sandwich board announcing her occupation. The two bystanders looked up but didn't attempt to escape. The guy in the saddle made no effort to stop, even after staring into the flashlight beams. His eyes were watery and unfocused with lids drooping. He just kept going at it.

Several seconds passed until Sergeant Hermann finally said, "Am I not standing here, or what? Back off!"

Reluctantly, the jockey did so. He was a forty-ish white man dressed in nightclub-black and so fried he didn't seem to know that his penis was hanging limp and ineffective as he struggled to put it away. The hooker was also white, way past her prime and obviously amped, probably on cocaine, the nightclub drug of choice. She was dressed confrontationally in a strapless black tube dress that stopped midthigh. Her makeup might be called theatrical if the theater was Kabuki. She wore stockings with seams, held in place by a partially exposed black garter belt, and she would've looked appropriate only at a Marilyn Manson concert.

"He wasn't hurting me," the hooker said. "In fact, I didn't feel nothing."

"That's your fault. I want my money back," the customer whispered, louder than he intended.

For the first time, the woman paid close attention to the cops and said, "I don't know what this man is talking about, Officers. There's no money involved here. This was just a spontaneous expression of love." Then she looked woozily at the man in black and said, "Ain't that right, honey?"

He caught on, staggered forward, and said, "That's right, Officers. This was not an act of prostitution. It was just—I don't know, a burst of mad passion. We shoulda gone to a motel."

"You should go to a clinic," Sergeant Hermann said. Then turning to the other two, she said, "How about you? Waiting to express your mad passion too, were you?"

One drunk, who was submitting to a pat-down search by Dana, said nothing. The other, who had already been searched by Hollywood Nate, said, "I just thought somebody was doing a Heimlich maneuver and I wanted to help. Can we go back to the nightclub now?"

Sergeant Hermann had the look of someone who wanted to be anywhere else, and after thirty-six years of police work, she definitely looked her age. She arched her spine with her hands on her hips, as though her back was killing her, looked at her watch, and said, "I'm hungry. Time for code seven."

"Go ahead and take seven, Sarge," Hollywood Nate said. Then to the hooker and her trick, he said, "You two are going to jail for lewd conduct." He looked at the drunken observers and said, "Anybody got outstanding warrants? You paid all your traffic tickets?"

The two observers mumbled an assent, and Sergeant Hermann waved at her cops and walked back through the alley to Vine Street, while Dana handcuffed the two prisoners, and Hollywood Nate filled out FI cards on the other two. They looked too prosperous to be wanted on traffic warrants or anything else, and their IDs were proper, so they were released.

Before they left, Hollywood Nate said, "If you go anywhere near your cars, you better have a designated driver. Understand?"

Sergeant Hermann had completed a long cell call while standing beside her shop by the time Nate and Dana were walking out of the alley with their two arrestees. Before the sergeant got back in her car, Nate and Dana saw her approach a shiny new Beemer that was illegally parked on Vine Street with the engine running.

They heard her say to the young black man in the driver's seat, "Move your car, please. That's a no-parking zone."

He looked lazily at her and said, "I'll only be a minute. My friend went in the club to find somebody."

"Move the car, sir," Sergeant Hermann said.

"This is some shit," the indignant driver said. "You're only messin' with me 'cause I'm young and I'm black and I'm good-lookin' and I got a cool ride. Am I right?"

Sergeant Hermann, who had heard this, or variations of it, hundreds of times in her long career, was feeling very tired and very old at the moment. She said to the driver, "I'm a senior citizen and I'm a Jew and I look like a manatee and my Ford Escort's nine years old. Where're we going with this bullshit?"

The driver wanted to fire back but was out of verbal ammo, so he dropped it into gear and drove away.

★ EIGHT ★

THE NEXT MORNING, Malcolm Rojas got out of bed and shuffled into the kitchen, holding his throat and swallowing hard, feigning illness so he could avoid going to his job at the home improvement center.

His mother was frying eggs for him, and his orange juice was on the kitchen table. She looked at him and said, "Sore throat?"

"Yeah," he said, "I can't go to work. I'll have to call in sick."

"Oh, sweetie," his mother said. "Are you sure you're too sick? You have a good job, and I'd hate to see you lose it. And today you'll get overtime pay."

"A good job," he said. "Slicing boxes open on a Sunday? Unpacking merchandise I can't afford to buy? A good job."

He sat at the table and took a sip of the orange juice.

"If you'd only gone on to City College like I—"

"Like you what?"

He couldn't stand it when her voice got shrill and whiny. He couldn't stand the sight of her in that shapeless nightgown with her tits hanging down and her fat ass sticking out, and that bleached frizzy hair in pins and two pink curlers, like somebody in a movie fifty years old.

"I was gonna say, if you'd gone on to a community college last year, it woulda been better than any entry-level job you could get at that mall. Your mother told you that."

The thing he hated most was when she referred to herself as "your mother," often accompanied by the stroking of his hair, which, thankfully, she hadn't done in months.

"First you say I shoulda went to college—"

"*Gone,* sweetie," she interrupted. "Shoulda *gone* to college."

"Okay!" he said. "Gone, gone, gone! How could I pay your damn room and board if I'da *gone* to college?"

"You wouldn't have had to," his mother said, putting the plate in front of him. "I woulda supported you for as long as you stayed in school."

He felt it coming again. The anger. He started to cut the fried eggs and take a bite, but his hands began shaking.

"Tell me something," he said. "Why is it *your* money? When Dad got killed, why did the lawsuit money go to you? Why not to both of us?"

"You were a boy, Malcolm," she said.

"I'm not now," he said. "I'm almost twenty. Why do you get the money and all I get is—"

"Room and board," she said, still with that country accent from her Oklahoma roots. "Which you should be glad to pay for, unless you wanna go to college or even a trade school."

Then her face softened and she stood behind him and, to his chagrin, reached over to actually stroke his hair, as though she'd read his thoughts and was taunting him. His breath caught. He could hardly believe it, and he said, "What're you doing?"

"You're still a boy," she said, stroking.

"Don't," he said. "Don't do that!"

"Why not, sweetie?" she said. "You have your father's lovely curls, and you're still your mother's darling little—"

Malcolm Rojas swept his breakfast off the table, sending the plate crashing to the floor. When he leaped to his feet, as though to hit her, she gasped and backed up to the sink.

"Malcolm!" she cried. "Have you gone crazy?"

He stood trembling, then turned and ran to his bedroom and slammed the door. Malcolm pulled on his jeans and a clean white T-shirt and didn't bother to call his boss before running out the door and down the stairs of the apartment building.

The last thing he heard from his mother was sobbing and her shrill voice calling after him, "Sweetie, what's wrong? Please! Let's talk about it!"

When he got to the carports, he jumped in his Mustang, backed out, and started driving aimlessly. Ten minutes later he was heading west on Sunset Boulevard, roaring past the morning traffic clogged in the eastbound lanes, heading toward the ocean without knowing why. He pulled over long enough to calm himself and to phone the boss's number, and he was glad to get voice mail and not the man. Malcolm wanted to explain how sorry he was that he had a fever and a sore throat, but he lost his nerve.

He put the cell phone away, reached into the glove compartment to remove the box cutter, and put it in the pocket of his jeans, deciding to go to his job.

That Sunday afternoon at roll call, the midwatch was down to four cars, with several cops off-duty. Sergeant Lee Murillo read the crimes and gave the usual admonitions and warnings about failure to complete the crushing load of forms that the consent decree entailed. Then he had to listen to the usual responses. These included some rational comments about the civilian firm that was getting richer from the audits, as well as some about the federal judge who would decide when the LAPD was in compliance. Then the heat started to rise, and of course the sergeant pretended not to hear the irrational suggestions delivered in stage whispers from one cop to another as to what the overseers should do with their audits, and what the federal judge should do with the consent decree, and what the judge's mother should have done with him, and which parts of him should be fed to the family cat. He knew that cop defensive humor was the equivalent of smacking someone in the face with a cream pie full of maggots, so he let it go.

Recalling some of the morale-lifting techniques of their late beloved senior sergeant, he ended roll call by saying, "There's nearly a Hollywood moon tonight." He gestured toward the framed photo hanging beside the door and said, "For you new people, a Hollywood moon is what the Oracle called a full moon, and tonight we're getting close. The team with the weirdest call gets an extra-large pizza with the works, compliments of Sergeant Hermann and my good self. Of course, we'll share the pizza with the winners. Too much of that stuff is not healthy for you."

"We had a weird one last night, Sarge," Johnny Lanier said. "A woman called us because her elderly father swallowed eight triple-A batteries."

"That's not so weird," said R.T. Dibney. "Poor old geezer probably just wanted to keep on going and going and going."

"Does it count for weird if we catch another stalker breaking into some house in the Hollywood Hills just to take a dump in a celebrity's toilet?" another wanted to know.

"Sorry, that's almost a cliché," Sergeant Murillo said.

Just before leaving, R.T. Dibney lifted the spirits of several of the male officers when he announced to the assembly that a rape report he'd taken the prior evening from a hooker on Sunset Boulevard contained a statement that the rapist had a "huge penis."

"The dude musta been real proud of his cruel tool," R.T. Dibney explained to all. "He took several photos of it to show off to the girls on the boulevard. And after he refused to pay and the hooker got lumped up, she grabbed the photos and ran. I got one of them here. Wanna see the big schvantz?"

That generated some interest, and several cops, females included, gathered around R.T. Dibney to have a look. It resulted in high fives and cries of "Yes!" from very relieved male cops who measured up. However, any urologist could've told them that the big schvantz was actually in the normal-to-small range. Like theirs.

At 5 P.M. that afternoon, Dewey Gleason, who was once again Ambrose Willis, was too occupied to remember the kid he'd met at Pablo's Tacos. He was busy being a Realtor. Half the morning and all afternoon, he'd been checking on a dozen foreclosure addresses that Eunice had downloaded. These and thousands like them had been damaging the local economy for months.

The runners he'd chosen for this job were unsavory. He'd needed a professional lock-picking burglar but settled for a pair of lowlife housebreaking tweakers whom he intended to dump as soon as possible. They were waiting in a battered old Plymouth parked at the curb in front of a modest house on Oakwood, in southeast Hollywood. Dewey couldn't remember their names, but it didn't matter. When he parked his car and got out, both thirty-something tweakers—one an inked-up Latino with a lip stud, and the other a sleazed-out, nearly toothless, shaky white guy with the sweats—got out of their car to meet him. The white guy gave Dewey a dozen keys.

"Afternoon, Mr. Willis," he said.

"Afternoon," Dewey said. "How many houses did you get done?"

"All six," the tweaker said, scratching his ribs, his neck, trying to reach his back.

Dewey gave him a look, and the tweaker smiled apologetically, showing the gaps in his grille, and said, "I'm jonesing. No sense lying to you. I need some ice pretty bad. Real bad, in fact."

"Let's see your work," Dewey said, heading for the door with the tweakers at his heels.

The sweaty tweaker pointed out the key to this house and Dewey tried it in the lock. It worked perfectly and he pushed the door open.

"We changed the front-door lock on all six houses, no problem," the tweaker said. "Can we get paid now?"

Dewey said, "How did you get in to change the locks?"

"Four had an unlocked window. One had a back door that you could slip with a credit card. One had the back door hanging wide open."

"Careless," Dewey said, shaking his head. "Everyone's so careless these days."

"Our pay, Mr. Willis," the sweaty tweaker repeated, and Dewey could almost smell the addiction on him.

Dewey opened his wallet and gave the tweaker $150.

"What's this?" the tweaker said. "We finished the jobs, changed the locks, and bought you extra keys."

"That's what we agreed on, one Franklin and one Grant per house," Dewey said.

"We did six houses," the tweaker said.

"So you say," Dewey replied. "As soon as I inspect them, you'll get the balance."

The Latino spoke for the first time. "So we say, man."

He said it so softly that Dewey was unnerved. Spittle was dripping over the guy's lip stud, and his eyes had narrowed.

"I'll meet you at Pablo's Tacos in three hours," Dewey said. "After I inspect the others."

"You ain't going nowhere with our money," the Latino said.

This guy didn't seem to Dewey like the spun-out tweakers he occasionally had to deal with. This guy seemed calm and focused and very serious. "Whadda you say about this?" Dewey said to the sweaty tweaker. "We've done business in the past. Whadda you say?"

"I gotta go along with my partner," the white tweaker said. "I got the joneses real bad. I can't wait three hours to buy me some crystal."

Dewey took another look at the Latino, who never blinked those slitted black eyes, and Dewey took seven more $100 bills and one $50 bill from his wallet. "I'm trusting you two," he said lamely.

"You can trust us, Mr. Willis," the sweaty tweaker said, snatching the money from Dewey's hand. "You got more jobs for me, just drive by the taco stand any morning after nine. I'll be there, looking for work. By the way, the keys were fifty bucks extra."

Dewey was furious, but he reluctantly gave the tweaker another $50 bill, and as they slouched away from the house, whispering to each other, he had a sudden stab of panic. What if they decided to kill him to take what was left in his wallet? What if that's what they were whispering about? Dewey was ready to run as fast as he could if they turned and came back at him. He was enormously relieved when they got in their car and drove off.

Dewey quickly locked the door, went to his car to retrieve a "For Rent" sign attached to a wooden stake, a roll of tape, a ball of string with brightly colored pennants attached, and a hammer. The sign said "Brad Simpson Real Estate," along with one of Dewey's cell numbers on it. He strung the pennants across the front porch posts and pounded the stake into the desiccated front yard.

Dewey drove to the next house on his list, desperately hoping that the tweaker had not lied to him. But he had. The second set of keys did not work, and he was positive that when he drove to the other four houses, they would still have the original locks in place. Fucking lying tweakers!

He hated them all. He hated this work. He hated thinking what Eunice was going to say when she found out he'd been fleeced.

Eunice, ever the anal planner, had made Dewey place the ads in the PennySaver and on craigslist from a computer that he'd rented for an hour at the 24/7 cyber café, where lots of drug dealers and hookers did business online. And because he was nearly computer-hopeless, she'd written detailed instructions for him on how to do it. Eunice later told him she'd quickly received several phone calls from eager prospective tenants who'd jumped at the rental price, so Dewey knew she'd now be impatiently waiting for his call, no doubt on her forty-eighth cigarette of the day.

"Good to go" was all he said when she answered.

She said, "I got several prospects dying to be the first one to see the places. I'll send a client to destination number one at six thirty."

"Jesus Christ!" Dewey said. "I've had a long day. I'll meet them tomorrow."

"People gotta work for a living," Eunice said testily. "You'll close the first deal this evening and then wait for number two. I'll have another good prospect there by seven thirty. The rest you can do tomorrow. Understand?"

He didn't have the nerve to face a broadside right this minute, so he said, "They're not all done yet."

"So?" she said. "Get somebody else to do them if the guys you picked won't do the job. What's the problem?"

He was silent for a moment and decided on a partial confession. "They made me pay them in advance for the others. I paid them for the whole job."

The line was dead for at least ten seconds before she said, "Made you? Made you? How?"

"They made me. That's all I can say right now." Then he lost his nerve again and lied. "But they're gonna go back and finish the jobs. They promised."

"Goddamn it!" Eunice said. "You accepted the promise of a fucking burglar? You'll never see them again!"

"I told you they made me!" he said, and now his voice had jumped a few frets and he hated her more for causing it. "It's gonna be okay!"

"How come nobody ever made Hugo do anything he didn't wanna do?" she said. "Tell me that!"

"They made him go to jail, didn't they?" Dewey yelled before clicking off.

It was all Dewey could do to keep from smashing that phone on the sidewalk in front of house number one. He went to his car, put the Brad Simpson Real Estate cards in his shirt pocket, and waited for the first good prospect to arrive for the appointment. Then he heard the chirp from one of the four cell phones he was carrying.

Malcolm Rojas was a half hour late in dialing the number of the man he knew as Bernie Graham. When he got his man on the line, Malcolm said, "I'm sorry I'm late, Mr. Graham. I've been real busy."

"Who is this?" Dewey said.

"Clark. You know, from Pablo's? You gave me your number?"

"Oh, yeah," Dewey said. "Did you decide you wanted a job?"

"In the late afternoons and evenings," Malcolm said, "after I leave my regular job."

"Gimme your number," Dewey said. "I'm busy right now, but I'll phone you later."

After giving his cell number to his prospective employer, Malcolm put the cell phone in his pocket and it clicked against the box cutter. He was on a residential street a few miles from that apartment with underground parking, on the other side of Hollywood. He wondered why he'd driven over here and why he was watching the women leaving the shopping center. He'd been sitting here in his car for more than an hour. He tried to concentrate on other things, such as the job he might be getting with Bernie Graham. He tried to imagine what it would be like to be making real money, not the shitty wage he was getting from the home improvement center for unpacking boxes.

Thinking of that made him look at his hand. Just before leaving work, he had sliced a tiny laceration near the base of his thumb with his box cutter while opening a crate containing power drills. It was small, but deep enough to sting. The boss had given him the first-aid kit, and he'd sprayed and patched the wound.

Then Malcolm felt it coming again. It always began in his belly and worked its way up until he felt that his face was on fire. His head would throb with it. In comic books, anger was often drawn in red, but his wasn't red. His was darker, black maybe. He felt almost smothered by dark vapors that made it hard to catch his breath. He could taste his rage, and it tasted like the blood on his hand. It scared him but he was excited by it.

Malcolm had seen dozens of women leave the shopping center and go to their cars, but this was the one he wanted. She drove an old gray Volvo sedan, and she was alone. He followed her, careful to keep a car between them like in the movies, and that part was thrilling. He knew that nothing was going to happen. He was only playing a game, a stalking game. She wasn't going to pull into an underground parking garage like the last one. It couldn't happen like that again. He was just fooling around, just passing the time until his anger subsided and he could go home.

Malcolm followed her onto a residential street six blocks east of the Wilshire Country Club. She lived in a bungalow, the type he'd seen in movies about old Hollywood. It was white stucco with a Spanish-tile roof. There was a tiny yard in front and there were lots of other small houses nearby. He parked half a block down the street, leaned back, fingers interlaced behind his head, and closed his eyes. He was just waiting to grow calm again. He needed a good night's sleep, he thought. Soon he was dozing fitfully.

The first "clients" arrived a few minutes before 6:30 P.M., and Dewey, with his best Realtor's smile, met them on the front porch, holding the door wide open. They were a young Latino couple, he with a pronounced accent, she with a slight accent and a baby in her stomach. Dewey figured they were no older than twenty, and they were shy.

The husband had the look of a gardener. He wore a khaki shirt and frayed jeans, and there was dirt under his nails. His naturally dark skin showed a decided tan line across his forehead, where his hat was usually worn.

Dewey held out his hand and said, "Welcome, folks! I'm Brad Simpson. Here's my card."

The young man shook his hand, and his wife spoke for them, saying, "We're the Valencias. We spoke to a lady in your office."

"Yes," Dewey said. "That was my secretary, Ethel. We've had so many inquiries in the last hour. She's called me on my cell four times. This one is going to be rented quickly. Come on inside."

Dewey saw their disappointment at the condition of the foreclosed house, and he said, "The last tenants were pretty awful. We haven't had time to clean the place. Also, we're going to paint the living room and the bathroom. Did my secretary tell you there's a little powder room just off the kitchen? We're going to wallpaper that as well as the kitchen. Everything will be done before you move in, if you decide to take the place."

They listened politely and then walked through the small rooms, until the wife said, "This could work for us, but we have one more house to look at."

Dewey said quickly, "How much did my secretary tell you the rent would be?"

"Twenty-four hundred a month," the young woman said.

"It'll go before the evening's over," Dewey said. "In fact, I have an appointment with a prospective tenant in"—he glanced at his watch—"thirty-five minutes." He looked at them thoughtfully and said, "You know what? I'd like you two to have this place. It'd be a nice street for your baby to grow up on. Gosh darn it, you remind me of how it was when my wife and me were starting out. I'm gonna take it upon myself to trim three—no, make it four hundred dollars off the rent. I know the owner won't give me any trouble when I tell him the place is not in good condition. He lives in Oregon and never comes to L.A., so I pretty much have total control over his property management. And I'll waive the security deposit. You write me a check for the first and last month and it's yours. You can move in on the first of the month, when the place will look fresh as a daisy, I guarantee you. Paint, wallpaper, plumbing repaired, the works."

Dewey smiled large and studied them while they talked quietly but enthusiastically in Spanish, and then the wife took a checkbook from her purse and said, "We accept and we thank you! Shall I make out the check to Brad Simpson Real Estate?"

"That'll be fine," Dewey said, thinking that four Clevelands would be a nice deposit to the account he'd just opened at the bank as Brad Simpson.

He filled out the rental agreement as fast as he could, figuring that the next "client" would probably also be arriving early for their appointment. After he said good-bye to the couple, he only had to wait ten minutes until the next appointment arrived.

This was a black couple, a bit unusual in that there were not many black people living in Hollywood. Every other ethnic group was more than proportionately represented, especially the growing Latino and Asian populations. These two were only slightly older than the last couple.

Dewey's professional smile broadened, and he extended a business card, saying, "Folks, you're just in time. The last appointment said they're coming to my office in the morning and will probably take the place, but until I get their first and last month's check, it's still open. My name is Brad Simpson and I'm very pleased to meet you!"

When the couple was looking at the kitchen, Dewey had a flashback to the last time he did the rental gag. On the first of February, six moving vans had arrived at the cottage he'd rented in mid-Hollywood. The street was blocked by the trucks, disputes raged, and the police were called. He happened to be driving by on his way to another "rental" and had to take a detour because of the traffic jam.

Malcolm Rojas could hardly wait until dark. He'd been watching the cottage for an hour. Dusky light blasted through the Hollywood smog, and the cottage where the woman had entered gave off a burnished glow. That light excited Malcolm. He was excited by everything around him, and even though the anger had not abated, he couldn't say for sure which emotion was stronger, anger or excitement.

No one else had entered the bungalow, no children, no husband, nobody. It was such a small house that he figured she lived there alone. Somehow that made him angrier. That bitch got a little house of her own, and he had to share an apartment with his mother, like a helpless child.

She had unlocked the front door and had carried her shopping bags inside but had not returned to the door. Maybe it wasn't locked now. Regardless, he was going in. If he had to, he'd ask her if his friend lived there. Who? Thomas, that was it. He'd ask if Thomas lived there. But if the door was unlocked, he was not going to ask anything. He was that angry and that excited. He reached into his pocket and stroked the box cutter.

She never heard him enter. She was in the kitchen, thawing a small steak in the micro when she heard him bump into a kitchen chair. When he rushed her from behind, he clamped his hand over her mouth, showed her the box cutter, and said, "If you scream even once, I'll cut your throat."

When he had her down on the kitchen floor, she began sobbing, her eyes on the box cutter that he held to her face.

She kept repeating, "Please don't! Don't hurt me! I'll give you money! Take the money from my purse! Take my car! Please don't hurt me!"

The bitch! She looked even older up close. He thought she was at least forty-five years old, maybe older. He looked at the roots of her strawberry blonde hair and could see gray. So she was maybe fifty years old. Look at her fat thighs! He pulled at her underwear, ripping it away from her while she said, "Please don't hurt me!"

"Shut up!" he said. "First you're going to suck me off, you fat old bitch!"

There was no doubt which team would win the Almost-a-Hollywood-Moon contest and get an extra-large pizza with the works from Sergeant Murillo for handling the weirdest incident, not after 6-X-66 got a call to the memorial park that night. One of the employees had returned to pick up a set of keys she'd inadvertently left on her desk, and she'd seen a door to the mortuary slightly ajar. She'd put in a 9-1-1 call on her cell and then informed the guard at the exit gate.

The cemetery was huge and far from 6-X-66's beat. And since the message from communications came in on their computer as "See the woman, open door," it didn't excite anybody, and no other cars responded to back them up.

"Watch three's got way more cars than we do," Aaron Sloane, the driver, said to Sheila Montez. "Where are they? Why do we have to roll all the way up here?"

"The lazy bastards gotta run to Seven-Eleven for a caffeine pick-me-up three times a night before they can even start thinking like cops," Sheila said irritably.

Aaron figured it was her monthly cycle making her cranky, but he'd been a cop long enough to know that absolutely the worst thing you could ever say to a woman officer who seemed to be in a bad mood was "Is it your time?"

Diplomatically, he said, "Maybe we could stop for a cup after we handle this call. You look a little...down tonight."

She glanced at him, looked back at the streets, and said, "I'm fine." Then, because he was not just any partner but the one who'd witnessed the Montez meltdown at the side of a dead baby's crib, she opened up a bit. She said, "It's just that you can't depend on anybody anymore."

Aaron hesitated and said, "Boyfriend trouble?"

That made her turn toward him and say, "If there is anything that nearly seven years of police work have taught me, it's that everybody lies, and you should never under any circumstances get involved with another cop."

He was crestfallen. "I thought you said you'd learned your lesson after your bad marriage to the sergeant from Mission Division. Have you been...dating another cop?"

"Who said anything about dating?" Sheila replied, and his heartbeat advanced ten beats per minute. "The Pope will samba at Saint Peter's before I ever date one again. But I was dumb enough to be one of three investors in a twenty-eight-foot powerboat. Don't ask me how or why. It happened right after I lost...lost the baby, and my divorce was final and...I don't know, I think I went crazy. Now my fellow investors — cops, of course — are bickering. And we're selling the boat, and I stand to lose almost eight thousand."

"Whoa!" Aaron said. "I'm sorry, Sheila. Is there anything I can do?"

"Are you independently wealthy, Aaron?" she said with that little sloe-eyed glance of hers that made his heart rate advance five more beats per minute.

He had gone from thinking that Sheila Montez was a very hot-looking woman to thinking she was drop-dead gorgeous. It was getting very hard for him to hide his feelings. "No," he said, "but I'd lend you whatever money I could."

She snapped out of it, smiled, and said, "I know you would, partner. You're probably the only cop I'd ever get involved with."

Then Aaron's heart rate increased another five beats, until she added, "In a business deal."

Aaron turned his face toward her and said, "I guess if I ever get married, it shouldn't be to another cop, should it?"

"Why do you ever have to get married?" she said. "Look around you. Just about all the married people at Hollywood Station are two- and three-time losers."

"I don't know," he said, trying to keep it casual, when it was anything but. "It gets lonely living alone, and it gets tiresome dating people that I don't even wanna be with. Don't you feel like that sometimes?"

She didn't answer him and didn't seem to notice his moonstruck look as they drove east on the cemetery road, his normal sixty-two-beats-a-minute heart rate approaching three digits. They met a security guard at the entrance who directed them to the mortuary. The guard was a sixty-ish wisp of a guy who looked as though he didn't want to be entering open doors in mortuaries after dark or, for that matter, at any other time.

Aaron cut the headlights when they were well down the road from the mortuary, and the black-and-white glided in and stopped a short distance away. Aaron and Sheila got out, leaving the doors ajar, and walked quietly to the side entrance of the mortuary, not expecting to find anything but a door left open by a careless employee. What's to steal in a mortuary?

After they were inside, Sheila was the first to hear them: male voices. She held up a hand, and both cops froze, drew their pistols, and listened.

"Yours is an ugly pig!" one voice said.

"Fuck you," the other said, giggling. "Yours is a hundred years old!"

"No!" Sheila whispered, looking wide-eyed at Aaron, her shocked expression saying, It can't be!

He nodded with a grimace, his expression saying, Yes, it can.

Aaron led the way into the mortuary, quietly creeping down a carpeted hallway to a room lit by lamps, where loved ones had been embalmed that day and cosmetic work had begun. There were two female corpses and one male corpse in the room, each on its own table. On top of the elderly female corpses were two Hollywood tweakers, both naked, both tatted out, both sharing a jar of Vaseline and a glass pipe full of crystal meth. They were side by side, having pushed the tables together for buddy bonding, and had gotten into the mortician's makeup box. One corpse had grotesque kewpie lips, while the other had eye shadow so thick she looked masked.

The scrawnier of the two white men said, "You got too much eye paint on her. She looks like a fucking raccoon!"

"Don't get me started on your shitty work!" the other said. "The fucking Joker looks more natural than yours." Then he turned his face to the corpse he'd mounted and said, "Goddamn it, bitch, can't you move a little bit? I feel like I'm fucking my ex-wife!"

Both meth-crazed tweakers were laughing hysterically when Sheila Montez switched on the overhead light and said quietly, "Please give me an excuse to kill both of you."

By the time they got the tweakers dressed and handcuffed and the night-watch detective and the watch commander were notified, two night-watch units had arrived and impounded the tweakers' car, which they found parked on the north side of the memorial park. When 6-X-66 finally got to Hollywood Station, they put one prisoner in a holding tank, a little room with a bench and a big shatterproof window. They walked their other prisoner into the detective squad room, where Compassionate Charlie Gilford was watching *Showbiz Tonight* on his own little TV, which he kept in a desk drawer.

The detective switched off his TV, stretched, yawned, and stood up. His rumpled Men's Wearhouse suit coat hung on the chair behind him, and for a few seconds, Sheila Montez had to gawk at the detective's incredible necktie, decorated with what were apparently meant to be some sort of cubist embellishments. Compassionate Charlie, who liked to go bargain shopping for Tijuana imports on Alvarado Street, had bought it from a Mexican street vendor who kept pointing to the design, saying, "Diego Rivera!" Except that it looked like something Diego Rivera might have sketched on a tablecloth during a bout of d.t.'s.

"Okay, so what's the big deal about this?" Charlie said to Aaron, while Sheila took the tweaker into an interview room.

"Didn't the watch commander talk to you about it?" Aaron said.

"Is this the cemetery deal?" Charlie said, cranky from being pulled away for more paperwork.

"It sure is," Aaron said.

The detective walked into the interview room, looked at the tweaker who sat in the chair nodding off, sniffed the air, and walked back out.

"That dude reeks," Charlie said. "What am I smelling?"

"Formaldehyde," Sheila Montez said, lip curling.

Sergeant Lee Murillo entered the detective squad room then and said to Aaron and Sheila, "Well, there's no doubt about it. You two get the Almost-a-Hollywood-Moon award. One extra-large pizza with the works."

Charlie Gilford glanced quizzically at the sergeant and said, "For what?"

Sergeant Murillo said, "For handling the weirdest call of the night."

Then the detective looked at Aaron Sloane and said, "Were those two hemorrhoids boning male corpses or female corpses?"

"Female corpses," Aaron said.

"Well, shit!" Compassionate Charlie Gilford scoffed. "You call that weird?" Then he repeated the mantra heard every day around the police station in that unique part of the world: "This is fucking Hollywood!"

NINE

GET UP!" Eunice yelled, and Dewey smelled smoke and and bolted upright, thinking the place was on fire. But the smoke he smelled was from the cigarette dangling from Eunice's mouth.

When he looked up at her, he said, "Oh, shit."

"Don't gimme that oh-shit look," Eunice said. "It's eight o'clock. This is the second time I've had to come in here."

Dewey said, "You're killing me, Eunice! Killing me! I can't work fifteen hours a day. Nobody can."

She stared at him and said, "You don't have to work at all, Dewey. This is Hollywood, U.S.A. You're free to sit on your ass all day long and watch *Girls Gone Wild* videos if that's what you want. But not in my apartment. Not in my life. Make up your mind."

"Goddamnit, Eunice, I don't have any morning appointments," he said, cursing himself for the whine that drizzled out every time she looked as serious as a stroke, as serious as poverty.

"What're you talking about, no morning appointments? You got houses to rent. I told you there was a ten-o'clock showing on the fourth house. And then you got two more appointments on that same house this afternoon and two more appointments tonight on the fifth and sixth houses. You claimed your burglar partners were gonna come through."

He swung his feet onto the floor and kept his head ducked, ready for the explosion. "There won't be a third, fourth, fifth, or sixth house."

"Do you mean what I think you mean?"

"The last thing I did last night before I came home was check on them. You were right. The guys I hired only changed the lock on one and lied about doing the others. They gave me dummy keys for the rest."

"Well, no shit, Dewey!" Eunice said, lip twisted in her supersneer. "Just like I predicted, whenever you hire tweakers."

"You think I can hire unemployed mechanical engineers, Eunice? It's the fucking world we live in. You can't trust anybody."

"Outsmarted by tweakers," Eunice said. "Well, no shit!"

"They didn't outsmart me! I told you, they threatened me. They coulda killed me, not that you'd care. I had no choice, Eunice. Sometimes that's what happens out there."

She stood smoking and looking down at him with contempt and said, "Well, get out on the street and pick up the noon delivery in Los Feliz. Do something to earn your keep, Dewey. That's all I can say to you. Earn your keep like I do. Consider it a warning."

"Here I lie, numb and helpless!" he said, using lines he'd delivered in dinner theater. "While a croaking albatross smothers me in its wings, plucking out my eyes, devouring my guts!"

"You sound like *such* a sissy when you go all theatrical," Eunice jeered. "If Hugo was here, he'd say you oughtta consider testosterone shots."

His head was throbbing when she stalked out of the room. He sat on the side of the bed for several minutes, listening to her computer keys begin clickety-clacking. He thought about his desperate life and how there didn't seem to be a way to change it. If only he still got calls from his agent. He'd take any job he could get, anything that paid a stipend. He would read for parts, even audition for those snotty kids making Internet films. He'd do dinner theater gigs in the suburbs. If only he still *had* an agent. He opened the nightstand drawer and took out the cell phone he used for Tristan and Jerzy.

When he was shaved, dressed, and heading out the door, Eunice barely glanced at him, except to snort at his Jakob Kessler getup. He turned the dead bolts and had a flashback of Eunice's face when his eyes had popped open that morning, of that dangling cigarette and that horrible scowl. Today she'd had the deepest furrows in her brow he'd seen in months. He felt so desperate and miserable and angry that he was emboldened to strike back somehow.

Before slamming the door behind him, he said, "You know, Eunice, your everyday scowl lines are especially mean and evil today. Why don't you call your dermatologist?"

"Dude, who won?" the forklift driver said to Malcolm Rojas when they were uncrating a washing machine in the warehouse.

Malcolm reflexively touched his face. The flesh was tender under his left eye where the woman had nicked him with her fist after she'd struggled to her feet. She was strong, that fat bitch, and she'd fooled him with her begging and crying, but then she'd made a quick move and was on her feet and almost got away.

"Some dude at the mall," Malcolm said. "He told me he wanted change for cigarettes and when I said, 'Get a job,' he suckered me. Man, I really kicked his ass." Malcolm showed the knuckle abrasions to the forklift driver.

The forklift driver, a young Latino, said, "What was he, a *mallate?*"

"Yeah," Malcolm said.

"Those South L.A. niggers," the forklift driver said. "They take the subway to Hollywood for dope and pussy. You're lucky he didn't pull a blade or something."

"He won't even be pulling his cock," Malcolm said. "I beat him *real* bad."

The forklift driver grinned and gave Malcolm a thumbs-up before driving away.

Malcolm's knuckles were hurting more than the small contusion under his eye. It was hard to remember exactly what had happened after he'd crawled forward onto her chest. He'd felt those big tits beneath him, and he was taking out his cock when she'd gotten her hands under his thighs and actually lifted him high enough for her to crawl out from between his legs. Then she was behind him, scrambling to her feet.

He'd spun and tackled her, and she went down and started screaming. She kept screaming even after he punched her, how many times, he couldn't remember. He did recall picking up the box cutter after she'd knocked it out of his hand. He remembered exactly how he'd been going to swipe it across her throat just as he'd swiped it across a thousand boxes he'd unpacked. But as he was ready to do it, he'd heard a car door slam and he panicked. He'd leaped up, run to the door, and was sprinting down the street to his car before he realized that the slamming car door came from the driveway next to hers, and that whoever had done it was already inside their house.

Malcolm had found himself thinking about that encounter a dozen times since it happened. Sometimes he tried to remember every detail, sometimes the broad strokes. It made his palms sweat when he thought about it. He knew that this new rage within him was very dangerous, and he knew that he should try to get it under control. If he had money, real money, he could afford things to help him, like a hooker. Maybe a hooker would give him what he needed and he wouldn't feel so angry all the time. Malcolm took out his cell phone and dialed the number of the man he'd met at Pablo's Tacos.

Dewey Gleason as Jakob Kessler was on Hollywood Boulevard across from Grauman's Chinese Theatre, sitting at a table, sipping a mediocre cappuccino, and waiting for Tristan and Jerzy. It was amazing how many Street Characters bothered to come out in the morning hours, but there they were, even duplicates. There were two Chewbaccas, and Dewey wondered if either was the one who'd gotten his ass thrown in jail last year. The newspapers had fun with it, saying that Chewie had crossed over to the dark side.

He saw a Spider-Man and a Batman, this one looking even fatter than the one who'd recently gotten the crap beaten out of him by a panhandler half his size. That dustup made the news as well. He didn't see any of the Marilyn Monroes this early in the day, and there weren't a lot of tourists with cameras, certainly not the coachloads of Asians who really spent the bucks posing with, and tipping, the Street Characters. Dewey suddenly had a dreadful passing thought that without Eunice he could possibly find himself someday inside one of those horrid costumes, surviving on tips. The last stop of a failed actor. Dewey Gleason as a diminutive Darth Vader? Even on this hot summer day it made him shiver, and he shoved the image from his mind.

The chirping of one of the cell phones brought him back into the moment, and as soon as he figured out which one of his characters the call was for, he answered, "Bernie Graham speaking."

"Mr. Graham, it's Clark," the voice said.

Clark, he thought. Clark. Then it came to him. Yeah, the dimpled Latino kid from the taco stand. "How you doing, Clark?"

"Fine, Mr. Graham," Malcolm said. "I'm ready to go to work."

"Right," Dewey said. "You have a day job, as I recall."

"If I could make enough money with you, I'd quit the day job," Malcolm said.

"I like your style," Dewey said. "Okay, I've got your number and I'll call you later today. Maybe I can use you this evening or tomorrow evening."

"Thanks, Mr. Graham," Malcolm said. "I'll be waiting."

Dewey shut the cell and checked his watch. What Eunice could accomplish without ever leaving their apartment never failed to intimidate him. He reckoned that his grudging awe for her abilities helped to keep him in bondage, as well as his dread of the future without her support. He had an address written on a Post-it Note that she told him to give his runners when they showed up.

After leaving home that morning, Dewey had personally checked out that Post-it Note address in Los Feliz. He had a three-hour window of opportunity when there was absolutely nobody home in the beautiful two-story Mediterranean-style house. The home itself, built in the 1920s heyday of old Hollywood, would arouse no suspicion from the delivery men, since the expensive merchandise was being turned over to a well-dressed man standing on the porch. Dewey wished he didn't have to be the man to take that risk. He wished he had runners who could pull it off for him, but of course that could never be. At that moment he spotted his runners.

If Eunice could see Jerzy Szarpowicz, she'd crap icicles. There he was, galumphing along Hollywood Boulevard beside his lithe and handsome sidekick. Jerzy was wearing a baseball cap, his usual black T-shirt that barely covered his bulging belly, and baggy jeans that were falling off his fat ass. Nothing could be done with a guy like that except to use him as a mail thief and Dumpster-diver.

Creole had possibilities. Dewey even liked his dreads because they made him look more like a Hollywood guy, an aspiring young actor maybe. And Creole could talk, whereas Jerzy just grunted. Dewey regretted he'd ever used Jakob Kessler with these two. Bernie Graham or even Ambrose Willis would've been better, and certainly easier on Dewey, especially on these hot days when Jakob Kessler had to wear a suit, dress shirt, and necktie.

The lifts in his shoes were already hurting Dewey's ankles, but he stood up rather than letting the runners sit. He said in his German accent, "Good morning, gentlemen. Walk me to my car."

His car was in the large parking structure on Orange Drive, and as they passed among the arriving throngs of summer tourists, Dewey handed Creole the Post-it Note and said, "Did you rent a suitable delivery van?"

"Yes, Mr. Kessler," Tristan said.

"Did you have any trouble with the driver's license when you rented the van?"

"We coulda," Jerzy offered. "The pitcher on the license you gave him had me worried. I mean, it sorta looks like Creole, but with the glasses on in the pitcher and his dreads airbrushed out, it didn't look too much like him today."

Tristan shot Jerzy one of those you-dumb-fucking-Polack looks, and sure enough, their boss jumped all over it.

Tristan heard the man say, "What? You didn't wear the glasses when you rented the van? And why were the dreadlocks showing? Don't you understand that there are reasons to alter your appearance?"

"He forgot the glasses," Jerzy said as they arrived at the parking structure. "And his little pinhead looked funny in my hat, so he didn't wanna wear it. There he was with his dreads hangin' out." Only then did Jerzy notice his partner glaring at him.

"I want my people to obey orders," Tristan heard his boss say in that Nazi accent of his. "Without discipline you jeopardize our work. We could've just let you use your own driver's license and had you assume the risk that would entail."

"It was just one of them — those things, Mr. Kessler," Tristan said. "It won't happen again."

"Don't worry about it, boss," Jerzy said. "The guy at the car rental was a fuckin' moron."

Both listeners allowed Jerzy's remark about someone *else* being a moron to pass without comment. Then Dewey said, "The last phone call from my office said that according to the tracking number, the delivery truck will arrive between twelve thirty and one P.M. You will park a block away and wait. When the truck drops the merchandise, you will drive quickly to the address on the Post-it Note I gave you, park at the curb in front of the house, and load the merchandise as quickly as possible. Then you will follow me to the storage facility. Do you understand?"

"Yes, Mr. Kessler," Tristan said.

This was the part that Dewey Gleason hated, waiting for the arrival of a delivery. What if some very alert employee had somehow flagged the skimmed credit card that bought the plasma TV with a sixty-five-inch screen, as well as the big Sony home theater system? What if the check Eunice wrote for the two computers — a bogus check she promised Dewey would sail through the Los Feliz resident's account that she "had thoroughly researched" online — had also been deemed suspicious? What if some cops from the LAPD's Commercial Crimes Division were in the back of the delivery truck, ready to bust anybody taking delivery? Dewey's white dress shirt was damp and sticking to his back and chest when he arrived at the Los Feliz address. He could feel the sweat running down his rib cage.

Dewey rang the bell and knocked at the door just as a precaution. As expected, there was no answer. He strolled out to the street to see if he could spot the van belonging to Creole and Jerzy, but it was nowhere in sight, and that worried him. He looked at his watch and removed his key ring from his pocket. The hand holding the key ring was trembling and his palms were damp. There was nothing to do but wait, since the imbeciles who checked the tracking numbers at the delivery services were never reliable.

Dewey felt his heart banging and his bowels rumbling when he heard the grinding of gears as a white delivery van began crawling up the steep residential street. This kind of anxiety wasn't worth it anymore. By the time he paid expenses and sold the merchandise to his usual receiver, he figured he'd be lucky to net $1,500 from this whole gag. One thing was certain: If men with badges leaped from the van after Dewey took delivery, he was going to offer a deal the moment they Mirandized him. He was going to ask the detectives to phone the DA's office, and in exchange for a promise of a plea bargain, he was going to give up Eunice and every runner they'd ever used. He would do all this right after he crapped his pants at the sight of them.

The Latino driver parked the delivery van in front of the house and got out with a clipboard. He quickly came up the walkway, seeing Dewey standing at the front door with a set of keys in his hand. Another trucker, this one a younger black man, got out of the van on the passenger side.

"Are you Mr. Harold Phillips?" the Latino said, looking again at the name on the delivery form.

Losing his German accent, Dewey said, "You caught me just in time. I'd gotten tired of waiting for you and was leaving."

"Sorry," the driver said. "We got hit with a couple of extra stops we hadn't planned for."

"It's okay," Dewey said. "You're here now."

Dewey signed "Harold Phillips" to the trucker's invoice, and the driver said, "One more signature."

"Of course," Dewey said, signing the second invoice.

Then both men walked back to the truck and opened the rear doors. No men with badges jumped out. Dewey looked both ways on the street but still didn't see Creole and Jerzy. The delivery team was carrying a Sony forty-six-inch HDTV up the three steps, when Dewey said, "Just leave everything on the front porch." Then for their benefit, Dewey spoke into his cell phone to an imaginary installer, and said, "Roger? Are you and Slim on the way now?" A pause and then, "See you in fifteen. Everything's here."

"The front porch?" the Latino said. "Don't you want this stuff inside the house?"

"I've got my geeks coming. They're gonna set up the plasma in the den, a Sony in the living room, and the other in my bedroom. Just haul everything to the porch and they'll bring it in as needed. Easier for them, easier for you."

The Latino shrugged and both men returned to the truck. It took four trips up the long walkway before everything was on the porch, including another Sony and a Pioneer sixty-inch plasma HDTV. Then the Latino hesitated, as though something wasn't quite right here. He said, "Why don't you let us—"

Dewey distracted him with a $20 bill, saying, "Thanks, guys. Stop and get yourselves a sandwich on me."

Both deliverymen smiled and thanked Dewey, then hurried back to the truck and were gone. Within seconds Dewey saw his runners driving down from somewhere near the top of the hill. They parked and got out quickly.

"You had me worried," Dewey said. "I couldn't see your car."

"You're not supposed to see our car, boss," Tristan said. "That's the idea."

"Let's get to work," Dewey said. "Our window of opportunity is closing."

After having loaded the merchandise into the rented van, Tristan and Jerzy were following their employer's car to the storage facility in Reseda, when Tristan said, "When we got to that house, did you notice somethin' funny about Kessler?"

Jerzy, who'd been dozing in the passenger seat, said, "Naw, he looked like the same butt-tight Nazi he always looks like."

"He was way nervous, man," Tristan said.

"Why not?" Jerzy said. "The fucker jist raided somebody's credit-card account for several grand and had some sweet fuckin' electronics delivered to the sucker's crib. Didn't you feel your asshole wink every time a car drove up the street?"

Tristan said, "Yeah, but when he was nervous, he didn't sound so much like Schwarzenegger. In fact, he sounded like a regular old citizen of the U.S. of A."

"What's your point, dude?" Jerzy said.

"That made me check him out a little closer, and I don't think his hair looked the same. His forehead looked higher."

"So, maybe the old fuck wears a rug," Jerzy said.

"He didn't look so old today neither," Tristan said.

"So he got a good night's sleep."

"I think he wears a disguise when we're with him."

Jerzy said, "I don't give a fuck if he decides to dress up like Wonder Woman and hustle tourists on Hollywood Boulevard. Jist so he pays us for the jobs."

"It might be worth our while to find out who he is."

"For what?"

"You never know. How about we follow him home and see where it's at?"

"In this fuckin' van?"

"Just leave it to me," Tristan said.

A ten-foot-high chain-link fence enclosed the storage facility, with wire strung across the top of it. The runners watched their boss stop outside and punch in an access code to open the car gate. They followed him in and waited while he stopped and presented his ID to a woman in an office adjacent to the storage rooms. After he returned to his car, they followed him to the rear of the facility, where he waved them to a parking area.

While they were unloading the van, their boss unlocked a double-size storage room and began shoving aside other crates and boxes to make room for the new merchandise. It only took a few minutes to carry it inside, and while his two employees were surveying the other stacks of crates to see what they might contain, their employer began counting currency he'd removed from his wallet.

"Two hundred for each of you and one hundred for the van rental," he said.

"We got somethin' more for you, Mr. Kessler," Tristan said, glancing at his partner, who looked perplexed.

"And what might that be, Creole?"

"Some very good mail. We worked the hills yesterday and did some Dumpster-diving outside a law firm on Wilshire Boulevard."

"Since I didn't order that service, how much are you expecting me to pay?"

"Real cheap. A hundred takes all of it."

They waited while their boss pondered before he said, "All right, let's have a look at it."

"It's not here. It's in my car," Tristan said. "Can we meet you back at the office late this afternoon?"

Dewey hadn't planned on going there, and Eunice still hadn't worked the last batch of mail they'd received, but the price was right, so he said, "All right, meet me there at six o'clock."

"We'll see you there at six," Tristan said.

When they were driving out the gate of the storage facility, Jerzy said to Tristan, "Now, what's this all about? We ain't got no new mail for him."

"We will have," Tristan said. "We're gonna make a quick run through the Hollywood Hills and grab what we can."

"Fuck you!" Jerzy said. "What, for a lousy Franklin we're gonna risk our ass again?"

"Trust me, wood," Tristan said. "After we sell him the mail, we're gonna tail him right to his crib. And that's gonna pay off in robo-bucks. I may jist take me a trip back to New Orleans to meet my cousins. My momma and me left there when I was five years old and came to L.A."

Jerzy mulled it for a moment. He hated to admit it, but this little nigger was smarter than he thought. Finally he said, "Whadda people in New Orleans do in their spare time besides drown?"

There was one crime that Sergeant Murillo read at roll call that got everyone's attention. After he went over the information concerning yesterday's attack on a woman who lived in the southeast corner of Hollywood Division, he said, "Of course, this has to be the same box cutter suspect. The victim in this one gave a description that matched, but she didn't see the guy as an Arab. She thought he looked Hispanic, but she couldn't say for sure. The box cutter nails it."

Dana said, "Sergeant, is this victim middle-aged? And do you happen to know if she's a blonde?"

Hollywood Nate jerked a thumb in the direction of the surfer team sitting on his right and said, "These days, who isn't blond?"

Everyone had a chuckle except Flotsam and Jetsam. Then Sergeant Murillo said, "I don't know if she's blonde. You might check with the sex crimes detail at West Bureau. It might be meaningful or maybe not. He might go after a brunette next time. One thing for sure, though, with a guy like him there *will* be a next time. He clocked her bad but didn't rape her."

"He didn't cut her?" Dana said.

"He dropped the box cutter during the struggle," Sergeant Murillo said. "She was lucky. After he was through punching and kicking her, he picked up the weapon and fled. This attack was a lot more violent than his first try, and the victim's in the hospital. I'm guessing we'll see a gathering storm of violence with this guy. Both times he struck in the evening, the same time that you're nice and fresh and ready to rock. It'd be terrific if one of you midwatch units were to stop a likely guy on a shake and come up with a box knife. If you do, I'll buy you pizza for a week. Hell, make it two weeks."

"Maybe we've got a shot," Dana said. "Same approximate time of attack. He's gotta be a local guy."

Sergeant Murillo said, "If you get him, I will also write you a fabulous attaboy, Dana. Or in your case, an attagirl. And it'll be so effusive that Napoleon's letters to Josephine will sound like mash notes in comparison. Now let's hit the bricks."

"Napoleon Harris is a good middle linebacker, but I didn't know he's a letter writer, did you?" R.T. Dibney said to Mindy Ling. "And who the hell's Josephine anyways?"

As always, after everyone gathered their gear, they touched the picture frame of the Oracle for luck before they left the roll call room.

TEN

DEWEY GLEASON WANTED to hook up with the new kid, Clark, before day's end, but that would've meant a costume change. He couldn't do that now because he had to go back to the duplex/office in east Hollywood to meet Creole and Jerzy and buy the new batch of mail that Creole claimed was so excellent. Eunice estimated that only five percent of the mail they bought from runners had any value whatsoever, and less than two percent had identity information that could make significant money for them. Still, she demanded lots of it and bitched if he paid too much to get it. Dewey knew he couldn't win with her, no matter what.

If it were up to Dewey, he'd just drive around with a laptop and pick up computer signals. He'd talked to lots of identity thieves at the cyber café, tweakers and crackheads mostly, who were doing just that. Then they'd go online and log in on the target's Internet service provider to access his computer and retrieve information they needed. Since there were so many businesses these days offering free Internet access, they could later log in on one of those ISPs to surf the Web and buy merchandise with stolen card numbers. Most people didn't bother to change their security codes with their ISPs, so it seemed to Dewey that it only made sense to update the way they were operating.

But would Eunice permit this safer and more sensible approach to their business? Of course not. It was too slow and uncertain for her. And she repeatedly said he wasn't capable of handling anything technical and could barely use a computer well enough to send e-mail. She preferred that Dewey do things the old-fashioned way, the way Hugo had done it, so she could get her "retirement fund" faster, and never mind the risks he had to take to get it done.

Eunice had lately set a target of $1,000,000 tax-free, after which they would quit the game and go to San Francisco, even though she knew that Dewey hated the city. He recalled an incident back when they were still sleeping in the same room. He was singing in the shower and changed the lyric of an old standard. He'd crooned, "Hate San Francisco, it's cold and it's damp, that's why the lady is a tramp!"

Then he'd dried off, grinned at Eunice, who was lying in bed, smoking, and said to her, "That's the way Rodgers and Hart shoulda written the song. That's the way I sang it when I did little theater in Santa Barbara. That was a great gig. Santa Barbara's really a nice town."

Eunice had snuffed out her cigarette and said, "You wanna stay in this hot smog belt after we earn the retirement fund? It's fine with me. Because Momma left her heart in San Francisco and can very easily leave your ass in Hollywood. Let's hear you sing that one, Tony Bennett."

It was an erection killer and the beginning of what he was certain would be an attempt by her to squeeze him out of the big payoff when the target was reached. Moreover, Dewey no longer believed he could stay out of jail long enough to accomplish her goal. He felt like the bomber pilots in the old war movies who had to fly during daylight hours over Germany, knowing that survival odds were getting longer with each mission flown. He was now ready to settle for far less than a million bucks, especially if he could ever devise a scheme where it went to him.

In the locker room prior to roll call, Jetsam resisted all attempts from his partner to find out what had transpired at Malibu Beach the morning before with the waitress from IHOP. While Sergeant Murillo was reading the crimes to the watch, Flotsam was relentlessly chattering in his partner's ear to no effect.

"Come on, dude," Flotsam whispered. "Something musta happened out there on the foamy for you to go all lock-jawed. Dial me in!"

Sergeant Murillo looked up from the reports at Flotsam and said,

"Would you mind discussing surf reports later. We've got a roll call to get through here."

It wasn't until they'd been out on patrol for thirty minutes that Jetsam relented and said, "Okay, bro, you carried the load when I went home early two nights ago, so I guess I oughtta tell you what went down with the IHOP hottie yesterday."

"Go, dude!" Flotsam said. "I got my ears on."

"Okay, bro, but I gotta tell ya, I'm noodled. I been beat down and ragdolled and launched by kamikaze waves in my time, but it ain't nothing compared to how that salty sister cranked me. And taking last night off didn't revive me."

"Are we talking chocka coolaphonic nectar sex?" Flotsam asked excitedly.

"No, bro, she showed up with a Barney in a sausage sling!" Jetsam said.

"What?" Flotsam cried, almost rear-ending a car in front of him on Highland Avenue.

"She tells me he's her cousin, out here on summer break from college in Kansas or Missouri or some fucking place where there ain't no ocean. And she apologizes and says she had no choice but to bring him, and would I, like, teach him some basic surfing maneuvers."

It was almost too grotesque for Flotsam to contemplate. "A shoobie in a Speedo? And she expected a real Kahuna to be seen on the same beach with him?"

"Roger that," Jetsam said. "A DayGlo green Speedo."

"Dude," Flotsam said with genuine sympathy. "I feel ya."

"First thing I did was I took that Benny aside and I go, 'Bro, you try to go out there amongst a horde of surf rats wearing that DayGlo banana hammock, and they just might banzai you with their boards and send you home to Iowa or wherever you come from in wires and plaster casts.' I ask him if he didn't bring some board trunks to wear on the beach and he tells me everybody wears Speedos where he comes from. And I go, 'Peachy, bro, but this ain't the Piney Woods YMCA swimming pool, or summer fun at Lake Suck-a-hot-one. This is Malibu-fucking-California!'"

"I can't adjust the focus here," Flotsam said. "That slammin' server from IHOP told us she surfs twice a month. She oughtta know the mini-mum fucking dress code for admittance."

"Maybe you just shouldn't trust someone who wears rings on her index fingers," Jetsam said. "And this dorky cousin of hers, he don't understand basic English. He blanks about half the time I'm talking to him. So I take our breakfast bunny aside and I go, 'Okay, I'll put your cousin out on a board and slip him into a nice gentle chubbie that don't have much of a break, but if them surf Nazis out there start looking at him with a kill-the-hodad death ray, I'm towing him back to sandy safety."

"So did you?" Flotsam asked.

"Yeah, I put him on the old log I keep in my truck and I rolled him around in the foamy. He tried standing up a few times, and he's all splashing and squealing and I'm thinking to myself, Why me? I drive to Oxnard twice a month to visit my mother and to Pacoima to visit the old man. And I send checks to both my ex-wives, mostly on time, even though the kid I thought was mine turned out to have the DNA of my ex-wife's dentist, who drilled into a lot more than her root canals. And I still stop and play Frisbee with my former girlfriend's dog, even though I can't say hello to my former girlfriend without getting spit at. So I, like, try to live a decent life, bro. What I wanna know is, why does God treat me like a butt crumb?"

"Dude," Flotsam said, "sometimes it just seems like God takes a day off to go to the track or something."

"Anyways, when I think it can't get no bleaker, the squid manages to stand halfway up on a mini-bump and he starts screaming, 'Cowabunga! Cowabunga!' "

"I'm speechless, dude!" Flotsam said. "Were you soooooo tempted to throw a choke hold on him?"

"Bro, I was, like, half a heartbeat from C-clamping his scrawny neck and letting him drift on down to San Pedro. But I see this pair of water monkeys paddling their boards right at us and I'm all, like, 'Okay, crusher, you and me're about to get spiked by a pair of seriously ugly sado creeps, so let's push the off button.' "

"You are truly lucky to be alive, dude," Flotsam said. "Bobbing on the briny unarmed with some spazzed-out hodad yelling, 'Cowabunga.' Next time get a Navy SEALs killing knife and Velcro it to your ankle."

"There ain't gonna be no next time," Jetsam said, "After we cruised on back to the IHOP honey, we find her all stretched out on these humongous beach towels under a big umbrella. But now she's all stripped down from her shorts and jersey into a sort of, like, old-school bikini."

"What, no thong?" Flotsam said. "That ain't right, dude."

"The retro bikini ain't the half of it," Jetsam said. "So we, like, sit there, and the cousin's all fired because he thinks he's ready now to star in *The Endless Summer, Part Four,* and then I catch a break, or so I think. The cousin says he's gotta be bumping on home, and I almost stand up and cheer. Turns out they came in two cars, and after, like, another eternity of surf questions, he bounces. The last thing he yells at me is, 'Farewell, O great wave rider! Farewell!' And at last I'm alone with my bodacious babelini."

"Oh, man!" Flotsam said. "This is the good part!"

"Just wait," Jetsam said. "She like, knew she owed me big time for what she put me through with cousin Horace, or whatever the fuck his name is, and she could see I'm all stoked from looking at her voluptuaries. And my inner slut is now totally in charge. And pretty soon I'm all sprawled there on the towel under the umbrella kissing her shoulder like somebody on the Lifetime channel."

"Wooka, dude!" Flotsam said. "Now you're rockin'!"

"So by and by I'm sort of eager for, like, harmless foreplay, given that our GPS location is not totally secluded. And then I find out why no thong bikini."

"Why is that?"

"She just had butt implants, and the incisions ain't healed up enough."

Flabbergasted, Flotsam said, "You mean that booty ain't the babe's?"

"No, it belongs to Dr. Strangelove or whoever the fuck gave it to her," Jetsam said.

"Then what?" Flotsam said, fearing the worst.

"I'm all heading upstairs on those magnificent mammaries, and she goes, 'Cease and desist, surfer boy!'"

"Don't tell me the bimbo decided to play Our Lady of Malibu?"

"No, the problem was, her saline or silicone or whatever they used to construct her implants was all leaking. And she's suing the plastic surgeon and can't stand to have them touched, let alone fondled."

"I gotta feeling this is gonna get worse," Flotsam said, getting sympathy pangs and gingerly feeling his own breasts.

"Roger that," Jetsam said. "Because by now I'm scared to touch any more of her below her chin for fear of what I might find that ain't really hers. Or like, maybe some part of her will fall off in my hand! And now she's all laying there with her eyes shut, and I'm, like, confused, sort of. So I say to myself, Go for it. And I pounce like a panther, and she is the recipient of one of those mega-long, steamy-hot, summertime movie kisses that the women in the chick flicks all swoon over."

"I never could see that part of the game," Flotsam said with a shrug.

"Me neither," Jetsam said, "but I locked on because her lips are, like, Scarlett Johansson–huge. Think of two all-meat tire tubes pressed together. And bro, I kissed and I nibbled and I licked with the darting tongue of a cobra! And then I started some sinister sucking on her lower lip with mucho enthusiasmo. But when I got no applause, no response, no nothing, I go, 'Don't you like this?' And she goes, 'Like what?' And I go, 'That ain't no casual kiddie kiss you just got, wahini. That was cooleoleol kissing designed to propel a lucky chickie to an advanced state of beach blanket bliss.' "

"And what did she say to that, dude?" Flotsam asked. "Though I'm almost scared to hear the answer."

Jetsam shook his head slowly and said, "She tells me that her lips are so plumped with implants gone bad, she didn't feel a thing. And that when she gets through with her lawsuit, her plastic surgeon's gonna be dressing as Alvin the Chipmunk and posing for tourists in front of Grauman's Chinese Theatre." Jetsam sighed then and added, "Bro, I ain't got my mind in the game tonight. I am like, way, way woefully noodled."

They rode for a while in silence, and finally it was Flotsam who said somberly, "Dude, we all know that Mother Nature is a pitiless cunt."

"A heartless bitch, bro," Jetsam concurred.

Waxing philosophical, Flotsam added, "But when a person chooses a surgical body shop to rebuild their own chassis, it's, like, bound to wreak collateral damage on innocent bystanders like you. Only one thing we can say about Spare-parts Suzie and your tale of terrible despair."

Flotsam paused and looked toward Jetsam, who took the cue. And they uttered the station mantra in unison: "This…is…fucking…Hollywood!"

Dewey got to the duplex/office just after 6 P.M. He hadn't had any jobs for the Mexicans in the last few days, so the place was unoccupied. He unlocked the door and had to sit there and wait twenty minutes before Creole and Jerzy showed up with a disappointingly small bag of mail.

"That's all you have?" he said in his German accent when they entered, looking almost as tired as he was.

"Yeah, but it's good stuff, Mr. Kessler," Tristan said, even though he didn't know what the hell they'd grabbed from the curbside mailboxes that afternoon.

"It isn't even sorted," their boss said.

"We been busy lately," Tristan said. "All we had time to do was toss the junk mail. I took a quick look and I know you'll be happy with some of the stuff we got for you."

Since Jakob Kessler never used obscenities, Dewey didn't tell them what he was thinking when he withdrew $100 from his wallet and grudgingly handed it over. "And now I would like to go home," he said.

"So would we, Mr. Kessler," Tristan said as he quickly left the apartment, with his partner shuffling along behind him.

They were in Tristan's old Chevy Caprice half a block away and spotted their employer exit the apartment, set the dead bolt, and walk to his car as though his feet were killing him, as indeed they were with those three-inch lifts in his shoes.

There was still plenty of daylight left by the time they were three cars behind him on Sunset Boulevard, and Jerzy said to Tristan, "I don't know what the fuck this superspy shit is gonna do for us."

"I don't either," Tristan said. "But I got real good instincts, wood."

They almost lost his car when, after turning north on Cahuenga, their target turned quickly west on Franklin Avenue. Tristan caught the red light and slammed on his brakes too late. They were in the middle of the intersection, initially blocked from a left turn by swift moving southbound traffic. Tristan made it all stop for him by making a reckless left turn that got brakes screeching and horns honking.

"Fuck!" Tristan said. "We lost him."

After barely escaping a head-on, Tristan was driving westbound on Franklin, when he encountered a stalled car half a block ahead. A dozen other cars were trapped behind it in traffic, their employer's car among them.

"We got him!" Tristan said, getting into the queue of cars that were waiting for the stalled car to move. Three Latinos who looked like gardeners got out of the car and pushed it to the curb.

Tristan drove past the traffic snarl just in time to see Jakob Kessler's car pull into a wide driveway, and when the gate opened, it continued under the upscale apartment building into the parking garage.

And that was when he heard a horn tooting behind him and looked up to see a light bar flashing.

"Shit!" he said and pulled over.

A moment later he was looking into the face of Dana Vaughn, while Hollywood Nate walked up on the passenger side of the car.

"License and registration, please," Dana said to Tristan.

"Did I do something wrong, Officer?" Tristan asked, deciding whether to show his real license or the bogus license he'd used to rent the van.

"Nothing except blow a red light and make a left turn against oncoming traffic that almost caused a head-on collision as well as a couple rear-enders. You were very lucky."

Tristan decided not to fuck with this bitch, so he gave her his legitimate driver's license and reached into the glove box for his registration. That's when Hollywood Nate made his presence known by coming right up to Jerzy and peering over his shoulder into the glove compartment as Tristan removed the registration and handed it to Dana.

"It'll be a few minutes, Mr. Hawkins," Dana said. Returning to the car, she checked on Tristan for wants and warrants, ready to write the citation for the red light and the left turn.

Hollywood Nate was looking at the tatted-out, surly-looking fat guy in the passenger seat, trying to decide whether to bother getting these two out of the car for a little more intensive investigation.

Then he saw the driver with the dreads turn to him with a pained expression and say, "Officer, I'm real sorry about what I done back there. I'm sure your partner is checking to see if I got any traffic warrants, but I don't. I'm really a safe driver, but my father died yesterday and I was thinkin' about Daddy and . . . well, it's not an excuse, but that's what happened. I wonder if you could gimme a break and only write me for just one thing instead of two?"

Nate leaned down and looked at Tristan's Mr. Sincerity expression and said, "Tell you what, have your friend drive."

"Good idea," Tristan said, nudging Jerzy.

"Okay by me," Jerzy said.

Nate said, "I'll tell my partner about it." Then to Jerzy, "And as long as you're gonna do the driving, let's just make sure your license is up to date."

Jerzy shook his head in disgust as he pulled his wallet from the back pocket of his jeans and gave Hollywood Nate his legitimate driver's license.

"You wouldn't have any tickets out there that you haven't paid, would you?" Nate said, looking at the unpronounceable name and the photo on the license.

"I'm sure you're gonna check to see," Jerzy said in resignation.

After Nate had walked back to the black-and-white to have Dana run the passenger for wants and warrants along with the driver, Jerzy said to Tristan, "Well, a lotta fuckin' good that done you."

"You ain't got no traffic warrants out there, do you?" Tristan said.

Jerzy said, "I did have, but I cleared it up last month. Cost me over four hundred bucks. Otherwise my ass'd be in the Hollywood jail tonight thanks to you and this dumb fuckin' *Mission Impossible* shit you got me into."

When Dana and Hollywood Nate were back on either side of the car, Dana said, "My partner told me about your recent tragedy, so I only cited you for failing to stop for the red light. And you'd better get your right taillight fixed. Sign here."

After Tristan scrawled his name on the citation, Dana tore off his copy, handed it to him, and said, "Now you can switch seats."

Both cops took a good look at Tristan and Jerzy when they got out of the car, walked around the front of it, and traded places. Jerzy was inked, but not sleeved-out with jailhouse tatts. Their movements and gaits did not indicate recent booze or drug use, so Nate gave Dana a your-call gesture.

"Our sympathies to your family," Dana said to Tristan and then winked at Nate before walking back to their shop.

While Jerzy was driving away, Tristan said, "We got the crib scoped out, even if it did cost me a traffic ticket."

"Do the rest of your spy chase on your own time," Jerzy said. "And by the way, neither of those cops believed for one minute about old Daddy. They used that to get my license and check me out for warrants, thanks to your big mouth."

"A little more inconvenience for you got me only one violation to pay for instead of two," Tristan said. "It was worth it, wood."

"Where is your old man, by the way?" Jerzy asked. "Alive or dead?"

"I never met him," Tristan said.

"Does your momma know which one he was?" Jerzy asked.

"Don't woof on my momma," Tristan warned.

That evening, shortly after most of the midwatch teams were getting ready for code 7, an eighteen-year-old Marine from Camp Pendleton was having a conversation with a street prostitute on the Santa Monica Boulevard track. That was a street normally used for unusual sexual encounters. There were always older gay men cruising in cars, looking for younger men walking. And the women, or those who appeared to be women, were usually transsexuals, either pre-op or post-op, or drag queens—some of who were obviously men—and a few others who could pass.

Whenever potential tricks would ask gender questions before closing the deal, the trannies and dragons would almost always say, "I'm a woman trapped in a man's body" to reassure the tricks that it wasn't *really* the same as a gay experience. A few of the dragons looked quite plausible, and even quite attractive, as women.

The Marine, whose name was Timothy Ronald Thatcher, had managed to hook up with one of the latter. The dragon was a slender, green-eyed, caramel blonde whose street name was Melissa Price. But in a prior life in a suburb of Denver, he was Samuel Allen Danforth, nicknamed "Sad" because of his initials and because of his loneliness as a bullied gay boy. In his high school yearbook, he'd said he was "going to Hollywood for a new and happy life where he would never be Sad again."

It was later learned by police that Melissa Price was lively and chatty and well liked by the other hookers who worked the Santa Monica track. Melissa had a tiny two-room apartment in Thai Town, where all tricks were taken. Friendly competitors of Melissa Price later told homicide investigators that after striking an acceptable deal with a john, Melissa would say, "Okay, darling, your Price is right, and she's all yours." Melissa Price, aka Samuel Allen Danforth, had been selling sex for a little over two months before meeting Timothy Ronald Thatcher, who was seven months younger.

Timothy Thatcher had come to Hollywood early in the evening with two other Marines, who were old enough to drink in the nightclubs on Sunset and Hollywood Boulevards. Young Timothy had asked to borrow the ten-year-old Dodge sedan belonging to one of the older Marines, saying he was "going out onto the boulevard to get me a hot woman."

The owner of the Dodge later told police that "as a joke on him" they suggested that Timothy Thatcher try cruising Santa Monica Boulevard, thinking he would notice that the hookers on the street had shaving bumps. One of the two older Marines later told police that he believed that Timothy Thatcher was probably a virgin and was trying to prove something to his senior companions.

Under subsequent intense questioning by military investigators, both older Marines stuck to their story and swore that they didn't know there was an M9 USMC-issue, semiautomatic pistol in the car. They claimed that PFC Timothy Thatcher must have put it there as protection for his first trip to Los Angeles. LAPD investigators believed that one of the older Marines, who had easy access to the sidearm, probably brought the pistol along, but their suspicions could never be proven.

The last witness to have seen Melissa Price, aka Samuel Allen Danforth, alive was a tranny with an eggplant-colored shag who'd been working the same block when Melissa got into the Dodge sedan. In fact, Melissa Price waved at the tranny with an OK sign that Melissa always gave after catching a trick who was cute or rich. In this case the trick certainly was not rich.

It was later debated whether Timothy Thatcher was overcome by remorse after his tryst with Melissa Danforth, or whether he truly did not know until it was too late that Melissa Price was not a female, but in the end it didn't matter much. Just before 8 P.M., the landlady of the small apartment building in Thai Town heard terrible screams and glass breaking and heavy objects striking walls in the little two-room apartment. And then a gunshot, followed by another, terrified every tenant in the building, and several calls were made to the police.

Timothy Thatcher did something extraordinary. He dialed his mother in Billings, Montana, on his cell, and when she answered, he said to her through tears, "Mom, I shot somebody! I didn't mean to do it, but when I found out this person was not a girl, I lost it!"

The Marine talked to his shocked and terrified mother for one minute and fifty seconds, telling her that he was "somewhere in Hollywood," and ended with, "Tell Dad and Billy and Mary Lou that I love them all." After that, he ran down the stairs and out to the street.

Six-X-Sixty-six was on the way to code 7 at Sheila and Aaron's favorite Vietnamese restaurant for tofu bun vegetarian salad and 360 Degree Beef. They were only a few blocks from Thai Town when the code 3 "shots fired" call was given to a unit from Watch 3.

"Let's jump this one," Sheila said, and she switched on the light bar long enough to get around boulevard traffic, then stomped on the accelerator. They arrived at the scene before the designated unit, just in time to be almost T-boned by the Dodge sedan driven by the escaping Marine.

"Hang on!" Sheila said to Aaron. "Gotta burn a U-ee!"

The black-and-white Crown Vic made a smoking, tire-scorching U-turn, and the pursuit was on.

An electronic tone sounded, followed by the announcement from a female RTO to all units that always set hearts racing: "Six-X-ray-Sixty-six is in pursuit!"

Timothy Thatcher, who did not know the area, drove in utter panic west on Hollywood Boulevard and then south on Western Avenue where he lightly sideswiped a Ford Explorer in the intersection, breaking his own right headlight, then headed west again on Sunset Boulevard where he encountered lanes clogged by nighttime Hollywood traffic. He made a squealing turn south on Van Ness that nearly lifted two wheels, skidded sideways, righted the car, and sped to Melrose Avenue where he turned west once again, brakes screaming. Unit 6-X-66 was sometimes as close as five car lengths behind, and Aaron broadcast the street names they were passing as well as the license number of the vehicle driven by a "white male." And as in all LAPD pursuits in the most car-strangled city in North America, there were moments when it was maddeningly slow.

Then they heard someone on the tactical frequency say, "Airship up!"

The Marine blew past Paramount Studios and made a tire-ripping right turn onto Gower Street, where he saw two black-and-whites coming at him from the north. The lead car belonged to the surfer cops, who'd switched on the light bar upon seeing him. That made a northbound Lincoln Navigator in front of Timothy Thatcher slam on the brakes, causing the Marine to crash into the SUV, giving the lone male driver of the Navigator a slight whiplash and all but demolishing the Dodge.

The Marine limped out of the car and ran north on the sidewalk away from Sheila Montez and Aaron Sloane but right at Flotsam and Jetsam and the Watch 3 team, who'd double-parked beside them.

Timothy Thatcher speed-dialed his mother once again, and when the panic-stricken woman answered, he said, "I love you, Mom. I love you!"

The mother of Timothy Thatcher later said that she got hysterical when she heard police officers shouting, "Get down! Down on the street!" And then the cell phone clicked off.

Johnny Lanier and his partner, Harris Triplett, had leaped from their car faster than the surfer cops, and the chunky black cop had a Remington shotgun at port arms as he raced forward. When he got behind Flotsam and Jetsam's car, Johnny Lanier aimed the shotgun over the roof, while a spotlight from one of the later responders lit the Marine.

Flotsam yelled to Jetsam, "Johnny's benching up with a tube! Get the fuck outta the kill zone!"

Then Jetsam shouted again to Timothy Thatcher, "Get down on your belly, goddamnit! Get down!"

And only then did all cops present see the M9 pistol that had been tucked inside the Marine's belt in the small of his back. PFC Timothy Ronald Thatcher swiftly drew that pistol and pointed it in the general direction of Johnny Lanier and his shotgun, only ten feet from the Marine. It was over in an instant: a roar, a flame, a fireball in the darkness, and a massive round of double-aught buckshot crashed into the Marine's throat and lower face, blasting chunks of bone and flesh all over the sidewalk beside the Hollywood Cemetery.

The senior sergeant Miriam Hermann was the first supervisor to arrive. By then, several other units were on the scene, trying to get traffic moving on the street. Johnny Lanier had returned the shotgun to their shop and was standing quietly with the surfer cops when the sergeant got there.

She had a few words with Sheila Montez and Aaron Sloane and walked over to Johnny Lanier's young partner to say, "Triplett, you and Lanier go to the station and I'll be there as soon as I can. You've got a long night of report writing ahead of you and lotsa face time with FID. The DA's rollout guys will be there as well."

"There was nothing we coulda done, Sergeant!" the rookie said, his voice quivering. "He didn't give us a choice!"

"I know, son," Miriam said, patting the young man on the shoulder. "Just get yourselves to the station now."

The magazine from the pistol was found on the floor of the Dodge, along with a live round that the Marine had ejected from the chamber. Timothy Thatcher apparently had wanted to make sure that no one else would die with him and Melissa Price that night.

It took thirty minutes for the mother of Timothy Thatcher to get through to the watch commander's office at Hollywood Station.

Sergeant Lee Murillo later said he would never forget that phone call, not as long as he lived.

The woman, becalmed by grief and from fearing the very worst, simply said to him, "Sergeant, I am the mother of Timothy Thatcher, who phoned me to say he'd shot someone tonight. I know that your officers caught up with him."

Sergeant Murillo was speechless for a moment, then stammered, "Ma'am, I, uh, I really don't have any details about the . . . the event. May I please have your number? Someone will call you as soon as we know something. Right now I just don't . . . I don't have—"

Her voice was controlled and implacable when she interrupted him to say, "Please, Sergeant, I must know one thing, and I won't trouble you further. Did your officers kill my son?"

After notifying the on-call homicide team to get on this suicide-by-cop ASAP, Detective Charlie Gilford grabbed his coat and car keys. If one thing could get the night-watch D2 out of the squad room, it was anything macabre or gory. Charlie Gilford sped directly to the scene of the officer-involved shooting to take a quick cell-phone photo of what was left of PFC Timothy Thatcher, whose face he described as looking like "a beef enchilada with way too much cheese and salsa."

Then he proceeded to the little apartment in Thai Town, where uniformed officers were protecting the scene until the detectives, criminalists, and body snatchers arrived. He stepped inside to take a peek at Melissa Price, aka Samuel Allen Danforth, lying on the floor, shot once in the chest and once in the face. The latter round caused grotesque damage to the left orbit but nothing like the trauma inflicted on Timothy Thatcher by the Remington shotgun at close range. The detective snapped another camera-phone photo and returned to the office, satisfied that he'd seen everything worth looking at.

By the time the first homicide detectives had arrived back at Hollywood Station from both scenes, they found that Compassionate Charlie Gilford had downloaded the grisly photos of both young men and had printed out and taped the images to the homicide team's computer. Below he had typed, "Sometimes it just don't turn out like that pup tent romp on Brokeback Mountain."

★ ELEVEN ★

WHILE AT HIS JOB the next morning, Malcolm Rojas decided to call the man he knew as Bernie Graham and ask him once and for all about that job. The man had been unreliable so far and had not called him last evening as promised. Malcolm had not slept well, his thoughts returning again and again to that woman who'd nearly gotten him caught. Every time he thought of the experience, anger welled. They were all alike and he hated them. But when he looked at his swollen left hand and the abrasions on his knuckles, the anger was mixed with stabs of fear and even shame. When she'd started screaming, he'd been terrified and hadn't known what to do. He should've slashed her throat with the box cutter to shut her up, and now he wished that he had.

Then he forced himself to think of Naomi, that tender, young girl with the shy smile who really liked him. Would she grow up to be one of *them?* Somehow he didn't think so. She had natural blonde hair, not like theirs, and she was sweet and kind, not like them. Her number was in his cell phone, and several times he'd been tempted to call her and see if she wanted to hang out. He thought he just might do that, but first he needed money. What he cleared from his job as warehouse helper was pitiful, now that he had to give his mother a third of his take-home pay. As soon as he made some real money, he'd call Naomi and take her to the beach in his Mustang. The car needed tires, but soon he'd have the money to buy tires, and lots else.

He dialed Bernie Graham, got his voice mail, and said, "Mr. Graham, this is Clark, the guy you met at Pablo's Tacos. I wanna talk to you about the job. Please call me."

After leaving his cell number, he resumed slashing open the tape on one side of the boxes, removing the merchandise, and slashing the tape on the other side to flatten the boxes for recycling. When he worked up a sweat, the intensity of his feelings became manageable.

Dewey got to sleep in late that morning, only because Eunice had an appointment with her gynecologist for a regular checkup. She'd tried to get him out of bed at seven thirty even though he had no morning meetings with runners, and of course that started the bickering.

Before she left the apartment at 8 A.M. Eunice had popped her head into his bedroom once again and said, "Dewey, if I call here in thirty minutes and you don't answer, I'll know you went back to sleep."

"Can't I sleep in for once, Eunice?" Dewey whined. "For once in my fucking life?"

"No!" she yelled. "You gotta go to the bank and write a check on the deposit I made from that rental gag. One measly rental check is all we get from that account because you couldn't manage to hook up with a housebreaker who was dumber than you. That means, Dewey, now you gotta open another account at another bank, unless you wanna risk using the same one and hope the renters haven't yet figured things out and called their bank. So get your ass outta bed!"

"Gimme a break, Eunice!" he'd moaned with his pillow over his head. That voice! She sounded like an old parrot with bronchitis. "One fucking break, one time. That's all I ask."

"I don't get a break," she snapped. "I gotta work from the crack of dawn till midnight sometimes. Why're you so special?"

"Speaking of cracks," Dewey said wearily, "are you having your annual pap smear?"

"Yeah, why?"

"Tell your doctor to say hello to your gizmo for me," Dewey said. "She sees it more often than I do."

"Asshole!" Eunice said, slamming the door behind her.

But at least she hadn't called to check on him. The 9:15 A.M. call on the Bernie Graham cell phone was what woke him. He picked it up but did not recognize the number before saying, "Bernie Graham speaking."

He heard a youthful voice say, "Mr. Graham, this is Clark, from Pablo's?"

"Clark?" he said, pausing until his head cleared. "Oh, yeah. Clark."

"I left a message for you. You said you'd call, and I thought maybe you lost my number."

"Sorry, Clark," Dewey said. "I'm very busy. Look, why don't I meet you today after you get off work? How about you come to the donut shop next to the cyber café on Santa Monica Boulevard at quarter after five? Know where it is?"

"I'll be there, Mr. Graham," Malcolm said.

After Dewey made his date with the kid, he lay there staring at the ceiling. He was losing his nerve and he knew it. So far he'd been very lucky. He'd felt confident that the trouble he went through, juggling his identities to keep his runners in the dark, was worth it, despite Eunice's constant belittling.

The incessant opening and closing of bank accounts with bogus IDs, and depositing bogus checks as well as legitimate checks from gags they'd pulled—all of that was bad enough. But having to be present for merchandise deliveries that Eunice ordered online or on the phone was nerve-racking. Yesterday, for example. Look how exposed and vulnerable he'd been on that porch in Los Feliz, but she didn't care. She was confident, cocky, even, because she was never out on the streets dealing with vermin, any one of whom might be cutting a secret deal with the cops to nail their employer: Jakob Kessler or Ambrose Willis or Bernie Graham.

He felt sure that none of the runners could direct the cops to a Dewey Gleason if they became police snitches. Even his car had been bought and registered under a bogus name at a bogus address, so if a runner gave the cops his license number, it wouldn't help them. No, it was those times when he had to be there to do the pickups and collecting that were making him old before his time. What if the college kid at the Pacific Dining Car had been popped at an Indian casino by security officers and had flipped? What if cops had been concealed out there in the parking lot, watching them when the kid had given back to him the bogus cards and other ID, along with his share from the casinos?

He'd been totally exposed that night for a very small payoff, but trying to explain that to Eunice was like talking to her ugly little bull terrier that keeled over dead last year, probably from a lifetime of breathing secondhand smoke. Dewey figured that's how he'd check out one of these days, gasping for breath and expiring in agony. One thing for sure, though, if he was ever diagnosed with a lung disease, he was going to lace her Whoppers and fries with potassium cyanide. There was no way that bitch was going to live after she'd killed him with exposure to those fucking death sticks.

When Dewey Gleason as Bernie Graham left his apartment that morning, he had another unpleasant task to perform. He had to meet his receiver at the storage lockers to complete the transaction he'd made telephonically for the merchandise that he'd put in storage the day before. What Dewey hated most about this aspect of his business was that he was especially terrified of the people involved in fencing the goods. The man who called himself Hatch was no exception.

Dewey had first encountered him at the cyber café, where he'd met most of his business associates. Hatch was clearly an ex-convict, the jailhouse body art attesting to that. He was a tall white man, bald, gimlet-eyed, and ripped, probably from pumping iron in a prison yard. He always wore a tight T-shirt, greasy jeans, and metal-studded boots. From watching prison documentaries, Dewey figured him for the Aryan Brotherhood. His facial art consisted of a spider on his forehead and tattooed drops that ran from the corners of his mouth down to his jaw line, like blood dripping from fangs. Under his lower lip was a thick soul patch. Dewey imagined that "Hatch" was short for "Hatchet" and that he'd probably earned the sobriquet.

The fact that Hatch appeared alone at their meetings was somehow more frightening than if he'd had an equally scary partner. Hatch would always show up on time in a black van. After Dewey got him admitted into the storage facility and the deal was consummated, Dewey would help carry the merchandise to Hatch's van. Being alone with him filled Dewey with dread and foreboding. As soon as his van was loaded, it would be easy for Hatch to cut Dewey's throat and clean out whatever merchandise he could carry alone. Dewey wondered how long his body would lie there in the padlocked room before the stench alerted other tenants.

When he drove over the hill to the San Fernando Valley and the storage facility in Reseda, Dewey found the black van parked on the street in front. Hatch sat behind the wheel, wearing mirror sunglasses and smoking a cigarette. Just the sight of him got Dewey's bowels rumbling. Dewey punched his driver's license number into the gate code and the gate opened. He waved at the woman in the office and pointed back to the black van with an OK sign. She nodded, and after going through the ritual of showing an ID to this woman whom he'd never seen before, Dewey, followed by Hatch's van, motored to the rear of the yard.

After parking, Dewey unlocked the storage room padlock and said, "Morning, Hatch."

"Bernie," Hatch said, nodding at him and flipping his cigarette butt onto the pavement in front of the double storeroom.

Dewey made a mental note to pick up that butt after Hatch was gone. They kept a clean storage facility here and Dewey didn't want any complaints about his guests. For an instant Dewey thought, Yes, I'll pick it up after he's gone. If I'm still alive. Then he told himself to get a grip. He'd dealt with Hatch and others like him for the past several years and he was still breathing. That brought it home to him yet again: Dewey Gleason was losing his nerve. He had to get out of this business.

"Do you have everything I ordered?" Hatch asked.

"Everything," Dewey said. "And I've got a few video cams I can sell you. Got them last month. Top of the line."

"Sure," Hatch said, grinning. "As long as you let me take them on consignment."

Dewey hadn't thought of Hatch as a tweaker, but the bastard had gaps in his grille. Crack maybe. Or maybe he got them knocked out in a prison rumble. The consignment remark was obviously meant as a joke, since nobody in their world did anything but cash business.

Dewey forced an obligatory guffaw and said, "Maybe next time. Just let me know in advance what you might need."

After Hatch took a perfunctory look at the merchandise and checked the invoice sheets, he said, "Let's load."

When they got the plasma TV and the home entertainment center into Hatch's van, he gave Dewey the agreed-upon price of $3,100 and said, "I can use as much of this quality as you can deliver."

"At the rock-bottom prices I charge, I'm sure you could," Dewey said, trying to smile, much relieved when Hatch got into the van and drove away.

After he picked up Hatch's cigarette butt, holding it by the ash end in case Hatch had a communicable disease, Dewey padlocked the storage room, got into his car, and drove away. He never saw the old Chevy Caprice parked on the street, a Chevy that had followed him from his apartment to the storage facility and was still shadowing him all the way back to Hollywood.

When Dewey pulled the Honda into the underground parking garage at his apartment on Franklin Avenue, Tristan Hawkins parked as fast as he could, got out of his Chevy, and sprinted to the security gate in front of the building. Tristan tried to stay concealed as much as possible behind a hibiscus plant beside the gate, and he watched his quarry emerge from the parking garage onto a common patio. He saw his man stop at a soft drinks machine, where he bought a can of soda, and climb the exterior stairway to the third floor, where he entered what looked to be the last apartment on the east side of the apartment building. For the first time, Tristan was seeing his boss in a different disguise, but he'd have known him anywhere.

Tristan went to the gate phone, chose an apartment number on the digital directory, beginning with number one, indicating the first floor, and began punching in the code next to the apartment numbers, most of which were no doubt occupied by tenants who were at work. It took three tries before he reached someone who was at home at that time of day.

Her voice was an elderly croak when she said, "Hello?" and Tristan knew she'd be no problem.

In Los Angeles, apartment dwellers came and went and seldom knew who was living next door, so he knew he could pull a name out of the air. "Hellooo, UPS," he said. "I've been trying to reach Mr. Brandon in apartment number one-twenty."

"This isn't number one-twenty," the old woman said.

"I know, ma'am," Tristan said, concentrating on keeping all traces of street from his diction. "I delivered a parcel there a few minutes ago just as he was leavin' for his job, and I stopped at the drinks machine for a Coke. And darn it, I left my keys on the table beside the machine. I'm locked outta my truck."

"Why're you bothering me with this?" the old woman said, and for a moment he thought it wasn't going to work.

"I tried six other numbers but there's nobody home. Look, would you mind walkin' to the machine and gettin' my keys and bringin' them to the gate?"

"Well...," she hesitated.

"Or better yet, ma'am, if you would please buzz me in, I'll get the keys myself. Please. I'm gonna get in trouble with my boss!"

"Well, all right," she said. "But you should be more careful next time."

"Thank you!" he said, hearing the electronic tone and the click of the lock.

Tristan hurried through the unlocked gate, scaled the outside staircase, taking the steps two at a time, and walked briskly to the last apartment on the east end of the third floor. It was number 313. He descended the stairs even faster, went back to the directory, scrolled the digital directory, and rang number 313.

"Hello," a familiar voice answered.

Tristan recognized Jakob Kessler minus the German accent, hung up the phone without a word, returned to his car, and called his boss on his cell phone.

The phone rang several times before Dewey could get out of the bathroom, his trousers at half-mast, and check the taped-on label on his GoPhone to see which of his characters the call was for.

"Jakob Kessler," he said, after getting the cells sorted.

"Mr. Kessler, it's Creole," Tristan said. "Do you have any jobs for Jerzy and me?"

"Not for the rest of the week, Creole," Dewey said. "I shall call you on Monday."

"Mr. Kessler," Tristan said. "I have somethin' to talk to you about. Can we meet somewheres this afternoon?"

"What is it about, Creole?"

"Nothin' I can talk about on the phone," Tristan said. "You're gonna be real glad to hear about it."

Dewey thought about his meeting with Clark, but there was no way to fit Creole in before that meeting, because Clark was expecting Bernie Graham, not Jakob Kessler, and a costume change was too much.

"I cannot do it today."

"Okay, Mr. Kessler," Tristan said. "How 'bout tomorrow?"

"I shall call you, Creole."

After closing his cell, Tristan mulled it over and thought, We're meeting *today,* Mr. Kessler, or whoever the fuck you are.

He got on his cell and speed-dialed Jerzy. He knew, by the way Jerzy answered, the dumb Polack had been woken up by the call, probably after smoking crystal or crack last night.

"Get some clothes on, wood," Jerzy said. "We got us some important work today."

"Where you at?" Jerzy said through a yawn.

"On Franklin at Kessler's crib. Meet me here in an hour. And stay on your cell. I may have to move to another location."

"What is this bullshit?" Jerzy muttered.

"Do it, wood," Tristan said. "It's about a *real* payday."

Eunice had been gone for most of the day, first to her gynecologist, afterward for lunch at her favorite restaurant on Melrose. Every once in a while she needed a day off, but when she arrived home, she was all business and intended to work well into the evening to make up the time. She didn't expect to find Dewey there.

"What the hell're you doing here?" she said with a sniffle, suffering from summer allergies exacerbated by constant smoking.

He pointed to the $3,100 on the table between two of the computers and said, "I collected for the TVs."

"And?" she said, taking a tissue from her purse and blowing her nose with a honk.

"And what?"

"And what else have you done today?"

"Aw, fuck!" he said. "I risked my life to collect from a thug you couldn't imagine in an acid nightmare, and I bring every penny of it home, and you ask me what else have I done."

"Why didn't you get online to the Assessor's Office? I told you there were loan documents I need, and I showed you how to do it. I wrote out everything so a child could understand."

"Yes, Eunice, I'm a computer re-tard. I know that. How could I ever forget it?" His jaw muscles flexed after he spoke.

"Why didn't you do a few lockboxes in the hills? I gave you cards with mag strips that'd work."

"I'm not a fucking burglar, Eunice," he said.

"I'm not asking you to ransack the houses and steal their TVs," she said. "But you could get valuable information if you'd look around in desk drawers. You got your real-estate business cards if somebody comes home. You only have to leave the door wide open, hand them a card, and say you're a West L.A. Realtor sizing up the property for a hot client. You're always bragging about what a great actor you are. But now you can't play a Realtor with conviction? Why can't you manage that, Dewey? Are you that gutless?"

He didn't answer for a long, painful moment. When she wanted to savage him, she'd always do it by reminding him that he was a failed actor, one of thousands out there on the streets of Hollywood. These days she seemed to be deliberately trying to drive him out of her life. She seemed to be looking for an excuse, but he wasn't going to give it to her. Not yet.

When he did answer, he said quietly, "I'm not entering a house where people live, and that's the end of it. It's too risky."

"Hugo would never hesitate to—"

Then he found himself in free fall. "I'm not Hugo, goddamnit!" he cried. "Hugo's in the joint, doing fifteen years because he did every fucking gag you dreamed up, and you finally got him caught!"

"Hugo had balls!" she said, sneezing twice, her allergies inflamed by a burst of emotion.

"I did too until I met you!" he said. "Just run what's left of my nuts through your crosscut shredder, why don't you? Just turn them into confetti, Eunice! They're no good to me anymore!"

"A drama queen," Eunice said. "After a real man like Hugo Beasley, I ended up marrying a drama queen. What the hell was I thinking?"

"There's such a thing as divorce, Eunice!" he blurted, but he wanted to grab those words back and swallow them, especially when she replied, "There certainly is, Dewey, and I've been thinking about it a lot these days."

When she went to change into her working clothes, she slammed the door to her bedroom, and Dewey felt the familiar rumbling in the bowels. It was even more intense than when he'd been alone in that storage room with Hatch. What if she did kick him out? Where would he go? How would he live? On the other hand, she needed him more than he needed her. He was the street performer, the artist who made all her computer machinations result in the profits that drove her, the treasure she lived for.

And that made him think about those bank accounts that she'd opened way back when she'd been married to Hugo. Every dime she'd salted with Hugo and later with Dewey had gone into them. Maybe he was being conservative, estimating them to have reached $500,000. Maybe she was close to her $1,000,000 goal! Maybe there was a way for computer-illiterate Dewey Gleason to learn the numbers and passwords to access the accounts. It calmed his bowels when he thought about it. But if he ever got the chance, he knew he wouldn't take only half. He deserved a lot more than that for putting up with that scowling shrew for nine long years.

When he was getting ready to go out again, Eunice was at a computer, looking as slovenly as ever.

"I'm going to work now," he said as pleasantly as he could. "I've got a new kid to meet. His name's Clark. Latino, with a great smile. I got a strong feeling he'll be a good runner for us."

She didn't answer, and he started feeling the fear again. She wouldn't really lock him out and call a lawyer. Would she?

He said, "Would you like a couple of Whoppers when I come back tonight?"

Without removing the cigarette from her lips she said, "Yeah, with fries."

Dewey Gleason smiled then. If there was a way to the witch's stony heart, it was by sticking a Whopper under her dripping nose.

"That's his Honda, but that don't look like him behind the wheel," Jerzy Szarpowicz said to Tristan Hawkins as Dewey Gleason's car pulled from the underground parking garage onto Franklin Avenue.

"That's because he's somebody else," Tristan said, giving the Honda time to get a few car lengths ahead. "He ain't Jakob Kessler today."

They followed the Honda when it turned south on Highland Avenue, and then it made several turns designed to get through some of the afternoon Hollywood traffic. Tristan almost lost the Honda twice before reaching Ivar Avenue and headed south until they were on Santa Monica Boulevard.

"This James Bond shit is wearin' me down, man," Jerzy grumbled. "How we're gonna make money from this is—"

"He's going to the cyber café," Tristan said.

"So what?" Jerzy said as Tristan drove toward the strip mall. "I still think that ain't him in that car."

Tristan got stopped at the next light, but there was no need for concern. He could see the Honda catch a parking place by the donut shop after a car pulled out. Tristan turned south and parked half a block from the strip mall.

"Let's go for a walk, wood," Tristan said.

The strip mall was busy. Lots of customers were at the 7-Eleven, and the donut shop was doing a brisk business. But the summer foot traffic coming and going from the cyber café was amazing even at this hour. Later, the tweakers and baseheads would be out in numbers, working the rented computers and meeting one another for surreptitious exchanges of money, drugs, stolen merchandise, and identity information.

There was a coffee-colored drag queen in an extravagant pink wig, a rhinestone-studded jersey, and second-skin shorts sashaying along the sidewalk beside the cyber café, hoping to catch a trick on his way home from work.

As they walked past the dragon, Jerzy leered and said, "Howdy, sweetness."

The dragon took one look at Jerzy, tossed her do, and said, "Fuck off."

When they were standing outside the donut shop, concealed behind an SUV, Tristan said, "Take a good look through the window. Is it him or not?"

Dewey was standing in line behind an agitated tweaker, and Jerzy said, "That dude's jonesin' bad. He needs a sugar fix."

"Forget the tweaker," Tristan said. "Is it Kessler or not?"

"That guy limps," Jerzy said. "And he's shorter than Kessler and younger. And his glasses have thick black frames."

"Is it him?"

"Yeah, it's him," Jerzy said grudgingly.

"I told you," Tristan said.

"That don't prove nothin'," Jerzy said. "The guy's a thief and also an actor, so what? Half the people in this fuckin' lot are probably actors or wannabes. And they're all thieves."

"We're gonna hang around a little while and see what role he's playin' tonight," Tristan said.

After Dewey got his coffee, he walked to a small table to wait for the arrival of Clark. Tristan and Jerzy strolled across the parking lot, where Jerzy had a cigarette and checked out the parade of hungry hustlers while Tristan kept an eye on the donut shop. Every time a customer went inside, Tristan would return to the same place behind the SUV to see if the customer was meeting with the man he knew as Jakob Kessler. Twenty minutes passed before Tristan saw a young Latino wearing some kind of employee work shirt and jeans enter the donut shop and head straight to the small table in the back. Tristan took a closer peek and saw the newcomer talking to their man.

"I'm so glad you called, Clark," Dewey Gleason said, shaking hands with Malcolm Rojas, who sat down at the table. "Would you like a cup of coffee? A donut maybe? They're pretty good."

"No, thanks, Mr. Graham," Malcolm said.

"I'd like to talk to you about the business we do, Clark," Dewey said.

"We have lots of venues to explore in order to find out how you might work best for us."

"I'm a hard worker," Malcolm said.

"I'm sure you are, but it's a matter of where you'd fit in. Let's go for a ride in my car and chat awhile about a few simple jobs."

Tristan and Jerzy scurried to the Chevy Caprice when they saw their man and the young guy leave the donut shop and head for the Honda. Tristan was in an all-out sprint to get to the car in time, and Jerzy cursed and puffed all the way, trying to keep up.

There was a moment when Tristan feared that they'd lost their target in the stream of cars on Santa Monica Boulevard, but they managed to catch up, and twenty minutes later they pulled into the shopping center's lot and parked three rows away.

When Dewey and Malcolm emerged from the Honda, Tristan said to Jerzy, "He's forgettin' to limp."

And then it was almost as though their man could hear them, because Dewey suddenly got into his Bernie Graham limp on his right leg, all the way to the store entrance.

Jerzy said to Tristan, "You wearin' a wire, or what? He musta heard you."

"He's takin' that kid to school, that's what he's up to, wood."

"What, like credit-card shit?"

"Yeah, what else? Let's take a look."

"Listen to me, Creole," Jerzy said. "I'm hungry and I'm tired and I'd really like to smoke a little glass right now, but I'll go along because I already come this far. But then you're gonna tell me what the fuck you got in your head."

It was a huge supermarket, one of many in the chain where Malcolm's mother always shopped. They walked to the long queues of shoppers pushing carts toward the dozen checkout counters, and Dewey said, "Clark, are you good with text messaging, like most young people these days?"

"Whadda you mean, Mr. Graham?" Malcolm asked.

"When you were in high school, were you able to sit at your desk and look at your teacher with your cell in your hand and text a girlfriend in another class without getting caught? That kind of thing?"

Malcolm Rojas hesitated to answer that one, the truth being that there was no girlfriend in that Boyle Heights barrio school, where he'd never belonged. Nor any boys whom he could call his friends either. Nobody ever had the back of the half-Honduran loner whom the other kids called Hondoo when they spat on his shoes.

Malcolm simply said, "I can handle a cell phone, if that's what you mean."

"Watch, Clark," Dewey said, gesturing toward a woman who'd reached the checkout and was loading her groceries onto the merchandise belt as the cashier rang them up. "She's the one I'd want to work on."

The woman was fortyish, well dressed, the only one in line wearing pearls, along with a tailored blazer, matching skirt, and sensible heels.

"Watch her purse," Dewey said.

"I'm not into snatching purses," Malcolm said.

"Nobody wants you to. Watch and learn," Dewey said.

While her purchases were being rung up, the woman opened her purse and removed her checkbook, placing it on the counter. She opened it as though to write a check, then, changing her mind, removed her wallet, took a credit card out, and ran it through the card reader. Then she put the card down beside the wallet and checkbook, not looking at them while she chatted with the bag boy and the cashier.

"I don't know what I'm supposed to learn here," Malcolm said, his frustration growing, wondering if he'd made a mistake trying to hook up with this man.

"See the guy standing behind her?" Dewey said. "Imagine if you were standing there shoulder surfing."

"What?"

"That's what it's called. The Colombians are really good at it. They can look at a checkbook and memorize an account number in a few seconds."

"I could never do anything like that, Mr. Graham," Malcolm said. "I don't have that kind of brain. I have to be honest with you."

"You wouldn't have to," Dewey said. "There's a better way. You could just stand there with your camera phone and pretend you're text messaging. But you'd really be taking pictures of the credit-card number, the checkbook, even the driver's license sometimes. A good shoulder surfer could've gotten all three photos from that woman, later pushed the send button, and downloaded the JPEG photos on his computer. Everything you could want is lying there in plain view. You don't have to snatch anything from anyone in this business, Clark. People will give their money to you. Why? Because you're smarter than they are."

"Is that what you want me to do, Mr. Graham? Shoulder surfing?"

"I'm just showing you one of the many possibilities that're open to you," Dewey said. "You'll start out doing more simple jobs."

Dewey and Malcolm returned to the car and headed for Mel's Drive-In on the Sunset Strip, where Malcolm Rojas was treated to a meal and thirty minutes of schooling that Dewey conducted like a game.

When Malcolm was halfway finished, Dewey tested him by suddenly saying, "What're the first numbers of an American Express card, Clark?"

With his mouth full, Malcolm said, "Three-seven."

"Visa?"

"Four."

MasterCard?"

Malcolm swallowed his food and said, "Five."

"Diners?"

"Six-oh-one."

"That's my boy!" Dewey said, toasting Malcolm with his soda. "You are a *very* fast learner. You should see some of the employees I've had to teach. My secretary, Ethel, would be impressed by you."

Sometime later, Dewey Gleason was to remember that impromptu comment to Malcolm Rojas, and it would then seem incredibly prescient.

TWELVE

SITTING OUTSIDE in the Chevy Caprice and watching the parking lot of Mel's Drive-In were Tristan Hawkins and Jerzy Szarpowicz, who was extremely pissed off at his partner.

"I'm outta here, Creole," Jerzy said. "You can follow Kessler and his little pal home and peep at them while they put on leather underwear with the easy-access zipper in front. But me, I'm outta here."

"This ain't what's goin' on here, wood," Tristan said. "This ain't no sissy pickup. Kessler's workin' this kid like he worked me."

"Okay, so what's that got to do with us gettin' rich behind it?"

"It's gonna take a little time to explain."

"Gimme the *Reader's Digest* version. I ain't got all night."

"Okay, so let's look at this Kessler, or whatever his name is. A big crime boss? Shit, he never made me, not one time, and I been followin' him all over town. He's nothin' but another little cyber café identity thief with a gimmick. Except he's in business with somebody smarter than him, somebody who's makin' those bogus driver's licenses and credit cards and writin' phony paper for the purchases we hauled to the storage yard. Where there was lotsa other goods squirreled away, you might remember. Kessler's jist a recruiter of runners like us, and a money collector. We gotta find out who his boss is and then we make our move."

"What move?"

"We're gonna become the junior partners."

"Take me home, man. Now."

"No, wait, dawg! We know where Kessler keeps the TVs and other shit he steals. We saw how he does that part of his game, and we know the address of the guy who's gonna get the bill for all that stuff we delivered. We know Kessler dresses up in disguises. We lean on him and let him know what we know, he'll faint tits-up like the bitch he is and either let us in or else buy us out. Think about it."

"We can't blackmail him. We been on jobs with him!"

"I'm jist sayin', we could tell him we'll rat him out to the cops about that house in Los Feliz, and where we took the stuff to his storage locker and all the other shit. He can't take a chance that we're runnin' a game on him, because he don't know nothin' about us, and we know lots about him. Especially we know where he lives."

"Maybe his boss ain't a bitch like him," Jerzy said. "What if he's partnered up with some bad motherfucker that don't want no junior partners?"

"That's why we need a little bit of patience. Maybe we do another job or two with him and we find out more, like who does he work for and where is that partner. Shit, it might be that whoever runs him works the business right outta his crib on Franklin. Then we got him. He won't be able to bounce on out in the middle of the night. We gotta know a little more about how it all works."

Tristan stopped talking then and looked at Jerzy. He figured the Polack must be burning up every little brain cell he had. The silence went on for nearly a minute and then Jerzy said, "Okay, let's get him to give us a job tomorrow. I ain't gonna play along forever, man. And one other thing you gotta know about me right now."

"What's that?"

"I ain't into violence unless..." He gave an ambiguous shrug.

"Unless what?"

"There's *real* money to be had."

Tristan held out his palm, and Jerzy slapped it without enthusiasm, saying, "Man, this could be a big fuckin' mistake."

Late in the evening, Officer Harris Triplett, the young patrol officer who'd recently completed his probation, was on temporary loan to the vice unit as a UC operator. He was posing as a trick and not having a good time so far. Harris wore his sandy hair so short and looked so youthful that the vice sergeant thought the young cop could easily pass for a sailor or Marine on liberty. The plan was to borrow a few cops to use as operators to get as many hookers as possible off the streets ASAP, because one of the local TV stations had been regularly featuring a spokesperson for the Restore Hollywood project who claimed that the LAPD was ignoring vice problems on the boulevards.

It was an informal three-day operation to quiet the critics, so Harris Triplett was not wearing a wire under his Aloha shirt, as a female UC operator would if she were posing as a hooker on the boulevard. Under the front seat of the Mercury Sable that he was driving were a rover and his service weapon.

The first drag queen he encountered on the Santa Monica track, aka the "fruit loop," was a mixed-race addict. The dragon, wearing a short gold dress and platforms, looked at him through the window and said, "So whatchoo lookin' for, dope or pussy?"

"What've you got?" Harris Triplett said, figuring if a good drug bust came his way, he shouldn't say no. He started sniffling and acting twitchy, his version of an addict, but he was far too hale and hearty to pull it off.

"You look like you could use some black," the dragon said with a knowing smile.

"Yeah," he said, figuring that "black" was tar heroin.

"Well, I ain't got no black," the dragon said. "Maybe I can get some liquid, though. I know somebody with a vial. That's sixty doses. You got that kind of sugar?"

"Yeah, I'll take it," Harris Triplett said, figuring that "liquid" was LSD or PCP.

The dragon let out a raspy chuckle and said, "You switched up on me to the other dope way too fast, baby. That means you're a cop. But you're a cute little puppy. Come back when you're a big dog."

The dragon laughed again and walked away.

The next streetwalker he encountered was a tall white transsexual, well known to the vice unit who'd arrested her in the past. And now that she was post-op, she could not be booked into a male facility. The tranny stopped on the sidewalk, holding back her shoulder-length natural-red hair and bent forward to look inside the car.

"This is a pool car," she said, "and you're a cop."

"What?" Harris Triplett said. "Me, a cop? I'm a Marine from Twenty-nine Palms."

"Kiss me if you're not a cop," the tranny said.

Harris Triplett hesitated and said, "I don't even kiss my wife."

"You only got one key in the ignition, sweetie," the tranny said before turning to walk away. "You should always use a key ring with at least a house key on it. I wish you weren't a cop. You're cute as a button."

Harris Triplett was starting to think that he was cute enough to clean up the streets of Hollywood single-handed if he just knew his ass from lamb chops. He put the vice unit's Mercury key on his own key ring and hoped he could manage to pop at least one hooker before his three-night loan to the vice unit ended.

He got on the rover to ask for permission from his cover team to try the Sunset Boulevard track, and permission was granted. And that did the trick. The first streetwalker he spotted on Sunset Boulevard was neither a dragon nor a tranny. She had real double-X chromosomes, and she appeared to be very young. And as it turned out, she was only fifteen years old. She was full-figured, bulging out of her little black dress, and wore her white-blonde hair in a bob, with blood-red gloss on her plump lips that made her look like a child playing dress-up.

She was only slightly more experienced than Harris Triplett at this game, and she smiled brightly when she saw his dewy grin, smooth, chiseled features, and short chestnut hair.

"Hi!" she said.

"Hi," Harris Triplett said. "What's up tonight?"

"Whatcha looking for?"

"Whatcha got?" he said.

"Do you have, like, a hundred bucks to spend?" she said.

"On what?" he said.

"I don't wanna, like, make you mad or anything," she said, "but I been told that I shouldn't negotiate until we get where we're going."

"So where we going?"

"My apartment. It's just up the street. I'll walk and you can follow me."

"How do I know you aren't taking me someplace where I'll get mugged?"

"There's a whole lot going on up in my apartment house, but it ain't got nothing to do with mugging," she said.

Harris Triplett didn't have enough for his violation yet, since she hadn't defined *negotiate* by offering sex for money, so he said, "Okay, start walking. I'll be right behind you."

When the girl had walked half a block north on the dark and quiet residential street, Harris picked up the rover and talked to his cover team, making the vice cops in charge of his security wish he'd been wired.

After some intense conversation between two teams of vice cops, the senior officer came on the radio and said, "Okay, Harris, we think we know where she's taking you. Go ahead and walk to the door with her, but try to get the violation outside. And take your gun. If she spots it and you lose the arrest, that's fine, it's only a misdemeanor. The second you get your violation, scratch your head. We'll be on the street, watching you through glasses."

Whispering into the radio, Harris Triplett said, "What if she won't talk unless I go inside?"

There was more uncertain conversation among the vice cops, and then the voice came back on and said, "Step inside if you have to, but for no more than one minute. If you don't get the offer that quick, open the door and walk away. If something goes wrong in there, yell loud, or throw something through the window if you have to. Sixty seconds after you close that door, you better come out, or we're coming in like the cavalry. Understand?"

Harris Triplett parked the Mercury and watched the young hooker ascending the outside stairway of the two-story apartment building already known to cops at Hollywood Station as "Middle Earth" because, as the vice cops put it, "we can't always figure out the species that inhabits the place."

The cover team parked their UC car half a block south, just as 6-X-76 happened to be passing on patrol. When Hollywood Nate Weiss and Dana Vaughn spotted two guys moving fast along the sidewalk, Dana hit them with the spotlight, and one of the guys held up his LAPD badge and waved them to the curb.

"Vice," Hollywood Nate said and pulled to the curb beside them.

The younger of the two vice cops, a Latino in a cut-off sweatshirt, khakis, and tennis shoes, said, "Stick around till we see what we've got here, okay?"

Dana informed Communications that 6-X-76 was code 6, meaning out for investigation, and they followed the vice cops to the apartment building where Harris Triplett had passed through an unsecured walkway.

Because his security team was so hesitant about his entering the apartment, Harris Triplett was more than a little nervous as he climbed the stairs, his Glock tucked under his shirt inside his waistband. The young hooker had opened the door and stood on the outside landing in the wash of light from inside, smiling encouragement to her young trick who was ascending apprehensively.

"Everybody's nervous about coming in," she said. "Don't worry, there's nobody here but you and me and one itsy-bitsy spider that lives under the kitchen sink."

When he got to the open door and peered inside a neat and tidy little one-bedroom apartment, he said, "What am I going to get for my hundred dollars?"

She smiled bigger and said, "Let's go inside. I been taught not to talk till we're relaxed and friendly."

Harris stepped gingerly inside, ready to go for his gun at the slightest provocation, and he started counting in his head to sixty.

"You're so nervous, it makes you more cute," she said. "Anybody ever tell you that?"

"You have no idea," he said, counting: fourteen, fifteen, sixteen . . .

"I just feel like kissing you, and I never kiss my dates," she said.

"I'm not really into kissing," he said. Twenty-eight, twenty-nine . . .

"What if I kissed your cock?" she said. "Would you be into that?"

"Well, that's a different story," he said. Forty-one, forty-two, forty-three...

She put her hand on his groin and said, "I think I'll fuck you till you beg me to stop. But first let's see the hundred dollars, darling."

"Fifty-two, fifty-three...," he said aloud now, alarming the girl, especially when he jerked open the door and started scratching his scalp with both hands like he had a head full of lice.

And suddenly they both heard a loud and terrible scream from the apartment next door, and the cover team, who also heard it, along with 6-X-76, came running fast, taking the stairs two at a time.

The hooker yelled, "What's going on?" and Harris Triplett was half in and half out of the doorway, pointing frantically to the next apartment, where they heard a cry for help.

The older vice cop, a burly white guy with a shaved head and a clamp-on hoop earring, banged on that door and yelled, "Police! Open up!"

They could hear several frantic voices inside, but no one came to the door. The older vice cop drew his pistol, stepped back, and kicked it open.

The four cops rushed inside, and the older vice cop yelled to three terrified men, "Everybody freeze!"

The older vice cop and Hollywood Nate ran along a hallway to the sound of moaning. The master bedroom was well lit and occupied by one naked man with lank gray hair and a gray mustache over a blue upper lip. He lay prone on the king-size bed and moaned, gasping for breath. Alongside the man, half hidden in the sheets, was a bloody object that looked to Nate like a totem of some sort.

"Call an RA," the vice cop said, and Nate drew the rover from his belt and requested a rescue ambulance.

Nate hurried back down the hallway to the large living room just in time to see Dana Vaughn come out of a bathroom with a bath towel while the Latino vice cop guarded three men, two of them already handcuffed together. The third man, a naked senior citizen with sad, baggy eyes, his body frail and fish-belly white, stood next to the fake fireplace with his hands in the air, sporting a tent-pole erection that would not subside given the number of potency pills he'd ingested with his martinis. His crimson countenance attested to the pills more than to his current embarrassment.

Dana said, "Cover that object, sir."

When she threw the towel at him, it landed right on his erection, and Nate said, "Damn, partner, it must take a lot of practice to do that."

Dana figured everybody at Hollywood Station would hear about the towel toss, given Nate's big mouth.

After advising the guests of their Miranda rights, the Latino vice cop said, "Write some FI's on these guys till we find out what's what. I gotta go check on our little operator."

He went next door, where Harris Triplett had placed the young hooker under arrest and handcuffed her while she cried her eyes out and tried in vain to convince him that she was not a juvenile and not a runaway.

Finally the girl said, "Okay, okay, you'll find out anyways. My name's Muriel Travers and I ran away from Canton, Ohio, two months ago."

"And how old're you?" the Latino vice cop asked.

"Sixteen," she said, dabbing at her tears with a tissue. "In four weeks."

While the vice cop went back next door to inform his partner that they had a juvie to deal with, Harris Triplett became filled with compassion for the weeping teenager, and he said gently, "I'm sorry, Muriel. I know how you must feel, but when you get home to your family, this Hollywood experience will seem like a bad dream. Do you want me to call your folks for you? Is there anything I can do to help you?"

"Yeah," she said, "you could take out your gun and blow your fucking head off, you narc cocksucker."

Meanwhile, in the next apartment, Hollywood Nate had himself a look at the decor. There were large framed photos of nude men wrestling and playing volleyball, and the resident was into Barbie dolls and Disney collections, which was not uncommon in Hollywood. On the fake fireplace hearth, a Mickey Mouse stuffed toy was riding a glass penis.

The two middle-aged men sitting quietly on the sofa in the large living room, handcuffed together, kept looking anxiously at the hallway leading to the master bedroom. One was a balding fat guy with Jack

Sparrow facial hair, wearing an orange wife beater, board shorts, and flip-flops, and anxiously crushing a blond wig in his hands, apparently part of his beach boy getup for this 1960s party. The other guest was a bit younger than the others, with a fringe of mousy hair, and teeth coated in porcelain veneer as white as a toilet bowl. He was dressed like a cheerleader in a letterman sweater, chinos, and saddle shoes. Both men were blitzed but sobering up from fright.

The cheerleader said, "Officers, we're not doing anything illegal here. We're having a harmless nostalgia party. We don't even use drugs, except for the strawberry martinis. Maybe we had too many." Then he pointed to the naked old guy with the erection and said, "Roger was down in the pool having a moonlight swim just before you arrived, and hadn't dressed yet."

"Must be awful hard water down there," Nate observed.

Dana said, "There's a guy in the bedroom who might dispute how harmless your nostalgia party is."

When they could hear the whoop and whine of the ambulance siren, the older vice cop left the man in the bedroom to enter the living room and whispered to Dana, "I think the guy's in big trouble. His ass is torn up, and he's got a couple vials of heart medication on the nightstand next to him. I think he's had a heart attack."

"Check out the beach boy," Dana whispered. "There's blood spatter on his shorts."

"Uncuff him and bring him in the master bedroom," the vice cop said. "I need to talk to him privately."

In the next few minutes, the paramedics arrived with their gurney and carried the stricken man out of the apartment, where they encountered a detective in a wrinkled suit and a horrible necktie. It was Compassionate Charlie Gilford, waiting at the foot of the stairs until the gurney got past. Only his instinct for the bizarre would get him out of the squad room when there were summer reruns of his favorite reality shows, but when he heard the watch commander talking about this one, he figured it might be worth a peek.

The detective entered and checked out the living room and then walked to the master bedroom with the older vice cop.

"This is what spoiled the party," the vice cop said, gloved-up and holding a twelve-inch bloodstained Barbie doll, with her one arm extended and the other broken off.

"Her ponytail's a mess," said Compassionate Charlie. "Let's hear it."

Back in the living room, where Hollywood Nate and Dana Vaughn watched the partygoers, Dana said sotto to Nate, "If there was a Hollywood moon tonight, we'd win the pizza."

When Compassionate Charlie returned from the bedroom, he beckoned Nate and Dana into the hallway away from the others, where he quietly explained things.

"Seems like the over-age beach boy shoved a Barbie doll up the host's ass to liven up the party and get a few giggles from the others," Charlie explained. "With the host's permission, he says. Except when the rubber band that held Barbie's little arms in place busted loose, they popped straight out, and her fingers are sharp. So, suddenly the guy on the bed doesn't love Barbie no more and doesn't find the joke very funny and he starts screaming. But the beach boy, who says he drank seven martinis, claims he got confused and thought it was a pleasure scream, not a pain scream, until the guy started clutching his chest and gulping like he's underwater and grabbing for his heart medication." After a pause, he added, "I imagine his love canal's gonna need to be resurfaced big time."

"Are we booking anybody here?" Nate asked, looking queasy.

"The guy was turning blue when I saw him last," Charlie continued. "And with his heart condition and all, he might just croak. So, even though this won't go anywhere, I'm gonna call this a mandated sexual assault case for now, and I'm gonna advise booking the Brian Wilson look-alike until somebody can interview the host tomorrow. If he lives."

"How about the others?" Dana asked.

"Let them walk, but we'll need a good crime report and transportation for the beach boy."

"What's the booking charge?" Nate asked.

Compassionate Charlie grinned and said, "How about assault with a deadly Barbie?"

Nate and Dana went back to the living room, thinking that things couldn't get much stranger, until the diminutive man called Roger let out a yelp, lost his wraparound towel, and scared the crap out of every-body. A purple oscillating object flew across the floor and stopped when it struck Nate's shoe, causing him to leap away like it was radioactive.

"Sorry," Roger said, picking up his towel. "I'm sorry to alarm you, but I held it in as long as I could."

"What the hell is that?" Nate demanded.

"It's a vibrating egg. I didn't want you to know it was there. I'm so embarrassed."

The detective ran into the living room and said, "Who yelled?"

Hollywood Nate, looking a bit pale, pointed to Roger, who was hold-ing the towel in front of him, and Nate said, "That dude shot me in the foot with an egg he had tucked up his ass!"

The detective shrugged and said, "So, chill. This is Hollywood, for chrissake."

"What?" Nate said. "You think it's an everyday thing when a guy lays an egg on your goddamn shoe?"

Backing her partner, Dana said, "Yeah, Charlie, wouldn't you find it a teeny bit weird if someone fired a rectal egg at *you?*"

Compassionate Charlie stroked his chin as though mulling over something momentous. And before exiting, he sucked his teeth and said, "I think it all depends on the size of the egg he laid. Are we talking pigeon or ostrich?"

When Malcolm Rojas left Mel's Drive-In that evening, he was excited about the money he was going to make. He considered quitting his job in the warehouse even before working a single day for Bernie Graham, but then he thought he'd better wait and see. It was still too early to go to bed, so instead of driving home, he parked on a side street near Holly-wood High School and impulsively dialed the number of Naomi Teller.

Her cell phone rang several times, and when he was about to give up, she said in a small voice, "Hello."

"Can you guess who this is?" Malcolm said.

"No," she said, stifling a giggle because she knew who it was.

"Do you have so many boyfriends you can't guess?" he said.

"Maybe," she said, even though she'd never had a real boyfriend.

"Take a guess," he said.

She said, "Josh."

"No, it's not Josh," Malcolm said, and he sounded so disappointed, she laughed and said, "I'm just kidding. I know it's you, Clark."

Malcolm was happy again and said, "I'd sure like to take you for a ride in my Mustang sometime."

"You have a Mustang?"

"It's an old one," Malcolm said, "but it runs good. "We could go to the beach."

"I'd like that," she said, "but my mom'd go all spaz if I went to the beach with a guy as old as you."

"How old do you think I am?"

"Twenty-one maybe," she said. "You sound older than you look."

"I'm nineteen," he said. "Is that better?"

"My mom'd still think you're too old for me. You're an adult and I'm a juvenile."

"What if we met at the mall and went to the movies?" he said. "Would that work?"

"Sure," she said. "As long as my mom doesn't know."

"I'm gonna call you on Friday and set something up, okay? We'll maybe see a movie and grab a pizza and get better acquainted. Can you do it?"

He could hear the excitement in her voice when she said, "For sure. Call me at about six o'clock on Wednesday, okay?"

"Okay, Naomi," he said. "I can't wait."

"Me too, Clark," she said.

Malcolm felt good when he closed the cell and dropped it on the passenger seat. It made a clicking sound when it bumped against the box cutter. Looking at it made him think that it was too early to go home. His mother would be sitting there watching one of her stupid TV shows if she was sober, and she'd insist on making him a sandwich even after he told her he'd eaten already. She wouldn't believe him. She never believed him. If she was drunk, she'd forget and call him Ruben, and she might even try to stroke his hair again.

He was starting to get angry just thinking about it. He felt like masturbating to relax, but instead, he found himself driving around the residential streets. Then he drove to the shopping center and cruised the lanes farthest from the store. The last row of cars was in a rather dark area, and in that part of the lot, the pole light was not working. He saw some customers walking toward their cars. One was a shapely young Asian with a stylish black bob, pushing a shopping cart. He glanced at her and drove past. Another was an attractive Latina who looked to be thirty-something. He drove past her as well.

Then he saw a middle-aged silvery blonde carrying two bags of groceries. He thought about his new boss, Bernie Graham, who had put so many ideas into his head that evening. He thought about Bernie's advice to always have a story ready when you approach someone to pull a gag, as Bernie called it. He felt it again: arousal mingled with fear. He put the box cutter in his pocket and got out. He approached behind the woman, who had the hatch open on her Volvo station wagon.

She looked alarmed when he said, "Ma'am, I think you dropped this."

He was holding a $10 bill in his hand. His broad, dimpled smile belied the rage and the exhilaration sweeping over him.

"I didn't drop that," she said.

"You must have," he said. "It was right there by your car."

"No," she said. "It's not mine."

"Finders, keepers, I guess," Malcolm said. "Can I help you with your groceries?"

"No, thank you," the woman said. "My husband is right behind me. In fact, here he comes."

Malcolm saw a man walking through the next row of cars and said, "Oh, okay. Have a nice evening." But when he was walking away, the man who she said was her husband got in a car and started the engine.

Malcolm spun around, but the woman was in her station wagon with the engine racing and the headlights on. The Volvo backed out of the parking space and sped away while Malcolm stood and screamed after her, "You bitch! You lying bitch!"

Then he looked around to see if anyone had heard him. He looked for the security officer who patrolled in a golf cart. He was trembling and felt weak and light-headed. The rage lit his face on fire. He knew he had to go straight home to his bedroom and masturbate right away and try to sleep. If his mother tried to stroke his head, he feared he might kill her.

At 11:15 P.M., Flotsam and Jetsam in 6-X-32 got a message that said, "Go to the station." Ten minutes later, they entered the sergeants' room, where Sergeant Lee Murillo sat at his desk. In a chair beside him sat Bootsie Brown, who'd tried to cash a dead man's check while the deceased sat in his wheelchair outside.

"That's the one, Sergeant!" the old black man said, still in the layered secondhand clothes he'd been wearing when last they'd seen him. He pointed at Flotsam and said, "The tall one with the funny-lookin' hair." Then he saw Jetsam and said, "They both got sissy-lookin' hair, don't they? Looks like they bleach it out, jist like the workin' ladies on the boulevard."

Flotsam was stunned, but before he could speak, Sergeant Murillo said, "Excuse me, Mr. Brown, let me take a few minutes with the officer to hear his side of this. While you're waiting, would you like a cup of coffee?"

"I certainly would, Sergeant," Bootsie Brown said. "And how 'bout a donut or somethin'? That food in jail ain't fit for a cock-a-roach."

Sergeant Murillo gave Flotsam a meaningful don't-ask-questions look and said to Jetsam, "Officer, would you please get Mr. Brown a coffee and a snack from the machine?"

"What?" Jetsam said, flabbergasted.

"Just do it," Sergeant Murillo said. "I'll explain later."

While Jetsam grumbled and bought Bootsie Brown his refreshments, Sergeant Murillo took Flotsam out in the hall and said, "He wants to make a one-twenty-eight on you. Says you called him a name when you arrested him."

"What's that grave robber doing here, Sarge?" Flotsam said. "Him and another homeless guy tried to cash a dead man's check."

"Yeah, I know all about that," Sergeant Murillo said. "I've read the reports and I'm doing my best to talk him out of the personnel complaint. We've got enough paperwork to do around here."

"But what's he doing outta jail?"

"The DA refused to issue a complaint. Two old bums trying to get drunk and give their dead buddy an Irish wake? Nobody wanted to take that one before a jury."

"Well, I never insulted the old bastard, not even once," Flotsam said. "And now we gotta buy him coffee and a Twinkie? This is bullshit, Sarge!"

"I'll reimburse you for the snack. Let's just get through this, shall we? He says you called him 'frogative,' whatever that is."

"What's 'frogative'?"

"I don't know, but he thinks it's a ten-dollar word that means he looks like a frog."

"Sarge, I appreciate what you're doing here, but I feel like I gotta call the Protective League and get lawyered-up! I never called that old bastard anything!"

"Okay, stay real," Sergeant Murillo said. "Do you remember him saying he was going to sue you?"

"I guess so. Hell, half the people we pop say that."

"And what did you say to him after that? Try to remember your exact words."

The tall cop's brow furrowed and he looked up at the ceiling while his supervisor waited, and then he broke into a huge grin. "Holy shit, Sarge!" Flotsam said. "Frogative!"

Three minutes later, while Bootsie Brown was contentedly munching on a Toll House cookie and sipping coffee, Sergeant Murillo and Flotsam reentered the sergeants' room.

"Mr. Brown," Sergeant Murillo said, "how's the coffee?"

"Not bad, but the cookie's stale. How 'bout a Ding Dong?"

"Let's talk first, Mr. Brown," Sergeant Murillo said. "Do you remember telling these officers you were going to sue them for false arrest?"

Bootsie Brown paused with the cookie halfway to his lips and said, "I mighta. It was a humbug arrest. That's why they let me and Axel outta jail in forty-eight hours. We was jist tryin' to have a Irish wake for good old Coleman."

"And what did this officer say to you when you threatened to sue him?"

"He called me that name."

"What name is that?"

"He said I was frogative."

"Officer," Sergeant Murillo said to Flotsam. "Please tell Mr. Brown what you said to him when he threatened to sue you and your partner for false arrest."

"I said, 'Your prerogative.'"

"Frogative, progative, it's all uppity bullshit!" Bootsie Brown said to Sergeant Murillo. "He wants to insult somebody, he oughtta have the guts to use normal words and call me a asshole or somethin'."

"You can go back to work," Sergeant Murillo said to the surfer cops. Then to the transient, he said, "Mr. Brown, I'm going to explain to you how things work around here."

"Does this mean I ain't gettin' a Ding Dong?" asked Bootsie Brown.

★ THIRTEEN ★★

TRISTAN HAWKINS HADN'T SLEPT well and had experienced strange and troubling dreams for most of the night. He'd smoked a blunt before going to bed in his east Hollywood hotel-apartment, where he'd lived alone since the first of the year. The smoke hadn't really mellowed him, and it came back on him later, resulting in sleeplessness and nightmares. Somehow the tropical colors that the landlord favored, along with the rank, humid cooking smells from the Cubans next door, reminded him of a whorehouse in Haiti, an unpleasant memory from his short stint as a steward on a cruise liner when he was eighteen years old. It was a good job, but he'd gotten fired for stealing $20 from one of the cabins being tended by another steward.

Tristan had been wide awake since daybreak and lay there staring at the mildew stains on the plasterboard walls. After their surveillance of Kessler the night before, he'd completely lost control of Jerzy, and he was peeved every time he thought of how the dumb peckerwood threatened to throw him out of his own car unless Tristan let him go "back home to his woman." And what was his home anyway? Just a shitty little two-bedroom house in Frogtown that Jerzy shared with a woman who was uglier than Shrek, and her four miserable brats.

If he had someone else he could use to help execute the vague plan he was formulating, he'd drop Jerzy in the time it took to make the call to tell him that his bitch looked like she belonged on *WrestleMania,* and that he'd take a bath in a tub of bleach if he had to sleep with that old hose bag. But he couldn't do that, and they were scheduled to meet Kessler at 5 P.M. back at the pest-infested duplex/office, where Tristan was supposed to tell him about the interesting new idea he had. The fact that he had no ideas at all wasn't of concern; it was how to handle Kessler after they informed the man that they were his new partners. The fact was, a little muscle might be needed to quiet Kessler down, and that was the main reason he needed the big Polack.

Kessler had been a letdown in any case. Tristan hadn't made $1,000 total in the weeks he'd been a runner, so even if the plan didn't work, he had very little to lose. His scheme was going to involve fast-talking and finesse, and that required his talents. Still, he wished he had one more ace to play. That's why he decided to return to Kessler's apartment today when he was certain the man would be away from it.

At 10 A.M., Tristan Hawkins was at a T-shirt shop on Hollywood Boulevard, where a non-English-speaking Guatemalan embroidered "Department of Water and Power" across a baseball cap that Tristan bought at the shop. For another $25 the Guatemalan stitched the same lettering across the pocket of the gray work shirt that Tristan had brought with him.

Just before noon, Dewey Gleason as Ambrose Willis was sitting in his car in the parking lot of an electronics supply house in the San Fernando Valley, working a pair of runners who were purchasing three wireless $1,799 Dell computers with bogus checks that Eunice had printed, along with altered ID that Tristan had stolen on one of his forays to the Gym-and-Swim.

His Jakob Kessler cell chimed, and he picked up and said in his German accent, "Jakob Kessler speaking."

"It's Creole, Mr. Kessler," Tristan said.

"Yes, Creole, what is it?"

"I just wanted you to know we might be a couple minutes late for our five-o'clock meet."

Sounding annoyed, Dewey asked, "What is the problem, Creole?"

"I'm workin' a deal this afternoon for you, Mr. Kessler," Tristan said. "If it goes like I think it will, I'll have some good stuff for you."

What time, then?"

"Five thirty?"

"All right, five thirty sharp."

"We'll be there," Tristan said. "By the way, where are you now?"

Suspiciously, Dewey said, "Why do you want to know?"

"We could meet you in the next hour if you're anywheres near Hollywood."

"No, I am not near Hollywood. I shall see you at five thirty."

When he snapped shut his cell phone, Tristan smiled. He thought he could hear traffic in the background and was certain that the man was not at his apartment on Franklin Avenue. But twenty minutes later, Tristan was.

He was wearing the Water and Power baseball cap with his dreads tucked under, as well as the newly embroidered work shirt. And he had a clipboard in his hand with official-looking documents attached to it. He rang the gate phone of the old woman he'd conned last time.

He recognized the same raspy voice when she said, "Hello, who is it?"

"Department of Water and Power," Tristan said. "We're replacin' meters and need access, please."

The old woman said, "Call the manager. She's in number one-three-two."

"I know that," Tristan said, "but there's no answer. I'm just goin' down the list, and you're the first one to answer."

"Oh, all right," the old woman said. "Are you going to have to come into my apartment?"

"No, ma'am," Tristan said. "We'll only need access to the meters."

The gate buzzer sounded, and the lock clicked open. Tristan entered, climbed the familiar stairway, and was standing at the door of the last apartment on the left, number 313.

He rang and waited twenty seconds before ringing again, and he felt sure that someone was looking at him through the brass peephole.

The door opened a few inches, and Eunice said, "Yes?"

He saw bloodshot blue eyes and gray-blonde tangles of hair, and she reeked of tobacco smoke.

"Department of Water and Power, ma'am," Tristan said with his most winning smile and taking great care with his diction and grammar. "Have you experienced a power surge today?"

"No," Eunice said. "Why?"

"We're havin' trouble with the load on this street," Tristan said. "People have reported computers crashin' for no apparent reason, and we're checkin' with every resident we can. Do you have a computer?"

"Yes," she said.

"Would you please turn it on and see if it's okay?"

"My computers are working fine," she said.

"You're sure?"

"I'm positive," she said.

"Okay, then, sorry to have bothered you."

When he walked away, he was excited. She had more than one computer. His hunch had been correct. She worked out of Kessler's crib. This woman was either a hired hand or his bitch, but for sure she was also his geek. Yes!

Dewey Gleason as Ambrose Willis was angry at himself after he paid off his shopping runner, a young aspiring actor, full-time parking valet, and part-time thief. The kid had talked Dewey into waiting for him outside Chateau Marmont by claiming that within one hour, he could enter the hotel and talk a wealthy female vacationer into buying him a drink in the bar, where he would collect all the information from her credit card without her knowledge. He claimed that he'd even obtain her driver's license information and checkbook account number. Dewey, who felt sleep-deprived, remained in his car, eventually snoozing. After an hour, he awoke and entered the hotel bar but found no sign of his runner. He figured the bragging little sociopath had probably hooked up with a rich vacationer of either gender and was up in the room fulfilling their Hollywood fantasies.

Thinking of that handsome, young aspiring actor made him remember that he was to meet the other good-looking kid at the office. However, it would be difficult, now that he had to be Jakob Kessler with Tristan and Jerzy, and he would have little time to turn into Bernie Graham. It was at moments like these that he wondered if the elaborate disguises were worth it. But if not, it would mean that Eunice was right again, and that was too hard for Dewey to accept. He decided to leave the hotel and go straight home, become Jakob Kessler, and gather the things he'd need to turn Kessler into Bernie Graham. Then he got on the cell and rang the kid he knew as Clark.

Malcolm was on his lunch break when the cell rang.

"Clark," Dewey said, "this is Bernie Graham."

"I hope you're not gonna change our appointment again, Mr. Graham. I need the work now. I can't wait any longer."

"I just need to push it back an hour," Dewey said. "Meet me at the address I gave you at six o'clock instead of at five. I'll put you to work tonight, and you can start earning some spending money right away."

"Six o'clock," Malcolm said. "At the office."

"Right, but like I told you, it's not really an office. It's an apartment that we use for meetings and other things."

"See you at six, Mr. Graham," Malcolm said. "For sure, right?"

"For sure, Clark," Dewey said.

Dewey drove straight home and found Eunice in a fouler mood than usual. He'd been hoping to lie down for another one-hour nap, but now he knew it would be impossible. She wasn't even happy when he told her that in the trunk of his car he had three laptops that he was going to deliver next Tuesday for $1,100 cash.

Eunice was wearing her favorite pink bathrobe and pajamas but no makeup, and it was 2:30 in the afternoon. "Nothing's going right today," she grumbled, moving the cigarette from one side of her mouth to the other with her tongue and teeth while her fingers flew over the keyboard of computer number three.

"What's wrong?"

"'What's wrong?' the man asks," Eunice said to the ceiling. "I'm stuck in this room working myself into an early grave while you're out all day doing God knows what and bringing home chump change. That's what's wrong."

"Jesus, Eunice!" Dewey said. "It's getting harder and harder to do business. There's stuff all over the papers and TV these days about identity theft, and everyone's being more cautious. And please don't tell me how Hugo woulda had no trouble, because I'm telling you that Hugo never had to run up against the shit I'm facing."

She looked at him and said, "Go in your bedroom and kill Ambrose Willis. You look even sillier than when you're doing the old Jew, Jakob whatsisname."

"Jakob Kessler. He's an Austrian. I don't know if he's a Jew. I never asked him."

"He sounds like a Jew to me every time I hear the phony accent."

"Aw, shit!" Dewey said. "Just one little break sometime, Eunice. If you ever give me one fucking break, I'll probably have a stroke and die on the spot."

"I should be so lucky," she said.

He went into his bedroom, slammed the door, and fell down on the bed, a bit alarmed by how his heart was thudding irregularly. Something had to be done. He was nearing the end of the line with her one way or the other. He desperately needed a nap, but he groaned to his feet and laid out his Jakob Kessler wardrobe and wig, along with the casual clothing of Bernie Graham that he'd take with him in an overnight bag. He knew that a quick change in the duplex/office would be tricky, but he didn't think that a kid like Clark would pay a lot of attention to details.

The door to his bedroom was opened abruptly by Eunice, who didn't know how to knock and had no intention of learning.

"Dewey," she said. "We should maybe think about moving to another place."

"Oh, Christ!" he said. "We haven't been living here that long, Eunice. It's such a hassle to move everything."

"A guy from Water and Power was here today. They been having problems around here with power surges."

"So? You have surge protectors."

"And I try hard to have everything properly stored and backed up, but you never know. He said some computers had crashed, and it's got me worried."

Trying to sound as blasé as possible, he said, "Just so our bank account information is always accessible. You never know when people in our business might have to make a very fast withdrawal or transfer of funds."

Her watery blue eyes narrowed, and she said, "Don't worry about the bank account, Dewey. It's safe."

As expected, she said *the* bank account, not *our* bank account. And she didn't use the plural this time. With as much sincerity as he could muster, he said, "Eunice, we're not getting any younger. In case a serious illness or accident happened to you, how would I access the funds? Let's say if they were needed for your medical care. Do you realize I have no idea where the funds are or what I could do to help you?"

"Nothing's gonna happen to me, Dewey," she said, expressionless. "Worry about your own health and well-being."

He was tired and under such strain that he said impetuously, "You act as though it's your money and not mine too. I've worked my ass off for you for nine long years, Eunice."

"Correction," she said. "We've been married for nine very long years. But for the first two and a half years, I supported you completely while you haunted the offices of second-rate casting agents. Back when you spent more time at Dan Tana's and the Formosa Café than the goddamn waiters and bartenders because you think screenwriters and moguls still hang out there. You live in the past, Dewey. You're about as up-to-the-minute as a spinning wheel. Old Hollywood is dead. But I spoiled you and let you have your way, hoping you'd outgrow it. Does this sound familiar? Am I opening the gate to Memory Lane?"

"I was working every minute in those days, Eunice," he said, feeling his resolve leaking away. "I filled legal pads full of script notes every moment I spent at Dan Tana's. I met some important people there and at the Formosa, and I got a few acting gigs out of it. I could've gotten more if you'd stood by me with patience and encouragement."

"You never needed encouragement, Dewey, you needed a mommy," she said. "Well, sonny boy, I got real tired of being your mommy. And now, six and a half years later, you still haven't learned the business like you should have. You still got your movie star dreams, and if I wasn't completely in charge of our affairs, we'd be broke. There are certain things for which you have a minor talent, but money management isn't one of them. It's much better this way, and that's how it's gonna stay, Dewey."

"And I have no say at all in the matter, is that it?" he said. "I'll never have money of my own except what you dole out to me, right? Everything in the bank account is yours to control forever, right?"

She lit another cigarette from the pack she kept in her bathrobe pocket and said, "As you well know, Dewey, before I ever laid eyes on you, Hugo and me had built up a tidy nest egg. And as you also know, the money you've brought in—because of *my* talents, I might add—is commingled with that other money. So I think you should be grateful for all of that instead of being whiny and petty and childish."

Her "talents"? He wanted to tell her she was nothing but a hacker and a forger and a thief. He wanted to tell her it was his innovative ideas in finding and working runners that brought in the money she craved and hoarded. He wanted to tell her that her "talents" were a dime a dozen and if he put his mind to it, he could find fifty hackers at the cyber café who would be more productive partners. Most of all, he wanted to tell her that he hated her guts like he'd never hated anyone in his life. But he didn't tell her any of it.

Dewey heaved an enormous sigh and said, "I don't even know how much we have in our account, Eunice. I don't know how many accounts the money is in. I don't know where the account or accounts are. And I'm your husband. How do you think all of that makes me feel? As a human being."

"It's just another concern that you don't have to deal with," Eunice said. "You should feel relieved that *this* human being takes care of important matters. That's how you should feel, Dewey."

Suddenly he cried, "You've taken my balls, Eunice! I have to live week after week, day after day, as a man without balls!"

She took a big puff on her cigarette, inhaled, and said, "Stop by Hollywood Prop Supply. You might find some you could rent." Then she blew the smoke into the room, turned, and closed the door.

Dewey Gleason knew then that he could bring himself to kill her if he could first discover a way to access the account or accounts. And he believed he'd never have a single conscience attack afterward. He was so emotionally drained that he did fall asleep for an hour despite her. When he woke up, he had to become Jakob Kessler for his meeting with Creole and Jerzy.

At roll call late that afternoon, Sergeant Lee Murillo and Sergeant Miriam Hermann were both sitting at the table in front of the room. After she read the crimes, Sergeant Hermann said, "The detectives on the sex desk at West Bureau got a call from an alert officer at North Hollywood desk about a mall incident last night. A young, curly-haired Latino who fits the description of the guy that attacked the two women here in Hollywood made a try for a woman putting groceries in her car. He attempted to give her a ten-dollar bill that he claimed he found near her car. She didn't buy into it, and he really freaked and started screaming as she drove off. If he's our guy, he seems to be getting more out of control with each encounter. Be supercareful with any young Latinos who fit the description we gave you. A fifty-one-fifty with a box cutter should be taken very seriously, and this one's out there stalking."

Dana Vaughn said, "Was the woman middle-aged, blonde, and a bit overweight?"

Sergeant Hermann said, "I don't know. It doesn't say in the note I got."

"Both of ours were," Dana said. "I checked with the officer who took the report on the woman who got beat up."

"That's a good question. I'll call North Hollywood and get back to you with the woman's description," Sergeant Hermann said. "There might be a specific MO being established here."

R.T. Dibney guffawed and said loudly, "If the woman's middle-aged, you can bet she's overweight, and she's probably blonde. All the middle-aged women I date or been married to are overweight, and all of them become bottle blondes sooner or later. It's the easiest way to hide the gray."

Dana Vaughn saw Mindy Ling cast a withering look at her partner for shooting off his mouth, and Mindy said, "From the looks of your sideburns and stash, R.T., you learned a few coloring tricks from your multitude of lady friends."

Everyone had a chuckle, until Sergeant Murillo said, "Okay, if we're all through with beauty tips by R.T. Dibney, let's go to work."

Of course, each of them touched the Oracle's picture before filing out the door.

Jerzy was even more unhappy than usual when he showed up in the parking lot by the cyber café and entered the donut shop, where Tristan was sitting at a table in the back.

"Get your sugar fix," Tristan said, nibbling on a chocolate donut covered with multicolored sprinkles. "Go ahead and load up. I'm buyin'."

Jerzy sat down without ordering and said, "I let you talk me into some crazy shit, but this takes the cake."

"Forget the cake. Have a donut," Tristan said, pointing to the plate in front of him piled with five assorted donuts. "This is gonna take a high energy level from both of us."

"I wish I had some smoke to sprinkle on the donuts," Jerzy muttered.

"Did you get the equipment?"

Jerzy automatically lowered his voice when he said, "Yeah, we're tooled up, and I ain't real happy about it."

Tristan lowered his own voice and said, "Where are they?"

"In the trunk of my car at the bottom of a box of birdseed and dog food that my old lady wants for the fuckin' zoo she keeps in her house."

"You can rent her a bigger house if this gag goes like I think it will. What'd you get?"

"An old snub-nosed revolver," Jerzy said. "Couldn't get my hands on a semiautomatic."

"Don't matter, dawg, it's only a prop," Tristan said. "It ain't loaded, is it?"

"Of course it's fuckin' loaded. It ain't that much of a prop."

"I think you should leave it in the trunk. Maybe it was a bad idea anyways. We don't need no gun."

"You said you wanna scare the guy."

"Not that much," Tristan said. "Did you get the other . . . tool?"

Impatiently Jerzy said, "Yeah, the buck knife was no problem. Every biker I know carries one in his saddlebag. I think I know why it had to be a buck knife."

"Readin' my mind again?" Tristan said.

"You figure that O.J. Simpson diced the white bitch and her boyfriend with a buck knife, right? And O.J.'s a national hero to you and all your tribe, am I right?"

"Fuck you, peckerwood," Tristan said. "It's a scary-lookin' knife, that's why. We ain't into force. Fear is our weapon. And the element of surprise. We're only gonna scare him, not shoot him, and not cut him."

"Element of surprise," Jerzy snorted. "Okay, break it down, master-mind. You got me breathin' hard."

"When Kessler shows up, I start talkin' shit for a minute and you jist make sure you're between him and the door. You understand how important that is, right?"

With his mouth full of donut, Jerzy rolled his eyes and said, "No I'm a fuckin' idiot."

Tristan thought, For once we agree, you fuckin' redneck. But he said, "Anyways, you gotta be the immovable object that the man can feel breathin' on him every second I'm talkin' to him. I'm gonna tell him what we know and what we want and what we're gonna do if he don't cooperate."

"And you're one hundred percent convinced he ain't gonna call our bluff and tell us to go ahead and rat him out?"

"Look at us," Tristan said. "We ain't got a Ben Franklin between us. He knows we got nothin' to lose. But Kessler and his geek got a whole lot to lose. You jist stand there like a statue and let me work it. He's gonna get so scared of my story that if you give him a peek at the buck knife, he'll mess his drawers."

"Okay, but if I get tired of listenin' to your shit, and if it ain't havin' the desired effect, I reserve the right to do it my way."

"And what might that be, wood?"

"You'll see."

"Puttin' your hands on the man is a last resort," Tristan said quickly. "And then only to make him sit down. We don't need no violence. He's jist a pussy playin' dress-up. He'll take it if you piss on his shoes. No need to tune him up."

"Maybe," Jerzy said, shoving a whole donut in his mouth, the powdered sugar turning his lips white.

As they were preparing to leave, a black-and-white pulled into one of the open spaces by the cyber café. Aaron Sloane and Sheila Montez got out and headed toward the donut shop.

Sheila speed-dialed a cell number and said, "Gotta make a quick call."

When she walked several paces away for privacy, Aaron felt the familiar pain. He was having a hard time with his emotions these days: sadness, jealousy, even despair. Yet, for all he knew, she was only calling her parents to set up a family dinner. He knew she came from a large Mexican family in Pacoima. It could just be that. But whenever she made a private call, he found himself imagining the worst: a yuppie stockbroker or maybe a lawyer in a perfectly tailored Hugo Boss suit, sitting at his desk in Century City with a cell phone in one hand, a bottle of Evian in the other, making plans with Sheila for a couple of days and nights on Catalina Island.

The captivated cop tried but couldn't come close to feigning insouciance until Sheila closed her cell and said, "I'll have coffee. You aren't gonna catch me eating one of those lumps of grease they call donuts."

"They're really good when you're hungry as I am," Aaron said. "I haven't had a thing all day except a bowl of cereal. These donuts really stick to your ribs."

"They stick to your thighs," Sheila said. "And to your butt. I think they're made of cellulite. I'll just have coffee and watch you harm your body."

"You don't have to worry about *your* body," Aaron said with that same lovelorn look he continually tried to repress.

Sheila didn't reply, but Aaron caught a glimmer of a smile in response to his compliment as they walked across the parking lot toward the donut shop, which all cops knew was frequented by hustlers and dopers from the nearby cyber café.

Tristan was giving last-minute, animated instructions to Jerzy while getting into the Chevy Caprice, when Aaron took a look at them and said to Sheila, "We can use a couple of shakes for our recap. Let's see if these dudes have one good driver's license between them, and maybe even a registration."

"Nobody'd steal a car that crappy," Sheila said, but she moved to the passenger side of the Chevy when Aaron approached the driver.

"Turn off the engine, sir," Aaron said, startling Tristan, who hadn't seen him coming.

"Somethin' wrong, Officer?" Tristan said, very grateful that the Polack had left the gun in his own car. But then he thought of the buck knife. He didn't need this shit right now.

"Your right taillight is broken," Aaron said. "I'd like to see your license and registration."

"Sure, Officer," Tristan said, glancing at Jerzy, who had that not-again expression going on. Tristan feared it might piss off the cops.

From past experience and urban legend about the LAPD, Tristan always opened the glove box very carefully, giving the cop on the passenger side a good look before reaching his hand inside for the registration.

"Here it is, Officer," Tristan said.

Aaron didn't like the looks of the sullen, fat white guy and was about to ask them to get out of the car, when Tristan smiled obligingly and said, "You're welcome to run a make on us if you want. But Officer Vaughn already done it, day before yesterday."

Aaron was mildly surprised. "How did you meet Officer Vaughn?"

Tristan reached inside his wallet and removed the folded copy of his traffic citation, handed it to Aaron, and said, "She gave me this traffic ticket and she checked out both of us for warrants and such. And she also told me to get the taillight fixed."

Aaron looked at the citation and then glanced at Sheila, who shrugged. Aaron said, "So why didn't you get the taillight fixed?"

"My daddy died," Tristan said. "I been tendin' to funeral arrangements. I'll go straight to a Chevy dealer and get it fixed tomorrow, Officer. So help me God."

Aaron handed the documents back to Tristan, again looked across the roof at Sheila, who gave a chin tilt, and said to Tristan, "Drive carefully."

When the Chevy was motoring away, Aaron said to Sheila, "Butter wouldn't melt in his mouth. He's one slick-talking dude."

"The donuts in this joint wouldn't melt if you hit them with a blowtorch," Sheila said. "Are you really gonna eat one of them?"

"Two," Aaron said. "Glazed and cream-filled, with extra sprinkles."

Tristan hadn't driven his Chevy two blocks before Jerzy said, "I don't like the way our luck's goin'. We're runnin' up against too many cops these days."

"We been in the wrong place at the wrong time, is all," Tristan said. "We gotta be more careful where we go until this whole deal shakes out."

Jerzy was quiet then, thinking about the risk they were about to take, and finally he said, "You know how cops give people's descriptions over their radio, like 'male white,' or 'male Hispanic,' or 'male black'? That kind of cop shit?"

"Yeah," Tristan said. "What about it?"

"Know what I heard a cop say to another one there at the cyber café when they were roustin' some of your south L.A. cousins?"

Tristan sighed and said, "No, but you're gonna tell me, I'm sure of that."

"Instead of sayin' 'male black,' he said, 'male *usual*.' Ain't that a giggle?"

★ FOURTEEN ★

HOLLYWOOD NATE WAS HAVING women troubles, and by now Dana Vaughn was growing accustomed to her role as adviser. The latest problem involved a secretary of a casting agent who, Nate was "almost positive," might cast him in a made-for-cable pilot for a cop show being shot on a soundstage in the San Fernando Valley.

Dana, who was driving, interrupted him to say, "Nate, the Valley is the porn capital of the universe. Have you checked out this production company?"

"This is a legit indie production," Nate said. "They're making it on a shoestring, but they're trying to hire a good features director."

"Whadda they want you to do?"

"They need a cop technical adviser, but the secretary told me I'm being considered for a scene that runs for five script pages. That's a significant part."

"So what's the problem?"

"Her name's Sharon. She's okay, but way alpha. My ex-wife was a man-eater too, and I just wanna run the other way when I meet another one like that."

"So what?" Dana said. "You're trying to get a job, not trying to get laid. Or am I wrong about that part?"

"No, you're right, but she has other ideas."

Dana stopped at Melrose and La Brea in the middle of a rush-hour traffic snarl, with people driving home from work in all directions, and she said, "Are you telling me that Hollywood Nate, the most talked-about male in the women's locker room except for George Clooney, isn't willing to *take* one for his acting career?"

"I must be getting old," he said. "These days I have to feel something for the women I sleep with."

When the light changed, Dana proceeded cautiously across La Brea, trying to get around a beer truck, and said, "Would you be mortified if I shared with one or two of the other girls that Hollywood Nate has at last got in touch with his inner child? Who's turned out to be that nice boy his mother always mistakenly thought he was when she glowed at his bar mitzvah?"

"Don't even think about doing it. You're my partner and sworn to secrecy."

"Okay, so what're you gonna do about this?"

"I was hoping you'd have some advice," Nate said. "I'm not sure she could kill the job if she got really pissed off, but I think she could make it tough. I'm expecting a call any day now with a contract offer from her boss."

"How old is she?"

"About your age," Nate said.

"Okay, I see your dilemma," Dana said. "Who in the hell would go to bed with a woman my age, right?"

"That's not what I meant, partner," Nate said. "You're a bona fide Betty. In fact, if I hadn't been forced to finally become a grown-up after the Oracle was no longer here to protect me, I'da tried leaving my house key in your ticket book."

"My life," Dana said melodramatically. "Always bad timing."

"Come on, help me out," Nate pleaded.

Dana considered it for a moment and said, "Okay, it's gonna be hard for a dreamboat like you to manage, but you're just gonna have to get less attractive to her."

"Don't expect fanny burps," Nate said.

"Worse than that," Dana said. "You gotta start subtly criticizing her makeup. Like maybe she uses too much or too little. Or maybe you don't think the color of her lipstick is quite right for her. And if you really wanna end her lust, start inviting her to the gym to work out with you. Tell her it's a good way to burn off the cottage cheese that clings to the thighs of *women her age*. Within a week she'll hate your guts."

Hollywood Nate thought it over and said, "I don't wanna be *that* snarky."

"Then leave off the cottage cheese part."

They were interrupted by a call that had just been given to 6-X-66.

"We can mosey over there as backup," Dana said. "If I'm all through being your shiksa auntie."

After their coffee and donut fix, the partners in 6-X-66 had been chatting pleasantly, until Sheila Montez started talking about a cop she'd met in grappling school last year.

"There we were," she said to Aaron Sloane, who was now driving east on Melrose Avenue, "supposedly learning street fighting. How to protect ourselves when we're on the ground, battling for our lives. He wasn't a big guy at all. More like my size. And after lying on top of each other for five days—you know, wrapping legs around each other—the sexual tension started building. On the last day of class, he says to me, 'Wanna go have a drink?'"

Feigning lighthearted curiosity, Aaron said, "And did you?"

"Of course," she said, and he could see her smile but didn't know how to interpret it. "Best affair I've had since my divorce."

And then she glanced sideways at him, smiling even more with that dusky, sloe-eyed way of hers, and he didn't know if she was kidding him or not. And she didn't appear to know about the stab he felt in his heart every time she mentioned another man to him, or how it could depress him for hours or even days.

The call that 6-X-66 received seemed benign enough: the ubiquitous "family dispute." It was at a medium-size shopping center with a large supermarket as its anchor. The premier mall within the boundaries of Hollywood Division was certainly the Hollywood and Highland mall, where the Kodak Centre loomed proudly. This particular shopping center was frequented by many of the people who spoke one of the more than two hundred foreign languages of Los Angeles, and two of them were speaking Spanish heatedly when Aaron and Sheila arrived.

They were a young Latino couple, both natives of Colombia, and there seemed no cause for alarm, nothing to make the cops more cautious than usual. After they saw police, the pair stopped yelling at each other, and the pregnant twenty-year-old mother began fussing with her thirteen-month-old baby in a stroller.

The police never did find out who placed the call and only learned later that it was a female voice speaking Spanish-accented English that had said, "Violence might happen."

Sheila was first out of the car, and while Aaron was emerging, she approached the young couple, who were standing quietly, awaiting their approach. As was her custom, Sheila spoke in English until she was sure that the citizens did not understand her, before she switched to Spanish.

"Good afternoon," she said. "We've received a call that there's a problem here."

The well-groomed and neatly dressed young man, who turned out to be the woman's occasional boyfriend, had no tatts, nothing that might suggest gang affiliation. The cops weren't sensing a threat until he reached down and grabbed a semiautomatic handgun concealed under a bag of disposable diapers. He pointed it at the baby.

"Get back or I will kill her!" he said in slightly accented English as the baby began screaming for her mother, who began screaming even louder.

Sheila froze, as did Aaron, who was approaching the couple from an angle to their right.

"Easy, sir!" Sheila said. "Easy! Just take it easy!"

Aaron reached for the nine on his belt, until the young Colombian yelled, "Touch it and I will shoot!"

Nobody moved then, and while the mother of the baby screamed, "Noooooooo, Arturo!" he kept the gun aimed at the baby's head and pushed the stroller toward the door of the supermarket, all the time turning back toward the cops as he walked forward.

Aaron was the first to grab his rover and make the call for assistance. Like all LAPD cops, he was instinctively reluctant to broadcast an "officer needs help" call — the equivalent of a mayday, and the most desperate call in the street cop's repertoire — especially since he was not convinced that the gun was real. The code of machismo said that a good cop should be able to take care of business without calling for code 3 backups, which would bring police from everywhere and mark the caller as a pantywaist if the help call turned out to be unnecessary. And nothing was worse for an LAPD male copper than to be labeled a pantywaist.

So he said, "Officers need assistance, man with a gun!" and stated the location.

Sheila Montez, who was not burdened by male machismo, and who was utterly horrified by the threat to the baby whether or not the suspicious-looking gun was real, cried, "Bullshit on assistance!" She grabbed her rover and said, "Six-X-ray-Sixty-six. Officers need *help!*"

Before they heard the siren of the assigned police unit speeding their way, they were both walking along at a medium pace, deployed wide apart, trailing the Colombian, who was still pushing the crying baby toward the supermarket door without taking his eyes from the cops.

"Stay here and wait for the officers!" Sheila said to the hysterical mother, who was beside her, wailing.

"Look, you're not in really serious trouble yet!" Aaron yelled to the Colombian. "Put the gun on the ground and let's talk!"

"So you can shoot me?" the young man shouted.

"Nobody wants to shoot you," Sheila said, approaching closer. "Put the gun down and let's talk."

Without breaking stride until he was only thirty feet from the glass doors of the supermarket, the young man said, "I am not going back to Colombia. They will kill me if I go back. I prefer to die here."

"Who's gonna kill you?" Aaron asked.

"There are very bad people in my country who hate me," the man said. "And they will kill me."

They had to raise their voices again in order to be heard over louder wails from the baby. The young man was ten feet from the entrance doors to the supermarket when the car that had been assigned the help call roared into the parking lot, siren yowling.

"You don't wanna hurt that baby," Sheila said. "Is she your baby?"

"No," the Colombian said. "She is yours." And abruptly he stopped and shoved the stroller directly at Sheila, who chased it and caught it just before it tipped over. The young man ran into the supermarket before Aaron's pistol was clear of the holster.

Within ten minutes, Sergeant Hermann, Sergeant Murillo, and two supervisors from Watch 3 had arrived and got on the air to call a tactical alert. In another seven minutes, there were twenty-two officers, some from neighboring divisions as well as a pair of motor cops surrounding the super-market, with SWAT on the way. And supermarket shoppers, who had not seen the action taking place outside the market, were baffled when police kept arriving and blocking the exit doors, refusing to let them leave.

Sergeant Hermann's car was parked near one of the entrances to the market, and she got on the PA to address all officers, saying, "The store stays locked down until patrons can be escorted outside!"

Another five minutes passed as more officers arrived, while angry and frustrated customers worked at triggering the opening device on the glass doors, yelling to the cops outside that they wanted to go home.

When Sergeant Hermann addressed the swell of customers at the door, saying, "Is there a man with a gun inside the store? Are you being threatened?" a dozen voices, both male and female, began shouting in several languages.

Those speaking English were yelling things like "There's no gunman in here!" and "Let us outta here!" and "My kids are getting scared!" and even "My goddamn ice cream's melting, you assholes!"

While this was going on, Sergeant Murillo and Sheila Montez were interviewing the mother of the baby in Spanish. After each exchange, Sheila would translate bits and pieces into English for Sergeant Hermann and Aaron Sloane.

Finally, Sheila said, "She's been dating the guy occasionally for six months. She knows him as Arturo Echeverría. He told her he's hunted by members of a drug cartel and has to carry a gun for protection, but she claims she didn't know it was under the diaper bag. He doesn't work at any job as far as she knows, and he doesn't have friends. He told her he lives alone in an apartment in Little Armenia, and that's all she knows about the guy."

Sergeant Hermann said, "Okay, let's let the women and kids out, escorted by officers. The men stay inside for now until SWAT arrives. Sloane and Montez, you two stay by each exit door. You're the only ones who know what he looks like."

The plan sounded reasonable, especially since nobody in the store was aware that the police were searching for an armed and desperate man in their midst. Both Sheila Montez and Mindy Ling got on the PA, Sheila speaking Spanish and Mindy speaking Mandarin, and told the patrons that women and children would be escorted outside ten at a time, questioned very briefly, and released.

One of the problems was that in Hollywood (called Babelwood by the cops who worked there) the police had no officers to make the same announcement in Arabic, Cambodian, Farsi, Russian, Korean, Vietnamese, Tagalog, Armenian, Thai, or any of the other languages spoken by the customers inside the supermarket at that moment.

Officers escorted outside the first ten women and kids, and none of those who understood their questions had seen a man with a gun. Then another ten were escorted out with the same result. Then all hell broke loose.

The man known as Arturo Echeverría, who had been very busy inside that store scurrying around looking for a way out, eventually finding himself in the storage area behind the meat counters, had decided that it was time to act. And for the first time, Aaron and Sheila and the other cops at the scene learned that the gun was indeed a real one.

Arturo Echeverría stood behind the mobs of customers at the west exit door, who were hollering and complaining, and he began firing! The customers heard five explosions behind them that shattered glass displays and ricocheted off concrete floors, reverberating from one side of the checkout counters to the other.

And then, pandemonium! Some customers crouched or hit the floor, women with children shielded their young ones with their bodies, and the masses decided, the hell with Sergeant Hermann's reasonable plan. They charged both exit doors. People screamed, people fell, people were trampled. And the cops stood helplessly while men, women, and children, shouting in languages the cops could not understand, stampeded from the store, shoving officers back as they ran from the gunfire. Aaron Sloane and Sheila Montez tried to visually examine each young man who ran from the supermarket, but it was hopeless.

Many of the men who fled were store employees in white shirts and dark trousers, some wearing aprons and badges, some black baseball caps with the store's logo on the front. And some others wore meat-stained white aprons as well as the black baseball caps. There were half a dozen of them, as panicked as everyone else, and, like everyone else, they scattered when they got past the first line of cops, running far enough to stop and gather in groups or to duck behind cars in the parking lot or simply to say in Spanish or Tagolog, "Screw this. I don't get paid to get shot." These last few raced for their cars in the parking lot.

As it turned out, one of those who fled toward the cars was Arturo Echeverría, dressed as a butcher in a long white coat, a meat-stained apron, and a black baseball cap with the store's logo on the front. He ran to a car, following behind one of the store's butchers, and as soon as the butcher unlocked his car, Arturo Echeverría said to him, "I need a ride, *compadre*."

When the butcher looked at him and said, "I ain't never seen you in the store before," Arturo Echeverría drew the gun from under his apron and said, "You see me now. *Vámonos*. And do not cry out."

The terrified butcher drove away with Arturo Echeverría behind him on the floor of the car, promising not to kill the man if he obeyed orders. The butcher was released at the corner of Beverly Boulevard and Vermont Avenue and was not robbed of his money or cell phone. The stolen car was later found in a parking lot near LAX, where the hunted man had no doubt flown out of Los Angeles and possibly the country.

Among the many officers who had responded to the help call that afternoon were Flotsam and Jetsam, who aided in the search of the building after the stampede of customers and market employees had ended. It was determined that nobody was hiding in the store and that none of the customers had been hit by gunfire. Some clothing belonging to the night-shift butchers was missing from a locker, but that was all. And after paramedics had treated several with minor injuries incurred in the stampede, the surfer cops were standing by their car, chatting with Hollywood Nate and Dana Vaughn, who had also responded to the help call.

Flotsam said to them, "You know, that was, like, a way cooleo escape. That dude? He deserved his freedom."

Sergeant Miriam Hermann, who was sweating and tired and feeling her age, was enormously frustrated that the man with a gun had escaped while she was in charge of the tac alert. And she happened to be walking past the unsuspecting surfer cops at that precise moment.

Sergeant Hermann froze in her tracks. "What...did...you...say? Repeat that."

Caught unawares, Flotsam turned. "Oh, hi, Sarge! I was only, like...I was sorta...I was just...just..."

"He was just leaving, Sarge," Jetsam said, grabbing his partner by the arm as they scurried to their black-and-white.

Watching the events at the shopping center along with hundreds of other spectators was Malcolm Rojas, who'd recently finished his workday at the home improvement center warehouse. He found it exciting when the SWAT team showed up with all their equipment. This was like reality TV, and he got so involved in the show that he almost forgot his meeting coming up with Bernie Graham. Malcolm had decided for sure that either he made some money with Bernie Graham tonight or he was through letting the man string him along. Part of him didn't care one way or the other because part of him wanted to quell the feelings that had been growing inside him all day, feelings that scared and excited him and demanded release.

Something that he'd been realizing more and more was that the stalking of those women was more exciting than the time he had them in his power. He always thought that the sex was what he wanted, but now he wasn't so sure. He hadn't gotten any sex yet, because the bitches were so...so...he didn't know *what* they were, other than clever and tricky. Stalking them was way better than jerking off, that was for sure. He loved the stalking part. But he knew he'd have to have sex with one of them sooner or later. Just so he'd know. But *what* would he know? It was all so confusing and frustrating that the rage began to stir within him.

"When was the last time you had a square job?" Tristan wanted to know as he drove to the duplex/office for their meeting.

"I was a hod carrier in El Monte for a couple months," Jerzy said after he opened his eyes to see if they were getting close to the east Hollywood neighborhood.

"When was that?"

"I don't know. Two, three, years ago. What the fuck difference does it make?"

"I worked at a Hollywood dance studio for almost three years," Tristan said. "I did the books and made all the appointments and I was learnin' to become an instructor. I even got all kinds of promises about becomin' a partner in the business. And then one day the boss and his wife were gone and the dance studio was taken over by the landlord, and all the promises were like the shit your momma told you when you were little. About how good life was gonna be. I ain't had a square job since."

Jerzy smirked and said, "Yeah, well, you can take your half of the money we're gonna make and go home to New Orleans and show your momma what a success her Creole boy is."

"My momma ain't in New Orleans," Tristan said. "And I ain't no Creole."

"And you ain't never been to college like you said, right?"

"Right," Tristan said.

"I figgered as much," Jerzy said. "Jist another refugee from Watts. Come to Hollywood after the fuckin' greaseballs took over your ghetto."

"I'm only a thief like you," Tristan said and then added, "but when we pull off this gag, I'm gettin' outta the game so I don't end up like you."

"You can never be like me," Jerzy said. "I'm a white man."

Tristan and Jerzy rode in silence and arrived at the duplex thirty minutes before their boss was due to arrive. They tried to slip the front door lock with a credit card but were unsuccessful. Then they walked along the driveway that led to rear carports and tried to open the bedroom window, finding that it was an old aluminum slider and could be pried open with little trouble.

Tristan got a screwdriver from the trunk of his car and gave it to Jerzy, who first pried off the screen with his buck knife and then used the screwdriver to pop open the slider. Then he boosted Tristan up and through the window, and Tristan opened the door for him. They brought in the six-pack of beer that Jerzy had insisted they buy on this hot summer day and were having a brew when a black-and-white, fresh from the siege at the supermarket, parked on the street in front.

Tristan peeked out the window and saw two cops, a tall one and another one, both with streaky blond hair, walking toward the apartment, as though they were expecting trouble.

"Cops!" Tristan said to Jerzy. "Get rid of the buck knife! Sit on the kitchen chair and stay cool, fool!"

Jerzy said, "Fuck! We can't get away from them! They're everywhere!" And he shoved the knife inside his boot under the leg of his Levi's jeans as Tristan opened the door before the cops reached the front step.

"Hi, Officers," Tristan said with a smile.

Both cops looked wary, and Flotsam said, "We got a call from a neighbor that somebody climbed in the window here. Was it you?"

"Sure was," Tristan said brightly. "We lost our key. Come on in. We appreciate that you're watchin' out for us."

Flotsam entered with Jetsam following behind. Tristan noticed that each cop had a hand very close to his pistol, and he said, "This here is my friend Jerzy. He boosted me in the window. Our friend Mr. Kessler is expectin' us here."

"Wait a minute," Jetsam said. "You mean you don't live here?"

"Take a look around," Tristan said. "Nobody lives here. There's a fridge in the kitchen and a table and two chairs and a fleabag chair in the livin' room, but that's it. There ain't no more."

The cops moved their hands away from their pistols but still were looking very cautiously at both men. Jetsam said, "All we know is you two climbed in the window."

"Him," Jerzy said. "My ass is too big to climb in windows."

"Okay," Jetsam said, "but until we figure out what's going on, we'd like to make sure you're not burglars." Then he said to Jerzy, "Stand up."

Jerzy was used to cops. He stood, moved his hands away from his body, and let Jetsam pat him down. Tristan did the same for Flotsam.

When the cops were through with the frisk, Flotsam said, "Your IDs, please."

Both Tristan and Jerzy gave the cops their legitimate driver's licenses, and Jetsam pulled out his rover and stepped outside the front door, only a few steps away.

"We're clean," Tristan said. "We already got a check run on us the other day."

"Yeah?" Flotsam said. "You two must be pretty busy to always be getting checked out by police."

"No, it was jist a ticket," Tristan said. "But I guess we look suspicious or somethin'."

"Everybody looks suspicious when they climb in windows," Flotsam said.

"I can see that," said Tristan. "You got a job to do."

When Jetsam came back in the apartment moments later, he said to his partner, "Mr."— he couldn't pronounce Jerzy's last name and pointed to him— "has been in jail a few times for drugs and grand theft. Mr. Hawkins has a misdemeanor record for petty theft and DUI."

"The petty theft was when I had to steal some milk for my baby sister after our family got foreclosed on," Tristan said.

Flotsam looked at Jetsam and said, "Why does everybody give us such lame stories?"

Tristan said, "Officers, is there somethin' in this here apartment to steal? We're waitin' for Mr. Kessler, who wants us to help him haul some furniture and fix up this place for his pregnant daughter and her husband. It's a hot day, so we decided to pop open the window and sit in the shade and suck on a brew till he shows up. No harm, no foul. Okay?"

Flotsam glanced at his partner, who'd finished writing FI cards on both men. Jetsam signaled by raising his eyebrows almost imperceptibly.

Flotsam said, "Okay, Mr. Hawkins, but maybe next time you should sit on the step outside to wait for your boss instead of scaring the neighbors."

"I hear you," Tristan said. "We're sorry."

When the cops had gone, Jerzy said, "So your name's Hawkins. What's your Christian name? Or are you a fuckin' Muslim?"

"Whadda you care?" Tristan said.

"I jist wanna know if it's a circumcised cock or an uncircumcised one that I'm gonna cut off and jam down your throat if you get me busted behind this crazy fuckin' scheme of yours."

During all the goings-on at the supermarket, and just after the surfer cops had departed from the duplex-office, Dewey Gleason as Jakob Kessler showed up, carrying an overnight bag, and unlocked the door. He'd never bothered to have the place alarmed, because there was nothing of value there. It was no more than a convenient spot to meet his runners, pay them, and receive the fruits of their labor.

He was surprised to find Creole and Jerzy Szarpowicz already inside, waiting for him. Creole was wearing a white Polo shirt and chinos, as though he was ready to work a job for him at a westside hotel. As usual, the Polack, in his black T-shirt, filthy jeans, and boots, looked like he'd just crawled off a Harley. Wearing his baseball hat backward made Jerzy even more repugnant to Dewey, if that was possible.

Dewey said in his accented Kessler voice, "How did you get in here?"

"Pried the window open with this," Jerzy said, holding a big screwdriver like a stabbing instrument as he stepped between Dewey and the only exit door.

"You did what?" Dewey said, his accent slipping a bit.

"It's a hot and smoggy day," Jerzy said. "We wanted to relax inside. In fact, we bought a six-pack. How 'bout a brew? They're in the fridge."

"This is an outrage!" Dewey said, not sounding as outrageous as he wanted to sound. "I want to know what game you two think you are playing."

"We ain't—aren't playin' a game, Mr. Kessler," Tristan said, correcting himself by force of habit when talking to this man.

"What *are* you doing, then?"

"We're formin' a partnership," Tristan said. "You're the senior partner and we're the junior partners. We're willin' to work real hard. Sixteen hours a day if you want. But we're takin' a percentage of what we make together. No more chump change."

Dewey turned as though to leave, but Jerzy didn't budge. He stood with his arms folded, looking down at Dewey. Then he showed Dewey a mirthless smile, and said, "Siddown. Take a load off. Lose the wig. Lose the glasses. And lose the fuckin' elevators. We saw you without them. You're kind of a cute little shit when you ain't playin' gestapo."

"I am leaving!" Dewey cried, and he pushed past Jerzy, who dropped the screwdriver and grabbed Dewey around the neck, driving his fist into Dewey's midsection. Then he did it twice more.

"Chill, wood!" Tristan yelled. "What the fuck you doin'?"

As Dewey slid to the floor, gasping and going fetal, Jerzy said, "I'm cuttin' to the fuckin' chase. I'm sick of this game. I'm gettin' his attention. You got a problem with that?"

Then he snatched the gray hairpiece, tape and all, from Dewey's head, jerked the steel-frame glasses from Dewey's face and tossed them on the kitchen table, and, for good measure, pulled the $600 elevator shoes from Dewey's feet.

"Look at these skates, Creole!" Jerzy said. "I put these on, I could look like Frankenstein."

You already do, you dumb Polack, Tristan thought, and you're about to fuck up my whole play here!

Then Jerzy grabbed the man by the front of his shirt and made a fist, as though he were going to move his facial bones around. Now the big Polack was scaring Tristan as much as he was the man on the floor.

"Don't go turbo, dawg!" Tristan said. "Step off! We don't wanna kill the man. We wanna work with him. Jist chill, okay?"

"Okay," Jerzy said. "But I got a feelin' this actor's gonna sing better if I tune him up."

"Help me get him in the chair," Tristan said, taking hold of Dewey's right arm.

Dewey's gasps turned to groans mixed with a few sobs when they each took an arm and, lifting him to his feet, put him in the overstuffed chair that Jerzy knew from experience was full of fleas. Then Jerzy grabbed a kitchen chair, placed it facing the door, and straddled it, arms crossed on the backrest.

"I'm sorry about the violence," Tristan said to Dewey. "I don't work that way, but you got my partner upset when you tried to bounce."

Jerzy pulled the buck knife from his boot, held it up beside his face as though to shave with it, and said, "In case you try again, Mr. Kessler."

"What name do you want us to call you?" Tristan said to Dewey, who was in pain with every breath he took.

"I don't...don't give a shit what you call me," Dewey said, unaccented. "Just take my money and get out."

"The man thinks we're thieves," Jerzy said. "Common fuckin' thieves. I'm insulted. How 'bout you, Creole?"

Tristan had not expected anything like this and was trying to readjust his approach, now that the dumb Polack had freaked out.

He said to Dewey Gleason, "What name do you want us to call you?"

"My name's Bernie Graham," Dewey said. "Whadda you want from me?"

"Like I said..., Bernie," Tristan said, "we're gonna be partners."

"I think you're both crazy," Dewey said and then winced again as he tried to move to a more comfortable position in the chair.

"We were very patient, buyin' into your Nazi act," Jerzy said. "Lettin' you take advantage of our hard work with the minimum wages you paid us. It's different now."

"Is this a kidnap?" Dewey said. "If it is, I don't have any money at home. There's about six hundred and change in my wallet. Take it and go."

"Who do you got at home?" Tristan asked.

"Nobody. I live alone."

"Where do you live?" Tristan asked.

"What difference does it make?"

"Don't make me get up," Jerzy said.

"I live in Sherman Oaks," Dewey lied. "In an apartment."

"Alone, huh?" Tristan said.

"I live with my dog." Another lie, and he winced again.

"Yeah, I seen her," Tristan said. "You got that part right."

Dewey said, "What?"

"You oughtta take her to a groomer once in a while," Tristan said. "Get her shampooed and fluffed up. She smells like an ashtray."

That got Dewey's attention. His eyes widened, and he said, "What's going on here?"

"And while you're at it, get yourself flea-dipped, Bernie," Jerzy said, "after sittin' in that chair."

"We know where you live," Tristan said. "On Franklin. And we know your geek, Miss Nicotine Fingers. How many computers is she runnin'?"

After a long silence, Tristan said, "And of course we know where your storage locker is. And we know about the job you did on the owner of that house in Los Feliz. Wait'll he gets his American Express statement."

"You were in on that," Dewey said. "You made money from that."

"Chump change," Jerzy said. "Chicken feed for pigeons."

"I got a friend at Hollywood Station," Tristan lied. "A detective who busted me a while back. If I was to call him now and tell him all I know about you, he'd see to it that I get a suspended sentence and probation for dimin' you."

"How about your partner?" Dewey said, his mind racing, trying to digest all of this. "Is he willing to go down with me?"

"Me?" Jerzy said. "I'd flip too and get the same deal Creole gets. The DA would probably buy us French dips downtown at Philippe's when we get through testifyin'."

"You won't call the cops," Dewey said, so scared that his teeth clicked together when he talked. "You don't wanna get arrested. There's nothing in it for you."

"Sure there is, dude," Jerzy said. "We get to take you way down and see you go to the joint, where some of Creole's dark-skinned cousins will turn you into a screamin' bitch. I would like that because I don't like you..., Bernie."

"You wouldn't let yourselves get busted just to bring me down," Dewey said painfully. "You're bluffing. This is all bullshit."

Tristan laughed out loud at that and said, "Sure we are, bro! You're too smart to think we'd go to jail even for a day jist to nail your puny ass. No, you and your geek can get outta Dodge tonight if that's what you wanna do. This crazy Polack and me, we're gonna sit up on your crib and watch the door. If you two go, all you can take is the clothes on your back and an extra set of underwear. Your computers, all your checks and credit-card equipment, all the files you prob'ly have inside there—all that precious information stays. Not to mention your storage room full of very valuable goods. The second we see you drive off, I'm gonna call the cops, like the good CI that I am. And then they make their big recovery of stolen goods and all the rest of the stuff you got at your crib. By the way, Bernie, CI stands for 'confidential informant' in cop talk. In case you didn't know."

"I'd like to take a piece of him to leave behind before he says good-bye to Hollywood," Jerzy said, pointing the buck knife at Dewey.

Ignoring Jerzy, who was wrecking the conversation flow by terrorizing the man, Tristan said, "I'll get in real good with that detective for providin' him with information that breaks up a criminal enterprise. It's always good to have a get-outta-jail-free card from a cop. How much is everything worth that you'll leave in the apartment and in the storage room? That's what you're gonna lose, along with the whole business you worked so hard to start up. Are you ready to give up your entire livelihood to keep from payin' your junior partners a reasonable percentage of what we can all earn together from now on? Are you that dumb, Bernie?"

Dewey was quietly watching Tristan. Then he looked at Jerzy and back at Tristan, and he said, "Were you the guy from Water and Power?"

"You ain't—aren't the only actor in Hollywood, Bernie," Tristan said with another hearty laugh.

"Get me one of those beers from the fridge," Dewey said. "Help me sit up and we'll talk."

Tristan said, "Get the man a beer, wood." And he helped Dewey sit up straight in the chair.

Jerzy said, "He oughtta get his own fuckin' beer. What am I, his personal negro?" But he did as he was told, grumbling as usual.

"Open that bag," Dewey said to Tristan, "and give me the hand towel and the loafers."

"Sure," Tristan said, putting the overnight bag on the kitchen table, opening it, and finding casual clothes neatly folded, a pair of Bernie Graham glasses, and the Bernie Graham mustache.

"Is this your props and makeup department, Bernie?" Tristan said. "Who are you when you change into this?"

"A guy named Bernie Graham," Dewey said. "That's what you can call me."

"Wanna put them on?" Tristan asked, fascinated now. "Would it make you feel better if we let you, like, get into character? Is that what it's called?"

"Just give me the towel."

Tristan threw the hand towel to Dewey. Then he and Jerzy pulled up kitchen chairs and sat watching.

"The spray bottle," Dewey said.

Tristan handed him the plastic bottle and he sprayed it directly onto his face and wiped the shadows from under his eyes and around his mouth, and then sprayed more onto the towel and wiped his sideburns free of the gray.

"I suppose you want your comb and brush," Tristan said, handing them to the man.

"Thank you," Dewey said, and he took the comb and brush and worked on his hair while Jerzy stood watching with Dewey's can of beer in his hand.

"What the fuck is this anyways?" Jerzy said. "The *Creole and Bernie Show*?"

"Let the man get into character," Tristan said. "Want your stash, Bernie?"

"Thank you," Dewey said, carefully sticking the mustache over his upper lip. "And my Bernie glasses, please."

"They busted when I tossed them on the table," Jerzy said.

"Those are my Kessler glasses," Dewey said. "I'll never need those again." And he held his palm below his eyes and removed both contact lenses, which had lightened his brown irises.

"Ain't that some shit, wood?" Tristan said with admiration. "I'm proud to be a partner of this man!"

Dewey said, "The reason I'm getting into character, as you call it, is because I have to meet a new runner here in thirty minutes. Would you please help me get into my loafers? I can't manage. I think I have a cracked rib."

"Puttin' the man's shoes on his feet is definitely a job for you, Creole," Jerzy said, handing the beer to Dewey. "There's some things a self-respectin' white man won't do."

After Dewey looked sufficiently like the person that his new runner was expecting to meet, he gulped some of the beer and said, "It's amazing how good a cold beer tastes after someone has just beaten the living shit out of you."

"Forgive and forget, dude," Jerzy said. "Close the book on that misunderstandin', but make sure there ain't another one."

"The first thing I have to say," Dewey began, "is that you're right. Just getting outta town with the clothes on my back is not in the cards. And neither is the partnership that you envision."

"Don't back up on us, Bernie," Jerzy said ominously.

"Let the man finish," Tristan said.

"But I think we can work together and come up with a plan that'll make you a lump sum far beyond what you could make working an entire year with me."

"Doin' what?" Tristan said.

"The geek, as you call her, is my wife. She's a brilliant hacker and has accounts that I have no way to access. In fact, I don't even know which bank they're in. If we could devise a way to make her give me some information I'd need, I'd be grateful enough to pay you half of what's in those accounts."

"And how much would that be?" Tristan asked.

"Maybe as much as eighty thousand dollars," Dewey lied. "You would get half of that amount."

"Forty grand?" Tristan said. "Whadda we gotta do? Torture it outta her? We don't do violence."

"You couldn't prove it by me," Dewey said, moving painfully in the chair.

"You mean you jist can't tell the bitch to give it up?" Jerzy said. "What kinda man are you, Bernie?"

"Not a confrontational one," Dewey said. "She was married before we met, and she had already set this up. She does all the secret banking online and in private."

"That's kinda like a prenup, ain't—isn't it?" Tristan said. "That you agreed to?"

"Her version of one," Dewey said. "It's her money, not mine, she says. But I think I've earned it more than she has."

"You said 'accounts,'" Tristan said. "You think there might be more than one bank account?"

Dewey was thinking fast, trying to sell his story to Creole, who was obviously the intellectual superior of the two.

"Of course we have lots of small bank accounts that we open and close under different names when we have to move money around. That's how I get cash for the runners. But the secret account is the one I'm interested in learning about."

"Could there be more than just the eighty grand?" Tristan asked. "You two do some pretty good business."

Dewey told a whopper, saying, "No, I don't think so. If you added up all the accounts she's opened and the ones I've opened, there might be another two thousand in there. Whatever there is I'll split with you if we can agree on a sensible plan for making her cooperate."

"Do you have a plan in mind, Bernie?" Tristan asked.

"This meeting today has opened certain doors and made it all very urgent. I need some time to think."

"We ain't got time for you to think," Jerzy said, getting his mind around a $40,000 payday. "So what if we was to, like, kidnap you? We could phone and tell her we're gangsters and we know all about your business and we're holdin' you for ransom. And we'll cut your fuckin' throat if she don't give up what's in the bank. Wouldn't she pay us to save the love of her life?"

Dewey flashed a weak, ironic grin, took a sip of beer, and said, "To tell you the truth, Jerzy, I think she'd go ahead and leave everything behind and be on the first flight out of L.A. I think that within six months she'd have another Bernie Graham working his ass off for her, and she wouldn't think twice about the husband she left in the hands of kidnappers. In fact, I think she might see right through your plan and figure that I was in on it. She's very cunning and clever."

Tristan, who'd been listening quietly and thinking, said, "There's not much use in goin' home and sleepin' on it. There's only one answer here."

"What's that, mastermind?" Jerzy said.

"We gotta kidnap *her,* not Bernie, and we gotta make it look good. We gotta put more fear in her than we put in Bernie today. And Bernie's gotta play his part and have very serious phone talks with her, where she's so scared she begs him to pay the ransom of, say, a hundred grand."

Jerzy snapped open another beer, guzzled most of it, pointed to Bernie, and said, "He says there's only eighty in the account."

"Dawg," Tristan said patiently, "if we ask for eighty, she'll know for sure Bernie's in on the game."

Now it was Dewey who appeared to be deep in thought, and he surprised Tristan when he said, "Don't ask for a hundred. Make it five hundred thousand. That's a nice round number. Why not be extravagant?"

Tristan paused just for an instant and said, "Why ask her for an amount that's gonna make her think it's all hopeless, Bernie?"

"It gives us a chance to pile on the bullshit during negotiations," Dewey said much too quickly. "You know, back and forth. The price gets whittled down, because that's what kidnappers do when they have to. She has to finally be convinced that you thugs are gonna settle for the eighty grand because you're satisfied there's no more in the bank."

"All this makes me not wanna pop the question to my bitch if this is what marriage does to people," Jerzy said with a bemused smile. "Anyways, she don't do drugs, so a mixed marriage wouldn't work."

Tristan stood up and said, "And what if your wife don't wanna cooperate, Bernie? Then what?"

Dewey finished the beer, groaned in pain, licked the foam from his lips, and said, "She will have to be made to believe you're for real."

"Bernie," Tristan said, "let's hope she believes our bluff. Far as I'm concerned, the game's over if she figures out it's you that's behind this thing. Or if she decides to die for her money rather than let you get your hands on it, I'm tellin' you right now, I'm outta there. I ain't gonna torture no woman. I'll walk away from this whole gag."

"How do you feel about it?" Dewey asked Jerzy.

"That's a lotta money to walk away from," Jerzy said. "I think we gotta convince her to talk. If you got her back with some minor damage, it'd be okay with you, huh?"

"I won't be getting her back," Dewey said. "If she doesn't give up the information, it's probably because she figures I'm in on it. She'll dump me, so I'll be gone either way with whatever I can get for the stuff in the storage room. Which of course I'll share with you fifty-fifty."

"You got a lot ridin' on this game, don't you, Bernie?" Tristan said.

"You forced the issue," Dewey said. "I have no choice. If it all goes sideways, the only good thing is, she can't go to the cops about us without going to jail herself when the whole gag is busted wide open. Anyway, I'm willing to try it if you are."

"You're a cold-blooded little motherfucker," Jerzy said. "I'm startin' to like you a lot. So how're we gonna go about kidnappin' your old lady?"

"That's gonna be easier than you think because you're gonna kidnap both of us," Dewey said.

"What?" Tristan said. "*Both* of you?"

"It's the only way it can work," Dewey said. "I have to be there as another kidnap victim to make her believe it. And I have to help persuade her to talk."

"And you think you can do that?" Tristan said.

"Yes," Dewey said, "because I'm a real actor, even if that bitch never gives me credit for it. When I perform, I can convince anybody of anything. Creole, I'll call you tomorrow afternoon with a foolproof plan."

"Somethin' bothers me about this," Tristan said. "If she gives up what you need to find her secret account, you ain't gonna be able to slide on into her bank and pull out the cash. You'll transfer the money to one of your runner accounts, am I right?"

"Yes," Dewey said, surprised.

"Well, if I remember right from when I helped do the books at the dance studio where I used to work, there's a ten-day waitin' period at the banks for big transfers to clear. Am I right?"

Dewey hadn't counted on Creole having a whole lot more between his ears than Jerzy, but now he could see how he'd completely misjudged his runner. If they suspected that Dewey was after Eunice's hidden treasure chest of *cash*, this whole gag could explode in his face.

Dewey wore his mask of sincerity when he said, "The bank where I'll transfer the funds to is a small independent bank that I've done lots of questionable business with. I know the manager exceedingly well. There won't be a ten-day wait. In fact, it'll take two days at most and we'll have our money."

Dewey figured that two days would be enough time for him to tie up loose ends and get the hell out of L.A. with Eunice's "retirement fund." He looked into Creole's amber eyes for any hint of disbelief but saw none.

Dewey watched him nod to Jerzy and say, "Can we hold her for two days, wood?"

"That's a long time to keep her," Jerzy said.

"That's a lot of money," Dewey countered, touching his ribs and grimacing.

"Okay," Tristan said, "but remember, if you decide to get outta Hollywood tonight, one of us will be campin' out right near your crib."

"I understand," Dewey said. "Now you can go ahead and leave. I'm expecting the runner any minute. You're welcome to sit out on Franklin Avenue tonight and watch my front door if you want, but I guarantee I'm going nowhere but to bed. If I can make it there. You boys have actually brought things to a head. I should thank you, and I will when it's over. For now, take two hundred from my wallet and have a nice meal on me."

"From what I saw of your woman, she's older than you, ain't—isn't she?" Tristan said.

"Yes," Dewey said. "Several years older."

Tristan grinned and said, "I saw a story on *Access Hollywood* that claims older women with younger guys makes for married bliss in this town, Bernie."

Dewey showed a crooked grin, adjusted his stick-on mustache, and said, "It's true that we've got an age spread like some famous Hollywood couples. But Demi Moore and Ashton Kutcher we are *not*."

★ FIFTEEN ★ ★

WHEN TRISTAN AND JERZY WERE BACK in the Chevy, heading to Pablo's Tacos for Jerzy to buy a taste of crystal meth, Tristan said, "Dawg, that half a million ransom we're gonna ask for means more than Bernie says it means."

"So what's it mean?" Jerzy asked.

"It means there's a whole lotta money that the woman is in control of, and he don't even know how much there is. He's fishin' to find out from her. He figures to game her for as much as half a million and only give us a measly forty grand. And another thing, I don't believe his bullshit about a deal with some banker so he don't have to wait ten days to draw out transferred funds. I think her money's in cash someplace. She ain't no different from dope dealers or anybody else on the game. She don't want money where the state or the feds or the IRS can grab it if she gets busted. What we gotta do is figure out how to take the real money away from him after he gets his hands on it."

Jerzy thought it over for a long while and said, "Damn, Creole, your daddy *musta* been a white man."

Malcolm found the door partially open when he arrived. Still, he knocked on it and said, "Mr. Graham, you there?"

Dewey said, "Come in, Clark."

Malcolm found Dewey still sitting in the chair where Tristan and Jerzy had left him. He was sweating and pale.

"Are you okay, Mr. Graham?" Malcolm asked.

"I had an accident," Dewey said. "I fell. I think a rib is broken. Maybe more than one."

Malcolm said, "Do you want me to call an ambulance?"

"No, I think I'll be okay by tomorrow. But could you help me get up?"

"Sure," Malcolm said, taking Dewey around the torso and lifting.

Dewey cried out in pain, and Malcolm said, "I better put you back down."

"No!" Dewey said. "Just help me walk out to my car. And please carry my bag for me."

Malcolm picked up the overnight bag and said, "You can't drive a car, Mr. Graham. You better let me call you an ambulance."

"Just help me, please," Dewey said, putting his right arm around the young man's neck, his left arm pressed close to his damaged ribs.

They weren't halfway down the walkway before Dewey said, "You're right. I can't drive a car. I'll give you fifty dollars to take me home in my car. I live on Franklin west of Cahuenga. I'll have my secretary drive you back to get your car."

"Mr. Graham," Malcolm said before he helped Dewey into the passenger seat of the Honda, "you got a couple little bugs jumping all over your head. Can't you feel them?"

"Oh, Christ!" Dewey whined. "I'm in too much pain to worry about fleas."

When they got to Dewey's security gate, he pointed to his remote and Malcolm pressed it and drove down below the apartment building into the parking garage.

"Put it in my space, number twelve," Dewey said.

Climbing the stairs, one at a time, brought steady moans from Dewey punctuated by sharp cries when Malcolm moved too fast. After they struggled to the landing, Dewey was wishing he'd let the kid take him to the hospital. What if a rib punctured a lung or something? He wanted to plot some sort of revenge for what the slob did to him, but for now he only wanted to lie down in bed and remain immobile.

"Ring the bell, Clark," Dewey said.

Malcolm pushed the button, and they waited. Dewey figured that Eunice was peering out through the peephole, so he said, "Come on, open the goddamn door. I'm hurt."

The door cracked opened a bit, and Eunice peeked out, cigarette dangling, and said, "What the hell's going on?"

"Open the door wide, for chrissake!" Dewey said. "I can't walk without help."

Eunice opened the door, stepping back, and she said to Malcolm, "I'll take over. Wait outside."

When Malcolm released his hold, Dewey's knees buckled and he said, "Don't let go of me, Clark! Take me to my bedroom. Hurry up."

"He can't come in here!" Eunice said.

"Just shut up and get outta the way," Dewey said. "Come on, kid, walk me straight ahead to the hallway, and we'll make a turn to the right."

Malcolm looked in astonishment at the computer screens that were lit and full of names and numbers. Then he walked slowly to the hallway, holding Dewey upright.

"The second room, Clark," Dewey said. "Just take me in there, and we'll try to get my ass on the bed without ripping my guts out."

Malcolm helped Dewey across the small bedroom to a double bed and helped him sit. "Easy, now," Dewey said. "Don't move fast. Just scoot me slow and easy, and let me lie down on my side. Then try to lift my legs up onto the bed without killing me."

The young man followed directions, with Dewey groaning incessantly. When his legs were elevated onto the bed, Dewey said, "Now just flip me from my side onto my back. Gently. Very gently."

When he was finally supine, Dewey said, "Okay, that's better. Now step outside into the computer room and ask my ... secretary to come in."

A moment later, Eunice entered and closed the door, saying, "Well, now you really did it, Dewey. That boy just had a good look at our operation. Whadda we have to do to keep his mouth shut? Adopt him?"

"The kid doesn't know anything, Eunice," Dewey said, staring upward. "He just wants to make a buck."

"The hell he doesn't know anything," she said. "He's a new runner, isn't he? What's he supposed to think about the computers and the files? And oh, yeah, I have credit cards scattered all over the table, most of which are almost useless thanks to the poor quality of material you're paying for these days. You just completely breached our security that I worked so hard to set up."

"He's a know-nothing kid," Dewey said. "Kee-rist, Eunice!"

"He only knows you as Bernie Graham, right?"

"Yeah," Dewey muttered. "And you're my secretary, Ethel, okay?"

"You really did it now, Dewey," she said, shaking her head.

"Okay, Eunice," Dewey said. "Go out there and kill him. Asphyxiate him with cigarette smoke. But then you can dispose of his body all by yourself because I...am...fucking...hurt! Not that you give a shit!"

"So, what really happened to you, Dewey?"

"I got in a beef with one of the runners. A slob called Jerzy who's not quite as big as a Humvee."

"The old guy? He beat you up?"

"No, that's Old Jerzy. I told you, he's gone. I got beat up by New Jerzy."

"Jesus Christ!" Eunice said. "Old Jerzy, New Jerzy, what the hell am I doing in this nutty fucking arrangement?"

"It was over a payment I owed him," Dewey said with a sigh. "He wanted more. He's a tweaker and he turned violent."

"Tweakers again!" she said. "No matter how many times I say no tweakers, you still end up working with them. Is that kid in the other room a tweaker?"

"That kid is a baby," Dewey said. "He's a nice, polite boy who wants to make some extra change. If he hadn't showed up, I woulda had to call an ambulance."

"Okay, so if you really think you got broken ribs, then let him take you to the ER at Hollywood Pres. I don't want paramedics coming in here to haul you out."

"My ribs're feeling a little better. I don't think they're broken. I just need a good night's sleep."

"So, what am I supposed to say to the kid?" Eunice asked. "Now that he's in a position to extort us?"

"Say good-bye," Dewey muttered, "after you drive him back to the office. And give him fifty bucks for his trouble."

"We better be planning to move," Eunice said before opening the door. "I hope you enjoy your nap, because I won't sleep a wink tonight." She made no effort to hide a little sneer, adding, "And Dewey, take off that stupid fucking mustache."

When she closed the door, Dewey lay still, thinking maybe he could persuade Jerzy to make the kidnapping look extra real by giving Eunice a few of his special knuckle shots to her fat gut. Just to see how she liked it.

Twilight had come to Hollywood and brought with it the endless streams of traffic. When they got trapped by two signal sequences at a stoplight on Hollywood Boulevard, Eunice said to Malcolm Rojas, "You can call me Ethel. What's your name?"

"Clark," Malcolm said.

"We better not waste time," Eunice said, "so I can hurry back and tend to the wounded. You may have noticed he doesn't suffer in silence."

Eunice drove and Malcolm sat quietly. Several times she found herself glancing over at him. He was a handsome kid, she had to admit that much. He was youthfully slender, with delicate features that made him look sensitive. She loved his curly hair and his heavy black lashes over those burning dark eyes. Yes, he was a really good-looking boy.

Finally she said, "Do you have a job, Clark?"

"Yes," he said, "I work at a home improvement center in the warehouse."

"Do you like the work?"

"No," he said. "It's boring. I'm hoping Mr. Graham can get me some work that's more—"

"Exciting?"

"Not really exciting, but—"

"Challenging?"

"Yes, that's it. Challenging."

"Mr. Graham is good at finding challenging jobs for young people," Eunice said. "Maybe he can accommodate you."

Malcolm surprised her when he said, "How about you? How long have you been Mr. Graham's secretary?"

"Nine years," she said.

"Is he a nice boss to work for?"

She had to smile. This boy! She hadn't been around anyone like him since, well, she couldn't remember when. "He can be nice," she said. "I'm sure he'll be nice to you, because you're nice."

She looked over at him and he smiled shyly at the compliment. They rode quietly again, but she still found herself glancing over. At last she said, "You have such gorgeous color. I was wondering, are you Hispanic?"

"No," he said quickly. "My mother was a Persian. Her family was wealthy but they had to get out of their country and come to America poor. She's dead now. My father was a French chef who worked in some of the best restaurants in New York. He's dead too."

Eunice didn't believe a word of it. Just another Mexican-American kid, she figured, but with a rich imagination. Touching. It was touching to be with him. She was feeling emotions she hadn't felt in years. She was feeling like a girl!

When they got back to the duplex, Malcolm said, "That's my car, the old Mustang."

"A Mustang!" Eunice said. "My boyfriend had a Mustang when I was in high school."

When she parked at the curb, she turned off the headlights. She had an uncontrollable urge to talk longer with this boy.

He started to get out, and she opened her purse and said, "Wait a minute. Don't you want your money? Mr. Graham promised you fifty dollars, didn't he?"

Malcolm said, "Yeah, but I can't take money for helping a man who was injured. Anybody should do that for free. Just tell him I'll be waiting for his call."

"Wait a minute, Clark!" Eunice said, stunned. When was the last time she'd dealt with anybody who'd turned down money? She closed her purse and said, "What kind of burgers do you like? I'm gonna get me a Whopper. Wanna follow me? I'm buying."

"Well...," he said. "Maybe I should—"

"Come on. You gotta be hungry," Eunice said. "I'm starved. We can talk about the business, if you like."

That did it. He wanted to learn more about what Bernie Graham might expect from him and how much money he could make. He followed her to Burger King, where they parked in the lot and went inside.

Malcolm stood examining the wall menu, deciding what he was going to order, while Eunice was in the restroom. When she returned, her hair was combed and she was wearing fresh lipstick and even some eye shadow. Malcolm didn't like it, seeing her made up like this. It made her look...flirty. He felt himself getting angry, but he had to control it if he wanted to work for her boss, Bernie Graham.

"I think I'll do like you and have a Whopper," he said, concentrating on the menu. "And a Coke, please."

After she ordered at the counter and their burgers were ready, she brought a tray to the table where Malcolm waited. Eunice put Malcolm's burger and drink in front of him, along with a paper napkin.

"There," she said. "You're too thin to be missing meals."

Malcolm said, "If you could explain to me some of the ins and outs of the business, I'd really appreciate it. I want Mr. Graham to be happy with my work."

"How old are you, Clark?" Eunice asked.

"Nineteen. But Mr. Graham said I could pass for twenty-one."

"That's astounding," Eunice said, smiling tenderly. "I can't remember the last time I talked to someone who wanted to look older."

Malcolm did not like the way she was staring at him. He didn't like the way the conversation was going. He suddenly experienced a wave of nausea and even fear, but he held it back, forcing himself to concentrate on the food.

"The burger is awesome," he said. "Thanks a lot, Ethel."

*   *   *

"You ever throw a rock at our car again and I'll kill you and everyone you know," Flotsam said to the Salvadoran kid who was sitting on the curb with three other Latino teenagers after 6-X-32 stopped and the surfer cops got out. They made all four boys kneel with their hands on their heads, and they kept flashlight beams on them while they patted them down.

"I didn't throw no rock," the kid said with a giggle.

Flotsam was pretty sure the rock had come from him, the one with the goofy grin. They were in a graffiti-tagged residential neighborhood in east Hollywood. The boy was thirteen years old, an aspiring member of MS-13, the world's largest gang. But at this stage he was just a play gangster, just a wannabe.

Jetsam motioned for them to get to their feet and put their hands down, and he said, "Who threw it, then?"

"I didn't see no rock throwed," the kid said.

"Maybe that was a hummingbird sailing over our car," Flotsam said.

"Maybe a bat," the kid said, giggling again. "There's lotsa bats flying around here."

The other kids chortled at that, and Flotsam said, "You ever hit our car with a rock and I'll kill you, your momma, and your dog."

"Our dog is with my brother, Chuey," the kid said, giggling again, as a tricked-out lowrider squealed around the corner from the boulevard onto the residential street. The kid turned to look in the direction of the car and said, "Yo, here comes Chuey now!"

Flotsam and Jetsam turned toward the green lowrider with gleaming spinner wheels, and when Chuey spotted the black-and-white, he floored it to the end of the street, where he made a screaming left turn.

The surfer cops jumped in their shop, ripped a rubber-burning U-ee, and went after the lowrider. Chuey had second thoughts and stopped two blocks away rather than try to escape. It was another dark residential street like the first one, with modest homes interspersed among deteriorating apartment buildings. Somebody was destroying eardrums in the house nearest to them, playing hard rock that neither cop recognized. Salsa music was competing with it in the apartment building next to that house, with a Marc Anthony CD cranked up to decibel overload.

Flotsam approached on the driver's side and Jetsam on the passenger side of the car, both moving cautiously, lighting up the interior with their flashlight beams. Neither of them saw Chuey's "passenger," who was lying down on the backseat.

When Flotsam got parallel with the backseat, Chuey rolled down his window and said to the tall cop, "Be careful, man."

Flotsam put his hand on his nine and said, "Careful of what?" and found out when a Rottweiler rose up and roared, lunging at the rear window that was open six inches for ventilation.

"Whoa!" Flotsam yelped and drew his Beretta reflexively.

Jetsam almost drew but relented when he saw that the dog could not get out. Then he said, "Bro, that is a major canine. Hugangus, I would call it."

Flotsam's hands were shaking when he holstered his pistol. "Step outta the car, dude," he said to Chuey.

"I can't," Chuey said, eyes red and watery, clearly tanked, which explained his initial panic.

He was no more than twenty years old and was inked up gangster-style. Of course, Flotsam directed his flashlight beam on Chuey's hands, and in this case he was looking for more than a weapon. He was looking for an MS-13 tattoo but he didn't see one.

"Whaddaya mean you can't?" Flotsam said.

"If I do, my dog's gonna come over that seat before I can close the door, and he'll go for you."

"He does and I'll shoot him," Flotsam said.

Then Chuey said, "You can't shoot him! That dog's like my brother, man!"

"That dog is smarter than your brother," Jetsam said. "We just met him back there."

"You shoot my dog, I'll sue your ass!" Chuey said.

"We're gonna give you a sobriety test, dog or no dog," Flotsam said.

"I'm warning you, man!" Chuey said.

"No, I'm warning *you,* dude," Flotsam said. "And for the last time, get the fuck outta that car."

Flotsam's tone got the massive canine growling and his fangs bared.

By the time that growl came from deep within the animal's chest to his throat and past his bone-crunching jaws, it was a lion's roar.

"Partner!" Flotsam called. "Come around here and cover me!"

Jetsam ran around the car, drawing his Glock, while Flotsam grabbed the door handle.

"You chickenshit motherfucker!" Chuey said. "You shoot my dog and there's gonna be payback! I'll find out where you live!"

Seeing that Jetsam had the man and dog covered with his pistol, Flotsam drew his side-handle baton from the ring on his Sam Browne. The batons were made of aircraft aluminum and were supposedly unbreakable under normal conditions. Flotsam figured this might turn out to be a real test of that claim.

"You on it, dude?" he said to his partner.

"Good to go, bro," Jetsam said, directing his flashlight beam and his gun on whatever came out that door in a hurry.

Flotsam jerked open the car door, and Chuey turned in his seat, trying but failing to stop the 140-pound animal. In fact, the surging Rottweiler shoved Chuey out onto the street flat on his face, a pint bottle of vodka he'd been concealing behind him spilling onto the asphalt. And then the dog paused for a few seconds on the front seat, snarling at the cops.

Flotsam dropped his flashlight and, instinctively holding the baton high in the air to deliver a hammer blow, said, "Here he comes!"

But suddenly the animal froze. The brute stopped growling. His huge mouth opened wide and his tongue lolled out. And he started barking, an excited bark, without menace.

Flotsam said, "What the fuck?" and stepped back.

The dog leaped onto the street while Jetsam aimed his pistol directly at the animal's massive skull. But the dog sat, looking at the taller cop and barking happily.

"Bro!" Jetsam cried. "The baton!"

"He can have it!" Flotsam cried. And then to the animal he said, "Okay, doggy! Fetch! Fetch!" And he hurled the baton with all his strength and heard it clattering to the pavement forty yards down the darkened street.

The Rottweiler yapped with joy and raced after the baton as Flotsam picked up his flashlight, and Jetsam grabbed Chuey by the back of his collar. They quickly handcuffed the prisoner and dragged him to their shop, throwing him into the backseat. Then both cops leaped into the black-and-white and Flotsam made a faster U-turn than he had when Chuey had tried to get away from them.

Thirty seconds later, the Rottweiler was running back to the car with the aluminum baton in his teeth. But when he saw the car had gone, he dropped the baton and chased the black-and-white, howling.

Chuey's brother and his friends were surprised to see the police car speeding back toward them, and the kid thought he heard a dog barking furiously farther north on the street. The barking seemed to be getting closer. It sounded like a big dog. It sounded like *their* dog, and he was coming their way.

Flotsam slowed and yelled, "Grab your mutt when he gets here! Your brother's going to jail for DUI."

Then Flotsam floored it again and circled the block until he was back to Chuey's lowrider. They stopped to lock the car and give Chuey his keys.

"I gotta find Excalibur!" Flotsam said, jumping out of the car with a flashlight, searching for his baton.

Jetsam said, "Make it fast, bro, before the dog figures out he's been gamed and comes looking for revenge!"

Flotsam yelled, "Eureka!" when he found the baton resting against the tire of a parked car. He picked it up and ran to their shop, giving the baton a kiss before putting it in the door rack. Suddenly, he was wiping his mouth on the shirtsleeve of his uniform.

"Gross!" he said. "I kissed dog slobber!"

When they were on their way to Hollywood Station, their silent prisoner made an observation, his first words spoken since being pushed out of his car by the Rottweiler.

Chuey said, "Fernando just wants to chase sticks, man. He can do it all day long."

Jetsam, coming down from the waning adrenaline rush, said, "Is Fernando the one with two legs or four?"

SIXTEEN

O<small>F COURSE</small>, neither Tristan nor Jerzy needed to watch the apartment of Dewey Gleason during the night. After Jerzy had been dropped off at his car, he'd driven home to Frogtown to smoke some glass and listen to his woman bitch at her brats. There was so much yelling and turmoil in the little house that he'd grabbed a blanket and pillow and gone out to drink some gin and find some peace in his car. The crystal, along with the gin and backseat sleeping, made for a fitful night, and his back was stiff and his neck ached when he woke up at 8:15 A.M.

Jerzy thought of the instructions from Creole to find a place in Frogtown where they could safely hold Bernie Graham's old lady for however long it might take to get the information. Jerzy didn't like the idea of keeping the woman in his own 'hood, but Creole convinced him that it should be in an area where people minded their own business, and this was as good as any place.

Frogtown was a strange little chunk of northeast Los Angeles, south of the junction of the Golden State and Glendale Freeways. It was quiet during the day, but at night, Latino gang members often emerged onto the streets like the frogs had done decades earlier, when the amphibians were still able to thrive in the L.A. River bordering on the east. The river in the summer was sometimes little more than a dirty stream running through a monstrous graffiti-tagged concrete trough, and no one had seen a frog in years.

After Jerzy did a gum rub with a few remaining granules of crank, he fixed himself a plate of scrambled eggs while his woman was gone on one of her constant trips to the middle school vice principal's office because of the latest fight one of her sons had started. Driving and canvassing the area, he spotted a "For Rent" sign in a window over of what had once been a *panadería*. On the wall of that defunct bakery was a vivid mural of barrio life depicting tattooed gang members alongside the Virgin of Guadalupe, who stood beside a canary-yellow lowrider Chevrolet with chrome spinners. It was the only wall on that part of the street that hadn't been tagged, so apparently the mural was respected.

What Jerzy liked about the building was that other than the little upstairs apartment, there were only commercial properties for two blocks, and the former bakery was a safe distance away from lofts occupied by the painters and sculptors who nowadays encouraged art walks and daytime visits from prospective clients. Jerzy figured that at night the closest commercial buildings would be empty of people and only occasionally visited by a private security service. There'd be little chance of anyone hearing something like a scream.

And that made him think of Bernie Graham's woman. It could come to that, a woman screaming. Creole didn't think so and didn't even want to plan for it, but Jerzy knew better. If the whole fucking game went sideways, it might come down to forcing the information out of her. He knew that Bernie Graham had the stomach for it even if the little nigger didn't. He phoned the number on the "For Rent" sign and learned that the tiny upstairs apartment could be rented, first and last month and security deposit, for a total of $2,500. He figured they were in business.

As bad as Jerzy Szarpowicz felt when he awoke that morning, he was in much better shape than Dewey Gleason, who'd slept perhaps two hours all night, in twenty-minute intervals. When he tentatively raised himself on an elbow and slid his legs over the side of the bed, he felt a sharp pain but ignored it and forced himself to stand. After that, he took a few hesitant steps to the bathroom, holding on to his midsection with both hands, as though something might drop onto the floor.

It wasn't as bad as he'd anticipated, and he even managed to take a shower and dress himself unassisted in a suitable Bernie Graham wardrobe: oxford cotton, long-sleeve shirt, tan casual pants, and Gucci knockoffs. He put the glasses and mustache in his shirt pocket and decided it was too hot and he was too sore to be bothering with a Bernie Graham blazer. When he gingerly entered the kitchen, Eunice was sitting at the table, drinking coffee and reading the *L.A. Times* with an ashtray full of butts in front of her.

She glanced up and said, "Well, well, look who's on his feet and breathing."

"Only breathing as much as I have to," he said. "For chrissake, why don't you open a window and let some smoke outta here?"

"The smoke eater's on the blink again. You gotta get it fixed."

"Just open a window, Eunice."

"Sure," she said, "may as well, now that you brought Clark here. I guess security doesn't matter anymore."

"I'm gonna call Clark today and hook up with him," Dewey said. "I'll make sure everything's cool with the kid."

Dewey opened the refrigerator and poured himself a glass of tomato juice while Eunice read silently. Then he opened a box of wheat bran and poured it into a bowl with some skim milk. He took it into the computer room just to get a short distance away from her cigarette, and he sat staring at computer number one. There was a page of indecipherable numbers on the screen and a list of names that meant something only to the woman in the other room.

He ate the wheat bran and fantasized about how, with a few movements and clicks of the mouse, someone with the right information could pull up the name of her bank and maybe transfer the funds to another bank anywhere in the world. If he could do that, his entire miserable life would be changed. Just like that.

Eunice interrupted his thoughts with her chronic morning cough and said, "Where you going today, Dewey?"

"I haven't seen the Mexicans in almost a week. They should be onto something by now. I was gonna track them down and then I thought I'd go to the second list of foreclosed homes and do the rental gag again." Lying, he added, "I got a new guy who can change the locks and make me some keys. This one's not a tweaker."

When he finished his cereal, he entered the kitchen and started to put the bowl and glass in the sink but then realized it would just give her something else to bitch about, so he put them in the dishwasher, and then went to the bathroom to brush his teeth. By the time he came out, Eunice was sitting in front of computer number three, tapping away with uninterrupted clicks.

"See you later," he said and opened the door.

"Dewey," she said, taking the cigarette out of her mouth.

He stopped in the doorway, expecting some more shit from her, and said, "Yeah?"

In an amicable voice the likes of which he hadn't heard in months, she said, "Did you say you were gonna see that kid today?"

"Yeah," he said. "Don't worry, I'll make sure everything's okay. I might give him some busywork and a couple hundred bucks to keep him happy."

"I was thinking," Eunice said. "Since he knows something now that nobody else does, we're gonna have to handle Clark with extra-special care."

"Yeah?" Dewey said. "You got a suggestion?"

"I was thinking that you better keep him close for a while."

"I don't think I'll have to adopt him," Dewey said.

"I'm just saying, maybe we should . . . get to know him," Eunice said.

"Like how?"

"Oh, how about we invite him to a nice restaurant tonight or tomorrow night? You know, talk to the boy? See where his head is? I sure wouldn't wanna pack up and move to another location real quick just because of him."

A look, a silence, and she returned to the computer keyboard, tapping the keys as though it had been a thought in passing.

"Maybe you're right," Dewey finally said. "I'll call and see if he's good to go for something like that. Maybe we could take him to Musso's. I can't remember the last time we went to dinner together."

"Okay," she said too casually. "Gimme a call and let me know if it's gonna happen."

By the time Dewey got down the steps to the parking garage, he actually laughed aloud, then looked around to make sure nobody was down there who could hear him. Dewey Gleason's pain was forgotten. This was an unbelievable stroke of good fortune. He only had to figure out how to make it work. Dewey was giddy with excitement. Eunice was falling in love!

It was payday, and Malcolm's boss did not look particularly happy when the young man asked to leave work two hours early for a dental appointment. He asked why Malcolm hadn't told him this before the day he was due at the dentist so that a suitable personnel adjustment could have been made. Malcolm apologized and said it would not happen again.

The moment he left work, he speed-dialed Naomi Teller and was overjoyed when she answered.

"It's Clark," he said. "Today's the day!"

"The day for what?" Naomi said.

"Where you at?"

"I'm at my girlfriend's house. We're gonna go swimming in her pool."

"Forget swimming," Malcolm said. "Lemme pick you up and we'll go to Mel's Drive-In on the Strip."

Naomi hesitated and then said, "Can I bring my girlfriend?"

"No way, Naomi," Malcolm said. "This is our special time, like I been promising. You're gonna like Mel's. It's not McDonald's, that's for sure."

"On the Sunset Strip?" she said. "I guess not."

"I can afford it," Malcolm said.

Again there was silence on the line, and then the girl said, "Okay, you wanna pick me up here?"

"Where is it?"

"On Hayworth, right near Fountain. Let me run and get the exact address. I'll have to think of some excuse."

"Tell her your cousin arrived from Boston and your mom wants you home right away."

"Who should I say is picking me up?"

"Your cousin from Boston."

"I think I can come up with a better story," she said. "Gimme a minute to get the house number for you."

"Goody!" Clark cried.

That made her giggle. "You're so silly," she said.

After Naomi came back on the line with the address, Malcolm said, "I'll see you in twenty-five minutes."

He clicked off and drove to a check-cashing service near the home improvement center to cash his paycheck. He wasn't worried about money anymore. He'd soon have plenty of it, now that he was in tight with Bernie Graham and his secretary, Ethel. He wouldn't really mind if his boss at the warehouse fired him.

Thinking of his warehouse job made him think of the box cutter in the pocket of his jeans. These days he was carrying it with him at all times. He took it out, opened the glove box, and tossed it inside.

Late that afternoon, Dewey Gleason as Bernie Graham rented the tiny upstairs apartment in Frogtown after receiving the call from Jerzy Szarpowicz. Within an hour of closing the deal and signing the check — using one of the small-business accounts that was nearly depleted — Dewey met with his co-conspirators at the property.

"It's a dump," Tristan said when he and Jerzy walked inside.

"You need fuckin' luxury to do a kidnap?" Jerzy said.

"It's got two rooms and a bathroom, and that's enough," Dewey said. "And it's not close to a residence. Good job, Jerzy."

Jerzy smiled slightly, at last feeling appreciated.

"Use duct tape and tape those blinds to the wall," Dewey said. "We don't want her seeing daylight, and we damn sure don't want her knowing where she is. This gag's gotta last two days."

Dewey assumed that after two days, when they wouldn't be able to reach him and figured out that he was gone for good, they'd simply release Eunice and go back to being the street scum they'd always been. What could Eunice do about any of it? Complain that her criminal employees had kidnapped her? Complain that her husband had stolen the money that she'd stolen from hundreds of people, much of it even before she'd met her husband?

He wondered if it was his imagination or if there was something suspicious in the way that Creole glanced around the apartment and said casually, "Yeah, this gag's gotta last two days. That's how long it'll take your banker pal to release funds, huh? That's a long time from our end."

"It can't be helped," Dewey said. "It's gotta be that way if this is gonna work."

"It's gonna work, Bernie," Jerzy said. "You got my guarantee that she'll give it up."

Those sinister words made Dewey Gleason feel more than a little uneasy. The big talk was over. Now it was going to happen and the Polack meant business.

"I don't think you'll have to get rough with her," Dewey said.

"We'll do what we gotta do," Jerzy said.

This time it was Tristan feeling it. "I told you two I ain't torturin' no woman," he said to Jerzy.

Jerzy pulled up the T-shirt hanging over his gut and showed them the two-inch Colt revolver. "You two are gonna do whatever has to be done to get that fuckin' money. Once this thing starts, it goes all the way and we ain't turnin' back."

Tristan glanced at Dewey, who averted his eyes. Jerzy's own eyes were glassy and slightly dilated. Tristan figured he'd been smoking ice for courage, and he didn't like that. The Polack was trouble enough when he wasn't high.

"One thing sure," Tristan said, looking at Jerzy. "We gotta stay clean and sober for this job or it ain't gonna work. We gotta main-tain at all times. I hope we agree about that."

Jerzy gave one of his scoffing snorts that Tristan had come to hate and said, "You two do your jobs. I'm sure as fuck gonna do mine."

"I'd suggest you rent the van at the same place under the same name," Dewey said to Tristan, eager to get the conversation away from Jerzy and the menace in his close-set little eyes.

"We'll need five Franklins to hold us till this goes down," Tristan said. "Then we might need more. Sleepin' bags for Jerzy and me. A metal bed that we can chain her to. Food for two days, and lots of little stuff, like toilet paper, bottled water, whatever."

"And room deodorizer," Jerzy said. "She's gonna smell like a cess-pool when we put the fear on her."

Dewey opened his wallet and took out $600 and handed it to Tristan, saying, "This is to get started." Jerzy reached over and snatched three of the $100 bills from Tristan's hand.

"We'll need all of that and maybe more, wood," Tristan said to his partner.

"Why should you hold it all?" Jerzy retorted.

"Okay, you wanna rent the van? Here," Tristan said, and he handed the remaining bills to Jerzy. "You wanna buy the bed and other shit?"

"Let's not start off squabbling!" Dewey said as Jerzy stared down at his smaller partner, whose eyes were directed at "Foo Fighters" in red across the chest of Jerzy's black T-shirt. "How about letting Creole handle the money, Jerzy? He's the one that's already set up with ID to rent the van."

Jerzy grunted and handed the money back to Tristan without further comment.

"Okay, then," Dewey said. "Unless you got a better plan, I say this goes down at the storage locker in Reseda."

"Like how?" Tristan said.

"You two are in there when I arrive with Ethel. You'll ambush us."

"How do you plan to get your old lady to the storage room?" Jerzy asked.

Dewey said, "I think I have a way. It's possible that we could be ready as soon as tomorrow night. Are you two good to go?"

"Holy shit!" Tristan said. Then he thought about it and said, "Why not? But how do we get in the storage room to ambush you?"

"If I'm able to set it up for tomorrow night, I'll meet you at our office in the afternoon at about two o'clock. We'll drive to the storage facility, where you will enter behind me just like you did last time. We'll park the van at the next row of storage buildings so there's no vehicle parked by our storage room when I arrive with my wife. You'll be hiding behind the merchandise boxes, and when we arrive, you'll jump us, tape her up, blindfold her, and one of you will run and get the van from the neighboring parking area."

Jerzy said, "How the fuck do we drag this taped-up woman from the storage room to the van without somebody seein' us? As I remember, there were other people comin' and goin' around there."

"There won't be at eight thirty at night," Dewey said. "There's twenty-four-hour self-storage access for customers, but I've seldom seen anybody there after dark, except for the security guard in the front office. After you get us in the van, you lock up the storeroom, take my keys, and leave my car where it's parked. I've seen customers' cars left there for two or three days after they took away their stored belongings in a rental truck. Just wave to the guard when you drive out. It'll be a minimum-wage employee who'll probably be too busy watching TV to even wave back."

"You're sayin' we gotta sit in that hot storage room for more than five hours?" Jerzy said.

"Yes," Dewey said. "I need time to get back to Hollywood and set up the gag for her to go with me to the storage room. I'm gonna get a phone call and say that our runners Creole and Jerzy called and need four laptops and a plasma from there to deliver for a very good price, and that I gotta do the pickup ASAP. It's not gonna be comfortable for you in that room, but you're gonna get a hell of an hourly wage for those five hours and for the following two days after it's all over."

Tristan, who was listening intently, said, "Okay, as long as you seem to be writer and director of this here show, have you worked out how the woman thinks we got in that room to pull off the ambush without you bein' involved?"

"Yes," Dewey said. "I've worked out the dialogue. She'll know that you're Creole and Jerzy, our runners. She's heard of you. She'll also know that you, Creole, were the guy from Water and Power, so she'll know you staked us out for this kidnap. When you throw us in this apartment, I'll tell her that you musta made a duplicate key when we transferred the merchandise from Los Feliz to the storage facility, and that I also shared the gate code with you on that job. She's never been to the facility before. She'll buy it."

"And did you write the dialogue for when we get your hysterical old lady up here?" Jerzy asked.

It took several seconds for Dewey to say, "That part will be mostly improv."

"And what the fuck's that mean?" said Jerzy.

"I want this to go down without her getting hurt," Dewey said.

"Yeah, well, I wanna fuck every waitress at Hooters," Jerzy said. "But I might jist end up in jail, fuckin' a package of lunch meat if this don't get done right."

"She talks tough, but she's not a brave woman," Dewey said. "Maybe if you let her know about that very impressive knife of yours, she'll fold. But first you'll have to beat me up."

"I'm gonna love that part!" Jerzy said.

"No, not *really* beat me up," Dewey said quickly. "But she's gonna have to believe that you did it. Remember, she'll be blindfolded and think I am too. You'll have to punch your fist into your palm several times, and I'll have to yell out and beg you to stop. I'll throw myself on the floor. That kind of thing."

"I'd rather make it more real with you," Jerzy said with that worrisome grin of his.

"Get your mind in the game, dawg," Tristan said.

Dewey ignored Jerzy and said, "After you pretend to beat me up, you'll take me outta the apartment for about twenty minutes. Then you'll take me back in, and since she'll have a blindfold on, I'll be able to convince her that I'm hurting, and I'll tell her that you asked for half a million to let us live. The important thing is that you never remove her blindfold. In fact, duct-tape it to her face."

"This is all good," Tristan said, "but I still don't see how you get the money outta her bank account and into your hands."

"I've already laid the groundwork," Dewey said. "If you can scare her enough and then leave us alone, it'll be a done deal."

"Like, how do you actually do it, Bernie?" Tristan said. "Tell me the steps involved."

"You don't have to worry about that," Dewey said. "It's a wire transfer."

Suddenly Jerzy stepped close to Dewey and said, "There ain't no secrets between us here, Bernie. You ain't Mr. Kessler no more. Now tell my little partner what he wants to know."

Dewey looked up at Jerzy Szarpowicz, then at Tristan, and said, "She'll give me the password and the account number and routing number if I need it. And whatever else she used to identify herself, like her mother's maiden name of the name of her first doggy, or whatever the fuck I need to order her bank to wire the funds to my bank. Satisfied?"

"Back off, Bernie," Tristan said. "We got a right to know all the details. Like, why is she gonna be content to be the one who stays with us, while you leave her for two days to do the deal?"

"Because you're gonna tell her that one of us stays and the other goes and gets the money, and I'm your pick to go."

"Don't tell me," Tristan said. "Lemme guess. You're gonna offer to stay, because no manly man would leave his wife to die with a couple of insane kidnappers, but we're gonna say, no, Momma stays. And you're gonna go and bring the money back to save her life."

"That's what we have to sell," Dewey said.

"I keep goin' back to the possibility that she won't buy it," Tristan said. "What if she's braver and smarter than you think? What if she's layin' there blindfolded and starts to think this might all be a gag that her rat-fucker husband arranged?"

Dewey turned then and walked to the window, looking at the blinds. Finally, he said, "Be sure to tape these to the wall."

"Yeah, yeah," Jerzy said. "We'll do the details. Now answer Creole's question."

"I'm a good actor," Dewey said. "I'll sell it."

"Yeah, but what if you ain't quite as good as you think you are, and she just smells somethin' that ain't right?" Tristan said, pressing the man.

Dewey paused for an even longer time. Then he said, "There's one thing that'll keep her from even considering the possibility that this is all a charade. It's something that'll keep her mind totally focused on her own survival."

"What's that?" Tristan asked.

"Pain," Dewey said, turning around and looking at Jerzy. "But it's a last resort. And I mean *last*."

"Okay, Bernie," Jerzy said with that grin again that gave Tristan chills. "I do believe we are finally arrivin' at the same page on this here script of yours."

"I don't like this," Tristan said. "I don't fuckin' like this. I said from the git that I don't do violence to no woman."

"Nobody's askin' you to do it," Jerzy said.

"I don't fuckin' like this!" Tristan repeated.

"You'll like the money when it comes," Jerzy said. "And you'll forget the rest of it."

"It won't have to come to violence," Dewey said. "I'm sure of it."

Malcolm and Naomi were seated at the counter at Mel's Drive-In, and he was very happy with how impressed she seemed.

"It's too cool for school!" she said. "A burger on the Sunset Strip!"

Malcolm said, "Want some ice cream for dessert?"

"I'm stuffed," she said, pushing the plate away.

"I like chocolate," Malcolm said.

"Me too," she said. "Especially frozen yogurt."

"Yeah?" Malcolm said. "I like frozen yogurt better than ice cream too. You and me, Naomi, we got lots in common."

Naomi smiled and said, "I'm real glad you called today, Clark. I was starting to think maybe it wouldn't happen."

"When I make up my mind, I stick to it," Malcolm said. "I'm gonna be getting a new job soon. Then I'll have more time and more money to do things I wanna do."

"What do you wanna do?" Naomi asked, and Malcolm loved the way she tossed her head to get her shoulder-length blonde hair off the side of her face.

"Oh, maybe get a newer car. I like Mustangs, but mine's pretty old. And I wanna buy you some things. Expensive things."

"Me?" Naomi said.

"Sure," he said. "You're my girl now. I feel like I know you better than anybody else in my life," Malcolm said. Then he repeated, "You're my girl."

Naomi was startled and confused, and she said, "Clark, I like you. I really do. But my mother'd have a litter of kittens if she knew you called me that or if she even knew I was here with a guy your age. Especially a guy she never met."

"I'll go straight to your house now and meet your mother," Malcolm said. "And I'll tell her how I feel about you."

He didn't like the look on Naomi's face then. And he didn't like it when she lowered her gaze and said, "Clark, don't talk crazy. I think maybe you should take me home now."

She managed an insincere smile but remained silent for a moment when he said, "Okay, but I hope I can come in for a few minutes and see how you live."

"See how I live?" Naomi finally said as Malcolm examined the bill and put money on the counter. "Whadda you mean?"

"I wanna see how a real American family lives. I didn't have that kind of family. My mother was a Persian, and my father was a French chef in New York before we moved to L.A., when I was a baby."

A moment passed and Naomi said, "How did you get the scrapes on your knuckles, Clark? And that little bruise on your face?"

"I got in a fight at work," Malcolm said. "Two big guys in the warehouse were picking on a little guy, and I stepped in and took care of business. I can't stand bullies, and I clocked both of them. They ended up in the ER."

Naomi did not comment further and was more than apprehensive during their ride and only spoke when she had to direct him to her house on Ogden Drive. He, on the other hand, chattered nonstop about music, often referring to the latest songs he'd heard on KROQ. When they were a few blocks from her house, he turned up the volume and began singing along with "Love Me Dead."

He knew the entire lyric, and he turned his brilliant smile on her when he sang about "the mark of the beast." And again when he sang, "You're born of a jackal." He smiled even bigger when he said, "That song's about me!"

Naomi Teller had begun trembling by then and felt enormous relief when he pulled up in front of her house, a well-tended home in an area where homes were upper-middle class, but to Malcolm Rojas they looked like mansions.

She got out of the Mustang quickly, closed the door, peered through the open window, and said, "Clark, I really can't invite you in now. I need time to tell my mom and dad how nice you are, even though you're an older guy. I just need . . . well, like, time."

"That's a beautiful house," he said. "Which room is yours? Upstairs in front, I bet, so you can see the street."

"Yes, you're a good guesser, Clark," she said. "Well, bye-bye."

"Next time I wanna meet your family and see how you live," Malcolm said. "Promise me, Naomi."

Naomi said, "Okay, Clark."

"Don't forget me, Naomi," Malcolm said. "Don't ever forget me."

"I won't," Naomi said. "That's for sure."

When she was feeling the security of her front door just a few yards away, she paused, turned again, and, looking back at the handsome young man in the Mustang, said, "Jones isn't a French name. You said your dad was a French chef."

Malcolm said, "You're right, Naomi. He changed it when he came to America because his name was too hard to pronounce."

"I took French in middle school," Naomi said, feeling bold enough now to challenge him. "I bet I could pronounce it. What is it?"

"I don't like to talk about my family," he said. "They both died in a car crash."

"Oh, that's sad," Naomi said. "Who raised you?"

"I was raised by jackals," Malcolm said, and he began laughing.

The laughter grew in intensity until he had tears in his eyes. Naomi Teller imagined she could still hear that laugh when she ran inside her house and turned the dead bolt.

Night fell with a thud, thanks to the summer smog. It got very dark very fast. Sergeant Miriam Hermann in 6-L-20, the senior sergeant's designated car, was cruising Hollywood Boulevard when she spotted the shop belonging to 6-X-32 parked on Las Palmas Avenue, just north of the boulevard. She saw that the surfer cops were talking to a white male pedestrian, so she pulled over to the red zone on the boulevard, showed herself on the radio as being code 6, and left her car to observe unseen.

Flotsam and Jetsam were both facing north and didn't notice their supervisor standing thirty yards behind them in the darkness of a doorway. Sergeant Hermann could see that the guy facing the two cops was hammered to the point of oblivion. She doubted that they'd gotten him out of a car, because he looked too smashed to walk, let alone drive.

Flotsam looked at the fiftyish fat guy, whose souvenir Universal Studios cap, walking shorts, and tennis shoes with dark socks said "tourist." He was doing his best to stand without staggering to one side or the other, and Sergeant Hermann heard the tall cop say, "Well, Stanley, even though you're more bombed than Baghdad, we'd like to give you a break and let you walk home. But I don't know if you can manage it. Where's home?"

"The R-R-R-Roosevelt Hotel," Stanley managed to say, with a pronounced slur and a stutter like Porky Pig's. "I...c-c-c-can do it! Honest!"

Jetsam looked at his partner and said, "I dunno either, partner." Turning to the drunk, he said, "Where you from, Stanley?"

The man looked at them like he couldn't remember, but he said, "Indi...Indi...Indian...aw, fuck it...apolis." Then he got the hiccups.

"Well, your hometown makes a difference," Flotsam said. "Most surfers have heard about the USS *Indianapolis*. It got torpedoed in the Big War. A lotta brave sailors got taken by the men in gray suits."

"What?" said Stanley, utterly perplexed.

"Sharks," Jetsam said. "Surfers don't like the men in gray suits. We know all the stories about them."

"Oh," Stanley said without the slightest idea what the hell they were talking about.

"I say we give him a chance," Flotsam said. "In memory of the *Indianapolis*. You down, partner?"

"I'm on it, bro," Jetsam said. Then he looked at the drunk and said, "It's a balloon test. Pass it and we'll let you go. You good with that?"

Stanley said, "L-L-L-Lemme blow in the b-b-b-balloon. I ain't that...that..." And he lurched to starboard, but Jetsam grabbed his arm before he crashed to the pavement, and said, "I think *drunk* is the word you're searching for, Stanley."

Flotsam said, "Anyways, you ain't the one that has to blow, Stanley." With that, he reached in his pocket and pulled out a yellow balloon.

He put it to his lips and blew it to the size of a cantaloupe, after which he pinched off the neck, held it in front of the drunk's face, and said, "Game on, Stanley. If you can catch it, you're a free man."

Then he let it go. The balloon soared and dove and smacked the pavement while Stanley pawed the air in a futile attempt to grab it, with Jetsam holding his collar so he didn't kiss the concrete.

"Best two out of three, dude?" Flotsam said to Stanley, who nodded eagerly and said, "Let her r-r-r-rip!"

Jetsam picked up the balloon, readying for another test, when Sergeant Hermann startled both cops by walking up behind them, saying, "What in the hell are you surfer goons up to this time?"

Both cops spun around, and Flotsam said, "Oh, hi, Sarge. We're just, uh, trying to, uh, figure out how drunk this man is."

Stanley said, "Come on, let's d-d-d-do it!"

"Let's not," Sergeant Hermann said. Then to her cops, she said, "You can't book him now, not that you ever intended to. You might have a bit of a problem explaining your balloon test to a judge."

"Well, Sarge...," Jetsam said, trying to come up with something plausible.

"Where do you live?" Sergeant Hermann asked Stanley.

"The R-R-R-Roosevelt Hotel," he said, swaying precariously, "for a f-f-f-few days. Then I'm going home to Indi...Indi...Indi...aw, fuck it."

"Take this man to the Roosevelt Hotel," Sergeant Hermann said. "And don't ever let me catch you two playing with balloons again."

Without a word, both surfer cops got Stanley by the arms and marched him to the backseat of their shop.

When they got him inside the lobby of the Roosevelt Hotel, Stanley said, "Don't leave. Let's have a n-n-n-nightcap in honor of the *Indi*... *Indi...Indi...*"

"Aw, fuck it," Flotsam said, finishing it for him.

SEVENTEEN

MALCOLM WAS GOING to treat himself to his second burger of the day, this time at Hamburger Hamlet, and he was also thinking about going to a movie. When his cell phone chimed, he felt sure it was Naomi Teller and didn't bother to look, so he eagerly said, "Hi!"

"Clark, it's Bernie Graham," Dewey said.

"Oh, yeah, how you feeling, Mr. Graham?"

"I'm a lot better than yesterday," Dewey said. "In fact, my secretary, Ethel, asked me to call. We'd like to take you to dinner as a sort of reward for what you did."

"It's okay, Mr. Graham," Malcolm said. "You don't have to do that. I only hope we can start working together soon."

"We will," Dewey said. "I need to mend a bit longer, but in the meantime, we'd like to take you someplace for a bite to eat after you get off work tomorrow. Do you know Musso's on Hollywood Boulevard east of Highland?"

"No," Malcolm said, "but I'll find it."

"It's a very old place with good, wholesome food like your mother used to make."

"My mother. Yeah," Malcolm said.

"What about meeting us at Musso and Frank at five thirty? Pull around to the back and park in their lot. Come in and look for Ethel and me at one of the tables near the bar."

Malcolm thought it over and said, "Okay, Mr. Graham, but I sure hope we can get started on my job real soon. I need the money."

"We will, Clark, we will," Dewey said and clicked off.

After Eunice returned from her banking excursion, one of many that seemed to last an unusual amount of time, Dewey said matter-of-factly, "Eunice, I made an early dinner reservation for tomorrow at Musso's. I thought we could use a little R & R."

As expected, she was dismissive. "Knock yourself out, Dewey. I'll stay here and earn a living for both of us. Bring me two Whoppers after you're through."

Then he said, "I was hoping you'd come this time. I invited the kid, like we discussed."

"Kid?"

"Yeah, the new boy, Clark. It's the least I can do for the way he rescued me after I got beat up by that meth-crazed runner. I think he'll turn out to be a good little moneymaker."

"Did the kid say he'd come?" Eunice said, her voice rising in anticipation.

"Yeah, he's coming," Dewey said. "It'll be fun to see the lad in a nice restaurant. A real treat for him. I wish you'd come along too. We haven't had a night out together in a long time."

She paused for only a few seconds before saying, "Well, it has been a while. I guess I can use an evening off. But why do you have to eat at the old places? Christ, drive down Melrose and pick one of the hot ones: Lucques or Bastide or All' Angelo. You think you can recapture your youth by dining at Musso and Frank or the Formosa Café? Get real, Dewey. Old Hollywood is gone with the wind."

He stared at her. There was nobody else on the planet who could come close to turning an invitation into an insult the way Eunice could. There was so much he would've liked to say, but all he said was, "The kid'll feel more relaxed in one of the old places that serve comfort food. Let's think of him."

"Okay, have it your way," Eunice said and lit another cigarette.

"Good," Dewey said. "I made an early reservation because the boy works at his job all day and he'll be starved."

"I guess we really should do this," she said. "He did you a big favor, all right."

Dewey went to his bedroom and left the door slightly ajar and turned on the shower in the bathroom. Then he crept to the open door and listened.

He heard Eunice dial a number, and when it was answered, she said, "Hello, Henri, this is Eunice Gleason. You gotta take me tomorrow for a cut and dye. And I'll need one of the girls for a manicure and pedicure as well."

Dewey listened while she got her response, and then she said, "No, Henri. It has to be tomorrow. It's important to me. I'll give you a tip that'll make you very happy."

There was another silence and she said, "Eleven o'clock, and noon for the nail work. Terrific! Thanks, sweetie!"

When she hung up, Dewey heard her actually start humming a tune. He had to close the door when she came toward the hallway, so he couldn't make out the song. With a grim smile he wondered if it was one from her childhood, like "Puppy Love."

Malcolm finished his hamburger and paid the bill, and when he was in the parking lot, he started thinking of Naomi. He was surprised how disappointed he'd been when it had been Bernie Graham on the phone instead of his girl. He'd been thinking about what it would be like to kiss Naomi and have her kiss him back. He intended to find out next time.

The only girls he'd ever kissed were those sluts he went to school with in Boyle Heights. Those *cholas* with their eyebrows plucked bare, wearing eye shadow and mascara that made them look like those old punk rockers with painted faces. The making-out part and the gropes he got from them had never excited him much, not even on the few occasions when one of them would strip naked in his bedroom when his mother was at work. They'd certainly never excited him enough that he could keep an erection long enough to get the thing done, and after one of them taunted him and asked if he was a homo, he never even tried again. That was just before Malcolm and his mother moved to Hollywood, and it was one of the reasons the move had secretly been such a relief to him. Those little bitches were spreading lies about his failed performances, he was sure of it.

There would be no such problems with Naomi Teller. He got hard just imagining how she'd look naked. Thinking of those developing little breasts and her narrow hips was thrilling. At her age, she was built more like a boy. And her nipples would be pink, not brown like the ones on those little east-side bitches who'd mocked him. But he would not rush things sexually. He only wanted to kiss Naomi romantically, and tell her she was his girl, and hear her say that he was her guy and that she would never forget him.

Malcolm sat in his car and impulsively phoned her. It rang four times, and just before he clicked off, she said, "Hello?"

"It's me," he said, smiling.

"I know," she said.

"I was wondering if you were thinking of me," Malcolm said. "I was thinking of you."

"In a way I was, Clark," she said, and her tone was not happy.

"What were you thinking?"

"I was thinking that I'm too young to be seeing you. My parents would be very upset, so I think you shouldn't call me anymore."

The silence on the line lasted ten seconds before she heard him say, "Tell me the truth. Did your parents put you up to this?"

"They don't even know about you, Clark. It's the way I feel. I'm sorry. It was a mistake. I know you'll find a girl your age and—"

"You little bitch!" he cried, his face reddening and his voice quaking. "I thought you were different!"

Stunned, Naomi Teller said, "Clark! I'm hanging up now! Please don't ever call me again!"

"You're just like—" But she clicked off before he could finish. He was in a rage. He tossed the cell phone onto the seat beside him and opened the glove box, taking out the box cutter. He snapped out the cutting blade. This was the same fury he'd last felt when he'd beaten that bitch with his fists. He withdrew the blade into the grip, put the box cutter in the pocket of his jeans, and sped from the parking lot of Hamburger Hamlet, heading west.

The code 2 call on Ogden Drive was given to 6-X-76, Dana Vaughn and Hollywood Nate. It came out as "See the woman, prowler there now."

Backing up 6-X-76 were Mindy Ling and R.T. Dibney, who'd just cleared from code 7.

The responding car pulled up to the curb with lights out in case the prowler was still at the scene, but Dana and Nate saw the exterior house lights were on. A man and woman Dana's age were standing on the front porch. As the backup unit parked behind their car, Dana and Nate got out and Nate said, "What happened?"

Martha Teller was small-boned and fair, like her daughter. Her husband was taller, prematurely bald, with rounded shoulders and the beginning of a paunch. He said, "I heard what sounded like footsteps on the front walkway. Then I heard someone yell, 'You bitch!' I looked out but I didn't see anybody. Then a minute later, this came flying through an upstairs window."

He held out his hand, and the cops saw a baseball-size rock similar to the decorative stones in the Tellers' front flower garden.

"How long ago did it happen?"

"Less than five minutes ago," Mrs. Teller said. "You got here fast."

"Who lives here with you?" Dana asked.

"We have two daughters," Mrs. Teller said.

Nate said, "Do they have any idea who it might've been?"

"Our ten-year-old daughter, Shelly, is on a sleepover with my parents," Mrs. Teller said. "That's her bedroom window. Naomi's fourteen, and she said she hasn't any idea who could've done such a thing."

With that, Dana turned toward Mindy and R.T. Dibney, who were out of their car, and held up four fingers, indicating code 4, no further assistance needed.

Mindy nodded and said, "We'll cruise the neighborhood, Dana."

"I'd like to talk to Naomi privately, if you don't mind," Dana said to the Tellers, and the cops followed the couple into the house.

"She's very upset," Mrs. Teller said.

"I understand," Dana said. "I have a daughter who's eighteen. Believe me, I'm sensitive to teenage issues."

Ogden Drive was a pleasant residential street with lots of trees on both sides. Shop 6-X-46 wasn't cruising for more than three minutes when

R.T. Dibney craned his neck sharply to the right, and Mindy uttered the line so often said by one partner to another when on patrol: "What'd you see?"

"Nothing," R.T. Dibney said, turning forward again, but when Mindy looked over her shoulder, she observed a shapely woman in a T-shirt and shorts walking from her car to a lighted portico.

"For God's sake!" Mindy said. "Can't you at least get your inner creep under control when we're actually looking for a suspect?"

"The kid's long gone," he said. "Just some brat pissed off at his girlfriend. Dana'll get the girl to give up his name, and they'll call his parents. It might make them reduce the little bastard's weekly allowance from fifty bucks to forty."

"What's this?" Mindy said, seeing the silhouette of a car coming south in their direction with lights out. Then the headlights flashed on and she saw it was another police unit, searching slowly. Both cars stopped, facing opposite directions, and Mindy was looking at Sheila Montez.

"A rock thrower," Mindy explained. "Busted out an upstairs window and GOA." By which she meant *gone on arrival.*

"We didn't see any peds roaming around," Sheila said. "Maybe it was a neighbor kid."

"I think I'll just cruise for another few minutes," Mindy said, to which R.T. Dibney grumbled something unintelligible.

"We may as well check around for a while too," Sheila said to Aaron. "Even the alleys around here are nice. No mattresses or fish heads."

"And people wave at you with all five fingers," Aaron said.

There were several cars parked in front of residences on Ogden Drive during the early evening hours, and 6-X-66 drove past one of them. An old red Mustang was parked all the way north, almost at the corner of Sunset Boulevard. Sheila Montez and Aaron Sloane were heading south and were parallel with a house two doors from the Teller home, when Sheila saw a silhouette move across a lawn, heading away from the Tellers'.

"I saw something!" she said, hitting the brakes.

"What is it?" Aaron said, head on a swivel.

Sheila pulled into a driveway, backed out, and turned north, saying,

"On your side. Turn the spot on the yards. I think I saw somebody moving through the trees."

Aaron turned on the spotlight as she slowed, and he said, "I see him! A rabbit!"

Sheila saw him too, a slender male figure darting into the darkness beside a property on the east side of the street.

"I'm bailing!" he said, and when Sheila stopped for an instant, he was out of the car, flashlight in one hand, baton in the other, running east through a residential property into the darkness.

Meanwhile, R.T. Dibney, in 6-X-46, was complaining to Mindy Ling, saying, "What's the use of trying to look for prowlers anyways with these politically correct little mini-lights?"

Mindy didn't answer. She was too busy counting the days left in this deployment period, after which she was definitely going to ask for a partner reassignment. She thought she might even take a few special days off in order to shorten what had come to seem like a jail sentence.

But then she heard the RTO's radio voice say, "All units in the vicinity of Ogden Drive between De Longpre and Sunset, officer in foot pursuit of prowler, eastbound through residential property, toward Genesee. Six-X-Forty-six, handle, code three."

Hollywood Nate, unaware of the prowler sighting, was writing a crime report and having a cup of coffee in the living room of the Teller home with Naomi's father, who he learned was a cardiologist at Cedars-Sinai Medical Center. Naomi's mother was up in the bedroom, cleaning up broken glass and patching the window with cardboard. Dana and Naomi were alone in Dr. Teller's study, where Dana had closed the door for privacy.

Naomi had continued to adamantly deny knowing who had yelled and thrown a rock through the upstairs window. Nor had Naomi told Dana Vaughn how guilty she felt because her bedroom was in the rear of the residence, and the bedroom that was attacked belonged to her younger sister. Something had made her lie defensively when Clark had asked if that was her bedroom facing the street, and now she felt cowardly and remorseful for having done it.

Naomi thought that the police officer was a very attractive woman with eyes that were alert, yet calm and patient. Even though she was fairly certain this officer would understand, Naomi just couldn't bring herself to look at her while they chatted.

Finally, Dana said, "Naomi, I think you might have some idea who threw the rock. Someone could've been hurt. Certainly your family is frightened. Why don't you tell me who you think it might've been. We won't go charging over to the person's house, but we'll take some steps to see that it doesn't happen again."

Naomi looked straight into Dana Vaughn's eyes and started to speak. But she stopped, looked away again, and said, "I just don't know who he was. Maybe some crazy boy from middle school that just doesn't like me. I really don't know."

Dana said, "Naomi, I'm sure you have a cell phone, don't you?"

"Yes."

"I'm going to give you my card with my personal cell number on it. I'd like you to give me your cell number. If you think very hard about it and decide you might have an idea who the rock thrower is, please give me a call. You don't have to tell your parents about it if you don't want to. We'll keep this between the two of us until we're sure we can quietly determine who actually did it. Is that a deal?"

"Okay," Naomi said in a voice barely audible.

"We'll help you, honey," Dana said to Naomi Teller.

R.T. Dibney had been dropped off on Sunset Boulevard. He was out with his mini-flashlight, searching in an alley east of Ogden Drive, not just for the prowler, but for Aaron Sloane, who hadn't been heard from since he'd leaped from the car and started running. There was plenty of chatter on the tac frequency that he was picking up on his rover but nothing from Aaron. He'd heard Sheila Montez talking to Mindy Ling twice, and Sheila's voice was growing desperate.

Then he heard Aaron's voice in bits and pieces, and Sheila's voice said, "You're breaking up!" and Aaron's voice said, "Can you... lost...can't...radio!" And everyone but Sheila Montez thought that at least he was probably okay even if his rover wasn't, but where in the hell was the prowler? And within moments, two more black-and-whites from Watch 3 were cruising slowly along streets and alleys, searching with spotlights.

R.T. Dibney saw an open gate in a rear yard. He entered and heard a dog bark but realized it was coming from the house next door. By now, several homes in the area had their exterior lights on, and residents were outside, trying to see what was going on. Then another dog barked, and it sounded like a big one. R.T. Dibney was ready to draw his nine, when he thought he heard a sound behind him. Before he could turn, somebody slammed a shoulder into him and he was propelled forward right into the unlighted swimming pool, where he sank to the bottom and lost both his rover and his flashlight. By the time he came up, sputtering, choking, and gasping for air, he neither saw nor heard anything but the dog next door barking wildly.

When Aaron Sloane finally showed up on Ogden Drive, his uniform dusty from climbing into three yards after a shadow, he was limping and frustrated, and he slashed at a hedge with his baton. He'd been close enough to the prowler to see that the guy had dark hair and wasn't very big, but that was all he'd seen.

When Sheila Montez spotted him standing alone in the moonlight beside a purple flowering jacaranda tree, she jammed on the brakes, leaped from the car, and ran straight at him, not knowing or caring that Mindy Ling was out on foot less than thirty yards away, shining her light into cars parked on the street.

Aaron was massaging his leg when he saw Sheila, and he said, "I pulled my hamster."

Sheila threw her arms around Aaron's neck, and he was astonished. He was even more astonished to see her eyes glistening and to hear her say, "When I couldn't reach you on your rover, I thought...I thought..."

"I'm okay, Sheila!" he said. "I'm okay." And now he wasn't even thinking about the prowler, or his injured hammy, and he didn't want her to stop holding on to him, and all of his anger at the prowler and his malfunctioning rover had morphed into unbridled joy.

Mindy Ling pretended to be searching very intently when the

partners of unit 6-X-66 got back in their shop, and Mindy saw the silhouette of their profiles only inches apart and closing.

Driving east on Sunset Boulevard, Malcolm Rojas was more excited than he'd ever been in his life. He couldn't contain himself and began laughing, overwhelmed by the unimaginable thrill of what he'd accomplished that night. He wished there were a way he could share it with someone, but of course he could not. He wished they all could've seen what he did to the cop. Especially all those *cholo* punks in Boyle Heights who'd bullied him and called him Li'l Hondoo. He wished Naomi could've seen it.

There was just a twinge of anger left in him when he thought about Naomi, but most of it was gone now. He'd go home and relive this evening in his mind and masturbate. And now he was actually looking forward to having a meal at a nice restaurant on Hollywood Boulevard tomorrow evening with Bernie Graham and his secretary, Ethel. That was exciting too because it would mark the beginning of his job. He felt now like he could accomplish anything he wanted to do. This was the start of a new life for Malcolm Rojas. He felt like a man. Then he thought he might legally change his name to Clark Jones.

Some of the cars belonging to residents and visitors previously parked on Ogden Drive had driven away by the time the searchers were ready to give up. A few of the drivers getting into those cars had been interrogated by police, but most had not, including the driver of an old red Mustang, who by then was nearly home.

It was 6-A-35 from Watch 3 that first spotted R.T. Dibney standing on Sunset Boulevard in his socks, holding his shoes in his hand as heavy traffic sped by and headlights lit him. His Sam Browne and holstered pistol were slung over his shoulder, and his uniform was still dripping. As soon as the extraordinary encounter between the prowler and R.T. Dibney was described on the tac frequency by 6-A-35, at least four cars sped to the pickup location. Half a dozen cops from Watch 5 and Watch 3 jumped from their shops to take cell phone shots of the soppy cop, now stripping off his T-shirt, with his Kevlar vest and uniform shirt spread across the roof of the first black-and-white to arrive.

There, under a bright summer moon and a relatively smogless sky over Hollywood, they chattered and chuckled and clicked photos like crazy while R.T. Dibney shook his fist and cursed them and the mothers who'd spawned them.

Dana Vaughn was one of the cops taking photos, and Hollywood Nate said to her, "I wish we had a video cam with a zoom lens. R.T.'s normally twitchy mustache is vibrating like an electric toothbrush."

★ EIGHTEEN ★

THE NEXT DAY WAS to be the most momentous in his life. At such a moment, he could face and admit who Dewey Gleason really was: failed actor, failed screenwriter, mediocre forger and thief. At such a time, all denial was stripped away. He thought of his brother and sister in Seattle, a civil engineer and a schoolteacher. Both had spouses and children and were ostensibly happy, yet he'd always felt he was smarter and more accomplished than either of them. For years he'd blamed his failures on the show-business bug that bit him during his high school years. Then later, he'd decided it wasn't a bug, it was a goddamn vampire bat that sucked Seattle right out of him and eventually steered him to Hollywood. And this was where it would all finally end, one way or the other.

Of course, Dewey had slept intermittently, and the sleep he did get was clouded by bizarre and unremembered nightmares. There were so many things that could go wrong, he'd finally stopped listing them. He'd faced the certain truth that if this didn't work, he and Eunice were finished as a team, whether or not she guessed he'd engineered the gag. She'd probably pack up and head for San Francisco without him. That is, if she *survived*. And that made him think of Jerzy Szarpowicz, and of how much he hated even being in the cretin's presence, let alone having his own freedom depend on him. As he faced his fiftieth birthday in extreme desperation, he felt old, as old as original sin. Dewey knew that his plan could lead to *extreme* violence. And that made him get out of bed before daybreak and make his fourth trip to the bathroom.

When he was sitting on the toilet, he made a mental note to call Creole to tell him that when they got their kidnap victim into the apartment in Frogtown, they must not let Eunice have a cigarette, no matter how much she begged. Dewey hoped that nicotine deprivation might be the torture that would break her faster than anything they could inflict.

Tristan Hawkins and Jerzy Szarpowicz met at the house near Frogtown that Jerzy shared with his woman and her kids. After that, they spent an hour renting a van, using the same bogus ID that Tristan had used before, and then drove to a thrift shop, where they bought a roll-away bed with a pancake mattress of jail quality. The bed was old but the frame was made of heavy steel that would fit their needs. They didn't bother buying a pillow and certainly didn't purchase sheets. The thrift shop manager threw in a blanket with cigarette burns in several places, and having seen their victim, Tristan figured that cigarette burns would probably make her feel at home.

Next they bought some lengths of chain at a hardware store, along with two padlocks, a roll of duct tape, and some large cleaning rags to serve as blindfolds. They made a trip to a sporting goods store for two sleeping bags for themselves, and then to a supermarket for cans of soup, packages of lunch meat, three loaves of bread, mayonnaise (because Jerzy insisted), an ice chest, bags of ice, bottled water, toilet paper, one bar of soap, and several rolls of paper towels. They bought a box of lawn-and-leaf bags to haul away all debris from the apartment after they were finished with their gag. And that completed the shopping list.

Or so Tristan thought until Jerzy said, "We forgot something."

"What?" Tristan said.

"We gotta go back to the thrift shop and get an old rug."

"We ain't settin' up housekeepin', dawg," Tristan said. "Next thing, you'll be wantin' a few pots of geraniums."

"The rug's for jist in case," Jerzy said.

"In case of what?"

"In case we gotta roll her up in it if things don't work out right."

Tristan started to say something but changed his mind. What good would it do? He'd told both Jerzy and Bernie enough times that he wasn't going to stand for violence, but he knew in his heart that he wouldn't be able to stop it if it got started. He'd grown up in the 'hood. He knew how *nobody* could stop violence once it really got started. He refused to go back inside the thrift shop, so Jerzy bought the threadbare rug for $65 and carried it to the rental van by himself.

Eunice was absolutely bubbly when she went off to Henri's for all the beauty work. She even mentioned to Dewey that she might stop by Macy's and pick up something to wear.

"We're only going to Musso's," Dewey said. "I've seen guys in T-shirts and tennis shoes having dinner there. In fact, that's the dress code for most of the half-ass movie and TV people around this fucking town."

"You're grouchy this morning," Eunice said. "And you got bags under your eyes."

"That'll provide a marked contrast to our young dinner guest," Dewey said.

"I forgot we even have one," Eunice said, and Dewey controlled the urge to smirk. "I don't suppose Clark'll be dressed up, will he?"

"Not ghetto-fabulous or anything like that, I wouldn't think," Dewey said, and added with feigned enthusiasm, "Okay, then, see you later when you're beautiful."

Malcolm Rojas brought a clean shirt and jeans to work and put them in a locker. He thought he'd shower and shave there at the end of the day. Actually, he really only had to shave every other day, and he'd shaved yesterday for that little bitch Naomi, but tonight was a special occasion. His mother hadn't been awake when he left in the morning, so at least he was spared her nagging, or an interrogation as to why he hadn't called her when he'd failed to come home for supper last night.

It had been hard for Malcolm not to tell someone at work about what had happened to him. He'd bought an *L.A. Times,* hoping to find some mention of the cop getting dunked in a swimming pool, but there was nothing there. He hadn't even thought to look in the paper to see if the other incidents had been mentioned. That's because he wasn't proud of how he'd failed on both of those occasions, but nobody could say he'd failed last night. He'd gotten away when it looked like half the cops from Hollywood Station were looking for him. It made Malcolm smile every time he thought about it.

When they awoke late that morning in her double bed, Sheila Montez said to Aaron Sloane, "How about some tortillas and eggs? I still cook like a Mexican. Hollywood hasn't changed me."

"Anything you say," Aaron said with his moonstruck smile. "I think I'm still dreaming."

When she got out of bed and walked naked to the bathroom, he looked at her and said, "You're even more beautiful in the daylight. If I ever run into that prowler again, I think I'll kiss him."

Sheila glanced over her shoulder with the dusky, sloe-eyed look that always enchanted him. Her heavy dark hair, no longer pinned up so as not to touch the lower edge of her uniform collar per regulations, was draped across one shoulder.

She paused at the bathroom door and said, "After my bad marriage, I promised myself that I'd absolutely, positively never get involved with another cop. And I've kept my promise until now."

"You'll *never* have a problem with me, Sheila," Aaron said earnestly, propped up in bed on one elbow, his blue eyes wide and artless. "I'm crazy for you and have been since our first night as partners. Now I can't wait to take you to my folks' house in Van Nuys for Sunday dinner. They're gonna fall in love with you too. In fact, I predict that my accountant father will tell us how much money we could save if we take the proper steps to file a joint tax return next year."

After digesting the import of his words, Sheila turned away from Aaron for a moment and he couldn't see her face, and it alarmed him. The besotted young cop had been so overwhelmed by the rapture of the moment that the words had just poured from his lips. But now he feared he'd said too much too soon, and he was trying to think of something, anything, to tell her that he was patient and he'd wait, and that he hadn't meant to blurt out what he was feeling so profoundly.

But when she turned again to face him, her eyes were glistening, as they had been last night under the summer moon. All she said was, "If you ever cheat on me, I'll kill you."

"Cheat on you?" Aaron cried in relief and elation. "That's impossible, Sheila! Not only am I mad about you, I'm scared to death of you!"

Prior to getting ready for work that afternoon, Dana decided to take her daughter shopping at Banana Republic and Nordstrom, spending on Pamela most of the money she'd been saving to buy herself a few things at the midsummer sales. Dana loved shopping with Pamela, seeing her so enthusiastic and excited about going away to Cal in September. Of course, Dana's feelings were mixed. She was proud that Pamela had worked hard and got the grades to be accepted at UC Berkeley, but she worried about her child living in a dorm five hundred miles from her.

When they'd talked about it over lunch during a break from the shopping frenzy, Pamela sensed her mother's anxiety and said, "Mom, I know you think I might get taken over by radicals from the People's Republic of Berkeley and turned into a campus terrorist, but not to worry. About eighty percent of my dorm mates will be brainy Asian girls with parents calling three times a day to make sure they're doing violin practice as well as studying every waking moment. I don't think there's much chance of getting into trouble up there. It'll be all I can do to keep up academically."

And Dana gazed at her daughter, eighteen years old now, who'd inherited Dana's wide-set, golden-brown eyes, firm chin, great cheekbones, and lovely long legs. Dana figured she was probably smarter than both her cop mother and lawyer father, who, Dana had to admit, was readily coughing up the money that their daughter needed to get college-bound.

Dana thought that someday she might actually be able to bring herself to a face-to-face with that lying, skirt-chasing asshole, and hear about his new family: a bucks-up wife with two sons of her own. Dana guessed that by now the boys must resent their stepfather for taking control of their trust-fund management, because Dana was sure that he would have. He was that kind of intrusive, controlling lawyer who could never stop beginning every ponderous pronouncement with "At some point in time." Dana hated that law school redundancy almost as much as she'd hated his philandering. How he'd managed to provide the seed to produce the splendid girl sitting across from her would always be a mystery.

Before they finished their iced tea, Dana's cell chimed, and when she picked it up, a tremulous voice said, "Officer Vaughn?"

"Yes?" Dana said, not recognizing the caller.

"It's Naomi Teller? From Ogden Drive?"

"Yes, Naomi," Dana said. "Thanks for calling. Do you have some information for me?"

"Yes," Naomi said. "I been thinking about it and I didn't talk to my mother or dad, but I'd like to talk to you. Could we talk in person? It's kinda hard to tell it on the phone."

"I go on duty late this afternoon. I can meet you just after six P.M. Do you want me to come to your house?"

"No. I'll just tell my mother I'm going up the street to visit my friend Liz, but I'll meet you at the corner of Sunset and Ogden. I'll start walking at six o'clock."

"See you there, honey," Dana said.

When Dana closed her cell phone, Pamela said, "Who was that?"

"A fourteen-year-old girl whose house got attacked by a prowling rock thrower last night. I think she wants to tell me who it was."

"Rock thrower?" Pamela said. "I didn't think you busy LAPD cops had time to be chasing around after rock throwers."

"This one's special," Dana said. "When we were looking for him, he sneaked up on one of our officers and tossed him into a swimming pool before escaping."

"Really?" Pamela said. "How mad was the cop?"

"You know how your electric toothbrush vibrates?" Dana asked.

At 3 P.M., Dewey Gleason in his Honda, followed by Tristan Hawkins and Jerzy Szarpowicz in a rented van, were at the car gate of the storage facility in Reseda. Dewey punched in his entry code while the office employee looked out the window. The gate buzzed and swung open. Both vehicles drove in, and Dewey stopped at the office, entered, and spoke to a woman he'd come to know as Bessie on other trips he'd made as Bernie Graham.

"Dropping off a van, Bessie," he said. "We're coming back later."

"Okay, Bernie," she said.

He often gave her small gifts, and this time he brought a few fan magazines to keep her occupied when he pulled out of the storage facility alone in his car.

They proceeded to the storage room, and while Dewey unlocked the door, Tristan drove the van around to the next lane of parking spaces.

While Tristan was gone, Jerzy said to Dewey, "I hope you don't plan to lock this thing up while we're inside."

"Of course I do," Dewey said. "My wife'll be with me when we come back tonight. What's she gonna say if she sees the thing unlocked?"

"I don't know what she's gonna say," Jerzy said, "but you ain't lockin' us in there."

"There's plenty of air," Dewey said. "And if you have to take a leak, just do it in there."

"You ain't lockin' us in there," Jerzy repeated. "Figure out somethin' else." And with that, he took the padlock from Dewey's hand and said, "I'll hang on to this."

"Shit!" Dewey said just as Tristan came jogging back from parking the van. He was carrying a flashlight, a roll of duct tape, and rags for the blindfolds.

"What's the problem?" Tristan said when he saw that they hadn't yet opened the storage-room door.

"He won't let me lock you in," Dewey said. "It'll look suspicious if I don't. It could wreck the whole gag."

"I ain't gonna be locked in that room," Jerzy said, "and that's final."

"Lemme see that," Tristan said, indicating the padlock.

Tristan hung the padlock over the metal door staple and closed the door and folded the hasp over it. "There," he said. "In the dark it'll look okay. Make sure your old lady's standin' behind you when you pretend to be unlockin' it."

Then he opened the storage-room door and said to Jerzy, "Come on, dawg, let's get inside and figure how we're gonna pull our ambush on this here victim and his woman."

"This isn't starting out right," Dewey said. "This is a bad omen."

"Fuck your omens," Jerzy said. "Just do what we say."

So now Dewey could no longer even pretend that he was in charge. These thugs had taken over. Dewey looked at Jerzy and nodded, forcing himself to think only of the money and of driving away from Hollywood forever. He imagined how he'd be laughing out loud every time he thought of this fat pig being left in Frogtown with nothing but his frustrated partner, his boiling rage, and Eunice Gleason.

There wasn't a soul at Hollywood Station that day who did not know about the assault on Officer R.T. Dibney the night before. When he came to work, everyone greeted him with a grin, a chuckle, or a wiseass remark. He even saw two Mexican janitors jabbering in Spanish, and one of them waved his arms in a swimming motion while the other cackled hysterically. The Mexican stopped swimming when he saw R.T. Dibney glaring at him.

R.T. Dibney was expecting more of the same after he changed into his uniform, but walking to the roll call room, he got stopped momentarily by the surfer cops, and they didn't make any wisecracks or swimming jokes.

"Dude, we're into cruising those westside reporting districts until we catch that prowler," Flotsam said gravely.

"Thanks," R.T. Dibney said with some suspicion.

"We're gonna get him before this deployment period ends, bro," Jetsam said.

Now R.T. Dibney was even more suspicious. It was one minute from the start of roll call. Why were they out in the hallway, offering this moral support?

Both surfer cops patted him on the shoulder in yet another show of solidarity and slowly made their way into the roll call room, where everyone was already seated in attentive poses, faces to the front. Both Sergeant Lee Murillo and Sergeant Miriam Hermann looked as serious as the troops. He couldn't figure that out either.

The surfer cops sat quickly and nobody paid the least attention to R.T. Dibney, who was the last man in, and he made his way to his usual seat.

But as he prepared to sit, Sergeant Murillo said, "Today, roll call training is about...swimming pool safety."

And there on R.T. Dibney's chair was a child-size, plastic life preserver with a little toy whistle attached to it, and a tag that said, "Next time, just whistle."

After the dozen cops and two supervisors got their laughter under control, R.T. Dibney, with mustache twitching, said to all, "I'm gonna find that guy. And when I do, I just might not be taking prisoners."

"You're a knockout!" Dewey Gleason said to Eunice when she emerged from her bedroom in a knee-length, wraparound, black-and-white flower-print dress from Macy's. Her strawberry-blonde hair was dyed and highlighted, making her more of a taffy blonde this time, and cut in a chin-length bob. Her nails were coated in clear polish, with the tips whitened for the more natural look, and she wore black, strappy heels that he figured must have set her back a few Franklins.

"I love your new shoes," Dewey said.

Eunice said, "Yeah, well, if I bought shoes to fit the occasion, Musso's would deserve old leather bedroom slippers."

"Anyway, you look terrific," Dewey said with less enthusiasm.

Eunice hadn't had a compliment from Dewey in so long, she didn't know how to respond. She removed the cigarette protruding from the left side of her freshly glossed lips and said, "A girl has to get gussied up once in a while to feel like a girl."

Waxing theatrical, Dewey said with a flourish, "Her flesh is luminous in velvet shadows. A figure from Rembrandt, who will turn all heads in Musso and Frank!"

Eunice looked at him and said, "Don't overact and go all burbly. When your chirp level gets elevated, you make me think you have ulterior motives, Dewey."

That wiped the smile off his face and gave him a jolt of alarm. The goddamn woman had a sixth sense! He'd have to watch every word he said tonight if he was to get her to that storage room in Reseda. The booze would help if he could entice her to swill it while she was busy flirting with the kid. Suddenly, the whole elaborate plan seemed half-baked, and he felt the confidence leaking out of him. But then he only had to think of that meth demon and his sly little partner and remember that they owned him now. That was enough to give him the resolve to get through this gag and hope that he really was the actor he'd always believed he was.

Malcolm Rojas was showered and shaved and wearing a lemon-yellow, long-sleeve shirt that his mother had ironed. He arrived early and was standing nervously in the parking lot behind Musso & Frank when Dewey drove the Honda in. Malcolm wondered why someone as success-ful as Bernie Graham didn't have a better car, but he figured it must be part of doing what the man always referred to as a gag, and not wanting to draw attention in any way. Malcolm couldn't understand the relation-ship that Bernie Graham had with his secretary, Ethel, and wondered if it was romantic. All Malcolm knew for sure was that he didn't like the way Ethel looked at him and smiled at him, as though she wanted to put her hands in his hair the way his mother had done until he'd put a stop to it. And then, when they got out of the Honda, there was something about Ethel, all dressed up with her hair really blonde now, something that made him think of his mother.

"What's wrong, kid?" Dewey said as he and Eunice approached Malcolm.

When they shook hands, Malcolm's palm was wet and clammy. "Oh, nothing," Malcolm said, and the image vanished.

Eunice smiled coquettishly and said, "Are you hungry, Clark?"

"Not real hungry," Malcolm said, "but I'm sure it'll happen when I smell the food in there."

Five minutes after they cleared from roll call, Dana Vaughn had a sur-prise for Hollywood Nate.

"What was it that the Oracle always told you about police work?" she said.

"He said that doing good police work was the most fun we'd ever have in our entire lives. He was nearly sixty-nine years old when he died, so I think he knew a few things about the Job."

"How would you like to do some pretty good police work tonight?"

"Like what?"

"Popping the guy who pushed R.T. Dibney into the swimming pool."

"What're you talking about?"

"The kid, Naomi Teller? She called me. I think she wants to give up the person who tossed the rock. I'm betting it's some little jerkoff from school that she doesn't want her mom to know about."

"You haven't told anyone about the phone call?"

"No, I thought it'd be cool to bust the kid ourselves and let you come up with something funny when R.T. Dibney finds out about it."

"Yeah!" Hollywood Nate said eagerly. "Maybe I'll text him and offer to trade the kid for the keys to his new Acura. Something like that."

"I thought you'd enjoy it, honey," Dana said.

Naomi Teller was standing on the west side of Ogden Drive just south of Sunset Boulevard at 6:10 P.M., as promised. She looked especially young in low-rise jeans, a cutoff "Pink" jersey, and tennis shoes, especially since she was still a year or more from acquiring the womanly curves that the style required.

Dana pulled to the curb and said to Nate, "You better take a short walk and let us girls talk it over."

"Roger that," he said, getting out of the car and holding the passenger door open for the girl to get in.

When Naomi was in the passenger seat next to Dana, she said, "I was wondering if pushing the officer into the swimming pool is real serious?"

"It's an assault on a police officer," Dana said. "People don't do it every day, that's for sure. Are you worried about what'll happen to the rock thrower?"

"No, I'm kinda scared about what might happen to me if I snitch. 'Cause I'm pretty scared of him. I think he's not quite right up here." She tapped her temple with a fingernail decorated by a little Walk of Fame star.

"Tell me about him," Dana said.

"I met him when I was walking home last week, and I gave him my number. And I went and had a burger with him yesterday when he called me after he got off work. That's all I did with the guy, but he's, like, nineteen years old. My mom'd have a fit if she knew I got in a car with a guy his age that I didn't even know."

"Did he say where he worked?"

"No."

"What kind of car?"

"A red Mustang. A real old one."

"What's his name, Naomi?"

"Clark. He says it's Clark Jones, but I don't believe he's a Jones. He looks like a Gomez maybe. He's real cute with great teeth and big dimples."

Dana smiled at that and said, "Why'd he throw the rock through the window?"

"Because after he bought me the burger, he thought I was his girlfriend or something. There was stuff kinda weird about him, and I got scared and wished I'd never got in his car. When he called me later, I told him he was too old for me. I did it, like, real nice and all, but he got way mad. He called me a bitch, and I hung up on him."

"Do you know where he lives?"

"No, he never said."

"When he called you at home, was it on your home phone?"

"No," Naomi said, "on my cell."

"Bingo!" Dana said. "You've got his cell number in your phone, then?"

"Oh, yeah," Naomi said. "In fact, I put it in the list the first time he called." She pulled her phone from the pocket of her jeans, scrolled to "Clark," and said, "Here. You can write it down."

Dana pulled out her notebook and did just that, and then she said, "Now I'd like the best description of him that you can give me. You think he might be Hispanic, and he's nineteen years old, right? How tall is he?"

"Not tall," Naomi said. "I'm five foot six, and he's only a couple inches taller."

"How much does he weigh? Take a guess."

"He's thin. So how much would that be?"

"About a hundred and forty or so. Any tattoos?"

"Not that I could see."

"How about the color of his hair and eyes?"

"Real pretty brown eyes with long lashes," Naomi said. "And real dark curly hair, almost black."

Dana made notes and then said, "Long hair, short hair?"

"Just a regular guy's haircut," Naomi said, "except it was thick and curly. It curled over his ears. Most girls would die for hair like that."

And then Dana Vaughn's demeanor changed, and Naomi thought her questions seemed a bit more urgent.

Dana looked at her notes and back at Naomi and said, "When was the first time you saw Clark?"

"Last week," Naomi said. "I forget what day. Maybe Friday?"

"What was he wearing then?"

"He wore a T-shirt and jeans and tennis shoes," Naomi said.

"What color was the T-shirt?"

"Blue. Light blue."

And now Naomi saw even more of a change in the officer when she leaned forward and said, "When you were having your burger yesterday, where were you?"

"At Mel's Drive-In on the Strip," Naomi said. "It was pretty expensive, I think."

"Did you notice anything different about him yesterday? Anything about his face or other parts of his body?"

"Like what?"

"Any fresh scratches or bruises anywhere?"

"Just skinned-up knuckles on both hands. And a little bruise under his eye. He said he beat up a couple of guys at his job that were bullies. I didn't really believe that either."

And now there was no question in Naomi's mind: This police officer was super-interested in Clark Jones. In fact, the officer looked as though she wanted to call out something to her partner, who was waiting twenty yards away on the sidewalk.

"Anything else?" Dana asked.

Naomi said, "I think Clark is kind of a bragger who makes up things. Like about his Persian mother and his French father. I didn't believe that either. We talked about guys like him in class. They have a mental problem, maybe because of drugs or something. It makes them behave...grandy-something."

"Grandiose?"

"Yeah, that's it," Naomi said. "He talks, like, way grandiose."

"If Clark phones you again, I want you to call me immediately," Dana said. "I'm not sure yet, but he may be involved in some very serious crimes against women."

"Now I'm really scared," Naomi said.

"Don't be afraid," Dana said. "I'm taking your information straight to my station and phoning detectives with it. I think Clark will be behind bars very soon. Would you like us to drop you at your house now?"

"I think you better," Naomi said. "I don't wanna walk alone. But I'd like to tell my mom about it myself. She might phone you later."

"That's fine," Dana said. "I'll be available."

After they dropped off Naomi at her house on Ogden Drive, Dana said to Hollywood Nate, who as yet knew nothing about Naomi's information, "Well, if the Oracle was right about doing good police work, we're about to have ourselves lots of fun, honey."

When Malcolm finished his steak, he said it was the tastiest he'd ever had. Eunice smiled tenderly and said, "Would you like another soda?"

"I don't think so. Thanks, anyways."

"Did you save room for dessert?" she asked.

"Sure," Malcolm said with his high-wattage smile.

"That smile of yours could light up the Vegas Strip," Eunice said, making Malcolm drop his eyes in discomfort.

Dewey, who hadn't eaten more than a few bites of his swordfish, signaled to a waiter for a recitation of the desserts. The waiter nodded but continued with other customers. It didn't faze Dewey, who especially liked the waiters at Musso & Frank, most of whom were aging brusque Mexicans dressed formally in black tie. They knew their stuff and didn't waste time or words stroking customers, unless the customers were Hollywood relics, those faded stars and almost-stars who still came to the old places for the fantasy of retaining continuity with a Hollywood that was no more.

"Do you like this place, Clark?" Eunice asked, tapping on the table with one of her newly lacquered nails, and Dewey knew she was dying to run outside for a smoke.

"Yeah, it's really nice," Malcolm said.

Eunice looked around, trying to see the place as the boy saw it. Musso & Frank was one of the old restaurants that didn't so much resist changes in style and decor. They simply ignored them.

"Have you ever been to a nice restaurant before?" she asked.

"No, not really," he said. "But like I was telling you, my dad was a French chef. He told me about the restaurants he worked at in New York and Paris, France, and London, England. He's dead now."

"A French chef?" Eunice said. "How about that. Is your mom still alive?"

"No, she passed away too. She was a Persian who was a distant relative of the royal family over there. I was raised by my dad's cousin, who was married to a man in East L.A. I didn't belong there, but there was nothing I could do about it. Now I live alone in Hollywood in an apartment. It's pretty expensive. That's why I'm so anxious to go to work for you and make some real money."

Dewey glanced at Eunice and knew that she didn't believe this kid's bullshit any more than he did, but by the way she smiled at the boy—and it wasn't maternally—he knew she didn't give a damn what he said. Eunice was utterly taken. Thank God for midlife crises, Dewey Gleason thought, and he looked at his watch.

Jerzy Szarpowicz, sweating in the oppressive darkness of the metal-and-concrete storage room, turned on his flashlight and also looked at his watch.

"It don't make the time pass no faster by lookin' at your watch every two minutes," Tristan said. They were sitting on top of cardboard crates containing large plasma TV sets that they fully intended to take away and sell when this was over.

"I'm burnin' up in here!" Jerzy said. "I wish I had a quarter of Go Fast. I even wish I had a dime bag of smoke."

"Get on the floor," Tristan said. "Heat rises."

"It's jist as hot down there," Jerzy grumbled. "This gag ain't gonna work. That motherfucker's gamin' us like he games everybody else."

"It might work, it might not work," Tristan said. "If they don't show up, we'll load all his merchandise in the van and take it outta here and sell it. Then we'll have more negotiations to conduct with Mr. Bernie Graham."

"If he ain't already outta Dodge," Jerzy said.

"He ain't," Tristan said. "He's locked into this gag. You can see it all in the man's eyes."

"See what?"

"Greed," Tristan said. "Like I see in your eyes."

"And how 'bout you? You ain't greedy?"

"Oh, yeah, dawg," Tristan said. "But somehow I don't think I'm desperate greedy like you and Bernie. I got my limits."

"You think too much," Jerzy said.

Tristan looked at his partner and said, "Wood, it jist occurred to me that I ain't never seen you in anything but a black T-shirt, jeans, and boots. Don't you have no other threads?"

"I got duplicates of these," Jerzy said testily.

"Your bitch must find you very easy to buy for," Tristan observed.

All pout, Jerzy looked at his wristwatch again.

Six-X-Seventy-six was back in the officers' report room at Hollywood Station. Dana had called to leave information for the sex crimes detectives, a job that had recently been taken away from Hollywood Detectives and given to West Bureau. She made a request that when the detectives got the warrant the next day, she be kept in the loop as to their arrest plans.

And while she was doing that, Hollywood Nate was apprising the acting watch commander, Sergeant Murillo, on what they'd learned from Naomi Teller. His supervisor was not just interested but very impressed.

When Nate was finished, Sergeant Murillo said, "Damn, I think you've nailed it. Clark Jones, or whatever he's called, has gotta be the rapist too."

"Dana nailed it," Hollywood Nate said. "A lotta coppers woulda just taken the original report for the busted window and turned it in and been done with it. Not her. She's gonna be one hell of a sergeant."

"No doubt about that," Sergeant Murillo said. "And though we're one day early for our full moon over Hollywood, this piece of police work deserves a large pizza with the works for you two."

"Which you'll help us eat," Nate said.

"Of course," said Sergeant Murillo. "And I think I'll call Miriam in to join us at the feast."

"If you're calling in Sergeant Hermann, don't you think you better get the super-large-size pizza?" Hollywood Nate said.

When Nate got back to the report room, Dana Vaughn was still writing. He watched her for a moment. When she stopped writing and glanced up at him, he said, "When your promotion and transfer goes through, I hope you'll come back here as our midwatch supervisor after you finish your probation."

"You gonna miss me that much?" Dana said.

Hollywood Nate said, "You're not a sixty-nine-year-old guy with too much gut and a crew cut right out of an old black-and-white movie, but by God, there's something about you that reminds me of the Oracle."

"Why, honey," said Dana Vaughn, "that's just about the nicest thing anyone around here's ever said to me."

After paying the check, Dewey said, "Will you two excuse me? Cocktails always excite my bladder."

"We don't need the details," Eunice said. "Just go."

When Dewey was gone, Eunice said to Malcolm, "Can you give me your cell number, Clark? I'll be needing it when we have to set up jobs for you."

"Sure," Malcolm said.

Eunice smiled at Malcolm when she punched his number into her own cell phone. He didn't like the way she was smiling at him and wished his boss would hurry back.

The moment he was alone in the restroom, Dewey pulled his cell from his pocket and speed-dialed. After one ring, he heard Tristan say, "Yeah."

"Call in exactly ten minutes," he said.

"Okay," Tristan said and clicked off.

Dewey's bowels suddenly rumbled and he ran inside a toilet stall just in time.

Eight minutes later, after Eunice had visited the restroom, she and Malcolm and Dewey were in the parking lot behind the restaurant, having said their good-byes. Dewey paid for his car and Malcolm's, and just as they were ready to go, Eunice, who'd drunk two cocktails more than usual, said, "Clark, don't go home yet. Let's stop and get a nightcap. Have you ever been to the Formosa Café? No, of course you haven't. It's another old Hollywood joint on Santa Monica that Bernie likes because Bogie drank there."

She saw the young man's blank expression and said, "Humphrey Bogart? Ever heard of him?"

"No," Malcolm said.

"Damn, you're young!" Eunice said.

Dewey looked at his watch. Less than two minutes! The kid had to be gone when his cell rang, or the whole gag could fail! "Ethel," he said, "this young man can't have a nightcap. He's not old enough to drink in bars, so why don't we let him go."

When she turned to face him, Dewey could see she was hammered, and only minutes away from belligerence. If she turned mean, it was all over. As he was trying to decide how to handle her, the kid saved him.

"Thanks, but I should go home now," Malcolm said. "I had a real nice time, but I still gotta get up early for my job at the warehouse." Then he added, "Which I hope I can quit real soon."

"Soon," Dewey said. "We'll start working in earnest late tomorrow afternoon. Keep your cell on and I'll call around noon."

"Good night, Mr. Graham," Malcolm said, walking to his car. "Good night, Ethel."

"Night," Eunice said and then turned to Dewey and said, "You can't let someone have a nice evening out, can you, Mr. Graham?"

He didn't need this shit, not now. He looked at his watch and held open the passenger door for her, saying as soothingly as he could without condescension, "Eunice, we had a very nice evening. The boy had to go home and—"

His cell chirped, and she heard it while she was lighting a cigarette and shooting a boozy glare at him.

He opened the cell and said, "Bernie Graham speaking."

He heard Tristan say, "Okay, I'll jist keep this goin' till you say good-bye."

Then Dewey said for effect, "Oh, shit! How did that happen?" After a long pause, he said, "Oh, Christ, I can't come now, and I don't have anybody else to send!" He paused again and said, "Okay, okay, how long will he wait?" After another pause he said, "I'll deal with it somehow."

When he clicked off, Eunice said, "Now what the hell's the problem?"

"That was our runner Creole. He works with Jerzy and they're stuck downtown at the interchange with a flat tire and no spare. I was depending on them to deliver three laptops and two small plasmas to a regular customer of ours named Hatch. You've heard me talk about him."

"They'll have to do it tomorrow," Eunice said.

"He said Hatch wants the merchandise by ten o'clock tonight or he's walking away from the deal. And he owes us three grand in addition to this delivery."

"What, you're giving easy terms to thieves now, Dewey? How the hell is it that he already owes us three grand?"

"It wasn't me. Creole did it last Thursday without my approval when he made another delivery to Hatch. I knew you'd get mad, so I didn't tell you. Anyway, Hatch is waiting in north Hollywood in Von's parking lot with almost five thousand dollars for us. That's if we make tonight's delivery by ten o'clock."

As drunk as she was, it made her stop and think, as Dewey had hoped it would. He knew he could always depend on her avarice.

She said, "And I suppose the goods are in the storage room in Reseda."

"Of course," he said, "and there's just barely enough time to pick up the stuff and deliver it to Hatch. I'm just saying, that's how it is."

She smoked and thought about it and said, "Okay, let's go. I mighta known I could never get a nice evening out without some major shit going down all wrong."

"It wasn't my fault, Eunice," Dewey said.

"Just drive to Reseda, for chrissake," Eunice said, taking a big drag from the cigarette and blowing it at the windshield. "And hurry it up, Dewey, or we'll lose it all and that'll make everything perfect. A perfectly fucked-up evening."

★ NINETEEN ★

THE STORAGE FACILITY was almost without customers by the time Dewey and Eunice arrived at 8:45 P.M. The light was on in the office, and the employee on duty at that time of night was an elderly ex-employee of a local alarm company who'd been pensioned off and was now supplementing his income. Dewey had met him on a few occasions but couldn't remember his name. When Dewey stopped at the gate and punched in his code, the man looked out and buzzed open the car gate. Dewey drove in and stopped at the office, leaving Eunice in the car while he went inside to check in.

The night man had more hair than Dewey did, but it was chalk-white. His face was splotchy with liver spots, and the skin on his hands was translucent. He had a small TV on the desk and was watching Dodgers baseball.

Dewey read the name on the shirt tag and said, "Evening, Sam. I'm Bernie Graham. Met you a couple of evenings last year, but so far this year I've only been coming in the daytime."

"Oh, sure, hi, Bernie," Sam said, but Dewey was sure the old guy didn't remember him at all.

"My employees left a van here today, did you see it?"

"Naw," Sam said, eyes darting back to the ballgame. "I been too busy to make the rounds."

"I'll be driving it out in a little while. Might be leaving my car here till tomorrow."

"No problem, Bernie," Sam said. "I'll open the gate when I see you leaving."

When Dewey got back to the car, Eunice was dozing, but she sat up, looking disoriented when he opened the door.

"You're at the storage room," Dewey said, "in case you're wondering."

"Oh, shit," Eunice said. "I was hoping this was only a nightmare."

"I'll need some help carrying the plasmas," Dewey said. "My ribs're still aching bad."

"What else?" Eunice said. "I may as well get a back sprain while I'm at it."

Dewey's hands were shaking when he pulled open the hasp and pretended to be unlocking the padlock hanging on the door staple. He dropped the key twice before he could complete the charade, causing Eunice to say, "Do you want me to do it? Next time drink Virgin Marys."

When he opened the door, he said, "I never come here at night. Let's see, where's the light switch? Can you strike a match over here?"

Grumbling, she walked inside, and then a meaty hand was clamped over her mouth and she was pulled to the floor onto her belly with a huge weight on top of her while duct tape was wrapped around her ankles.

She heard Dewey cry out, "Owwww! You're breaking my wrist! Put the gun away, Creole! Why're you doing this?"

A man whose breath smelled like rank onions and beer said in her ear, "If you make one fuckin' sound, I'll bury my knife in your belly and gut you like a pig. Now lay real still."

Then, while she whimpered, her wrists were duct-taped behind her back, and a cloth blindfold was wrapped around her face and duct-taped in place with barely enough of her nostrils exposed for breathing.

Eunice heard Dewey say, "Okay, I can't move! You don't need the gun, Creole! Take the merchandise! Take our money! You can have the goddamn car too!"

Then she heard a smacking sound, like fist striking flesh, and Dewey cried out in pain. And she heard a thud against the metal wall of the storage room and then a low moan from Dewey.

His voice was guttural and choked when he said, "Go ahead and hit me if it makes you feel better, Jerzy. But for God's sake, don't hurt my wife!"

To Tristan Hawkins, the man looked like some fucking radio actor in one of those old movies about people performing to a microphone. He was cooking way too much ham here, so Tristan decided to take control.

"Shut the fuck up," Tristan said. "I'm sick of hearin' you."

Unable to surrender the stage, Dewey moaned again and said in a stage whisper, "Okay, I'll be quiet, but please, please, don't hurt her! That's all I ask!"

Then Eunice heard footsteps and knew that one of them had gone out and closed the door behind him. She started crying and had trouble stifling her sobs even when Tristan said, "Lady, you better turn off the faucet, or I'll tape your mouth shut."

The next sound Eunice heard was the van pulling up to the storage room. Then the door creaked open and footsteps came near her and she was lifted by the man with the big hands and dragged along the floor. She heard the van door slide open, and the man grunted as he lifted her onto the floor of the van and rolled her to the back of the cargo space.

Then Dewey moaned aloud and said, "Ohhh, my ribs. They hurt!" as he pounded the floor of the van and made sounds that he thought indicated he was also being manhandled.

Tristan was getting really concerned now. He was sure that Bernie's performance was way over the top, so he jumped into the passenger seat of the van, reached behind him, and grabbed Dewey's shoulder, saying into the man's face, "I want...you...to...shut...the...fuck...up. And, dawg, this ain't a woof, it's a warnin'. You feel me?"

Dewey seemed to get the message and was silent after the van door was shut. Jerzy got in, dropped it into gear, and drove to the exit gate. Sam didn't even look out but hit a button and the car gate swung open.

Tristan saw the Polack turn around and grin, his meth-stained donkey teeth glinting in the bluish glow from the security lights. Then they were out onto the street and heading to Frogtown.

*   *   *

The sex crimes detective at West Bureau called from home to Hollywood Station at the same time that Dana Vaughn and Hollywood Nate were enjoying their celebratory pizza with Sergeant Murillo and Sergeant Hermann in the lunchroom.

Dana took her call in the watch commander's office and was talking to D2 Flo Johnson, whom she knew from her days working narcotics.

"That's terrific work, Dana," the detective said. "I'll run it by my D-three. I think this might be worth some Saturday overtime for my team. I can write a brief search warrant, and after I get a judge to sign it, I'll fax it to Clark Jones's cell provider. Then we'll be in business."

"You don't wanna get on it now?" Dana said, disappointed. "It's kind of personal. In addition to attacking the women, he dumped one of our Hollywood coppers into a swimming pool. You know about that?"

"I did hear something about that," Flo Johnson said, "but we should wait till tomorrow, when we're more prepared. If we can't reach the guy at his billing address, we'll need to use Major Crimes Division to triangulate from the cell towers. I can't get all this going tonight."

"What if he figures the girl may have dimed him and he dumps his cell?"

"Let's hope he's home at his billing address on a Saturday. That'd make it easy."

"We'd like to be there," Dana said. "If you don't already have him by tomorrow night, will you call us? We're Six-X-Seventy-six."

"Tell you what," the detective said. "We'll be on this tomorrow, and if we don't have the guy in custody by ... What time do you clear from roll call?"

"Eighteen hundred."

"If we've got nothing by eighteen hundred, you can come with us to where we'll be setting up on the billing address. That's assuming he's a local boy."

"I think he is," Dana said.

"Deal," said Flo Johnson. "I'll be in touch with you tomorrow."

"Roger that," Dana said. "And thanks for keeping us in the loop."

"I'm the one who owes you the thanks," the detective said.

Dana reentered the lunchroom with a smile, until she saw only Sergeant Murillo and Hollywood Nate picking at the remains of the crust.

"Damn, you guys ate all the pizza!" Dana said.

Hollywood Nate pointed toward the empty chair and to the doorway, indicating that the departed Sergeant Hermann was to blame.

"Don't look at me, Dana. I ordered the super-large," Sergeant Murillo said apologetically. "You can be sure I'll be writing you that glowing attagirl as soon as the guy gets popped. In the meantime, can I buy you a burrito?"

Malcolm Rojas had gone to bed very early and was watching TV, as was his mother in the living room, a wine bottle beside her chair. He'd been reliving in his mind this very exciting day, especially the dinner at a real Hollywood restaurant. His rage at Naomi Teller had faded to an annoyance. She wasn't worthy of his anger. When he made a lot of money with Bernie Graham and bought a new car, he might drive by her house sometime and toot the horn. Then she'd see what she'd missed by being a little bitch.

He was dropping off to sleep when something occurred to him. Naomi had his cell number! Suddenly he was wide awake. He wanted to call her right now. Maybe he could say he was sorry for getting angry on the phone. And maybe she would tell him about the broken window, and of course he would deny knowing anything about it. Or knowing anything about a cop being pushed into a neighbor's swimming pool.

Then he calmed himself by trying to use logic. What if she did mention him to the cops as possibly being the rock thrower? They couldn't prove anything. And they sure couldn't prove that he shoved the cop into the pool. And even if they could, how serious a crime was that for someone who'd never been arrested in his whole life? A broken window? Back in Boyle Heights, people broke other people's windows every day.

And cops had a lot worse things happen to them back there than getting pushed into a swimming pool. Even now he had to laugh whenever he relived that amazing moment. Thinking of how he'd been brave enough to do it, as noiseless as a spider, and elude all of them and escape unseen like a ghost. It was incredibly thrilling. He masturbated again and then went to sleep.

Jerzy parked the van beside the steps leading to the upstairs apartment. This part of Frogtown was quiet, although it was widely known that gunshots fired by gang members could often be heard on quiet evenings in this part of Los Angeles. There was an unusual hum of cicadas in the air, making one wonder where they were coming from. There was sparse vegetation around the old commercial buildings, and the nearest house was a block away, but the hum was surprisingly strong.

Tristan got out and, using his flashlight, ran up the outside staircase and unlocked the door. He came back down and walked out to the street, looked both ways, and then slid open the side door of the van. He pointed at Dewey to begin emoting.

If Dewey hadn't been so nervous, so downright scared, he would've objected to Tristan's assuming the role of director. But now Dewey began striking and kicking the wall of the van before he hopped out, moaning as though his body were being roughly dragged. For good measure he cried out when his feet hit the pavement, as though a vulnerable part of his body had made contact with the ground.

"Turn it down!" Tristan whispered. The man was over the top again.

Eunice had stopped crying halfway to Frogtown, and she hadn't uttered a sound since, except for her very heavy breathing. Jerzy dragged her out onto the sidewalk, and with Tristan lifting her legs, they carried her up the staircase, both men straining and puffing before reaching the open door.

When they got her inside, Tristan switched on the overhead ceiling bulb and they hoisted her onto the bed, dropping her on her side.

"Woman, you better call NutriSystem," Jerzy muttered. "My fuckin' back is broke."

Jerzy made considerable noise descending the stairs while Tristan stayed watching Eunice. Jerzy and Dewey clumped back up the steps, Jerzy panting as loud as he could, and Dewey moaning as though in agony. Dewey flopped down on the floor beside the bed, Eunice's back to him, and continued groaning while the two kidnappers walked to the door.

Jerzy said, "We'll be right back, and if either of you moves, you'll suffer for it, believe me."

Then they went out, closed the door, and stood right outside on the porch.

Eunice's breathing was so loud, it sounded like snoring, and Dewey said, "Eunice! Can you hear me?"

She didn't answer, and he sat up from his reclining position and said, "Eunice! Are you conscious?"

"Yes," she said in a feeble voice, "but I can hardly breathe."

"What is it?" he said. "Why can't you breathe?"

"I think it's an asthma attack," she said.

"You don't have asthma," he said.

"Or emphysema," she said. "I been having...having lotsa trouble with my lungs lately."

"Oh, God!" Dewey cried. Her breathing sounded like a hacksaw cutting through steel—like the steel bars of a jail cell! What if she stopped breathing? What if she had to be rushed to an ER? All this for nothing? Everything screwed because she had to smoke eighty fucking cigarettes a day for the past thirty years? He said, "We gotta get you outta here!"

Her sawlike breathing was a little less raspy now, and she said, "How...how do you plan to do it, Dewey? I can't move. Can you?"

"No," he said, "but we gotta think of something."

After several seconds she said, "How...how did those goddamn... thugs get in our storage room, Dewey?"

He said, "I hate to admit it, but...well, they outsmarted me. I led Creole and Jerzy there today, like I usually do. They followed me in their rented van to pick up Hatch's delivery. But when we got there, Creole said that Hatch just phoned him and called it off till later, not sure how many laptops he wanted. I left them there at the storage room to wait for Hatch's decision."

"You...you left them there?" she said, the extra stress making her breathing more difficult again.

"I didn't wanna sit there waiting with them. You and me were going out to dinner, and I wanted to go home and freshen up. So, yes, I left them there, Eunice. They called me later and said an emergency came up and they had to make a run somewhere and they'd keep me posted. How could I know it was a lie and they were gonna hide in there and pull this shit?"

"What?...what're they pulling, Dewey?" Eunice asked. "Maybe you can tell me, because I'm pretty confused by all this."

"I don't know, Eunice," Dewey said. "I guess they saw through my Jakob Kessler act. I guess we'll find out soon enough." Then he remembered his bogus pain and said, "God, he hurt me, Eunice! I think I'm bleeding from my ear."

After another long silence, she said in more measured tones, "Why did the one you called Creole have Hatch's cell number? Do you delegate your responsibility to runners now?"

She was sounding stronger and asking the right questions, and Dewey felt his confidence waning. He stalled by groaning in pain some more. When he finished emoting, he said, "Not usually. But today was a special day. I gave Creole Hatch's cell number and I called Hatch and said Creole would be handling the transaction tonight. I did it so we could have a nice long peaceful evening away from all this...this awful fucking business we do. Okay, so they outsmarted me. I admit it and I'm gonna pay the price for it, not you."

"Whadda you mean, you're gonna pay the price?"

"Whatever they want, I'm gonna refuse them unless they take you outta here and drop you unharmed somewhere. I'll let them keep me here and I'll pay the price. Whatever happens, you'll be safe." After a few seconds he said, "God, I ache all over!"

She was quiet again, and he could almost hear her thinking. It worried him. He wished she'd start crying again. Then they heard heavy footsteps and the door opened.

Tristan and Jerzy entered, and Dewey nodded at them and said, "For chrissake, tell us what this is all about. Whadda you want from us?"

"We want money, of course," Jerzy said.

"I always treated you right," Dewey said. "Did I ever fail to pay you for your work?"

"You paid us shit," Jerzy said. "But now you're gonna make up for it. And we want more than you got in your wallet."

"How much do you want?" Dewey said.

"About five hundred thousand should do it," Tristan said.

Dewey looked at his watch. He'd rehearsed this moment several times in his head, and he'd decided that the period of silence should last a full ten seconds. After that pause he said, "Have you been doing acid? Or too much crystal?"

Then Dewey pointed at Jerzy and closed his fist, making a gesture of punching his left palm. Jerzy nodded and smacked his left palm with his big right fist and Dewey grunted and moaned again and said, "Please, Jerzy...please don't hit me again!"

Tristan thought that both Jerzy and the man were getting into their roles with way too much gusto, so he tried to pull them back by saying, "Okay, dawg, shut it down."

Dewey's moans were punctuated with gasps and even a few whimpers until Tristan said, "Let's be businessmen here. Turns out we figured out the whole game you been runnin' with old Ethel here, and we figure we own you now and we're gonna steal a lotta the money that you stole from other folks all these years. And we think about five hundred thousand is reasonable. We decided we're gonna keep one of you, and the other one is gonna get the money from wherever you keep it, and then everything's cool and you won't see us no more. And you can go back to business as usual."

Dewey spoke in what he thought was a painful whisper and said, "You're fucking lunatics."

Jerzy said, "Okay, we tried being gentlemen. Now we're gonna show you how the wolf eats the rabbit."

"What're you doing?" Dewey said. "Ohhh, stop!" And then he let out a cry of pretend pain.

Way over the top! Tristan thought. Next thing, somebody driving by might hear it and call the cops! He shook his head and mouthed the words "Too much!" at Dewey.

Dewey quieted down to steady but subdued moaning punctuated by an occasional sob. He finally said, "Please...please don't do that again.

How much…much do you want? Five grand? Maybe…maybe Ethel could scrape up five thousand if you let her go. Please, Creole, let her go!"

Dewey looked at Eunice lying there on her side, knees drawn up, blindfolded and silent, not whimpering, not even complaining. And he looked at Tristan, shook his head, and shrugged.

Tristan took the cue and said, "Jerzy, how 'bout takin' him down to the basement for some serious talk. Call me with good news when you get it." Then he said, "Dude, I'm afraid I gotta leave you alone with Jerzy. He'll take the gloves off and put some serious hurt on you, but you ain't givin' me no choice."

Jerzy and Dewey both began shuffling and grunting their way to the door and before it closed behind them, Dewey said, "Creole, at least take the tape off her. Have some compassion!"

When they were outside, Dewey and Jerzy descended the staircase and went to the van, where they got inside and sat. Jerzy opened a can of beer and Dewey looked at his watch. It was 1:25 A.M.

"We'll give them twenty minutes," he said to Jerzy, who was unresponsive.

Dewey could smell days of body odor. He opened the door of the van, and Jerzy said, "Where you goin'?"

"To take a leak."

"Well, don't go far," Jerzy said.

"It's my wife that's your prisoner," Dewey said. "Not me."

"That sorta depends how you look at it," Jerzy said. "So piss here beside the van. I won't peek at the little worm when you let him outta your pants."

Tristan said, "Look, lady, I don't wanna see you or your old man get hurt bad, but you gotta understand, you ain't leavin' here till we get what we're after. And my peckerwood partner, he's a violent dude. Do you see that?"

Still, Eunice did not reply. All Tristan heard was her breath rattling. It was making him nervous, and he said, "Do you have some kinda lung problem?"

There was no answer, so he said, "Do you wanna go to the bathroom?"

And at last Eunice spoke. She said, "Yes."

Tristan said, "Okay, what we're gonna do here is, I'm gonna cut the tape off your ankles and your wrists. You're gonna go in there and do what you gotta do, but do not touch the blindfold. If you do, I'm gonna whap you upside the head with a lead pipe I got in my belt, and then I'm gonna tape up your wrists and your ankles and your mouth. And you might jist suffocate. You understand?"

Eunice nodded her head, and Tristan said, "Goddamnit, woman, say the words!"

"I understand," she said.

"Okay," Tristan said, and he took a penknife from his pocket and began sawing through the tape on her ankles. He left the tape sticking to each leg when he got through and said, "You can go ahead and move your feet if you want. Must be cramped up by now." Then he began sawing through the tape on her wrists.

She moaned in relief when she could move her hands to the front of her body, and she stripped the duct tape from each wrist and threw it behind her into the middle of the room.

"Get up," Tristan said, and he held on to Eunice's right arm as she slid her legs across the bed until her feet were on the floor.

"One of my heels is broken off," she said.

"Well, I'll send you a new pair of shoes when I get the money," Tristan said. "Now stand up, and I'll lead you to the bathroom and you can feel where the toilet is and the sink."

Eunice stood and kicked off both shoes, walking barefoot to the tiny bathroom. Tristan turned her so that her back was to the toilet and said, "You can sit down when you're ready. The toilet paper is up on the sink to your right. There's a bar of soap there too, but I forgot to bring paper towels."

"Would you please close the door?" Eunice said.

"Ain't no way in the world that's gonna happen," Tristan said. "But I'll turn my head away if that makes you feel better. I ain't interested in watchin' somebody on a toilet, trust me."

"How do I know that?" Eunice said. "I can't see."

"You can take my word for it, woman," Tristan said. "Because I'm the only one here that can keep my crazy fuckin' partner from doin' some things you won't like at all. You can think of me as your protector, if you cooperate."

Without responding, Eunice reached under her dress, pulled her panties down, and sat carefully on the toilet seat. After hearing the stream for twenty seconds, Tristan said, "Yeah, you did have to pee, all right."

A moment later she was standing in front of the sink, where she found the faucet, cold only, and washed her hands, drying them on her dress. Then she felt Tristan take her arm again and lead her back to the bed.

"You aren't gonna tape me up again, are you?" she said.

"No, but I'm gonna chain your wrists to the bed. I was gonna chain your ankles too, but I'll see how things work out. If you or your husband don't cooperate, your ankles will get chained and then I'll have to let Jerzy do what he does."

"Where is my husband?" Eunice said.

"In the basement of this here place," Tristan said.

"What's happening down there?"

"You can guess, can't you?" Tristan said.

Eunice was silent again until he wrapped the chain around each wrist and locked the links together with the padlocks. The chain encircled the steel frame of the old bed.

When Eunice spoke she said, "Why do I have to wear this blindfold? My husband knows both of you very well. Why the blindfold?"

"Because we don't want you to have any idea where you're at," Tristan said.

"I can understand why you did that when you were driving us here, but now that we're at the destination, why can't you take it off? All I'll see is the room."

He wasn't ready for a question that logical asked so dispassionately. The woman was thinking, and Tristan was starting to conclude that she might be way smarter than her old man.

"If you could see where a window is at, you might be tempted to take a flyin' leap at it next time I take you to the bathroom. The blindfold stays on."

Tristan's cell rang and he opened it and said, "Yo."

Jerzy on his cell said, "We're comin' up now."

"Five more minutes, wood," Tristan said. "Gimme five more minutes."

"Okay, but then we're comin' up and I'll take over," Jerzy said.

Tristan clicked off and said, "Lady, my partner ain't had the success he hoped for with your husband and now he wants to start on you. Why not save both of you a lotta pain and tell us how one of you can get us our five hundred grand. You can get outta this in one piece and go out and steal another five hundred grand from people the way you stole this batch. You ain't stupid. So don't do somethin' real dumb here, okay?"

"Would your partner take me down in the basement too?" Eunice asked.

Damn! Tristan thought. Does she suspect something? Maybe that there's no basement and that Bernie is in on this gag? He said, "Whether he does it here or in the basement, you ain't gonna like it either way. Jist get us what we want."

"We don't have five hundred thousand dollars," Eunice said.

"How much you got?"

"Very little. We might be able to come up with the five thousand that my husband offered you. Maybe a little more."

"Don't say that to my partner, woman. That's all I can say."

"Would you let me go so I can get some money from the bank for you?"

"Oh, yeah," Tristan said. "We'll drop you off at Bank of America or somewheres and let you and him bounce inside to make a withdrawal."

"I didn't mention him," she said. "You could keep him in the basement as a hostage."

It was at that moment that Tristan Hawkins began to get a very strong feeling that doing the gag his way was doomed. And that only Jerzy could get the information out of her, by doing it his way.

That's when he heard the heavy footsteps, bumping sounds, and whimpers from Dewey. The door opened and Jerzy stomped in, playing his part to the hilt, and Dewey, now a balls-out method actor, dragged himself across the floor and fell heavily onto his stomach with a plaintive "Ohhhhhh."

"Tell you what," Tristan said. "You two have a nice little talk and we'll be back in ten minutes for your final answer. By the way, man, would you like to take a leak?"

"He already did," Jerzy said with the snuffling giggle that Tristan had come to hate. "Look at the front of his pants."

"Let's give them some space," Tristan said.

After the door had closed, Dewey gradually quieted down, erupting in a sob only every so often, when he felt the timing was right. He knew that this was his last chance to persuade her, and he wanted her to speak first. But she was silent.

A moment passed before she said, "Are you blindfolded, Dewey?"

Perfect, he thought. She didn't ask how badly he was hurt or what they'd done to him. She's thinking of how to escape! "Of course," he croaked, followed by a whimper.

More silence, until she finally said, "Are you hurt bad?"

He thought about trying wry laughter but wasn't certain he could pull it off. Then he said, whispery, "I don't hurt *good,* I can tell you that!"

"So, what did he do to you?" she said without emotion.

"He's very good at those fucking body shots. Now I know I got cracked ribs. And he loves to squeeze my balls until I'm...I'm...crying like a little girl and puking my guts out." And then Dewey surprised himself by actually crying. It was coming back to him as good as it ever had. He was Dewey Gleason, kidnap victim. He was absolutely in character. He still had the old acting chops!

"Were you able to get some idea of where we are?" she asked after he calmed himself.

"I think...think it's a two-story house. All I could smell was mold and mildew in the basement. And him. You can smell him more than...than anything. I...I don't want him to touch you with his filthy hands, Eunice!"

She didn't reply for another agonizing minute, and then she said, "How do they think they can get away with this, even if we gave them money?" Eunice said. "These're guys you know."

Dewey sighed and said, "Oh, God! I don't know what's hurting more, my ribs or my nuts. What? What did you say?"

"I'm saying that you could help the police to find these two, and they know it. Do they plan to kill us after they get the ransom, or what?"

"They know more about us than we do about them," Dewey said. "They believe we'd never dare go to the police, no matter what they do to us. They think they could tell enough about us to get the cops unraveling our business and retrieving what's on your computers. Where there's enough data to send us away for twenty years for grand theft and forgery. That's what Jerzy told me between our little sessions down there. They don't feel like they have to worry about cops at all. Pardon the pun, but he says they have us by the balls."

"Did he specifically ask questions about my computers?" Eunice asked calmly.

Dewey felt like screaming, but he just raised his whisper a few octaves and said, "Goddamnit, yes! They found my Bernie Graham ID in my wallet. And I told him what I know, which isn't much. And I woulda told him anything else he wanted to know. And so will you if that bastard starts working on you."

"Okay, get a grip," Eunice said. "We gotta figure out a way to pay them a little something. They know they'll have to let one of us outta here to accomplish that."

"They want five hundred thousand, Eunice. They're not gonna settle for a little something."

"When they come back up here, I'll bargain with them," she said. "They're your runners. They're petty thieves, not killers."

"Jerzy's got the instincts of one," Dewey said bleakly. "Don't underestimate him, Eunice. I'm begging you."

"Let me handle it when they come back," she said. And then she said quickly, "What time is it?"

He glanced at his watch and said, "Quarter to two." And then he added, "More or less. Jerzy told me it was one thirty when he dragged me in here."

She was quiet again, and he was furious with himself for looking at his watch and blurting out the time. When he spoke again, he said, "I don't have the same opinion of Jerzy that you have. Not anymore. I hope you'll buy me outta here, Eunice. Don't leave me here and just hope for the best."

"I'll take care of things, Dewey" was all she said.

When the door opened again, Tristan and Jerzy entered, the Polack wearing a leather jacket even though the night was still warm. Dewey saw a look of grim determination on Creole's face.

Tristan said, "We ain't wastin' no more time with you two. We want the five hundred grand, and you're gonna tell us how to get it."

"We don't have five hundred thousand," Eunice said.

"No?" Tristan said.

"We have twelve thousand and change," she said. "That's all there is."

"Really?" Tristan said. "And we can have it, huh?"

"Yes," Eunice said, "if you let us go."

"What's gonna happen now ain't my fault," Tristan said. "It's your fault. We're gonna take one of you home. And the other one's gonna stay."

"Let her go, Creole," Dewey said. "She'll keep her word."

"You're the one who's goin' home," Tristan said. "Get on your feet."

Dewey made struggling sounds and stood up. He said, "I'm begging you! Let Ethel go! Keep me here!"

"We're through with all that," Tristan said. "It's time for all us thieves to learn how our world turns bad sometimes."

Dewey stood looking back at Eunice, blindfolded and chained to the bed, and wanted to say something to her but could not.

Still grim, Tristan said, "Say good-bye for now to your old lady, Bernie. You and me, we're gonna go to your crib and have a little nap till we get a call. Then we're gonna get the money, and it ain't gonna be no twelve grand and change."

"Can I have a cigarette?" Eunice said, still strangely composed.

And Dewey was certain now that she either had not bought into this gag or she could not make herself believe that their former runners would actually torture her. Dewey looked into Tristan's eyes and saw that Creole agreed with his assessment.

"I need me a smoke too," Jerzy said, pulling off his baseball cap and dropping it onto the floor. His hair looked like a colorless tangle of fishing line.

"This ain't no time to be burnin' a pipe," Tristan said when he saw Jerzy take the glass meth pipe from his jacket pocket and put it on the kitchen counter.

"Oh, yeah, this is the time," Jerzy said. "I gotta get in the spirit of things to come." And when he looked closely, Dewey saw fury in the big man's bloodshot eyes.

"Main-tain, dawg," Tristan said with real concern in his voice as he and Dewey walked to the door. "A dead woman ain't no good to nobody."

"Don't hurt her!" Dewey said, his voice tremulous, and this time he was very close to meaning it.

When the door was closed, Jerzy walked to the bed, and when Eunice could actually smell him, she lost some of her aplomb and said, "How about a cigarette, Jerzy? Let's you and me have a smoke and talk things over."

By way of an answer, he took the roll of duct tape from his jacket, bit off a ten-inch strip, and taped her mouth shut.

And at last Eunice Gleason trembled in fear.

He said to her, "Now I'm gonna burn a pipe. And when I'm finished smokin' glass, I'm gonna rip off that tape for two minutes. And in that two minutes, you're gonna give me the right answers. 'Cause if you don't, I'm gonna put that tape back on your mouth and go to work on you. And when the tape comes off again, you're gonna beg to tell me the right answers."

He saw sweat beading like pearls on her forehead. That pleased him.

★ TWENTY ★

WHILE GETTING READY for work the next morning, yet another overtime shift, Malcolm Rojas was nervous and anxious. His mother had been complaining again about not receiving her share of his recent paycheck.

After he'd eaten the cooked breakfast she'd prepared for him at 6 A.M., he said, "If you don't stop nagging me about money, I'm gonna move in with my friend Phil."

That stopped her, and she looked worried when she said, "Who's Phil?"

"A guy I work with in the warehouse," Malcolm said, trying quickly to come up with details about a fictional friend to make his threat more plausible. "Phil and me been talking about sharing the rent. His mom's always nagging him too."

"I'm not always nagging, sweetheart!" his mother said, pouring him more orange juice. "But money's not easy to come by, and it's not cheap living here in Hollywood. You know that."

"Maybe it'd be better for both of us if I move out," Malcolm said. "And pretty soon I'll have enough money to do it. I'll be getting a new job."

"You're not thinking of quitting your present job?"

"Pretty soon I am," he said.

"For what? Where you gonna work?"

"I have . . . prospects," he said.

"Where? Who with?"

"I'll tell you when it happens," he said. "Now I gotta go or I'm gonna be late."

After he brushed his teeth, his mother was waiting at the door with his lunch in a paper bag. "Please don't do anything yet, sweetie," she said. "Let's talk it over about you quitting your job. And don't worry about giving me any money this time. Okay?"

"Okay," he said, pleased at how he could still manipulate her.

When she reached up and put her hands in his hair, about to kiss him on the cheek, she said, "My sweet boy."

He grimaced and said, "Don't do that! How many times do I gotta tell you?"

She jumped back so fast she bumped her head on the door frame. "I'm sorry!" she said. "I'm sorry, sweetie. Sometimes I forget how grown-up you are."

When he was driving out of his parking space, he felt miserable, and it was all because of her. He vowed that when he started working for Bernie Graham, he really was going to move away from her forever. Her touch gave him an icy-cold feeling that would usually be followed by heat. He could feel it coming already. He knew the heat would grow as the day progressed. It might turn into the thing he couldn't control, the burning sensation in his belly that worked its way up to his skull when he thought of all those bitches.

Tristan Hawkins fell onto Eunice Gleason's bed, fully clothed. Dewey tried to get some sleep in his own bed but could not, suffering from severe acid reflux, which seldom troubled him like this. At 6 A.M., Dewey was dressed and in the kitchen making coffee when Tristan shuffled in, yawning and scratching.

"Jerzy shoulda called us by now," Dewey said. "I don't like this. I got a bad feeling about this."

"Shut the fuck up and pour me some coffee," Tristan said. "I got enough to worry about. Anyways, this was mostly your plan."

"I thought she'd fold 'em the second she saw you two," Dewey said. "I was wrong."

"How long you been married to that woman, Bernie?"

"Nine years."

"Nine years and you ain't figured out yet that she's twice as smart as you and ten times the man?"

Dewey poured two cups of coffee and said, "The milk's in the fridge. The sugar's in the cupboard there."

After sipping his coffee, Tristan said, "Lemme ask you somethin' about that woman. Would she stick big money in a bank account somewheres, knowin' full well that if your business enterprise ever got brought down, the cops could find that money without a whole lotta trouble? Especially if they got all the records around here, and what must be stored in those computers out there in the other room? Would she do that?"

"I know what you're getting at," Dewey said. "Don't you think I've looked for evidence of a safe deposit box?"

"Bernie," Tristan said, dead-staring him. "Did you ever think she might do what you do? Like maybe take the cash to some nice fireproof, earthquake-proof, safe and secure storage locker? A place where she could go in and clean it out in a minute and boogie on outta town?"

Dewey's eyes flickered just for an instant, but it was enough for someone as streetwise and sly as Tristan Hawkins. Dewey looked away and had a sickening thought that in this unholy foursome, he might actually be the dumbest!

"Speak to me, Bernie," Tristan said. "This ain't the time to be gamin' me. Your old lady might be past talkin' at this point. We may be on the verge of grabbin' what we can and gettin' the fuck outta Dodge."

At that moment, the resolve of Dewey Gleason melted. He was so far out of his depth, he was ready to join forces with this wily young man sitting across from him. He said, "I did find a key in her wallet one time, and yeah, it looked like a padlock key."

"And where's that key?"

"I don't know. It was gone the next time I looked."

"That means," Tristan said, "I was right when I told the Polack that you had no intention of transferrin' funds and havin' a way to beat the wait period, and all that bullshit you said. You hoped to get that key and whatever information you needed to get in her secret place and clean it out and leave poor Creole and the dumb Polack with nothin' but your half-dead wife."

"Don't say 'half-dead,'" Dewey murmured, and Tristan thought he was about to start blubbering.

"Get used to it, Bernie," Tristan said. "She might be fully dead by now, because I seen how the Polack gets when he smokes crystal, and it ain't pretty."

Then tears did well in the eyes of Dewey Gleason, and Tristan said, "So, all in all, it might jist be you and me against the fuckin' world right now. And I'm ready to tear this place apart to scope out a key and try to find the lock it belongs to."

Dewey said, sniffling, "She drove me to this! I'm not a violent person. I never hurt anybody in my —"

"Me neither," Tristan interrupted, "but if you don't main-tain and get hold of yourself, I jist might do some violence on *you*. Now wipe your fuckin' nose and let's get to work!"

They had begun ransacking Eunice's closet, searching in the pockets and linings of every hanging piece of clothing, when Tristan heard the man sob.

Eunice was startled by Jerzy's snores. He was lying on his sleeping bag still clothed in his black T-shirt and filthy jeans, but he'd removed his boots and she could smell his feet. With the blindfold removed now, she was able to see light through the cracks in the blinds. She'd never needed a cigarette more. She'd been lying there for four hours and had not yet been harmed. If he had not chased his pipe full of crystal with a cocktail of downers, she knew the night might have ended in horror.

At 2:30 A.M., he'd sat astride her with a buck knife in his hand, wired from the methamphetamine, and said, "Do you and me have this heart-to-heart, or do I cut your left nipple off to start with?"

With tears soaking the blindfold and her mouth taped shut, she'd nodded her head vigorously, and he'd said, "Okay, I'll play along for one question and one answer. Here's the question: Are you ready to pay us five hundred thou to get away from here?"

Her nodding was so robust it made him laugh, and he dug his nails under the tape and ripped it off her face, along with some dermis at the corners of her mouth. But she did not cry out in pain.

"You got some balls, woman," he said. "That musta stung."

With as much composure as she could muster, Eunice said, "Now the blindfold, please. And a cigarette. We'll talk, and you won't be sorry."

Jerzy emitted a loon laugh and said, "Momma, you totally are a devil-woman! If you wasn't so old, I'd prob'ly fuck you jist to absorb some of your test-tosterone! Maybe I'll let you gimme a blow job before we say good-bye if you promise not to gnaw my cock off."

She felt his fingernails again and the blindfold was pulled and twisted and finally torn away, along with some of her hair, but again she did not utter a sound. She looked up at the naked lightbulb in the ceiling fixture, blinked several times, and then looked at Jerzy's face. It seemed like his dilated eyes were all pupil with no iris showing. She turned her head for a glance around the empty room.

"It could use a woman's touch," Jerzy said. "But I don't think you'll be here long enough, one way or the other."

That was when he'd gone to his leather jacket crumpled on the floor and removed a plastic bindle from a zip pocket and shaken several capsules into his large, filthy hand. He'd swallowed them down with a pint of gin from the other pocket. When he raised the bottle, his T-shirt was hiked, and she could see a gun inside the waistband of his jeans.

"Please unchain one hand so I can smoke on my own," she'd said.

That was the moment. He'd reached for her left wrist, but she'd jerked her right hand forward and said, "This one's killing me."

It made no difference to Jerzy which hand he freed, and he'd unlocked the padlock that joined the link around her right wrist, the one that was so tightly cinched that she knew she had no chance of slipping out of it. But when Creole had linked her left wrist, he'd put the padlock through the chain one link looser, and Eunice thought there was maybe a chance with that one.

Shaking his head in admiration, Jerzy tossed the padlock onto the floor and said, "If I ain't careful, I'm gonna ask you to divorce Bernie and marry me!"

When her right wrist was free, she lowered her arm painfully and said, "Thank you, Jerzy. I don't think I'll be looking for another husband, but I will definitely be eliminating that son of a bitch who put you up to this. Can I have that cigarette, please?"

Jerzy Szarpowicz didn't know what the hell to say to this woman now! So she'd figured out that her old man was in on the gag! He could hardly wait to hear what she said next. He walked over to the kitchen counter to her purse, and she only had a few seconds when his back was to her, but she used her right hand to manipulate the chain encircling her left wrist. She thought she just might be able to pull free. It was possible!

He dropped the purse beside the bed, and when he gave her a cigarette and lit it, she took the biggest pull on a smoke that he'd ever seen, and she said, "Bless you, Jerzy."

"Yeah, well, you better hold your prayers till we talk."

Between desperate puffs, inflating her lungs with smoke, Eunice watched the downers already having an effect on Jerzy, despite the meth he'd smoked.

"How close are you to Creole?" she asked.

"We ain't in love," Jerzy said.

"I wanna make a deal with you and you alone," Eunice said.

"Ain't you takin' advantage of my kindness with all your wants?"

Eunice said, "If you will kill my husband, I'll give you three hundred and fifty thousand dollars. That's all I've got. If you wanna share it with Creole, that's up to you. But I have a feeling you're too smart for that."

Jerzy took one of the cigarettes from Eunice's pack, lit it, stood up and started pacing, and said, "Fuck me! You are one evil-eyed, cold-blooded, backstabbing devil-woman!"

"I know I'm in no position to make deals," she said. "I'll lead you to the money this morning, after you kill Bernie for me. I want him dead."

"Any other requests?" he said. "You want me to run down to the market and get you some peppermint ice cream?"

"There's a key," she said. "It's in my apartment. I'll tell you where I hid it. Take a taxi there. Deal with Creole any way you want, but kill that son of a bitch I'm married to. Use your knife to keep it quiet. Bring the key back here, unchain me, and I'll drive with you to the storage facility where the money is."

Jerzy was wishing he hadn't mixed the downers with the glass. His head was spinning and he was having trouble following the conversation. Then he said the one thing she hoped he would not say. "Why don't you jist tell me where the key is, and I'll phone Creole and he'll bring it here along with Bernie. And after you tell Bernie how to get the money outta storage, I'll take the money away from him at the storage place and kill him for you. I never liked the motherfucker anyways."

"Won't work," she said quickly. "Nobody can get into the storage facility but me. There's a real security guard in the office where you check in. He's even armed. He'll never let Bernie or anyone else in there without me. Is it safe to kill Bernie here in front of Creole? Will he permit it?"

"You think I'm gonna leave you here alone while I taxi to your crib?" he said.

"There's nothing I could do," she said. "You can chain up both my wrists to the bed and tape my mouth again. But I wish you wouldn't. My lips hurt like hell."

Eunice forced herself to breathe normally as she watched him thinking. She was counting on his greed and the fact that his brain was drug-addled. Nearly a minute passed before he spoke.

"Where's the key?" he said.

"There's a little pocket that I sewed in the drape over the window in his bedroom. The key is in it. You could get it without Creole even knowing about it."

"You mean the key is right there beside his bed?"

"That's right," she said. "The last place he'd ever look."

"A devil-woman," he said admiringly. "And where's the storage place?"

"It's called North Hollywood Storage," she said, unable to come up with the name of an existing storage facility other than the one from which she was kidnapped. This was a hazardous moment for her if Jerzy was smart enough to pick up his cell to look for a phone number under that name. "It's not too far from our apartment. I put a lotta furniture in that storage room to make it look legit. The money's in the dresser drawers."

"I gotta figure out how to make all this work," Jerzy croaked. "Right now I can't think too good."

It was then that he'd said he needed to take a nap to clear his head.

When he awoke three hours later, Eunice could clearly see dawn through the cracks in the blinds and in those three hours, she'd formulated her plan. He snuffled and snorted and dragged himself to his feet and stumbled to the bathroom to urinate.

When he came back, Eunice said, "Are Creole and my husband at our apartment?"

"Yeah," he said.

Eunice saw the ox nodding, still half asleep, and she thought it was now or never. She said, "God, I gotta go to the bathroom bad. I'm about to poop my pants."

"I hope you ain't too modest," Jerzy said, "because the door stays open. And make it quick." Then he unlocked the padlock on her left wrist.

Eunice stood up with a groan, bowed her back and rotated her hips, and walked slowly to the bathroom. On the way, she saw bread and a mayonnaise jar on the kitchen counter. Jerzy stood outside the door, glancing inside while Eunice, actually constipated from stress and fear, gave her own acting performance, grunts and all. Needing an eye-opener, Jerzy shuffled over to his leather jacket on the floor and took a swig from the gin bottle.

When she was finished, she washed her hands, leaving them wet, and returned to the bed. She put her left wrist back into position and kept her right hand down by her hip, the hand with the bar of soap in it, which she slid beneath her wrinkled dress. She held up her left wrist to be chained.

As soon as he clicked the padlock through the same link as Creole had used before, she said, "Call a taxi and get over there. Ring them on the gate phone, and when they let you inside, act like you're panicked. Say you killed me accidentally and everyone better get outta town. Get

Creole out of there somehow and then kill my husband and get that key. Taxi back here and we'll go together to the storage facility to pick up my husband's car for the rest of our business."

"It might jist work," Jerzy said, looking at his buck knife.

"It will," she said. "But you better call Creole now and say something to keep them from driving over here. The element of surprise is what's gonna make it all happen for you."

"What should I say?" Jerzy asked, and Eunice believed she almost owned him now. She was thirsty and knew he must be parched, given all the booze and drugs he'd ingested.

"Tell Creole to stay there and wait for your call. Say that you might be on the verge of getting the info but that I'm a tough cookie."

"You got that part right," he said.

"Okay, Jerzy, you saw Bernie do his acting bits often enough. Let's see you do it, but first, please get me some water."

He went to the kitchen and came back with a plastic bottle of water, removed the cap, and handed it to her. When she drank, it seemed to remind him how thirsty he was, and he returned to the kitchen for another. When he did, she poured water on her left hand and wrist.

He returned and retrieved his cell from his jacket and speed-dialed, and then he did just what she was depending on. He turned away and walked to the kitchen to give his performance without an audience. Dewey would have stayed there, relishing an observer, but Jerzy was not an actor, and she knew instinctively he'd want privacy.

She heard him say to his partner, "I need more time. She's bad, man. Her old man's a pussy, but she ain't. Gimme another hour."

And while he talked, she soaped up her left hand and wrist, moving herself into more of a sitting than reclining position so that he would not see the soap slime running down her bare arm. There was one more movement she was depending on: a bowel movement, a real one this time. His. She needed him in that bathroom. But as she twisted and pulled, her hand was not slippery enough. It wasn't working!

He came back from the kitchen and said, "Okay, I gotta call a cab, and I'm gonna have to chain you up real good and tape your mouth. Sorry about that."

"Jerzy," Eunice said. "I'm about to faint from hunger. Before you go, can I have something to eat? Anything."

"All we got is some bread and a package of salami."

"That sounds great," Eunice said. "Please bring it here."

Jerzy went to the kitchen and came back with the package of meat he hadn't opened and the loaf of bread.

"You wouldn't have anything to put on the bread, would you?" she asked.

"I got a jar of mayo in there," he said.

"That's perfect," Eunice said.

When he came back with the jar of mayonnaise and a plastic butter knife, she'd already torn open the meat package and was making a sandwich. "Would you like one?" she asked.

"Naw, I only get the munchies when I smoke pot," he said. "When I get the money, I think I'll switch to blow. I'll be able to afford first-class booger sugar after you make me rich."

"Can you open the jar for me?" Eunice asked.

He opened the mayonnaise jar and handed it to her, watching her spread a small dab on the sandwich with the plastic knife.

"Don't try stabbing me in the throat," Jerzy said with a revolting leer.

Eunice wished she'd had a cigarette to calm herself, but with as much self-control as she could manage, she said prosaically, "Maybe you need to have a poop too before you leave here, Jerzy. You're gonna kill a man with a knife. And it won't be a plastic knife like this one."

He stared at her fiercely, and she froze, shivers shooting through her. Had she gone too far and made the dolt suspicious? Or was he just contemplating the impending murder, something he'd never done before?

Finally he said, "Yeah, I gotta admit I'm a little nervous about guttin' your old man, but once I start..."

Jerzy stopped talking and lumbered into the little bathroom, leaving the door open. She heard him unbuckle his belt, and as soon as his bathroom noises began to tell the story, she reached into the mayonnaise jar and scooped out a handful, slathering it on her left hand and wrist. Then she rotated her wrist and pulled, all the time trying to hold the chain in her right hand to keep it from striking the steel bed frame. The mayonnaise oozed down her arm as she twisted her wrist and tugged. And suddenly, her left hand slipped past the linked manacle! She sat upright, and when she heard him grunting, swung her feet to the floor, grabbed her purse, and bolted for the door.

Jerzy saw her flash across the open bathroom door and yelled, "Hey!" Then he leaped to his feet with his jeans down around his boots, and fell forward onto his knees and then onto his face, yelling, "I'll kill you! Now I'll kill you! You're a dead woman!"

But he was yelling into an empty room. Eunice was already halfway down the steps, not knowing what part of L.A. she was in, running barefoot along the sidewalk in Frogtown, absolutely certain that if she let him get close, he'd shoot her dead.

Tristan Hawkins and Dewey Gleason were exhausted from having ransacked the apartment for hours. They had not found a key, nor any evidence of a storage facility, a safe deposit box, or anything else to provide a clue as to where the money could be.

Tristan was slumped in Eunice's chair in front of one of the computers, and he said, "Maybe we gotta admit the possibility that your old lady put all the money in a bank account. Or maybe more than one account. If she did that, we're gonna have problems."

Dewey, who looked to Tristan like a man facing a firing squad, said, "I don't understand how she could be holding out so long. What could he be doing to her?"

"We're way down the road past all that," Tristan said. "We gotta depend on the Polack to make her talk, and that's the end of it."

"I wish I had it to do over," Dewey said with a bleak stare into the abyss.

"Well, you don't," Tristan said, "and I'm sick of hearin' you say that."

And that was when Tristan's cell rang, and Dewey said, "Thank God! Maybe she's talked!"

"Yo," Tristan said into the phone, and Dewey studied him, seeing the alarm grow on his face as he listened to a long monologue from Jerzy Szarpowicz.

Then Tristan said, "No, don't come here! Catch a cab to...to the office. Yeah, wait there. We'll clean out the storage room and take the stuff there in the van."

When he closed his cell, Dewey looked at him and said, "Is she dead?"

"No, she escaped!" Tristan said. "And if I can get my hands on his gun, I'm killin' that motherfuckin' Polack as soon as all this is over."

"How could she escape?" Dewey said.

"Never mind how. We gotta get outta here. You and me're goin' back to the storage room and loadin' up every fuckin' thing in there. Does your old lady know about the office?"

"She knows about it but not exactly where it is," Dewey said.

"Okay, Bernie, we're gonna store the merchandise in the office for a few days, and you're gonna sell all of it to your fence, and we're gonna split the money three ways. Because that's all any of us is gonna get from this fuckin' gag."

"She can't call the cops," Dewey said in despair.

"I ain't takin' no chances," Tristan said. "She figured out this gag from the git, and at this point she might be ready to go to jail herself jist to see you go down. If you wanna pack a bag, hurry the fuck up. And I wouldn't advise you to argue about any of this, because the Polack is about ready to kill the first person that crosses him. But before you pack up, let's check somethin' out."

Dewey followed Tristan into his bedroom and watched, perplexed, as Tristan went to the window and carefully examined the drapes, running his hand over every inch. When he was finished, Tristan said, "Like I thought. No key. And I don't have to look. There ain't no such business called North Hollywood Storage."

"What?" Dewey Gleason said in confusion.

Five cars containing motorists on their way to work drove past Eunice Gleason when she ran into the street, waving frantically. The sixth one, an old Pontiac driven by a middle-aged Mexican woman heading to her job at a restaurant in Silverlake, stopped for her.

Eunice wasn't sure how much English the woman understood, but Eunice told a tale of having been picked up by a man in a bar and literally held captive by him after she'd refused him sex.

The woman kept repeating, *"Policía?"* when there were breaks in Eunice's tale, but Eunice looked out at the street, shook her head, and said, "No, no police. Just drop me there at Denny's, *por favor.*"

When she got out of the car, she tried to give the woman a $20 bill, but the woman refused to take it, once again saying, *"Policía?"*

Eunice smoked a cigarette in front of Denny's restaurant and looked in her compact mirror. She had what looked like a swath of sunburn across her mouth and chin where the tape had been ripped off. Her new hairdo was tousled and tangled, and there was no makeup left except around her eyes, but she felt surprisingly relaxed when she approached the door. Nobody in Denny's seemed to notice that the disheveled woman who entered and went to a booth was barefoot.

Without looking at a menu, she said to the waitress who brought a pot of coffee to her table, "Hotcakes, crisp bacon, two eggs over easy, and tomato juice. When you get a chance."

The salty-looking waitress said, "Rough night, huh?"

"You wouldn't believe it," Eunice said, realizing that she was feeling something close to elation.

The whole kidnap might have been a Dewey Gleason gag, but the presence of Jerzy Szarpowicz was real. She had escaped torture and, finally, death. She had done it with brains and guts, and now she was free of that miserable little son of a whore who at this moment was probably trying to figure out how he could scrape together enough money to run for his life. Now that the weasel had realized what a formidable woman he'd married, he was no doubt panic-stricken. Well, her retirement had just arrived ahead of schedule. But it would be retirement for one person, not two, so she'd get by. She had to get back to the apartment and take the hard drives from the computers, along with all the incriminating files.

After that, she'd pack up and be on the first flight to San Francisco, where she'd establish a bank account and have the $945,000 moved from the four Hollywood banks in which she'd made deposits over the years.

She thought she'd wait until the real-estate market improved before selling the family home on Russian Hill. She wanted to finally own a condo, maybe near North Beach, with its nightlife and people having fun. It was about time she started enjoying herself after so many years of hard work.

Eunice knew now that Dewey had actually bought into the many hints she'd dropped whenever he got frustrated, intimations that she'd hidden piles of money in a secret cache, like some Latin American drug lord. That was so like him. Limited talent, limited intellect, and limited imagination. Hugo could've eaten him alive. Eunice was actually smiling when she took the cell phone from her purse and dialed a number she'd been given last night.

Malcolm had his box cutter in his hand and was slashing open a crate containing video games when his cell chimed. He'd been working extra hard all morning, trying to quell the anger that was still simmering.

"Hello," he said.

"Clark," Eunice said. "It's me, Ethel. Would you like a job today?"

"Yeah," he said, "but I'm at work right now."

"That's okay," Eunice said. "I'll need the rest of the day to get ready. I'd like you to come to the apartment and help me do some work."

"I can't get there till after six," he said.

"Can you make it earlier?"

"I'll try," he said. "Will Mr. Graham be there?"

"No, I'll explain it to you when you arrive. You're gonna be well paid for your labor."

"Okay, I'll be there," he said.

After he clicked off, he noticed that his battery was getting low, so he turned off the cell until he could get to his car and charge it. When he was back slashing open boxes and crates, he didn't really feel much better for at last getting a job from Bernie Graham. The tormenting memory of his mother's touch had made this an uncommonly terrible day for Malcolm Rojas.

There was some telephone debate that Saturday between the sex crimes team at West Bureau and their lieutenant after Dana Vaughn's former colleague D2 Flo Johnson phoned the lieutenant at home to explain the entire case. The lieutenant had recently come from a staff meeting with West Bureau brass where once again complaints from self-styled "community leaders" concerning minority-group harassment had been discussed. As usual, things ended with dispiriting lectures about the federal consent decree and fears of allegations from black and Latino citizens.

The lieutenant said, "Okay, the rock-throwing prowler generally fits the description of the guy that attacked the women, but there're a lot of young Hispanics with curly hair that would also fit."

"How about the light blue T-shirt and jeans?" Flo Johnson said.

The lieutenant replied, "Common clothing for young guys. And that girl Naomi isn't even positive which day she met her guy."

"How about the damaged fists following the day when our guy attacked the second victim and put her in the hospital?"

"That's more...convincing," the lieutenant said. "But we still have to be careful not to stir up any more complaints about minority-group harassment."

Flo Johnson sighed and said, "My maiden name was Trevino, Lieutenant. I'm second generation from Sonora, and this isn't about annoying the Hispanic community. This is about a vicious rapist who's gonna kill somebody sooner or later."

And so it went until someone with more rank and more spine listened to the detective and gave her the okay to proceed. D2 Flo Johnson went to the website that links cell numbers to their providers. Then she wrote a search warrant and faxed it to the district attorney's weekend command post, which faxed it to an on-call judge at home, who signed it and faxed it back.

The cell provider had given the name of Madge Rojas, with an address on Maplewood Avenue in east Hollywood. It was early afternoon when four detectives went to the Maplewood address, but they found nobody at home. After that, Flo Johnson and her partner sat in their car on Maplewood Avenue and sweated in ninety-degree heat. Her D3 back at the office contacted a D3 at Major Crimes Division and explained the urgency of the case, and he agreed to go up to a satellite link and wait for whoever possessed that number to turn on his cell phone.

As this was going on, Madge Rojas enjoyed a matinee with pop-corn and soda at a multiplex cinema while her son, Malcolm, worked his overtime shift on a busy Saturday at the home improvement center. Malcolm's mother decided not to rush back to their apartment. He seldom came straight home from work anymore, especially on a weekend. She'd given up questioning him about where he went at night. He'd get so angry, he was starting to scare her. She made a mental note to contact one of the free clinics about psychological counseling for her son. Meanwhile, she thought there was no reason she couldn't stay and see one of the other movies at the multiplex after this one. No reason at all.

At 3 P.M., when Dana Vaughn was about to get a shower and start preparing for work, her cell chimed.

"Dana? It's Flo Johnson," the detective said. "It's been a real busy morning and afternoon. How come all the good stuff happens on weekends?"

"Did you get him?" Dana asked, trying not to sound disappointed for not having been in on it.

"Not yet," the detective said. "The phone bill goes to a Madge Rojas at an address on Maplewood. Autotrac ran the name, and credit info indicates she lives with her nineteen-year-old son, Ruben Malcolm Rojas, who has no criminal record. We did get the license number of his Mustang, and I've already phoned the Hollywood watch commander to pass it on at roll call to Watch 3 and Watch 5. We'll be waiting for the cell phone ping as soon as it's turned on. I'll personally ask your boss to let you help back us up if we ping it to a Hollywood location."

"Too cool!" Dana said. "I'll wear a fresh uniform. I work with Holly-wood Nate Weiss, and he'll figure a way to get us some press coverage if we're in on this one."

Flo Johnson chuckled and said, "A little extra color instead of our usual drab lipstick shows up better on TV."

TWENTY-ONE

LADIES AND GENTLEMEN and those of you who do not fit either category, I have an announcement to make," Sergeant Lee Murillo said by way of beginning roll call. "There is a real Hollywood moon tonight. And as you know, a full moon over Hollywood brings out the beast rather than the best in our citizens. The car that comes back with the weirdest encounter of the night will get an extra-large pizza with the works. And now to training material. Last time it was how to address our Hollywood citizens of various nationalities who speak many languages. This time it's how to address our Hollywood citizens of various genders who speak our same language. For example, you must never address or refer to a transsexual as a tranny."

R.T. Dibney raised his hand and said, "Is it okay to call them transtesticles?"

After the guffaws died down, Sergeant Murillo said, "And you must not address or refer to drag queens as dragons."

"If they're ugly, can we call them drag-goons?" Flotsam asked.

Sergeant Murillo ignored him, saying, "And post-op transsexuals will be searched by female officers, pre-op by male officers. Booking in either the men's or women's jail will also depend upon their medical status and condition. And you will not refer to Santa Monica Boulevard as Sodom-Monica because of the number of male prostitutes there."

Jetsam said, "Boss, it's way confusing out there. We need an organization chart to know how to talk to these people."

Flotsam pointed to young Harris Triplett, back from his loan to the vice unit, and said, "The last night Triplett was working for the vice unit, a deaf guy on Santa Monica Boulevard handed him a note that said, 'Can I have a blow job?'"

That actually got people interested, and Hollywood Nate said, "Did you bust the poor guy, Harris?"

Reluctantly the young cop said, "Uh-huh."

Then several of the saltier cops booed and chimed in with remarks like "Harris the Harsh!" and "Harris the Horrible!" and "Enemy of people with disabilities!"

While everyone was jeering and having a rollicking good time, R.T. Dibney leaned over to Harris Triplett and said, "Kid, always be careful how much you drink if you do the Hollywood nightclub scene. You might get hammered and pick up with what you think is some smokin' hot chick and wake up with a hairy scrotum across your nose."

Sergeant Murillo flapped his hands palms-down to get them quieted, then pointed to a license number and car description on the board behind him and said, "We do have some real police work to take care of tonight. Dana Vaughn has done some work that might result in the arrest of the box-cutter rapist who we think is Ruben Malcolm Rojas, Hispanic, nineteen, five eight, one forty-five, brown and brown. He lives with his mother on Maplewood, just west of Kingsley. West Bureau detectives, assisted by our gang units, are out there right now, waiting for cell phone pings that could very well track the guy right to your beat. Listen to the tac frequency and watch for that old red Mustang. I think it'd be just dandy if one of you midwatch units took him down. And remember, the Oracle said that doing good police work is the most fun you'll ever have in your lives. So go out there under that Hollywood moon tonight and have yourselves some fun."

At the end of the forty-five-minute roll call session, everyone touched the picture of the Oracle for luck as usual, like parishioners dipping their fingers into a font of holy water, and headed downstairs to the kit room to line up for their nonlethal weapons. When Hollywood Nate was loading the war bags into the trunk of their shop in the parking lot, he heard the surfer cops jawing with intensity.

"Did I or didn't I?" Jetsam asked Flotsam.

"Dude, I wasn't watching, but it's, like, something you always do, so I'd say you did it."

"Did what?" Dana Vaughn asked.

"Touch the Oracle's picture," Flotsam said.

"You were behind me, Dana," Jetsam said. "Did I touch it?"

"I was talking to Nate," Dana said. "I didn't see."

Hollywood Nate said, "I didn't notice either."

"I better go back up and touch it," Jetsam said.

"Dude!" Flotsam said. "Ain't that taking superstition a little too far?"

Jetsam paused and looked as though he was about to get into the car, until Dana with a wink at Nate said to Jetsam, "It's a tradition and it's about luck. And tonight there's a Hollywood moon. I wouldn't tempt fate, honey."

That did it. He ran back inside Hollywood Station.

When the taxi delivered Eunice to her apartment on Franklin, she was so sure that Dewey and his friends had fled that she didn't ask the driver to accompany her inside. However, after entering, she did take a cursory look in every room before closing the door. It was only the irrational doper, Jerzy Szarpowicz, who worried her at all.

The fact that they'd ransacked the place did not surprise Eunice. Her gag with the key was enough to make the morons conduct a frantic search. She removed the hard drive from each computer and then pulled three flattened cardboard boxes from under her bed, which she kept for this purpose. She put them together and began loading them with hard drives, files, credit cards, and forgery paraphernalia that littered her worktable. She planned to drop each box in one of several trash Dumpsters behind various commercial establishments on the way to the airport.

She then sat down and wrote a letter to the apartment manager, describing how the sudden death of her father in Florida had made it necessary to leave immediately to care for her aging mother. She invited the manager to keep the security and deposit fees and to dispose of all property left behind as she saw fit, including clothing and personal items belonging to her husband. She broke into a smile when she wrote that part of it. After finishing the letter, there wasn't much to do but pack as much as she needed, leaving older articles of clothing behind. San Francisco definitely required a whole new wardrobe anyway.

After she showered and did her makeup, hiding the damage that Jerzy and his duct tape had done, she felt positively giddy. Wearing a new lace-trimmed bra and thong panties like those she'd bought for her dinner at Musso & Frank, Eunice went to the kitchen, lit a smoke, and poured herself a Bombay martini. She felt her excitement grow while waiting for Clark to arrive. She couldn't decide what to wear for the trip. She felt free. She felt . . . young.

"I wish I had the Polack here instead of you," Tristan said to Dewey Gleason as they staggered from the storage room to the van, carrying a thirty-six-inch TV console that required two rest pauses before they could move the box fifty feet.

"I might be able to pull my own weight if that son of a bitch hadn't driven my ribs halfway to my backbone," Dewey said, leaning on the box and panting.

It was almost impossible to contemplate that the goods he had stored in this room were the sum of all he possessed in life. He was certain that Eunice was already leaving the Franklin Avenue address, now that her elaborate security was blown. He didn't know for sure if she'd get out of Los Angeles or find another Dewey Gleason and set up at another location, but he believed she might've bought herself a gun by now and would shoot him dead if she ever set eyes on him again. Dewey had a passing thought that if he had a gun of his own, he might save her the trouble. He was alone. He was lost.

"You ready, Bernie?" Tristan said. "We shoulda had this job done hours ago."

"I got pain shooting through me," Dewey said.

"You're gonna have a bullet shootin' through you if we don't get back to the office before dark. The Polack ain't a patient man."

"That actually sounds comforting," Dewey said, picking up his end of the load with a moan that sounded like the lowing of a cow.

Jerzy Szarpowicz was literally bouncing from wall to wall in the little duplex/office. He would stride across the room, turn his back to the wall, and push off toward the other wall. He was muttering aloud, mostly a string of incoherent obscenities, aimlessly directed at Bernie Graham's woman, at Bernie Graham himself, at Creole, and at the Mexican at Pablo's Tacos who wouldn't front him a little crack or crystal after he'd done business with the greaseball for three years. The taxi rides had eaten up almost all his cash, and in fact, he was $1.45 light on the fare after he had the driver take him from Pablo's parking lot to here. The taxi driver, one of those camel fuckers Jerzy despised so much, had started bitching about it until he got a good look at Jerzy's snarling face and red-rimmed blazing eyes, and then he'd just dropped it in gear and sped away.

Jerzy had been pacing with the buck knife in his hand, indulging in violent fantasies until he tired of that. Then he pulled the snub-nosed revolver from his jeans and passed the time by aiming it at the imaginary heads of those he hated. Two of those he hated interrupted him by driving up to the curb in the rented van and in the Honda just as the Hollywood moon began to rise.

Tristan and Dewey each carried a box containing a laptop to the door, which was held open by Jerzy, who'd tucked his weapons inside the waistband of his jeans, under his T-shirt.

"Where the fuck you been?" Jerzy growled.

"Don't start," Tristan said. "I might as well've loaded the van by myself, all the help Bernie gave me. My ass is scrapin' the ground."

"I need money right now," Jerzy said to Dewey. "Call your fence and start sellin' this shit."

"I have a call in to him," Dewey said, "but I don't think my receiver's gonna run right over here this minute."

"Come on, dawg," Tristan said to Jerzy. "Help me carry all those boxes inside. Bernie, you keep callin' the guy till you reach him. Tell him this is like a big garage sale if he's got plenty of cash."

Dewey sat down on a kitchen chair, cell phone in hand, and said, "I'll keep trying."

Jerzy looked like his central nervous system was short-circuited, and he seemed ready to start tearing the wallpaper off the walls. Dewey tried his best to avoid eye contact, but Jerzy said to him, "Bernie, if you don't get me some money tonight, I'm gonna start rememberin' how much I hated Jakob Kessler."

Dewey tried speed-dialing Hatch one more time while Tristan and Jerzy walked to the van under an unusually clear summer sky in a bright glow of moonlight.

"Yeah, we got us a Hollywood moon up there, dude," Flotsam said when he walked back to the shop with the license belonging to the driver of a Lexus hardtop convertible. "Did you see what that guy's wearing?"

Jetsam, who had walked up on the passenger side, flashing the beam from his mini-light onto the dash to let the driver know he was there, said, "I think I saw a coat and tie, right?"

"You didn't look low enough. He ain't wearing pants. But he's got nice wingtip shoes on and socks."

"Where's his pants, bro?" Jetsam said as Flotsam put the ticket book and flashlight on the hood of the black-and-white and started writing.

"On the seat beside him," Flotsam said. "With his underwear. He was probably jerking off, and that's why he was late on the red light."

"What did you say to him, bro?"

"I asked to see his license."

"What did he say?"

He said, 'Yes, officer.'"

"Is that, like, okay with you, bro? I mean, maybe he was flashing somebody in the lane next to him."

"That's a seventy-thousand-dollar ride. If he wants to jizz all over it, that's his business."

As Flotsam finished writing the ticket, Hollywood Nate and Dana

Vaughn turned the corner onto Gower, dimmed the headlights, and pulled next to the surfer cops.

"Keep looking for an old red Mustang with a Latino kid driving," Dana said. "I just checked where they're setting up and they don't have him yet."

"That was great work, Dana," Jetsam said. "You rock, girl."

Dana said, "I'm gonna be notified by detectives if he goes home, but I think it'd be super-cool if one of us busts him on the street before they do. Stay on the air and listen for Six-X-Seventy-six."

"Roger that," Flotsam said. "We'll be all over it."

When Dana and Nate were gone, Flotsam said, "Now, dude, you wanna waste our time investigating a possible weenie waver who's, like, suffering the effects of a Hollywood moon? Or do you wanna be ready to jump with Dana and Nate if the big ping happens somewheres around us?"

"You're right, bro," Jetsam said. "Why should I give a shit if a driver don't have pants on? Sometimes I forget where I'm at." Then he looked at his partner and they said in unison, "This is fucking Hollywood!"

When the driver signed the citation, Flotsam tore off a copy, handed it to the man, and said, "Drive carefully, sir, and please try to keep *both* hands on the wheel."

Eunice, having started on her third Bombay martini, was wearing a tiger lily silk blouse and Ralph Lauren white jeans that she could hardly squeeze herself into, and toeless wedges. She'd had trouble deciding on a lipstick but had finally settled on something called Flirty Burgundy. She hoped it didn't draw attention to the damage that the duct tape did to the skin around her mouth. She was considering another change when the phone rang.

She picked up and heard him. "Hi, Ethel," he said. "It's Clark."

"Come on up," she said and touched a phone button to open the gate.

Eunice took one more look in the mirror before opening the door with a huge smile.

"Hi!" she said, thinking he looked very hot, sweaty, and tired. But also thinking there was something very sexy about that. She had an image of herself helping him out of his T-shirt and drying his chest and shoulders with a towel. She imagined that his skin would be hairless. She knew his body would be firm and smooth. She said, "You look like you could use a cold drink, Clark."

"Is Mr. Graham here?" Malcolm asked.

"Mr. Graham is definitely not here," she said. "And won't be coming back."

"He won't?" Malcolm said. "Where is he?"

"Like old Hollywood, he's gone with the wind," Eunice said.

"I don't get it," Malcolm said. "I'm supposed to work for him. He promised!"

"You can work for me," Eunice said, finishing the martini in a gulp. "At least for today. We gotta get these boxes and luggage down to your car. I need you to take me to the airport." As he looked at the suitcases waiting by the door, she said, "I hope we can fit all my bags in your Mustang. Is the trunk very big?"

"I gotta see Mr. Graham!" Clark said. "He made a lotta promises to me. Is he at the office?"

"The office?" she said. "Oh, yeah, the apartment where he meets with the runners. He might be there, but he can't help you."

"He's gotta help me!" Malcolm said. "I better drive over there and talk to him."

"Look, Clark," Eunice said. "Lemme get you a cold drink. How about a martini? Bet you never tasted a real Bombay martini."

"I gotta go find Mr. Graham," Malcolm said and started for the door.

"Sit down, Clark," Eunice said. "I've got something to tell you."

Malcolm hesitated while she pushed a computer chair on wheels toward him and lit a cigarette. The smoke in the apartment was making him nauseated and she looked like she'd had too many martinis, but she had urgency to her voice, so he sat.

"Okay," he said. "I'm sitting."

"Clark," Eunice said, "Mr. Graham isn't in charge of our business.

Mr. Graham is just a glorified runner. I'm the boss of our operation, and I'm shutting things down for a while. I'm leaving town and won't be back for a few months." Then she added, "I'm going to New York."

"How about Mr. Graham?" Malcolm said.

"Fuck Mr. Graham!" Eunice said. "Pardon my French. He tried to cheat me, so I fired him. He's out." Malcolm looked so distressed that she felt sorry for him and said, "I'm gonna come back here and start a new business in a few months, and I could use a smart boy like you. I'll stay in touch and tell you when and where to meet me. But for now, I want you to help me get rid of everything in those boxes. We'll have to find Dumpsters for them and then return here to get my bags. I can see now that we'll never be able to squeeze the boxes *and* the luggage into your car."

Malcolm's disappointment was palpable even to Eunice in her deliriously happy, three-martini state.

"You called me here to be your taxi?" Malcolm said, hardly moving his lips when he spoke.

"Not my taxi, my loyal employee," Eunice said. "It's important that we get rid of all the stuff in those boxes. I'm gonna pay you two hundred dollars, Clark. With maybe a bonus if we can dispose of everything and get me to the airport in two hours."

"This is not right," Malcolm Rojas said. "I gotta go to the office and talk to Mr. Graham about this. This is not fair."

When he stood abruptly, Eunice said, "Clark, Clark, cool down. I'll pay you three hundred. And after I get settled, I might just send you a plane ticket to come visit me. How would you like that?"

She stood and reached up slowly and buried her left hand in the beautiful curls over his ear. His dark eyes were so fiery and intense she felt her own heat rising.

"You can make plenty of money with me, sweetheart," she said with a long sigh, tugging at his curls, thinking his nose was cute and pert and his dimples were divine.

When she pushed closer to him he could smell the gin, and it disgusted him, and her touch disgusted him, and when she called him sweetheart, it enraged him. "I'm not your sweetheart," he said.

"What...what's wrong?" she said, looking at his face flush. "I'll bet you never had a mature woman treat you right, have you, Clark? I'll treat you right and pay you good money to boot. All for a little help this evening."

Malcolm felt her left hand scratching and tugging, and then her right hand moved down his body to the front of his jeans, and he felt her touching his crotch, rubbing it, feeling gently with her fingers, her recent manicure badly damaged by the chains that had bound her. "Just sit back down, Clark," Eunice said. "And let Momma teach you a few tricks."

With that, Malcolm Rojas shoved her so hard in the chest that she staggered back and fell onto the kitchen floor. "You bitch!" he said. "Don't you ever put your hands on me! You fat old filthy bitch!"

Eunice was livid. She pulled herself up by grabbing the kitchen counter, unsteady from the martinis, and yelled, "Who the fuck do you think you are, you Mexican dimwit? Get the fuck outta my apartment! Get out, you pathetic little greaser!"

She started for the door to jerk it open when she felt the strike to her throat—an instant of burn, and then she couldn't breathe. She threw her hands up and blood washed over them, running down her arms. She instinctively started to run, trying to breathe, but she could not breathe. Nor could she scream. She ran to her bedroom, slammed into the door-jamb, and fell to her knees. There was no air! She tried harder to breathe but nothing entered her lungs except blood.

Malcolm stood with the box knife down by his leg, looking at her. The tiger lily top was now a burgundy that matched her lipstick. She toppled onto her side, hands clutching at the air, as though she were trying to paddle up and away from there, blood streaming and finally bubbling from the widening gap in her throat. In less than a minute she stopped thrashing. Her body jerked twice and then was still except for little twitches. Malcolm couldn't take his eyes off her, utterly amazed. It was the most astonishing thing he'd ever seen. And then he turned and ran for the door, hurtling down the steps, running to his Mustang.

While driving aimlessly east on Franklin Avenue, he was startled by the dried spatter on his right hand. He started to wipe it onto his jeans but then paused and looked at it. The blood was arousing conflicting emotions in him. He knew that later tonight in bed he would have to relive this event as best he could. Right now he was too rattled to remember the instant that he'd slashed her. He hoped he could remember it while lying alone in the dark. He did not feel remorse. She had left him no choice, the way she'd screamed at him and handled him like he was nothing. Like he was a helpless child that she could fondle as she wished. He was only sorry there wasn't some way he could tell his mother what he had done—not to grieve but to gloat.

But then fear began to overwhelm him. He didn't know what the police could find at crime scenes. On TV it was like magic. The scientist-cop could almost trap your shadow and use it to catch you somehow. He hadn't worried about things like fingerprints when he'd attacked those other bitches. He never really touched anything but their fat bodies. And since he'd never been arrested, they couldn't find him, even if he left a bit of fingerprint somewhere. But this was different, what he'd done today. He was trying to think of what he'd touched in that apartment. Nothing. Only the door handle. It was a lever and he'd opened it with his palm wrapped around it. Could they get a print from his palm?

Then he remembered! He'd braced himself against the wall when she was trying to swim away from him through the air. His entire left hand with all five fingers might be imprinted on the wall beside her body! Did they take a thumbprint when he got his driver's license? He couldn't remember. If they did, was it the left thumb or the right thumb? Or was it his index finger? Would they have that to compare with the handprint he'd left in the apartment?

He took his cell from the charger and clicked it on to call Bernie Graham. Maybe the man was leaving Los Angeles too, just like Ethel. Malcolm needed someone to tell him what to do. Maybe Bernie Graham would take him along, and they could set up the business in some other city. Then he remembered the office. She said he might be there. Malcolm was more frightened than he'd ever been in his life. The fear was exploding into outright panic.

Dana Vaughn, who was riding shotgun with her cell phone pressed to her ear, closed the cell and said to Hollywood Nate, "Flo Johnson said they got a ping!"

"Where is he?" Nate asked.

"She doesn't know exactly. She's being given quadrants. Santa Monica Boulevard between Wilcox and Cahuenga."

"Better get on tac and tell Flotsam and Jetsam and Sheila and Aaron."

"How about Mindy and R.T. Dibney?"

"Okay," Nate said, "but we may have to taze R.T. to keep him from shooting the guy on sight."

By the time Malcolm reached the duplex in east Hollywood, the moon was large and full and high enough to make the street glow, the way he'd seen the boulevard glow in reflected glare from the huge spotlights during red carpet events. There was a van parked in front and no parking for half a block north, where he managed to find a space. He wondered if any of Bernie Graham's runners were there. He needed to speak to the man alone. He was feeling light-headed and giddy, like when he smoked pot. His thoughts were fragmented, and he kept seeing her doing her dog paddle, trying to swim away while the blood splashed onto the floor.

He dialed the Bernie Graham number.

Dewey Gleason felt a sliver of hope when the cell rang. He didn't even look at the caller ID. It had to be Hatch, the man with the money!

"Bernie Graham," Dewey said anxiously.

"Mr. Graham, it's Clark," he heard the voice say.

"Oh, shit," Dewey said. "I can't talk to you now. Call tomorrow."

"You *have* to talk to me, Mr. Graham," Malcolm said. "I'm outside the office in my car."

"Get outta here, Clark!" Dewey said. "I'm busy. Call tomorrow."

"You'll wanna talk to me," Malcolm said. "It's about Ethel. I was with her."

Dewey was silent for a moment and then said, "Okay, come in."

"Are you alone?" Malcolm asked.

"No, but we'll talk privately. Come in."

Malcolm closed his cell and put it in the glove compartment with the box cutter. He thought about it for an instant, then put the box cutter in the pocket of his jeans. He felt calmer just having it there. The box knife made him feel...large. When he stepped from the car, a dagger of moonlight stabbed at his eyes. He looked away from the glowing white ball in the black-velvety sky over Hollywood.

"Who the fuck was that?" Jerzy Szarpowicz asked.

"A runner," Dewey said. "He's outside."

"You told him to come in?" Tristan said. "I can't believe it."

"You'll wanna hear what he has to say," Dewey said. "It's something about my wife."

That silenced them. All three were waiting when Malcolm tapped on the door. Dewey opened it, and Malcolm stepped inside, out of the bright moonlight. He looked at the boxes and crates stacked wall-to-wall.

"Hello, Mr. Graham," he said with a shy smile. "I knew you were still in business."

"Whadda you know about his wife?" Jerzy said to Malcolm.

Malcolm looked warily at the ferocious man and back at Dewey. "This is real confidential, Mr. Graham," he said.

"Okay, let's go in the other room," Dewey said.

Dewey led Malcolm around the maze of stolen merchandise to the single bedroom at the rear of the apartment.

Dewey turned on the ceiling light, and before he closed the door he heard Jerzy say, "I ain't happy about this."

He heard Tristan reply, "I ain't happy about nothin' right now."

After the door was closed, Dewey said to Malcolm, "What about Ethel?"

"She lied to me, Mr. Graham," Malcolm said. "She told me your business was all through, and she wanted to pay me to drive her and all her stuff to the airport. But I didn't do it."

Flabbergasted, Dewey said, "She called you?"

Nodding, Malcolm said, "She said she was the boss and you were...nothing. She was in a hurry to leave and go to New York. I bet she stole some of your money."

"All of this happened at our apartment?" Dewey said.

"Yeah," Malcolm said. "I came straight here afterwards. I'm glad to see everything's okay. I can help you sell the stuff in there and then we can leave L.A. and start making real money like you said. You can find another secretary better than Ethel."

This boy! Dewey could only gape at him, at his earnest and intense gaze, the dark, liquid eyes somehow different tonight, with a kind of... glint in them. "Did she say anything else, Clark? Anything about... about how she spent the night after the three of us had dinner?"

"No," Malcolm said.

"How did she look? The same as at dinner?"

Malcolm thought and said, "She had a lot more makeup on."

"Okay," Dewey said. "So you left her and came here?"

"That's right," Malcolm said.

"That's fine, Clark," Dewey said. "But you can run along now. I'll call you on Monday and we'll get some jobs going. Okay?"

"I can't wait, Mr. Graham," Malcolm said. "I want you to leave L.A. with me and teach me the business. We'll be a good team."

"I couldn't leave L.A. even if I wanted to," Dewey said. "I'm short on cash right now."

"You have to," Malcolm said.

Dewey was losing patience. He said, "Why do I have to?"

"Because you'll be in trouble when they find Ethel in your apartment."

"Whadda you mean, 'find her?'"

"Find her dead."

Neither spoke until Dewey said, "What the hell're you talking about, boy?"

"She made me kill her," Malcolm said. "I had no choice."

Dewey could only shake his head in exasperation. He could see from the beginning that the kid was a bit strange and creepy, but he should've realized sooner that the boy was a real mental case. He opened the bedroom door and said, "Then she won't be needing the apartment anymore, will she? Maybe I'll just move back in until the rent runs out."

"Don't go out there yet," Malcolm said. "You think I'm making this up, but I'm not. I cut her throat. She bled all over the place. She's dead, Mr. Graham. You and me, we gotta make plans."

"This is ridiculous," Dewey said, but he felt an ominous shiver in the sweltering room on this warm summer night. He shook it off. "Ridiculous," he repeated.

Dewey walked out to the room where Jerzy and Tristan waited. He said to Jerzy, "Clark's leaving. He needs to go home and rest. I think maybe he's having some kind of...episode."

Less than a block away, no fewer than three unmarked cars were double-parked, including one containing D2 Flo Johnson. Behind the most recent arrival were 6-X-32, Flotsam and Jetsam, and 6-X-76, Dana Vaughn and Hollywood Nate. Two detectives were on the front porch of a residence adjacent to the red Mustang with the pinging cell phone in the glove box. Three detectives were covering the rear of the house, and the bluesuits were backing the detectives in front.

A very old immigrant from the Dominican Republic who did not speak English and was thoroughly confused opened the door. Flo Johnson spoke to him in Spanish for a few minutes and then said to the others, "This isn't where he is. Do you wanna set up on the Mustang or start knocking on doors?"

The detectives were trying to decide on their next move when 6-X-66, Sheila Montez and Aaron Sloane, arrived, followed by R.T. Dibney and Mindy Ling in 6-X-46.

Dana looked at the cops emerging from their shops and said, "The midwatch is well represented. Let's find this bastard. He's gotta be in one of the houses on this block."

The surfer cops approached Dana and Nate, and Flotsam said, "On Wednesday we got a call half a block south on this side of the street to an apartment almost empty of furniture. There were two guys there with bad news written all over them. Might be setting up a crack house or something."

"A big fat white guy that looks like a biker," Jetsam said, "and a light-skinned black guy with dreads."

Dana looked at Nate and said, "We wrote a ticket to a pair like that. The driver's name was...let's see...Tristan something."

"That's him!" Flotsam said. "We wrote shakes on both of them."

"What the hell," Dana said, "shall we stroll down the street and see if they have a guest tonight?"

"Why not?" said Hollywood Nate. "Birds of a feather?"

"Be careful, honey," Dana said.

"What did I jist hear you say?" Jerzy Szarpowicz said to Malcolm Rojas.

"I said I'm not leaving," Malcolm said. "I got nowhere to go. I'm in trouble."

"You're gonna be in a lot more trouble if you don't get your ass outta here," Jerzy said.

"Look, kid, run along," Tristan said. "We're expectin' an important call."

"I promise I'll phone you tomorrow and give you a real job," Dewey said. "Go home, Clark."

"I left a whole handprint on the wall," Malcolm said, emotionless. "I can't go home. The police might be there already."

Tristan looked at Dewey in puzzlement, and Dewey tapped his head and said, "He claims he murdered Ethel."

"I ain't got time for fuckin' bullshit!" Jerzy said. "We got business to do, and if I don't get me a dime of rock pretty soon, I'll be doing the killin', and I'll start with *you!*"

With that, he grabbed Malcolm by the back of his neck and swung him toward the door, which he crashed into, and he dropped to his knees.

"Get out, Clark!" Dewey said.

Malcolm stayed on one knee, looking up at Jerzy Szarpowicz, and said, "I'm not afraid of you because you're big. I can deal with big men now. I can deal with anybody."

"You little fuckhead!" Jerzy said, and he stepped forward, intending to kick Malcolm with his boot, but Malcolm was on his feet, leaping sideways and swiping through the air with his box cutter.

It didn't catch Jerzy in the throat, as Malcolm had intended, but sliced open a deep gash across his right cheek, and Jerzy screamed in pain and fury. When Malcolm lunged at him again with the box cutter, Jerzy had the two-inch .38 revolver out of his waistband, and he fired two rounds a few feet away into the young man's chest. Malcolm Rojas looked down at his body, dropped the box knife, and fell into a sitting position, leaning against one of the crates. Then he gazed up with shuddering breaths, while the other three, their ears ringing from the explosions, screamed incoherent obscenities at one another.

Tristan was the first to recover and shouted, "I'm outta here!"

But when he jerked open the door, he saw a crew of uniformed police running toward the sound of gunfire. The street was hemorrhaging blue!

"Cops!" he yelled, slamming the door. And then he shoved Dewey aside and ran for the back door, with Jerzy right behind him, gun in hand.

The police heard the back door crash open, so Dana and Nate sprinted along the walk beside the duplex to the rear of the lot, followed by the surfer cops.

R.T. Dibney and Aaron Sloane kicked in the front door of the duplex and found Dewey Gleason with his hands up and Malcolm Rojas dying on the floor.

Tristan Hawkins tried to leap the chain-link fence dividing the properties but fell back hard, and Hollywood Nate shined a light on him and yelled, "Stay down or die!"

Jerzy Szarpowicz powered through the doorway at that instant, firing his last four rounds at anything that had a human form, on his way to the rear alley. Hollywood Nate returned fire almost simultaneously, and the last thing Jerzy Szarpowicz saw were three orange fireballs that lit the darkness, two rounds hitting him in the right chest and one in his forehead, killing him instantly.

The surfer cops were yelling, and Hollywood Nate was yelling, and Tristan Hawkins was facedown on the walkway, crying, "Don't kill me! Don't kill me!"

In a moment, he was handcuffed tight, palms outward, dragged to his feet, and hustled along the walkway to the front of the house, while Hollywood Nate, still leaking adrenaline from the gunfight, yelled into the house, "Is it okay in there?"

"Okay!" Sheila Montez shouted, and she appeared backlit in the doorway, holstering her Glock.

Hollywood Nate then shakily holstered his Beretta and trotted along the walkway to the front of the house, where Dewey Gleason had now become convinced that what the boy had told him must be true, and Dewey was yelling at anyone who'd listen, "I had nothing to do with her murder! Clark did it!"

Tristan said to Jetsam, who clutched his arm, "Officer, get me to a detective quick! I wanna make a deal. I'll tell you everything I know about these crazy fuckin' people."

It was then that Hollywood Nate said, "Where's Dana?"

Mindy said, "Didn't she cover the back door with you?"

By now all of the detectives had arrived and were milling around the property and talking on cells, while the bluesuits were gathered in front of the duplex with their two handcuffed prisoners.

And Hollywood Nate said again, "Where the hell's Dana?" Then he switched on his flashlight and ran back along the walkway to the rear of the duplex, with the surfer cops right behind him.

Flotsam spotted her first with his flashlight beam. She was lying in a flower bed behind a short hedge that partially concealed her body.

"Here!" Flotsam yelled. "Call an RA!"

Hollywood Nate leaped the hedge and was down on his knees in the dirt, turning her onto her back, and crying out, "Partner! Partner!"

Flotsam shined his light onto her face and saw her eyes open in slits, and he said, "It's bad, Nate! It's bad!"

"No!" Nate shouted in denial, unable to see a bullet wound. He started doing chest compressions through her Kevlar vest, when Jetsam came running toward them, and Flotsam showed a distraught face to his partner and shook his head.

Then Nate stopped the chest compressions and, tilting her head back, raised her chin and placed his mouth over hers. He began breathing into her mouth, his left hand now wet with blood leaking from the bullet wound that severed her spinal cord at the cervix, just above her vest, killing her in seconds. By now other cops were there, lighting the scene with flashlight beams, and both Sheila Montez and Mindy Ling were crying.

Nate began doing the chest compressions again, his left hand slippery with her blood, and he began sobbing and murmuring, "Please don't, Dana! Please don't!" And both surfer cops turned way, Flotsam looking up at the Hollywood moon while the yelp of the ambulance siren drew closer and Hollywood Nate begged Dana Vaughn not to die.

TWENTY-TWO

BECAUSE HER MOTHER had not been religious, the daughter of Officer Dana Vaughn chose the Hollywood United Methodist Church for the funeral service after the coroner released her body. The Gothic church could be seen from the intersection of Hollywood Boulevard and Highland Avenue, arguably the heart of Hollywood, and had been used in movies, so Pamela thought that her mother would've chuckled and approved of her choice.

She told this to Hollywood Nate Weiss during a phone conversation when she asked him to be one of the pallbearers, four of whom would be old friends of hers, male and female officers. Another choice that Pamela made was Leon Calloway, the officer from Watch 3 whose life was seconds from ending one dark night when Dana Vaughn had taken a risky head shot to save him. He fervently thanked Pamela for according him such an honor.

When she called Nate, Pamela had said that although Nate and Dana had been partners for only a short time, her mother talked of him often, always with affection and a mischievous gleam in her eye. Nate told her he'd be proud to serve, and he was very thankful that it was a phone conversation. He knew he might've cracked if he'd been face-to-face with this brave girl who so sounded like her mother.

Nate had spent an agonizing week after that extravagant police funeral complete with a graveside honor guard firing volleys, a bugler for taps, a lone bagpiper on the hillside, a helicopter flyover, and hundreds of cops in class-A uniforms. There was a moment at graveside when a rookie officer in uniform suddenly appeared beside the LAPD chaplain to read a prepared message. Nate didn't know who she was, but pallbearer Leon Calloway knew. It was Officer Sarah Messinger, limping slightly but almost ready for her return to regular duty. She stood at attention before the microphone, simulating a modulated RTO voice they might hear on their police radios.

"Attention all units," she began. "This is an end-of-watch broadcast for Police Officer Two Dana Elizabeth Vaughn, last assigned to Hollywood Division patrol."

And then Sarah Messinger read a short summary of Dana's career, including her saving the life of Officer Leon Calloway. When Nate saw the big cop's shoulders tremble and heard a sob come from him, he almost lost it and had to say to himself, Hang on, hang on, hang on!

The "broadcast" concluded with "Officer Vaughn is survived by her daughter, Pamela, and every member of the Los Angeles Police Department grieves with her this day."

Then Sarah Messinger saluted very slowly and said, "Officer Dana Vaughn, you are end-of-watch."

Nate spent days asking himself what he could've done better that night. This, even though the investigators from Force Investigation Division and the District Attorney's Office, as well as every officer at the scene, said there was nothing anyone could have done better. Yet he kept tormenting himself by reliving every second of the event, and after he was cleared to return to duty, he used up several of his overtime days to sit at home alone and brood.

He hadn't been back to duty yet, when a second visit was scheduled for him with Behavioral Science Services in their offices in Chinatown. Like most cops, he distrusted shrinks and psychiatric testimony in general, often bought and paid for in courtroom trials. And like all cops, he ridiculed the MMPI test: "Do you want to be a forest ranger? Do you want to walk in grass naked? Have you ever thought of wearing women's underwear? Is your stool black and tarry?" He would never have gone to the BSS shrink if not ordered to do so.

The first visit had been pointless. The psychologist was a man in his forties with a rosy, well-fed look who'd had a spot of mustard on his upper lip that Nate would've found distracting if he'd been even slightly interested in the questions. Nate was asked about sleeplessness and anxiety and anger, questions always asked of cops who've killed someone, and he'd denied experiencing any of it. He'd said his only regret was that he couldn't have killed that bastard twice.

When the shrink got to the other routine questions about his relationships with parents and siblings, he'd said to the man, "What do my parents have to do with my partner getting hit by a fucking bullet from a Saturday-night special that couldn't have found that particular mark again if the asshole had stood three feet away in broad daylight with a truck full of ammunition?"

The BSS shrink made notes about unconscious anger that had not been worked through and integrated and recommended this second annoying visit, which was on the day he returned to duty. It turned out that he was scheduled with a woman psychologist. This PhD was younger than Nate, barely thirty he guessed, tall and bony, with hair as straight and dull as straw and glasses with black rectangular frames. Her eggshell-white dress could only be called institutionally nondescript. In an earlier time, she would've been wearing Birkenstocks and rimless spectacles with her hair in a snood. She made him think of buttermilk.

The psychologist introduced herself as Marjorie, and she said to Nate, "I understand you're an actor. What if you were to compose a scene that you wanted to tape and play back to see if it worked as intended? If I asked you to compose and play a scene describing Dana Vaughn, could you do it? Pretend that you're all alone with your own tape machine and give it a try."

"I don't have a tape machine," Nate said drily. "And cops're too suspicious to talk to recording devices."

Marjorie smiled and said, "But you're an actor, Nate. I'll lend you my pretend machine. And when you're finished, you can take the pretend tape home with you."

The shrink had such an unassuming manner and seemed so easy to ignore that Nate had to restrain himself from telling her that he truly did feel alone in the room. But after a moment of silence while he considered her goofy idea, he was surprised to discover that he *wanted* to talk about Dana Vaughn to an imaginary tape machine in an empty room. And when he started, the words tumbled out of him.

Nate gazed into space and said, "She had sparkling, golden-brown eyes and a special throaty chuckle that somehow ended with a tinkling sound like a wind chime, and she wasn't afraid of raising a kid by herself, or of gray hair and laugh lines, or of guys with guns, or of anything else in this shitty world. And she was smarter than me and a better cop, and she called me honey, and it irked me at first, but now I miss it a lot."

He fell silent then until Marjorie said, "And tell the machine what you regret now that she's gone."

That's when Nate's eyes welled and he finally said, "That the only time our lips ever touched was when I was trying to breathe life into her, and that I never said 'honey' right back at her, because she would've chuckled in that special way of hers, and that ... that ... she died all ... all alone out there. Under that ... fucking ... Hollywood ... moon."

Then he wiped his eyes, stood abruptly, and said, "Thank you, Marjorie. The reading is over, and I don't think I'd ever give me the role in whatever play you're directing. I think I'd like to go to the station now. And may I say thank you for the loan of your pretend machine. I was able to talk to it more easily than to any of the humanoids around here."

The body of Malcolm Rojas was released to his grieving mother after the postmortem, and though his mother would never believe in his guilt, both of the women he'd attacked identified their assailant from photos taken in life and in death.

The body of Jerzy Szarpowicz was cremated at the request of a brother in Arkansas, and the ashes were returned home by FedEx.

Of course, Hollywood Nate and everyone else at the station knew rather soon that Dewey Gleason and Tristan Hawkins would be charged with numerous counts of grand theft, forgery, and other property crimes. But despite three deaths having occurred at the crime scene, including the first-degree murder of a police officer, the District Attorney's Office had not yet decided how to finally charge the two defendants. Although they were principals in immediate flight after the commission of felonies, their particular felonies did not meet the test for charging murder in the first degree of a peace officer. In fact, since neither defendant had personally used a firearm or other deadly weapon, even a charge of second-degree murder seemed a waste of taxpayer money. It was especially problematic for prosecutors that Ruben Malcolm Rojas was a wanted sexual psychopath and killer who had burst onto the scene and triggered the tragic events. Both defendants claimed that they were only trying to get away from him, not from the police, and fled in panic after Jerzy Szarpowicz, who they had not known was armed, began firing.

On the day following their arrest, just after TV footage of the suspects had been shown on local channels, a landlord in Frogtown called detectives at Hollywood Station to report that he'd rented an apartment to the one identified on the news as Dewey Gleason. That led to the discovery of the bed, chains, padlock, duct tape, and the rest. In hopes of striking a good plea bargain, the prisoners competed vigorously to reveal more information on each other as low-level confidence men. Up until then, neither arrestee had mentioned the kidnapping, but now each decided to amend his confession upon being confronted with the new Frogtown evidence. This occurred the day after the detectives had succeeded in marrying them to their former, less complex admissions.

Then both Dewey Gleason and Tristan Hawkins had to tell their versions of the kidnapping of Eunice Gleason, insisting that no one had any intention of harming Eunice, who Dewey maintained was the ringleader of their posse but not known by her low-level employees and bogus kidnappers. According to them, it was all an elaborate scam for Dewey Gleason to get some of the money from his ruthless wife, money that was rightfully his.

"It was just us little scammers trying to scam the big boss" was how Dewey put it to the detectives. "And it all went sideways."

The Public Defenders Office and a court-appointed criminal lawyer argued that both clients were hardly more than identity-stealing scalawags whose confidence scheme directed at their boss, Eunice Gleason, had gone awry and resulted in a terrible but unforeseen tragedy not of their making. After conversations with jailhouse lawyers concerning prison overcrowding, coupled with their relatively innocuous arrest records and eager cooperation, Dewey Gleason became more sanguine, convinced that he would not serve more than eight years, and Tristan Hawkins less, considering their time served before sentencing and good behavior in prison.

It was pointed out to Dewey during an attorney visit that Symbionese Liberation Army urban terrorist Kathleen Soliah, aka Sara Jane Olson, who'd been a fugitive for twenty-four years until her capture in 1999, hadn't served much longer than that, even though her gang had murdered a woman in a bank robbery and planted explosives under two LAPD police cars with intent to murder the officers. Dewey felt much more confident after that particular jailhouse chat.

In fact, during the last interview he had with D2 Viktor Chernenko, a Ukrainian immigrant famous at Hollywood Station for mangling American idioms, Dewey said to the hulking, moon-faced detective, "Someday the fortune that my wife stashed somewhere is gonna be found. And when it is, I'm putting in a claim for it."

"That is the fruit of your criminal enterprise," Viktor Chernenko replied. "I do not think you will be successful."

"We both worked as honest people for years," Dewey lied. "Nobody can prove which of the money is dirty and which is clean. So okay, maybe I'll give up some of it to Uncle Sam and retire on the rest."

Viktor Chernenko arched his bushy brows and said, "If I were you, my friend, I would not count my ducklings before they quack."

Hollywood Nate was welcomed back warmly at his first roll call with hugs and quiet words of sympathy and encouragement. Perhaps because of Nate's return and the memories it evoked, roll call was subdued despite the efforts of Sergeant Lee Murillo to inject a bit of levity from time to time.

Nate was to have worked with R.T. Dibney that night, but R.T. had unexpectedly requested a special day off for reasons that some cops guessed had to do with a certain waitress that he'd been sniffing around. It was R.T. Dibney who'd introduced Aaron Sloane to the

Iranian jewelers Eddie and Freddie, who'd sold Aaron a real diamond ring, not a $200 zircon like the one that R.T. Dibney bought from them to trick his wife. Aaron's ring cost nearly $4,000, but the Iranians swore that Aaron was getting it at a fifty percent police discount.

Sheila Montez had not worn the ring to Hollywood Station yet because she and Aaron were afraid that one of them would get transferred per Department policy as soon as word got out that they were to be wed in December. They wanted to work together for as long as they could. But Sheila would wear it when they visited his parents or hers, and they'd admire it every night before going to sleep, when they would talk excitedly about buying a house in Encino now that the real-estate market had almost bottomed out.

With R.T. Dibney gone for the night, Sergeant Murillo asked Hollywood Nate if he'd mind helping out at the front desk with the regular desk officer from Watch 3, and Nate said he wouldn't mind at all. Sergeant Murillo noticed that Nate's eyes had lost their old luster, and it worried him. He met with Sergeant Hermann in the sergeants' room and asked her what she thought the Oracle would've done to help restore their troubled cop.

Sergeant Hermann said she'd think about it, and an hour later she said to Nate, "How about a cuppa joe at Seven-Eleven?"

Hollywood Nate was a Starbucks man but he said okay, and they rode in the sergeant's car to the mini-mall, where Sergeant Hermann bought the coffee and looked longingly at the sweets but patted her size 38 Sam Browne and shook her head sadly.

"Want a goody to dunk?" she asked.

"No, thanks," Nate said listlessly.

"Look at you," she said. "You don't have to count calories and fat grams. You still working out?"

"Not since...not for a couple of weeks," he said.

They took their coffee outside, and Sergeant Hermann said, "I'd like to ask you something personal. Did you go to temple after Dana Vaughn was killed?"

"What?" Nate said sharply. "Has the federal judge put a box on our ratings reports for religious attendance?"

"I'm just saying." Sergeant Hermann held up her palm in a peace gesture.

Hollywood Nate took a sip of coffee and said, "Okay, since I went to temple for the first time since my bar mitzvah and said my half-assed version of Kaddish when the Oracle died, maybe I oughtta do more mumbo-jumbo to mourn another Gentile cop. I guess it's no dopier than touching the Oracle's picture every day, and we all do that. So what's your point, Sergeant?"

"That sometimes gestures like that help us to keep old connections with ourselves, that's all," Sergeant Hermann said. "So we don't go adrift and get lost."

Nate was silent, but Sergeant Hermann had more. She said, "I'm gonna tell you what nobody but a woman who wears this badge truly understands. Thirty-seven years ago, when I served at the old stations, there weren't even proper locker rooms for women. I remember at one station I dressed in the janitor's broom closet. There was an air vent in there, and I could hear the guys in their locker room talking about us women, and what they said wasn't nice. We woman got buried in shit every day and pretended it was sunshine. We had to be better than the men but keep our mouths shut so they wouldn't notice when we passed them by. To think I've lived long enough to see cup holders in police cars."

"Is this about Dana?" Nate said impatiently.

"It's about you," Sergeant Hermann said. "You don't get it that Dana Vaughn and all the other women with time on the Job understand our history because they still live it to some extent. She was senior to you. She was on the sergeants list and might've been your supervisor one day. It's not your job to stay Velcro-close to a partner unless you're a training officer with a probationer. If you'd been partnered with a man that night, you'd still be feeling deep sorrow but not what else you're feeling."

"You don't know what I'm feeling," Nate said.

"Nathan," she said, "there was danger out there that night, and your job was to stop the son of a bitch who started shooting, and you did it. You wouldn't be punishing yourself now if you'd been partnered with a senior officer like R.T. Dibney, or Johnny Lanier, or one of the surfers, because you can't get past thinking of Dana Vaughn as a woman. And thinking that you shoulda been Super Glued to her before, during, and after the gunfight. Well, son, she wasn't only a woman, she was a cop, and a good one. And she'd be ashamed of you for feeling you somehow failed her. And she'd hate it because that...*diminishes* her."

After a long pause, he said, "Anything else, Sergeant Hermann?"

"Yeah," she said, tossing her cup in a receptacle. "Why're old farts like me such creatures of habit? Why the hell didn't I take you to Starbucks? I won fifty bucks in a scratch-off yesterday. I could afford that freaking designer coffee."

When they were back at Hollywood Station and Nate had returned to the front desk, Sergeant Hermann entered the sergeants' room, where Sergeant Murillo was writing a report.

She said to him, "Lee, how about we let Nate work third man in a car for the rest of the night rather than vegetating at the desk? Maybe with Flotsam and Jetsam?"

Sergeant Murillo considered it and said, "Very good idea."

After placing a call for 6-X-32 to come to the station, Sergeant Murillo called Hollywood Nate to the sergeants' room and conjured a quick story, saying, "Nate, I just got another call from a citizen that the Street Characters are doing some real aggressive panhandling in front of Grauman's. One of them grabbed a woman by the arm to complain about his tip, and another got in somebody's face and intimidated them. How about you go up there with Flotsam and Jetsam and walk the boulevard for a few hours? Maybe a show of force will convince Batman, Darth Vader, and the rest to curtail their dark and evil ways."

The only thing that Sergeant Lee Murillo said to Flotsam and Jetsam privately was "Take Nate with you for a few hours. Help him get his mojo back."

"How do we do that, boss?" Flotsam asked.

"Be your usual zany selves," said Sergeant Murillo.

Twenty minutes later, Nate was sitting in the backseat of 6-X-32 when it parked on Orange Drive. The panhandlers, hustlers, and purse picks didn't like the sight of three cops getting out to stroll among the tourist throngs, so a few of the curb creatures decided to call it a night, pronto.

One of these was Two-Dollar Bill, so named because you know he exists but you seldom run into him. He was a bug-eyed scarecrow Nate's age who looked older than Sergeant Hermann. His grille was gapped and yellow, his eyes were rheumy, and the rusty tumbleweed frizz growing from his head was sprinkled with psoriasis. Two-Dollar Bill was the kind of tweaker who was better off in jail, and a part of him knew that, because in recent months he was always unconsciously running to, instead of away from, the law. And nowadays he was always ready to allow searches and ready to make admissions from the git-go.

"Oh, shit!" Flotsam said when Two-Dollar Bill practically ran into them.

Since the physical condition of this tweaker made cops automatically glove-up, Flotsam reached into his pocket and drew on a latex glove in case touching was necessary. "Bill," he said, "somehow I think you ain't never gonna earn a blood bank T-shirt."

"Just going home," Two-Dollar Bill said. "Don't wanna miss *American Idol*."

"It ain't on, Bill," Flotsam said. Then to Nate, "Last year we popped Two-Dollar Bill when he had a pay-and-owe sheet stuffed in one sock and thirty-three grams of flake in the other. They kicked Bill outta jail too soon."

Two-Dollar Bill said, "It wasn't my flake or my owe sheet. I was holding it for some guy. I don't know his real name but everybody calls him Planters."

"Why do they call him Planters?" Flotsam asked.

"Because his body's shaped like a peanut," said Two-Dollar Bill.

"I don't suppose your socks are dope-free tonight, are they, Bill?" Jetsam said, but Flotsam quickly clamped his gloved hand over the tweaker's mouth to keep him from answering.

"Didn't you learn anything in court last time, Bill?' Flotsam said sotto. "Cop a 'tude or something. We got other business tonight."

Flotsam shot Jetsam a look that said wasting their time by popping Bill again was not gonna help Hollywood Nate.

Jetsam nodded subtly, and when Flotsam took his hand away, Two-Dollar Bill said, "You won't find nothing in my socks but a few tits-up bedbugs. I can't keep them outta my socks and underwear. When I got underwear."

"Home is where the heart is, dude," Flotsam said, giving Two-Dollar Bill a little shove, sending him scurrying off into the night.

While they continued along the boulevard, Flotsam and Jetsam were as garrulous as usual, talking about getting Nate out to Malibu for evening surfing, but Nate was generally unresponsive, still mulling over the import of what Sergeant Hermann had said to him.

As they approached the Kodak Centre, Flotsam said to him, "Dude, when was the last time you rented a midget to bowl with?"

"I only did it once," Nate said.

"We been thinking," Jetsam said. "If we gave you the rental fee, could you get your midget and bring him back to the bowling alley in the Kodak Centre on Wednesday night? We figure he'd attract enough bowling alley Sallys for all of us."

Nate said, "I haven't seen him in a while."

"Well, do you have, like, anyone else you could invite?" Jetsam asked.

"Yeah, dude," said Flotsam. "A man with your hormonal ingenuity oughtta be able to come up with another idea to get them Sallys mega-stoked."

"Downright stokaboka is how we want them," Jetsam said to Nate. "Invite anyone but a clown."

"Dude!" Flotsam yelled it so loud at Jetsam that he startled Nate.

To change the subject, Jetsam quickly said, "Hey, this juicehead is faced."

A balding tourist with a double chin and cheeks flushed to bubblegum pink was staggering along the Walk of Fame, definitely tanked. The front of his "Hollywoodland" souvenir T-shirt looked like it had been washed in mai tais, and his fly was unzipped, the tail of his tee protruding.

"Whoa there, pard," Jetsam said, grabbing his elbow as the man tried to lurch past. "How many drinks you had tonight?"

"I'm perf...perf...fectly sober!" the tourist said, reeling.

"Don't try to okeydoke us, dude," Flotsam said. "Answer the question."

"What was the question again?" said the tourist, wattles twitching.

"How many drinks you had tonight?" Jetsam repeated. "The truth bus or the bullshit bus. Which one you taking?"

The tourist hiccupped twice and said, "About fifteen or twenty drinks, maybe. Beers mostly. I been pissing barley and hops all night."

Flotsam said, "Dude, that answer makes you just about the most honest man in all of L.A., so we're gonna give you a chance to prove your sobriety. Now pay attention."

A few minutes later they were in the privacy of the parking lot west of the tourist masses in Grauman's forecourt, and Hollywood Nate was mystified when Flotsam pulled a balloon from his pocket and blew it up. On his second try, the tourist actually slapped the balloon as it dove past his nose, prompting Flotsam to say, "You got game, dude."

Ten minutes after that, the tourist was boarding a bus to his hotel in Universal City, having put forth satisfactory effort in a two-out-of-three balloon test to satisfy the forces of law and order that he was a real trouper.

Nate was still chortling when Jetsam said to him, "Hey, bro, let's see if any of them Main Street Crips or Rolling Sixties are up from south L.A. They'll be hanging around the subway station dealing crack."

"We might find a gun," Flotsam said to Nate. "You down?"

"I got your back," said Nate.

"The game's afoot, dude!" Flotsam announced.

"Rock on, bro!" Jetsam concurred.

This was the camera's favorite time, called "magic hour" in the movie business. The summer sun was plunging into the ocean off Malibu, and onshore winds chased tumbling clouds to the east, inflamed by streaks of color from dying solar fire. The sky over Hollywood Boulevard was transformed into a blazing palette where any fool could gaze up breathless and dream of painting a new self-portrait, and maybe this time get it right. After a moment, Nate found himself stepping out with just a touch of foot-beat swagger, slipping through the crowds, giving the stink eye to

Batman and Darth Vader, striding over marble and brass stars along the Walk of Fame. The surfer cops strolling behind him gave each other a knuckle bump, and Flotsam whispered, "Dude, I think Nate just caught a blast of mucho mojo!"

Nate glanced into the Kodak Centre as they were passing, and he halted, turning his face to the darkening west, letting that sea breeze cooled by the Pacific sigh in his ears and blow through his hair, bringing with it a breath of great possibility, perhaps even redemption.

"About that Wednesday night bowling?" he said. "I'm good to go. And I'll see about renting us a midget."

Upon hearing this news the surfer cops beamed. "Midgets rule, dude!" said Flotsam.

"We're gravy, bro!" said Jetsam.

Then Flotsam's grin melted like a Slurpee on the sidewalk when Hollywood Nate said, "But will somebody please tell me, why no clowns?"

ABOUT THE AUTHOR

JOSEPH WAMBAUGH, a former LAPD detective sergeant, is the bestselling author of eighteen prior works of fiction and nonfiction. In 2004, he was named Grand Master by the Mystery Writers of America. He lives in Southern California.